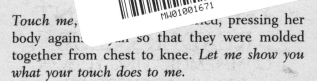

Touch me, ~~she cried,~~ pressing her body against him so that they were molded together from chest to knee. *Let me show you what your touch does to me.*

Ryan knew she hadn't spoken, but he wasn't surprised to hear her demands in his mind. She did not have to put into words what she wanted him to do now. He dropped his hands to her waist and slid them beneath her T-shirt, reaching her breasts, cradling them.

He could feel her craving for his touch. Her need was so strong, so palpable, that his hands were trembling as he stroked his thumbs upward.

Whatever fearful mystery lay in the shadows of the past . . . whatever dark danger awaited them on passion's burning path . . . one thing was now clear to Shana and Ryan as they came together in this moment of part magic, part madness. . . .

ANNOUNCING THE
TOPAZ FREQUENT READERS CLUB
COMMEMORATING TOPAZ'S 1 YEAR ANNIVERSARY!

THE MORE YOU BUY, THE MORE YOU GET

Redeem coupons found here and in the back of all new Topaz titles for FREE Topaz gifts:

Send in:

 2 coupons for a free TOPAZ novel (choose from the list below);

- ☐ THE KISSING BANDIT, Margaret Brownley
- ☐ BY LOVE UNVEILED, Deborah Martin
- ☐ TOUCH THE DAWN, Chelley Kitzmiller
- ☐ WILD EMBRACE, Cassie Edwards

 4 coupons for an "I Love the Topaz Man" on-board sign

 6 coupons for a TOPAZ compact mirror

 8 coupons for a Topaz Man T-shirt

Just fill out this certificate and send with original sales receipts to:

TOPAZ FREQUENT READERS CLUB-1ST ANNIVERSARY
Penguin USA • Mass Market Promotion; Dept. H.U.G.
375 Hudson St., NY, NY 10014

Name_____

Address_____

City_____ State_____ Zip_____

Offer expires 5/31/1995

This certificate must accompany your request. No duplicates accepted. Void where prohibited, taxed or restricted. Allow 4-6 weeks for receipt of merchandise. Offer good only in U.S., its territories, and Canada.

TOUCH OF MAGIC

by

Carin Rafferty

A TOPAZ BOOK

TOPAZ
Published by the Penguin Group
Penguin Books USA Inc., 375 Hudson Street,
New York, New York 10014, U.S.A.
Penguin Books Ltd, 27 Wrights Lane,
London W8 5TZ, England
Penguin Books Australia Ltd, Ringwood,
Victoria, Australia
Penguin Books Canada Ltd, 10 Alcorn Avenue,
Toronto, Ontario, Canada M4V 3B2
Penguin Books (N.Z.) Ltd, 182–190 Wairau Road,
Auckland 10, New Zealand

Penguin Books Ltd, Registered Offices:
Harmondsworth, Middlesex, England

First published by Topaz, an imprint of Dutton Signet,
a division of Penguin Books USA Inc.

First Printing, March, 1995
10 9 8 7 6 5 4 3 2 1

 Topaz is a trademark of Dutton Signet,
a division of Penguin Books USA Inc.

Printed in the United States of America

In memory of Isolde Carlsen,
a dear friend who is sorely missed.

The Fool (Reversed)
Folly

October 31—Samhain

Loneliness. It had been Shana Morland's companion for so long that she rarely noticed the emotion. Tonight, however, it was suffocating her, closing in on her as tightly as the thick Pennsylvania forest surrounding her. She tried to shake off the feeling, but it clung to her tenaciously.

With a heavy sigh, she leaned a shoulder against the tree beside her. As she watched the festivities taking place in the meadow buried deep in the woods, her loneliness became more unbearable. It was Samhain—All Hallow's Eve—and the members of her coven were gathered around the bonfire in celebration of the beginning of winter. Families were clustered on blankets and laughing together. Lovers were dancing around the fire or lingering in the shadows, sharing surreptitious kisses.

Shana knew she could approach any of the families and they would welcome her into their circle. But being welcome wasn't the same as belonging, and she hadn't felt this alone since her parents' deaths ten years ago. With another sigh, she pushed away from the tree and decided to go home. Her shoulders sagged at the realization that no one would even miss her.

"Stop wallowing in self-pity," she chided herself as she headed into the forest and began the short walk home. "Life is going to get better. Soon, you'll find a mate, and with any luck it will be a mortal who will take you away from Sanctuary. You'll finally be able to see the world, and you'll build a new life for yourself. You'll be a part of a family again, and you'll be deliriously happy."

Unfortunately, her pep talk didn't bolster her spirits, because she recognized the inherent problems in it. Although the council of high priests had recently given permission for members of her coven to seek mortal mates, unmated witches were still not allowed to leave coven boundaries. The only mortals with whom she came into contact were tourists visiting Sanctuary, and most of the men were married. She knew her chances of finding a mortal mate were serendipitous at best.

But if she couldn't find a mortal with whom to share her life, she would have to mate with a warlock. Unfortunately, the chances of that happening seemed just as slim. Most of the warlocks in her age group were already mated, and those that weren't simply didn't appeal to her.

By the time she arrived home, she concluded that she would be alone forever. She wanted to rant and rave at the unfairness, but she was too depressed to summon up the energy to do so. Instead, she wandered through the house, trying to remember what it had been like when her parents were alive and she had belonged. But the memories she sought had faded with time, and they were as elusive as her dreams.

"I wish there was some way I could know the future," she murmured as she stood at the kitchen window and stared morosely at the full moon. "Am I going to fall in love? If so, will it be with a mortal who will take me away from Sanctuary? Or will I spend the rest of my life imprisoned in this miserable monotony of coven life?"

If that is your future, can you face each day with the knowledge that this is all there will ever be? an inner voice asked.

She raked a hand through her hair, rattled by the question. Could she deal with that knowledge? Yes, she grimly decided, because not knowing was worse. She was almost twenty-seven years old, and she was tired of living in limbo. If there was just some way that she could find out what the future held, then she could come to grips with her life. But there was no way to determine the future.

What about the enchanted Tarot deck?

The thought had come from nowhere, and it startled her that she could even think something so blasphemous. Even more disturbing, however, was the titillation the thought evoked. If she did use the enchanted Tarot deck, it would tell her everything she wanted to know.

"Don't be ridiculous," she scolded herself. "The enchanted Tarot deck is cursed!"

But the curse will only go into effect if the deck is used by someone in love. Since you're not in love, it wouldn't apply to you.

"I couldn't possibly use the deck," she told herself firmly. "It's against coven law."

And who's going to know you used it?

Temptation stirred inside her. Did she dare use the deck?

"Surely one quick peek at my future wouldn't be dangerous," she assured herself. "And I am the caretaker of the deck. If nothing else, I should check to make sure it's still in its hiding place."

She headed for the special room in her home that served as the coven's repository. When she entered the room, she was barely aware of the hundreds of items cluttering tables and filling display cases. Her attention was focused on the fireplace, where the enchanted Tarot deck was hidden.

As she approached the fireplace, she nervously rubbed her hands against her thighs. What she was about to do was against coven law, and if she was caught. . . . She closed her eyes, refusing to think about the harsh penalty that would be imposed.

"All I'm going to do is use the deck to learn my future," she stated, hoping that by saying the words aloud it would ease her worried conscience. "It isn't as if I'm going to endanger anyone."

And what about the curse?

Shana involuntarily shivered at the reminder. Then she gave an impatient shake of her head. "For the curse to work, I have to be in love, so it doesn't apply to me."

With newfound determination, she slid her fingers across the cool bricks of the fireplace until she found the trigger for the secret panel. When she pressed it, a stone in the hearth slid open, revealing a palm-size wooden box.

Staring at it, she caught her breath in awe. Its surface was engraved with symbols so old she suspected no one remembered their meaning. But it wasn't its beauty that captivated her. It was the magical power she could feel emanating from it.

Tentatively, she touched the lid, and she immediately snatched her hand back. The wood felt oddly warm—almost alive—and she would have sworn she felt a heartbeat.

"You're being silly," she mumbled, chafing her hands against her arms as goose bumps scattered across her skin. "It's impossible for inanimate objects to have heartbeats."

Her declaration didn't alleviate the eerie sensation. As she continued to stare at the box, she knew that the sensible thing to do was close the secret panel and forget the Tarot. Everyone else had to wait for their future to unfold. Why should she have an advantage over them? The answer, of course, was that she shouldn't have an advantage.

"But I'll go crazy if I don't have some indication of what I can expect in life!" she fretted. "And even if there is something strange going on here, I don't meet the criteria to fulfill the curse. What could it hurt to just take a peek? I won't do a full reading. I'll only do enough to find out if I should resign myself to spending the rest of my life in Sanctuary. Once I have the answer, I'll put the Tarot away.

"But I have to hurry!" she reminded herself as she felt the magnetic pull of the witching hour. All the members of the coven were at the festival bonfire, but they'd soon gather for their midnight ritual. Once their power combined, they would learn what she was doing and stop her.

Despite her urgency, she cautiously trailed her fingertips across the lid of the box. It still felt oddly alive, but there was no sensation of a heartbeat. She sighed in relief. It had only been her imagination.

Lifting the box, she quickly carried it to the center of the pentagram, which was built into the hardwood floor. After setting the box down, she hastily gathered the sacred candles that were stored in the hiding place with the box. Then she lit and placed a candle on each of the five points of the star forming the inside of the pentagram. When she was done, she returned to the center and sat cross-legged beside the box.

She drew in an excited breath. Tonight the veil between this world and the spirit world was at its thinnest. All she had to do was summon the spirit of the ancient witch, Moira, who had cast her spell over the Tarot more than five hundred years ago. With Moira present, the cards would accurately foretell her future.

Drawing in another breath, she opened the lid and reached for the deck, which was wrapped in white silk yellowed with age. When she touched the silken packet, she was hit with a surge of energy so strong it felt like a high-voltage electrical shock arcing up her arm.

Jerking her hand back, she rubbed at her tingling arm and eyed the deck warily. What had happened? It felt as if the Tarot had power, and until she summoned Moira that was impossible! Was there a spell over it to keep it from being read? Recognizing that was a good possibility, she mumbled a frustrated curse. She couldn't come this close and fail!

Hesitantly, she reached for the packet again, expecting another jolt. When nothing happened, she couldn't decide if she was relieved or alarmed. Obviously, there wasn't a spell in place, so what had caused that surge of energy?

Though she wanted to attribute it to an overactive imagination, she knew it wasn't true. She was also forced to admit that whatever had happened was beyond her realm of experience. She was, after all, dealing with magic that hadn't been practiced in hundreds of years, and only a fool would use the Tarot. She had to put it away.

Wistfully, she ran her fingers over the silk. Like the box, it felt oddly alive. She couldn't help wondering what the cards looked like. Since they were so old, they wouldn't resemble a modern deck. Surely it wouldn't hurt to take a quick look at them before she put them away.

Just a look, she promised herself as she carefully unwrapped the silk and removed the deck.

Fanning the cards out in her hand, she frowned. Their backs were solid black. When she turned them over, she discovered that the faces were also black. Even more puzzling was that the stack was so small she automatically counted the cards. There were only twenty-two instead of the seventy-eight needed to comprise a full deck. Where were the remainder of them?

Just shuffle the cards.

Shana started as the order echoed in her mind. Suddenly, the cards seemed to move in her hand, and a shudder of alarm raced through her. She looked down at them, and they moved again, a slithering, sinuous motion that reminded her of a snake. As the hair on the back of her neck prickled, she realized that there was only one reason for the cards to come alive. *Moira.*

"That's not possible!" she gasped, fearfully glancing around the room. She hadn't summoned Moira, and a spirit couldn't come without a summons.

Just shuffle the cards!

As the demand again flashed through Shana's mind, the flames on the candles flared higher and began to undulate. The air seemed to crackle with expectancy. Even as fear threatened to overwhelm her, excitement stirred inside her. If Moira really was here, then so were the answers to her future.

Her common sense insisted that she put the Tarot away before it was too late, but she reminded herself that she was protected by the pentagram. No one—not even a powerful spirit witch like Moira—could enter it uninvited. As long as she remained within its boundaries she was safe, so what would it hurt to lay out a couple of cards?

She began to shuffle the deck. When she was done, she turned the first card over and her heart skipped a beat. The face of the card was no longer black. She was staring at an image of herself dressed in a black robe and wearing a strange peaked cap. Resting on her shoulder was a bundle suspended from a stick and she carried a bloodred rose in her hand. She was standing on the edge of a cliff and staring rapturously up at the sky, as though unaware that her next step would take her over the edge. There were no words on the cards, but she didn't need words to know she was being depicted as The Fool, and the card was in the reverse position.

She tried to give it a positive reading, but she knew instinctively that the real interpretation was folly—an imprudent venture that would have disastrous consequences.

New fear began to bubble inside her as her self-protective instincts screamed, *Put the deck away!*

She wanted to do exactly that, but her hands seemed to have become spellbound. No matter how hard she fought against them, they continued to lay out the cards. When they finally stilled, she had lain out the remaining twenty-one cards in an unfamiliar spread resembling an inverted pentagram. Even more bizarre, however, was that except for The Fool, the other cards remained black.

Before she could speculate what that meant, the air outside the pentagram began to shimmer and a form began to take shape. It was as dark and faceless as the cards; yet, it was as incorporeal as a ghost.

Her fear escalated to terror. Moira *was* here. But how had she come without a summons? Even as Shana asked the question she knew that *how* it had happened wasn't important. What mattered was, *why* Moira had come, and there could only be one answer. Moira was here to lay claim to a soul so she could again exist in this world. Since Shana was the person who had brought her here, it stood to reason that it was her soul the ancient witch wanted.

But she can only claim the soul of a person in love, Shana reminded herself, trying to curb the panic exploding inside her. Since she wasn't in love, Moira *couldn't* harm her.

"Don't you want to know why you can't read the cards?" Moira suddenly demanded, interrupting Shana's frightened musing.

Don't answer! Shana warned herself. If I pretend that she doesn't exist, maybe she'll leave. If she doesn't, it won't be long before the coven meets. They'll figure out what's going on and send her away.

Even as she offered herself the reassurance of a rescue, she realized that it might not be true. Moira had been the most powerful witch who had ever lived. Since she had been able to cross over without a summons, it was possible her magic was greater than the coven's. As much as Shana wanted to ignore her, she knew she was better off knowing what she faced.

With a frightened gulp, she proposed, "I can't read the cards because they belong to you?"

"So does the future, and now yours will be mine!" Moira replied triumphantly, pointing a shrouded arm toward the cards.

There was a brilliant flash of light, and Shana reflexively closed her eyes against it. When she opened them, both Moira and the cards were gone.

Wrapping her arms around herself, she fearfully whispered, "I'm not in love, so she can't hurt me. She can't!"

At her words, an unearthly cackle filled the air, and the card of The Fool appeared above her head. It hung suspended for several seconds, and then it drifted down to fall at Shana'a feet.

· CHAPTER ONE ·

The Chariot (Reversed)
Downfall

April 30—Beltane Eve

Everywhere he looked, there were eyes staring at him. Eyes filled with pain and fear. Eyes that begged for help. Eyes that condemned. And, most horrible of all, eyes filled with trust that faded to the empty sheen of death.

As the eyes closed ranks around him, he heard the woman call to him. Though he couldn't understand the words, he knew she was offering him refuge from the eyes. Slowly, he turned toward the sound of her voice. She was standing in the distance, her form so indistinct she was no more than a ghostly shadow. Her arms were extended in a welcoming pose. All he had to do was run to her, let her enfold him in her arms, and the nightmare would be over.

But even as he yearned to run to her, he couldn't find the energy to move. He was trapped in the world of the eyes, and they wouldn't let him go. Would never let him go, he fatally accepted, as they swarmed in on him until he could no longer see the woman.

As he lost sight of her, her voice began to fade until there was nothing left but a deafening silence and the eyes. They were his punishment—his torture—and they'd be there always and forever.

*   *   *

Ryan Alden bolted upright in bed. His body was slicked with sweat and trembling uncontrollably. As his gaze flew around the dark room, it took him a moment to remember where he was.

When he finally recalled that he was in some shabby motel room in the foothills of Lancaster County, Pennsylvania, he drew in a ragged breath. Then he dragged his hands across his face, trying to dispel the remnants of the nightmare. But even as he performed the act, he knew there was only one sure way he could escape the dream. He had to outrun it, just as he'd been outrunning it for the past six months.

Switching on the bedside lamp, he climbed out of bed and hurriedly donned the clothes that, according to his watch, he'd shed only an hour ago. Thankfully, he hadn't even unpacked his shaving kit, so he could leave immediately. Grabbing his motorcycle helmet and his duffel bag off the floor, he headed for the door.

Outside, his Harley Davidson gleamed in the light of a full moon. He strapped the duffel bag onto the back, pulled on his helmet, and swung astride the bike. Moments later, he was on the road, with the warm, spring air flowing over him. He didn't know where the road went, but as long as it took him away from the eyes, he didn't care.

The leashed power of the bike vibrated beneath him like an eager stallion begging for its head. Ryan recognized the danger of giving into the allure of speed. He was on an unfamiliar, twisting mountain road at night. One mistake and he could end up dead.

That in itself was an enticement, because that's why he had bought the motorcycle. He wanted to challenge death until it finally claimed him. What could be a better challenge than taking on this road at night?

With a grim smile, he leaned into the wind and gave

the bike full throttle. It hesitated for a moment, and then it leaped forward at such speed that he felt as if he were flying. Exhilaration and fear shot through him. He could feel that old bastard, Father Death, riding on his shoulder. He could sense how badly he wanted him, and Ryan was determined to best him yet again. He didn't mind dying, but if Death wanted him, he was going to have to put up one hell of a fight to get him.

Narrowing his eyes, he concentrated on the twists and turns illuminated in his headlight. He was subliminally aware that he was going deeper into the woods. His only conscious thought, however, was of the road and the unknown dangers it had in store for him. He rode the Harley uphill and down, dodging rocks and potholes, never once reducing his breakneck speed. He was running the race of his life—*for* his life—and, by damn, he was winning it yet again!

As he reached a fork in the road, he instinctively took the one on the right. When he did, a voice inside his head whispered, *Now you've found sanctuary. Your journey is at its end.*

The voice, more than the words, startled him, and he almost lost control of the bike. It was the woman's voice from his nightmare. How could she be speaking to him when he was awake? And what did she mean that his journey was at its end? Was he finally going to die?

The thought should have pleased him. Instead it scared the hell out of him, because he was sure he'd spend eternity with those damnable eyes. But his fear wasn't strong enough to make him slow down. Whatever lay ahead, he would meet it full throttle. After all, his future couldn't be any worse than his past.

As she watched her friends and family dance clockwise around the bonfire in the center of the meadow,

Shana absently toyed with a blade of grass. It was Beltane Eve, and their dance would bring good luck to the coven and protect them from illness. Tomorrow was Beltane and they'd dance around the Maypole, celebrating birth, fertility, and the renewal of all life.

With a despondent sigh, she leaned back against the trunk of the old oak tree she was sitting under and glanced toward the sky. A warm, spring breeze stirred the leaves overhead, and she stared at the full, silver moon suspended above the horizon. Of all the Greater Sabbats, Beltane was her favorite, but she couldn't get into the spirit of the festivities. She felt as if something evil was hovering over her, and her instincts were telling her that Moira was back.

She shivered as she lowered her gaze and surveyed the dark forest surrounding the meadow, looking for some sign of the ancient witch. In the six months since Samhain, she'd had no contact with Moira. She had assumed the old witch had been forced to return to the spirit world. However, like Samhain, during Beltane Eve the veil between this world and the spirit world was thin. Shana couldn't shake the feeling that Moira had again managed to cross over without a summons.

"But I'm not in love, so there's nothing she can do to me!" she whispered fretfully.

It was a hollow claim, because she wasn't sure it was true. The legend of Moira's curse had been passed down for five centuries. It was possible, even probable, that the details had been altered. She knew how her people enjoyed embellishing their legends. Somewhere along the line someone may have added the love angle simply to make the story sound more romantic. Indeed, many of the details of the curse could have been fabricated, which meant there was only one absolute she could depend upon. The curse was real or the Tarot would have never been banned from use.

Resting her head against the tree trunk, she closed her eyes. Why had she so foolishly broken coven law? If she were a warlock, she could be cast out of the coven for using the Tarot.

However, witches were never exiled. As far as she was concerned, their punishment was worse, and she shuddered at the reminder of what would happen to her. She would be stripped of her powers and shunned. She'd have to live alone in the small, barely habitable shack at the furthermost corner of coven land for at least a year. When she was allowed to return, she would remain powerless until a warlock fell in love with her and chose her as his mate. Then it would be up to him when, or even if, she would have her powers restored, which would be sheer misery. A witch's life with a warlock was difficult enough with her powers intact. It was why she had hoped to be one of the coven members allowed to seek a mortal mate. According to Ariel Morgret, who was her best friend and a mortal, men were often chauvinistic, but they were less domineering than warlocks. And if anyone would know that for sure, it was Ariel. She had mated with the high priest, Lucien Morgret, eight months ago, and one of her most frequent complaints was his dictatorial attitude.

Ironically, at this point Shana knew she would willingly suffer through the degradation of a shunning and the loss of her powers. If it would rid her of Moira, she'd even happily mate with the most domineering warlock alive. Why had she been so foolish? Why hadn't she just let the future take care of itself? Why . . .

She stopped herself. Recriminations wouldn't solve her problem. What she needed was a plan to deal with Moira.

Opening her eyes, she searched the crowd. When she spotted Lucien, she considered going to him and confessing what she'd done. As high priest, he would have to deal with Moira, and she wouldn't have to worry about her anymore.

But as much as Shana yearned to turn the problem over to Lucien, she couldn't. Ordinarily, a spirit could harm only the person who had summoned it, but she hadn't summoned Moira. She'd come to the conclusion that the Tarot had done so. Now, because of her impatience to see the future, Moira had the enchanted cards. Through them, she might have enough power to claim any soul within the coven.

But for Moira to contact anyone else, that person had to acknowledge her existence. That's why Shana had spent the past six months living in daily fear that someone would discover the Tarot missing. Once it was learned the deck was gone, everyone would know that Moira might be loose. With that type of acceptance, there was no telling what havoc Moira would create.

Shana heaved a sigh of resignation. If Moira was here, it was her responsibility to get the Tarot back. The best way to start was go to the house and summon Moira from the safety of the pentagram. Once she made contact, she'd try to figure out a way to straighten out this mess.

Rising to her feet, she furtively slipped into the forest. Her familiar, Portent, waited not far away. The huge, white stallion would get her home quickly. With any luck, she would have the Tarot before the witching hour, and Moira would return to the spirit world where she belonged.

When Shana arrived at Portent's hiding place, he whinnied softly in welcome. She took a moment to wrap her arms around his neck and rest her cheek against it. As their minds connected, she frowned. Portent also sensed evil, which meant the other familiars probably sensed it. If they began communicating their unease to their masters, she might be caught.

With a muffled curse, she stripped off the white ceremonial robe that covered her clothes. Tossing the robe across the front of the saddle, she mounted Portent and urged him to hurry home. Since his main purpose as her familiar was to be her protector, he automatically resisted.

She heaved an impatient sigh and said, "Portent, if I don't get the cards back, Moira is going to lay claim to my soul. You have to take me home so I can try to stop her!"

When he again whinnied, she argued, "There is no guarantee that if I go to Lucien for help I'll be safe. I brought Moira here, so I'm the one who has to defeat her. And the best way to do that is to get the cards back before she starts causing trouble. Now, take me home!"

He let out a snort of begrudging agreement and began to maneuver his way through the trees. A few minutes later, he entered the meadow edging the dirt road leading to her home.

With a toss of his head, he began to race across the meadow. Shana automatically leaned in close to his neck, reveling in the smooth, controlled power of his body moving beneath her. When he reached the road, he veered to the center of it and began to gallop. She felt as if she were riding the wind, and despite the ominous meeting awaiting her, she threw her head back and laughed in exhilaration.

When they rounded a bend at breakneck speed, her laughter died, and she screamed in terror. A motorcycle was coming toward them so fast that Portent couldn't get out of the way. To avoid collision she would have to conjure a protective spell around them. She didn't know, however, if she could invoke the spell in time.

Urgently, she began to chant. Just before she reached the end of the spell, the motorcycle rider, who was no more than a foot away from them, suddenly jerked on his handlebars. The motorcycle careered toward the ditch. Shana recognized that at the speed he was traveling, the crash would kill him.

Just as the motorcycle hit the ditch and the driver flew into the air, she finished the protective spell and propelled it toward him. When spell-lightning circled around him, he was already swiftly falling toward the ground. Shana knew it would cushion his body against serious injury, but it was too late to slow his descent and protect him from minor injury. Even with the spell in place, he hit the ground with enough force to make Shana flinch.

Portent came to a stop, and she quickly climbed off the horse and ran toward the man, whom she'd already determined was a mortal. A warlock would have connected with her mind and helped conjure the protective spell instead of taking a suicidal turn toward the ditch.

Why hadn't she sensed him on the road? she wondered in bewilderment as she jumped across the ditch. For that matter, why hadn't she or Portent heard the motorcycle's engine? And quick contact with Portent assured her that he hadn't heard or sensed anything, either.

When Shana arrived at the man's side, she discovered her answer, and she let out a horrified gasp. The light from his crashed motorcycle spotlighted him. He was lying on his back with his arms outstretched. A Tarot card rested in the center of his chest.

Fear paralyzed Shana as she stared at the card,

which was The Chariot in the reversed position—the symbol of downfall. Though the chariot driver's face on the card was unfamiliar, she was sure it was the image of the motorcycle rider. There was no other reason for Moira to place the card on his chest.

"But what does it *mean*?" she whispered, frantically glancing around in search of Moira. Since the card was here, she had to be here too. "What does he have to do with me?"

Suddenly, an unnatural and bitterly cold wind swirled around her. But it wasn't the wind that made her shiver. It was the words that echoed through her mind. *The future is mine, and soon yours will be mine.*

The wind died as quickly as it had arisen, and Shana knew that Moira was gone. She also understood that by bringing the mortal here, Moira had set the future in motion. It was too late to stop her. All Shana could do was follow the path Moira had set and pray that she could save herself and protect the coven.

With a heavy sigh, she knelt beside the mortal and probed his mind, confused by his unconscious state. Though he'd hit the ground hard, the impact shouldn't have been enough to make him lose consciousness.

Worriedly, she probed more deeply into his mind. The signals from his body indicated that though he was suffering from several aches and pains, the only real injury he'd sustained was to his right leg.

She glanced toward his leg and saw that it was at an awkward angle. Leaning forward, she held her hands over it. According to the energy patterns she received, the leg wasn't broken. There was, however, some muscle damage to his knee. It wasn't serious enough for him to need medical attention, but she suspected it would be several days before he could walk properly.

Gently, she straightened his leg. Then she removed

the Tarot card from his chest and studied his picture, deciding that he fit the fierce image of a chariot driver. He had dark blond hair that nearly reached his shoulders, which surprised her. Though long hair was normal among warlocks, she'd found that most mortal men wore their hair short. It was his face, however, that intrigued her. It was composed of sharp, angular features that taken separately were unattractive. Combined, however, they made the man strikingly handsome. There was also an element of recklessness in his dark brown eyes that give him a decidedly dangerous aura.

"Well, whoever you are, it looks like you're trouble. Of course, considering that Moira brought you here, I suppose I shouldn't be surprised," Shana stated dryly as she tucked the card into the back pocket of her denims. Then she began to gently remove the man's helmet.

As she did so, she again meshed with his mind, trying to figure out why he was unconscious. At first she received nothing but the aches and pains being telegraphed by his body. Then, without warning, she suddenly found herself being sucked into a whirling, dark vortex.

She tried to recoil from the darkness and was both startled and frightened when his mind wouldn't let hers go. How could this be happening? Mortals didn't have the mental powers needed to trap another's mind!

This had to be Moira's doing, she realized, as she was swept deeper into the blackness. Her head was spinning and her body felt as if it was weightless, nonexistent. She knew her eyes were open, but she couldn't see. Her ears were filled with a frantic keen that she sensed was coming from her own mouth, though she had no physical knowledge of making the sound. She could feel herself gasping, as though tortured for breath, and her heart was racing at such high speed that she was sure it would explode at any moment.

But it wasn't her physical distress that terrified her. It was the emotional emptiness surrounding her. She was trapped by a mind that had no soul, and those who had no soul had nothing to bind them to this world. Their fondest wish—their greatest fantasy— was death.

Was that why the man was unconscious? Was he willing himself to die? Was he going to take her with him?

No! I am not going to die! It is not my time!

The future is mine, and now yours will be mine!

Moira's taunt caused Shana's terror to escalate. She began to mentally struggle to break loose from the mortal's mind. She was a witch. She could break away from him. She *had* to break away from him! But even as she fought against the hold he had over her, she felt herself falling deeper into the vortex.

The darkness began to wane, and in its place came a new horror. She was surrounded by eyes. Eyes that accused and beseeched. Eyes that pleaded and condemned. Eyes that were filled with pain and fear. And, most horrible of all, eyes that were filled with the emptiness of death.

She tried to get away from them, but no matter what she did, they continued to surround her, to close in on her. They wouldn't let her escape, would never let her escape. She was going to die, and they were going to torture her forever.

No! I am not going to die! It is not my time!

The future is mine, and now yours will be mine!

Again she began to tumble deeper into the vortex, and again, the darkness waned. But this time it wasn't horror that awaited her. She was lying naked in a meadow. Kneeling between her legs was the mysterious mortal, wearing nothing but moonlight and an expression of lust so intense that her entire body quivered with a resonating chord of overwhelming desire.

With a guttural groan, he dropped a hand to the ground on either side of her head and lowered his lips to hers. As his mouth branded her with his passion, his hips flexed and he sheathed himself inside her with one quick, hard thrust. She cried out in wonder at the feel of him—so big, so blunt, so *male*!

And then he began to move inside her with a measured stroke that sent her reeling toward climax. She clung to his shoulders, begging him to go faster so she could reach the crest. But instead of meeting her demand, he lessened his pace until he was moving against her in a slow, languorous motion that was sure to drive her mad. When she couldn't endure the sensual torture a moment longer, he began to thrust into her urgently. She closed her eyes and cried out again as her climax overtook her.

But even as her body began to shudder in release, she felt him leave her. Her eyes flew open, and she frowned in bewilderment. They were no longer in the night-shrouded meadow. It was nearly dawn. He was standing precariously on the edge of a cliff, and she was several yards behind him. Panic surged through her, because she sensed that he was going to jump. She tried to cry out to him, but no sound came from her mouth. With a sob of frustration, she began running toward him. She had to stop him from doing this. It was her fault. If she just hadn't . . .

Before she could complete the thought, the scene again changed. She was on the cliff edge with him, but this time she was the one in danger. He had an iron hold on her arms, and he was pushing her toward the edge of the cliff. He intended to throw her off it!

"Why?" she screamed at him.

Instead of answering, he released his hold on her and pushed. As she felt herself falling into space, her eyes locked with his. She would have sworn she saw a flicker of triumph flash through them, and then there was nothing reflected in their depths. She was falling to her death, but she recognized that he was already dead, and she'd been the one to kill him. If she just hadn't . . .

"If I just hadn't what?" Shana whispered frantically, when the terrifying vision suddenly ended and her mind was set free. What could she have possibly done that would make him want to take his own life, and in the end take hers instead?

As Shana stared down at the man, who was still unconscious, she knew that Moira had just given her a glimpse of the future. She wasn't sure how much of that future was real and how much of it was due to Moira's manipulation. There was, however, one aspect of the vision that explained why Moira had waited until now to reappear. She was in possession of the Tarot, so she had been able to read Shana's future. She had known that on Beltane Eve, the mortal whom Shana was destined to fall in love with would arrive.

Shana stared at the man's face in horrified dismay. "So, that aspect of the curse was right. She has to claim the soul of someone in love, and considering the way we were making love in that meadow, it's just a matter of time before I'm madly in love with you. But you aren't going to make it easy, are you? That's the meaning of the Tarot card Moira left on your chest. You're to be my challenge, and if I fail, you'll be my downfall. But what kind of challenge are you going to present?"

Portent whinnied nervously behind her, and she glanced over her shoulder at him, shaking her head. "It wouldn't do any good to cast a spell to send him away. No amount of magic can change destiny, Portent. And, like it or not, this mortal is my destiny."

Returning her attention to the man, she frowned. Why was he still unconscious? Cautiously, she brushed against his mind, leery of again being sucked into that vortex. She could feel its darkness—its evil—whirling at the edges of her mind. She easily held it at bay, which convinced her that it had indeed been Moira who had trapped her in his mind earlier. To her frustration, she couldn't find a physical reason for the man's unconsciousness. It appeared that he simply didn't wish to wake up.

With a resigned shake of her head, Shana closed her eyes and summoned Lucien Morgret. As high priest, he would have to give her permission to take the mortal home and care for him. She just prayed that when he arrived, he wouldn't realize that magic from the spirit world was at work here.

· CHAPTER TWO ·

The Devil
Black Magic

Shana was so busy fretting over the mortal's condition that she didn't sense Lucien's arrival. She let out a yelp when he said, "What's going on, Shana?"

She leaped to her feet and turned to face him. When she did, she couldn't help but shiver. Lucien was the high priest, and she respected him. There was also a part of her that was afraid of him. His shaggy, shoulder-length black hair and sharp, angular features gave him a more dangerous appearance than the average warlock. But it wasn't his looks that made her so apprehensive. It was his eyes. They were a pale, silver blue that seemed to pierce you right down to your soul, and there was no leniency in their depths. If he ever found out what she'd done . . .

Deciding that there was no sense borrowing trouble, she quickly quelled the thought and said, "I'm afraid there's been an accident. I was riding Portent. When we came around the bend, this mortal was coming toward us on his motorcycle. He swerved to miss us and crashed. His knee is hurt and he's unconscious, but I can't find any physical reason for him not to wake up."

"I see," Lucien responded stepping to her side. As

he stared down at the man, he raised his hand to the crystal hanging from a chain around his neck. When the crystal began to glow, Shana nervously rubbed her hands against her thighs. If anyone could pick up on Moira's presence, it would be Lucien. He was a half-breed; his mother was a mortal. The interracial mix had weakened his natural powers, and he had to use the crystal to augment them. Though many considered his need for the crystal a handicap, Shana knew it made him as powerful as a full-blooded warlock. As the high priest, he also had the additional advantage of being able to draw upon the powers of the entire coven.

"What's wrong? Is he okay?" she asked in alarm when Lucien suddenly chanted a spell, creating an energy barrier of warmth to form around the man.

"He's suffering from shock," Lucien answered.

"Shock?" she repeated in disbelief. "How could he be in shock? He isn't bleeding."

Lucien glanced toward her. "A mortal can suffer shock from extreme emotional distress, as well as bodily trauma. Since you cast a spell around him, it can't be physical. What was so upsetting that it would cause him to lose consciousness?"

"I don't know," Shana said, raking a hand through her hair in bewilderment. "I told you what happened. He swerved to miss Portent and me and crashed. I managed to cast a protective spell around him, but there wasn't enough time to cushion him completely against the fall. That's why he injured his knee. When I got to him, he was just like he is now."

"And you're sure that's all that happened?" Lucien questioned doubtfully. When Shana nodded, he frowned. "It must have been the spell-lightning that frightened him."

Or something Moira did to him that I don't know about, Shana thought grimly.

As she regarded the man, she gnawed anxiously on her bottom lip. For Moira to interact with him, wouldn't he have to acknowledge her existence? Or did those rules apply only to her race?

"What?" she said, jerking her head toward Lucien when his voice penetrated her troubled musing.

"I said I'll go get the car and take him to the hospital."

"No!" When Lucien arched a brow at her shrill protest, she lowered her voice. "The hospital is so far away, and he isn't seriously injured. Wouldn't it be better if we took him to my house? I can look after him until he wakes up."

"And then what are you going to do with him? He has a badly sprained knee, Shana. When he wakes up, he won't be able to walk."

"So, I'll take care of him until he can walk."

Lucien shook his head. "We don't know anything about him. He could be dangerous, and I can't risk the coven's safety by letting him stay here."

"Lucien, he won't be able to walk. How could he be a threat?"

He stared at her suspiciuosly. "What are you up to, Shana?"

"I'm not up to anything." It wasn't a lie. Moira was the one who was up to something. "I inadvertently caused his accident, so I feel responsible for him. I just want to make sure he's all right."

"If we take him to a hospital, he'll be fine."

Shana again raked a hand through her hair. She couldn't tell Lucien about Moira, so what could she say that would make him agree to let the man stay? The truth, she realized, or at least a portion of it.

"Even if we take him away, he'll be back," she informed him. When he shot her an inquiring look, she quickly explained, "When I was checking his injuries, I briefly connected with his mind. I had a very strong psychic vision, and I learned that this mortal is meant to be my mate."

If Lucien was surprised by her claim, he didn't show it. Instead, he glanced from her to the mortal, and then back to her. "You're sure? Or is this just hopeful wishing? We all know how badly you want a mortal mate so you can get out of Sanctuary."

Shana gave him an exasperated look. "It isn't hopeful wishing. It's the truth. The vision I had was extremely intimate, but if you'd like me to share it with you to prove what I'm saying . . ."

She purposely let her voice trail off, praying that Lucien wouldn't take her up on the offer. Sharing the lovemaking scene with him would be embarrassing, but he might pick up on the other scenes as well. If he realized the man might be a threat to her life, she'd have to tell him about Moira. It was bad enough that Moira was using a helpless mortal in her deadly game. Shana wasn't about to compound the problem by putting Lucien in danger, even if he didn't take her seriously.

She sighed in relief when Lucien said, "That won't be necessary. I'll take your word for it, and I'll let him stay for now. However, I'll have to cast a spell that will make him forget us if he leaves."

"Why would you do that?" Shana asked, startled. She couldn't let Lucien cast a spell over him! If he became the mortal's spellbinder, they'd be mentally connected. And if Moira did have power over the man, she might be able to get to Lucien through that connection.

"He's a mortal, Shana. That means he's unpredictable, which makes his future unpredictable," Lucien explained. "Regardless of what you saw, there is no guarantee that it will come true. I have to consider the coven's safety, and the only way to ensure it is to spell-bind him. That way, if he leaves, he won't be a threat to us."

"Then *I'll* cast the spell."

"No, Shana. If you cast the spell, you'll share an emotional bond with him. I know from personal experience that that can backfire on you. It would be best for me to do it. Then, if things don't work out between the two of you, you won't be tied to him."

"And if things do work out between us, there will always be a part of him tied to you," Shana protested.

Lucien frowned. "If things work out, I'll release him from the spell."

"You know as well as I do that once you become someone's spellbinder, you can never completely sever the connection between you," she argued. "At times of intense emotion, your minds will automatically connect. I'm sorry, Lucien, but I don't want you knowing whenever my mate and I make love or have a fight. If anyone is going to cast a spell over him, it's going to be me."

"And what if it backfires?" Lucien challenged. "What if you fall in love with him and he walks away from you? Are you willing to spend the rest of your life alone and grieving over a lost love? Are you willing to forgo the chance to mate with someone else just so I won't be privy to the intense moments of your personal life? That sounds like a terribly high price to pay for a little privacy, particularly when you don't know for sure that you'll even need that privacy."

"Damn it, Lucien! Stop trying to intimidate me!" she cried in frustration. Everything he was saying was true, and how could she argue with the truth?

"I'm not trying to intimidate you. I'm trying to make you listen to reason. We're dealing with a mortal, and they don't play by our rules. For that matter, they don't play by their own rules. The only reliable thing about them is their unreliability, and that's particularly true of men. They are ruled by ego and libido, Shana. I'm sure you can satisfy the latter. It's the former that worries me. You're too impulsive and headstrong. You simply don't have the finesse required to deal with a mortal's delicate ego."

"How dare you say that to me!" Shana gasped in outrage. "You make me sound like a child!"

"In some ways you are a child," Lucien responded impatiently. "You've spent your entire life in the coven, and you're naive when it comes to mortals and their behavior. I just don't want to see you ruin your life when it isn't necessary."

"You're the high priest, Lucien, and as such, I vowed to give you my loyalty. I did not, however, accord you the right to make personal decisions in my life," Shana stated, truly angry. It was exactly this type of warlock overprotective arrogance that made her yearn to escape Sanctuary. Since she was orphaned, every warlock within the coven took it upon himself to protect her.

"Shana, I'm only trying to do what's best for you."

"I'm almost twenty-seven years old, Lucien, and I'm tired of being treated like I'm seven. I'm also tired of being told that I'm naive. If I am, it's because every warlock in town is forever trying to do *what's best for me*, instead of letting me make my own mistakes."

"You may have a valid point," he conceded. "However, this is one instance where making a mistake could be self-destructive."

"It's also an instance where letting you do what you consider 'best for me' could affect my entire life. As I said, I don't want you privy to the intimate details between my mate and me. So, if anyone spellbinds the mortal, it will be me. If it backfires, I'll have to live with the consequences."

Lucien glared at her. Shana glared right back, determined to hold her ground. Her determination wavered, however, when he said, "I could alleviate this entire problem by refusing to let him stay."

"If he leaves, I'll leave with him," Shana stated staunchly, even though Lucien's threat rattled her. However, her anger was too strong to sway her from her resolve. She'd started out wanting to protect Lucien from Moira, but now she was fighting for her own autonomy. Instinct told her that if she didn't make the stand now, she'd never be in control of her own life.

"Don't be ridiculous," Lucien scoffed. "You can't leave Sanctuary without my permission."

"You're wrong, Lucien. I can leave without your permission. I just can't come back if I do."

He gaped at her in disbelief. "You feel so strongly about the issue of privacy that you'd risk banishment over it?"

"If you were in my place, wouldn't you?"

He stared at her for a long moment, before grudgingly admitting, "I suppose I would."

"Then you'll let me cast the spell?"

He glanced toward the mortal and frowned. "It's against my better judgment."

"I didn't ask about your better judgment, Lucien. I asked if you were going to let me cast the spell."

He returned his attention to her. "I suspect I'm going to regret this, but yes, you can cast it. I just hope you don't end up regretting it, too."

"So do I, Lucien," she conceded, willing to acknowledge that his concerns were valid. "But if I do, it will be because of my choice, not because of yours."

"I'll go get the car so we can take him to your house."

When he was gone, Shana knelt beside the mortal and muttered, "I just risked banishment for you. You had better be worth it."

It took Lucien a good fifteen minutes to return with the car. By the time he arrived, Shana was worriedly pacing the edge of the road.

Before he came to a full stop, she was pulling open his door. "He's still unconscious, Lucien, and that isn't normal."

As he climbed out of the car, he smiled sardonically. "Welcome to the world of mortals, Shana. Nothing about them is normal. Is there any other change in his physical condition?"

"No."

"Then stop worrying about him. When he's ready, he'll wake up."

He strode toward the man, and Shana quickly followed. "When we get him home, is there anything special I should do for him?"

"Keep him warm and give him something for the pain in his knee. That should do it," he replied as he clutched his crystal with one hand and waved the other over the man. The energy barrier disappeared. "For now, however, you need to cast a spell to immobilize his knee. We don't want to injure it further."

With a nod, Shana focused her gaze on the man's knee and began to chant. As she reached the last word, she waved her hand in a counterclockwise motion, and then flicked her fingers toward his leg. Spell-lightning flashed briefly around his knee.

"You are probably the most adept spell-caster in the coven, Shana."

"Thank you," Shana said, glancing toward him in surprise. It was rare for a warlock to compliment a witch's magical skills. They considered their powers superior, and in some ways they were. In everyday magic, however, most witches were better.

He leaned down to lift the man into his arms. "Let's get him settled. I need to get back to the festival and Ariel."

"I'll ride Portent home and meet you there," Shana said, following him to the car.

Lucien put the man onto the backseat, straightened, and shut the door. "Mortals are obsessed with their cars, Shana. It seems as if everyone owns one, and they drive them everywhere. If you want to live in their world, you're going to have to get over your fear of automobiles."

"Yeah, well, I'll work on that," Shana grumbled, irritated at his reminder that she was ill-prepared for the mortal world.

By the time she and Portent arrived home, Lucien was leaning against the front bumper of the car with his arms crossed over his chest. She expected him to issue another gibe, but, thankfully, he didn't. He merely retrieved the mortal from the backseat and followed her to the house.

As she led him to the bedroom, he said, "While you go mix a potion for his pain, I'll undress him."

"You don't need to do that," Shana objected. "I can take care of him from here. As you said, you need to get back to the festival, and you really shouldn't leave Ariel alone for too long. She is eight months pregnant."

"I'll get back to her as soon as he's undressed. He's heavy, Shana."

Shana rolled her eyes. "Lucien, I'm a witch, remember? I have the same physical strength that you do. I'm perfectly capable of undressing him."

"I said he's heavy."

"Warlocks!" Shana mumbled, heading for the

kitchen. "Why do they have to make everything a battle of superiority?"

Unfortunately, that was a question witches had been asking since the beginning of time. To date, not one of them had come up with the answer.

When she returned to the bedroom, Lucien had undressed the man and covered him. After she poured the small glass of herbal medicine into the man's mouth, she turned to Lucien. "Thanks for your help. I really appreciate it."

"Well, let's hope you're feeling that way in a few days," he stated grimly. "Cast the spell over him before he wakes up, Shana. I want to make sure that when—*if*," he corrected at her frown, "he leaves, he remembers nothing about his time here."

"I'll cast it the minute you're gone."

"Good. If you need any help with him, let me know."

"I will. Now, you'd better get back to the festival and Ariel."

He nodded and walked out. As he disappeared, Shana was hit with a sudden urge to run after him and ask him to stay. But if she did that, he'd sense something was up. He'd start questioning her, and she'd probably blurt out the entire Moira fiasco.

"You got yourself into the mess, and it's up to you to get yourself out of it," she said, turning back to the mortal. "And the first order of business is to get this spell out of the way."

Opening the charm bag she wore at her waist, she retrieved a small vial of amber liquid. Popping off the lid, she said, "Well, my friend, I guess it's time for a touch of magic. Don't worry. You won't feel a thing. You heard what Lucien said. I'm the most adept spellcaster in the coven.

"I also hope you aren't modest," she went on as she grabbed the edge of the sheet, "because to get the best results, I need to rub the contents of this little bottle all over your body. Well, maybe not over all of it, but a good portion of it."

She tossed back the covers and let out an appreciative sigh as her gaze traveled from his neck to his thighs. She knew from the lovemaking vision they'd shared that he was well-built, but he had been wearing moonlight and shadows. Lamplight revealed the full extent of corded muscle and sinew.

"I'm sure glad I didn't let Lucien cast this spell," she told him as she sat on the edge of the bed and poured the liquid onto his smooth chest. "I have a feeling that if we do end up as mates, we're going to have a *lot* of intense emotional moments. We'd have probably driven him crazy. I also think that I'd better get this over with quickly, or I'm liable to drive myself a little bit crazy."

She fell silent as she quickly rubbed the potion over his chest and down to his hips, trying to keep her eyes from straying into intimate territory, but failing miserably. As she eyed his male endowments, she felt a small stab of desire. Quickly, she returned her gaze to his face. If he was a warlock, she'd simply connect with his mind and play out her sensual fantasies. But he wasn't a warlock. He was a mortal with a very troubled soul.

After she finished rubbing the potion into his skin, she placed one hand over his heart, and the other in the center of his forehead. Then she murmured the incantation. She felt energy shoot down her arms and enter his body, and then it returned up her arms in a warm rush.

She removed her hands and gave him a wry smile. "Well, now you're spellbound. I sure wish you'd wake up so I could find out your name. We have a lot to talk about."

When his only response was a soft snore, she stood

and tossed the covers over him. Then she carried his dirty clothes to the laundry room and put them in the washing machine. When she returned, he was still out, and she sat down in the chair next to the bed and started her vigil. A short time later, he started shifting on the bed. A quick brush against his mind confirmed that her mysterious mortal was finally waking up. Shana shot to her feet, feeling both nervous and excited. In a moment, she'd be talking with the man who was to be her mate.

As Ryan began to surface from the blackness, he shifted his body. When he did, a sharp, tearing pain shot from his knee, causing him to groan.

"I know it hurts, but the injury isn't too serious. Just lie still," a woman murmured as he felt the mattress dip beside him.

He knew that voice! It was the woman from his nightmare! His eyes flew open, but everything was blurred. It took a moment for him to focus on her face. When he did, he stared at her in disbelief. In his nightmare she was no more than a shadow, and he'd never considered what she looked like. It was just as well he hadn't, he now determined, because nothing he could have imagined would have done her justice.

Her dark brown hair hung in a silken fall to her shoulders. She had a heart-shaped face with flawless features. Her large brown eyes were framed by long, thick lashes. Suddenly she smiled at him, and he realized that she had a perfect cupid's-bow mouth. Without a doubt, she was the most beautiful woman he'd ever seen. She was also a stranger. So why was she in his nightmare?

She interrupted his confused reflection with, "I'm Shana Morland, and I'm sorry that my horse and I caused you to crash. Do you remember what happened?"

Ryan frowned as the events leading up to the crash came rushing back. He recalled the nightmare and his death-defying drive along the mountain road. He remembered taking the fork, and a few minutes later he'd come around a bend and found himself practically on top of a racing horse. He'd realized that a collision was imminent, and he'd jerked the bike toward the side of the road.

From there, everything became muddled, though he had the oddest recollection of lightning circling around him. That must have been his imagination. In order for there to be lightning, there would have had to be a storm. He definitely recalled that the sky was clear.

"I'm sure things are confused right now. You took quite a fall," the woman said.

His frown deepened. She was right. He had taken quite a fall. In fact, considering the speed at which he'd been traveling, he should be dead, not lying here looking at a beautiful woman.

"Where the hell am I?" he muttered, trying to sit up.

She placed a hand against his shoulder to hold him in place. "Please lie still. I've given you something for the pain, but it will take awhile for it to work. The less you move, the less pain you'll have until then. And you're in Sanctuary."

Her use of the word "sanctuary" conjured up another memory. As he'd taken the fork in the road, he'd heard her voice whispering that he'd now found sanctuary and his journey was over. How had she been speaking to him in his mind?

"What's your name?" she asked, again breaking into his thoughts.

"Ryan Alden," he answered, glancing around him. He was in a fairly large room that reminded him of a castle he'd once visited in Scotland. The walls were made of stone. There was a small window positioned high on the far wall, through which he could see a star-studded sky and a full moon.

He continued his survey of the room, noting that old candle sconces had been converted to light fixtures. However, there were so few of them that they couldn't penetrate the dark corners. The only furniture he saw was the large bed he was lying on, a rough-hewn nightstand, and an equally rough-hewn chair. The room was as strange as the woman.

Again he tried to sit up. This time she let him. As another tearing pain shot from his knee to his groin, he almost wished she hadn't. When the covers fell to his lap, he suddenly realized he was naked beneath the covers. He wasn't sure what upset him the most. The fact that he'd been so out of it that he hadn't known he'd been undressed, or that there was a good possibility this woman had done the disrobing.

"Where the hell are my clothes?"

"They're being washed."

"Who undressed me?"

"Lucien."

"Who's Lucien?"

"He's the high priest."

"I'm in a convent?" he gasped. That would explain the strange room, but surely a woman this beautiful couldn't be a nun!

She laughed softly. "No, you're not in a convent. I told you, you're in Sanctuary."

"And what is Sanctuary?" he asked as he cautiously moved his leg. When he was hit with another wave of pain, he closed his eyes against it. He wanted to examine his knee to see what was wrong with it, but he'd have to toss back the covers. He wasn't about to do that in front of a strange woman, and he meant that both literally and figuratively. How could she have been haunting his dreams for the past six months?

"Sanctuary's a town in Pennsylvania," she said. "You know, if you'd lie still, you wouldn't be in so much pain."

"Yeah, well, you know what they say, no pain, no gain," he muttered. "I'd appreciate it if you'd bring me my clothes."

"As soon as they're dry, I'll bring them to you."

"Just bring me my duffel bag. I have plenty of clothes in it."

She blinked at him, as if he were suddenly speaking a foreign language. "Duffel bag?"

He released an impatient breath. "Yes, my duffel bag. It's strapped to the back of my bike. And speaking of my bike, where is it?"

"It's where you crashed."

"You left it lying on the side of the road?" he exclaimed in disbelief. "What's wrong with you, lady? That's an expensive bike. Someone will steal it!"

"My name is Shana, not lady, and people don't steal in Sanctuary."

"People steal everywhere."

"Not in Sanctuary."

"Fine," he snapped. "People don't steal in Sanctuary. Just get me my clothes so I can get out of here."

"But you can't walk," she objected. "Your knee is sprained. As I said, it isn't a serious injury, but I suspect it will be several days before you can walk on it."

Several days? That was totally unacceptable. He had to keep moving. If he didn't, the eyes would catch up with him. He shuddered at the thought.

"I dont' have to walk," he informed her. "All I have to do is sit. Now, get my clothes. The faster I get out of here, the better."

"How are you going to leave?"

"The same way I arrived. I'm going to get on my bike and hit the road."

"I'm afraid you can't do that. Your motorcycle is damaged."

"What do you mean it's damaged? What's wrong with it?" he demanded, a sense of panic stirring inside him. He had to have his bike. It was the only way he could outrun the eyes.

"I don't know the proper terminology, but I can show you," she answered.

"Fine. Get my clothes and we'll go."

She shook her head. "You can't walk, remember?"

"I'll manage," he snapped. "Just bring me my clothes!"

"But—"

"I don't want to hear your buts, lady. I want to go see my bike, and I want to do it now. So, go get my clothes so we can leave."

"We don't need to leave," she said impatiently. "If you insist on seeing your motorcycle, I can show it to you from here."

Before he could respond, she placed her hands against his temples. A peculiar jolt shot through him, making him feel as if he'd been invaded. Every self-protective instinct he possessed began screaming at him to pull away from her touch, but no matter how hard he tried, he couldn't move.

Suddenly, her eyes took on a strange glow, as if some inner power was pulsing inside her. He gulped and real fear shot through him. Who was she? *What* was she?

Relax, Ryan. Nothing I do will hurt you. Relax.

He was staring at her face, so he knew she wasn't speaking. How could she talk inside his head? It simply wasn't possible! He had to fight her. He had to get away from her. He had to . . .

Relax.

Despite his determination to escape her, he felt his body growing slack. Her eyes became so luminescent that he felt as if he were looking into a pair of head-lights on high beam. Oddly, he didn't feel blinded by the light, but drawn to it in mesmerized fascination.

Look, Ryan.

At her words the light vanished, and he was staring down at his bike. The headlight was on, but even as he watched, he saw it grow dimmer, the life draining out of it. The front wheel and fender had been torn away. The back wheel was twisted so that it pointed skyward. The body of the bike looked as if some huge hand had tried to rip it in two. He didn't need an insurance appraiser to tell him it was totalled.

Panic surged through him. How was he going to outrun the eyes if he didn't have his bike?

Now you've found Sanctuary. Your journey is at its end.

No! That wasn't true! If his journey had ended, he wouldn't be alive. He'd be down there with his bike, his life draining away. Why wasn't he down there with his bike? How was he going to outrun the eyes?

Come to me, Ryan. Let me help you.

The voice came from behind him and he spun around. The shadow-woman from his nightmare stood in the distance. She was wearing a long, black robe with a hood that covered her head. Though he couldn't see her face, he now knew who she was. Her name was Shana, and she was offering him sanctuary. As she stretched her arms toward him, he wanted to go to her but he knew the eyes would never let him go.

The eyes aren't here, Ryan. Come to me. Let me help you.

He glanced around him in confusion. It was true. The eyes weren't here. Where had they gone?

Come, Ryan. I will help you, but you must hurry before it's too late!

Her words were compelling, and he started running

toward her. As he drew closer to her, a sense of unease stirred inside him. There was something wrong with her, but he couldn't pinpoint what it was. He slowed his step, wishing he could see her face, but it was shielded beneath the robe's hood.

Ryan, if you want me to save you from the eyes, you must hurry! she insisted when he stopped several feet away from her.

Again, her words were compelling, filling him with an overwhelming need to rush into her arms. But as he began to take a step forward, some primitive instinct made him step back instead.

The moment he did, he recognized what was wrong with her. He couldn't see her face, but he could see her eyes glowing from the depths of the robe's hood. Though they had the same luminescent sheen as Shana Morland's, there was a paradoxical quality of smothering darkness lurking beneath the surface.

Who are you? he demanded, taking another step back.

I'm Shana, and you must hurry, Ryan. Look behind you. The eyes are coming.

With a shudder, Ryan glanced over his shoulder. It was true. They were bearing down on him with such speed that in a matter of moments they would overtake him.

Ryan, please. Come to me. Let me help you!

He jerked his head back toward her. She still had her arms extended. All he had to do was go to her, and she would protect him—provide him sanctuary.

He took a step toward her. When he did, he saw a flash of triumph flare through her eyes. At that moment, he knew who she was, and a combination of fear and hatred surged through him.

He lunged for her, determined to destroy her, but just as he reached her, a voice yelled, "Ryan! Wake up!"

At the urgent order, the shadow-woman vanished and Ryan found himself staring at the woman named Shana. Her brow was contracted in a worried frown, and he knew her concern wasn't real. She was trying to deceive him just as she had before. But he knew better, because he could now sense her evil. She would never fool him again.

Looking her in the eye, he said, "I killed you once, and I'll do it again. You'll never defeat me. Never."

Shana stared at Ryan in horrified disbelief, though she couldn't decide what was more alarming. His threatening words or his face. He didn't even look like the same man. It was as if his entire facial structure had undergone a metamorphosis.

She blinked several times in rapid succession, sure that it was just her imagination. When she again focused on him, the image hadn't changed. His eyes were set deeper into his face and had an almost Oriental cast to their edges. His cheekbones were higher, more pronounced. His nose seemed to have lengthened and taken on a slight hook at the end. His cheeks were more hollow, his chin more pointed, and his jaw more square. Even the color of his hair had darkened. He had the same fierce looks of a warlock! What was going on?

Whatever it was, she'd better figure out a way to deal with him and fast! He was glaring at her with so much hatred that she knew it was only a matter of moments before he'd act on the emotion. She was also sure that when he did, he'd make every effort to carry out his threat to kill her.

Though her survival instincts were telling her to get away from him, she reminded herself that she was a witch and he was a mortal. Her powers would protect her against him. Reassured, she tried to probe his mind. When all she encountered was the emotional emptiness she'd experienced following his accident, she quickly pulled away. Moira had trapped her in that soulless desert once. She wasn't about to let her do it again.

"Who are you?" she asked, deciding that talking might help her figure out what was going on.

His eyes narrowed to dangerous slits. "You know who I am."

She shook her head. "No, I don't. You're a stranger to me."

"You still think you can fool me, don't you? You can't. I can recognize your evil no matter what guise you wear. You'll never trick me again."

"I'm not trying to trick you. I just want to know who you are. It's only fair that I know the name of the man who wants to kill me."

"I'm the man who *will* kill you," he stated.

"If that's true, then it won't hurt you to tell me, will it?" she countered, shivering at his words. He'd issued them with such cold certainty.

He frowned, as though confused by her logic, and then he said, "I am Aric."

Aric? Shana felt as if she'd been punched in the stomach. That was the name of the warlock who had killed Moira and then taken his own life. He was the reason for the curse! What in the world was Moira up to?

The future is mine, and now yours will be mine.

As Moira's familiar litany flashed through Shana's mind, Ryan-Aric slumped back onto the pillow. Shana watched, dazed, as his features slowly returned to normal. When the transformation was over, his slack expression told her he'd lapsed back into unconsciousness. Anxiously, she tried to probe his mind, but there was nothing there. She didn't even encounter the emotional emptiness she'd found earlier. If he hadn't been breathing normally, she would have been convinced he was dead.

"What have you done to him, Moira?" Shana asked, leaping to her feet and propping her hands on her hips.

There was no answer, but she didn't need one. A Tarot card magically appeared on the edge of the bed. It was The Devil, and his face was Ryan's. Black magic was at work here.

· CHAPTER THREE ·

The Star (Reversed)
Stubbornness, Pessimism and Doubt

"Oh, come on, Moira, you can do better than this!" Shana declared, snatching the card off the bed. "I don't need a Tarot card to tell me I'm dealing with black magic. That would be obvious even to a mortal. And speaking of mortals, why have you involved this one in your game? Could it be that you aren't as powerful as you want me to believe?"

She hoped the taunt would goad Moira out of hiding, but she wasn't surprised when it didn't. If Moira was as powerful as Shana believed, she had nothing to gain by responding. And if, by some slim chance, she wasn't that powerful, she'd never confirm it.

"So what am I going to do about you?" Shana muttered, tucking the new Tarot card into her back pocket as she returned her attention to Ryan.

Her first impulse was to summon Lucien again. Then she realized that was probably why Moira had pulled this stunt. She wanted Lucien to know about her presence so she'd have more souls to stalk.

"I am not going to tell Lucien about you, Moira,"

Shana said, searching the room for some sign of her nemesis. To her frustration even the shadows were still, though she knew Moira was here. She could feel her lurking presence. "This is between you and me, and I will not sacrifice anyone else, including this mortal. So you release him from whatever enchantment you've cast over him, and you do it right now."

Even as she issued the order, she knew Moira wasn't going to heed it. Still, she glanced toward Ryan expectantly. When nothing happened, she released a sigh of resignation. She was going to have to break the enchantment over him. Unfortunately, she'd never heard of one that reduced a person to total mindlessness, so she had no idea how to counteract it. She also knew that she had to be careful. The mortal psyche was fragile. If she used too much power on Ryan, she could end up destroying his sanity.

"Why didn't I pay more attention in school to the lessons on magic and its effect on mortal physiology?" she grumbled. Because she had been too busy daydreaming about escaping Sanctuary and seeing the sights in the mortal world. That pastime had been more fascinating than a dry recitation on the physical and mental limitations of their race.

"You know, Ryan, you could make this easy by just fighting against Moira and waking up on your own," she said, frowning at him. "She is a spirit, so her real power is in her ability to make you believe what she wants you to believe. In order to truly spellbind you, she'd have to be alive."

When he didn't even twitch a muscle in response, she heaved an aggravated sigh. She had to come up with a way to reach him, but how?

Suddenly, she recalled Lucien claiming that men were ruled by ego and libido. She didn't know Ryan, so she couldn't appeal to his ego. His libido, however, was a different matter. From the moment members of her race hit puberty, they were encouraged to explore their sexuality through dream lovemaking. She'd had enough dream lovers over the years that she was confident she could incite Ryan's baser nature. If Lucien's premise was true, then sexual arousal might be enough encouragement for Ryan to break loose from Moira's hold over him.

Her quandary, however, was how to proceed. She was sure that the fastest way to reach him would be to insert the vision she'd seen of them making love into his mind. She quickly discarded that option, however. It might trigger a recollection of the violent scenes that followed. Considering that he'd been threatening to kill her when he passed out, she wasn't about to chance resurrecting any hostile emotions. She was just going to have to make up her own lovemaking scenario. Hopefully, men shared the same sexual fantasies as warlocks.

Sitting on the edge of the bed, she brushed her mind against his, confirming that there was still nobody home. She shivered at the disconcerting sensation, and she couldn't help wondering if she was doing the right thing. Moira already had control of his mind. What if her own manipulation was too much for him? She didn't think she could live with herself if she destroyed him.

The alternative, however, was to involve Lucien and possibly put the entire coven at risk. But surely there was *someone* who could help her. Of course! She should summon Lucien's cousin, Sebastian Moran. Sebastian was the troubleshooter for the high council, which was composed of the high priests from all the covens around the world. Lucien was able to draw upon the power of all the coven members, but Sebastian was able to draw upon the power of all the high priests. He was, quite simply, the most powerful war-lock alive. Surely he could defeat Moira.

And what if he can't defeat her? What if Moira claims his soul and his powers transfer to her? Remember, she was the most powerful witch who ever lived. If she has retained her own power and it combines with his, what kind of evil will you be loosing upon the world?

"I hate moral dilemmas!" Shana declared with a groan. She also knew that as unacceptable as it was, she only had one choice. She had to take a chance with Ryan. The alternative was far too dangerous to ignore.

Drawing in a deep breath, she closed her eyes and began to concentrate. Since the vision they'd shared had taken place in a meadow, she decided to use a similar outdoor setting so he'd have something familiar to ground him. She chose a favorite spot of hers beside the mountain stream flowing through Sanctuary. Beavers had dammed a portion of it, creating a deep pool that was perfect for swimming on a hot summer day. Instead of nighttime, she visualized a hot, lazy afternoon.

As the details took form in her mind's eye, she began to concentrate on the sensory particulars—the sound of water rushing by, the intermittent singing of birds, and the low buzz of insects. The smell of rich earth and fragrant trees and bushes. The sight of sunlight streaming through the thick boughs of oak trees and dappling the water with shimmering golden circles. When the clarity of her mental vista became real to her, she envisioned Ryan swimming naked in the pool, his strokes powerful and the water sluicing over his body. Within moments, he had become as real to her as the setting.

Drawing in another breath, she let her mind connect with his. The feeling of absolute emptiness was so startling that for a moment she almost lost her concentration. Quickly, she forced her attention back to the pool and let herself become absorbed in the fantasy. As she watched him swim, catching a glimpse of a strong arm, a muscular back, and tight, hard buttocks, she gave free rein to her emotions.

Desire was simmering inside her when he finally swam toward shore and began to emerge like some pagan water god. His tanned skin gleamed gold. The sun turned the water droplets clinging to his hair and skin into sparkling diamonds. As he strode toward her, her gaze traveled from the sleek cap of his wet hair to his groin, and she caught her breath. He was fully and magnificently aroused. She yearned to touch him, cup him, stroke him until he was quivering in her hand, and then she'd . . .

"You'd what?" he murmured, coming to a stop in front of her.

Reluctantly, she dragged her gaze to his face, not in the least disconcerted that he'd evidently read her mind. As her eyes met his, the lust she saw burning in their depths ignited her own passion.

Her voice was no more than a soft exhalation as she replied, "Anything you want."

"Anything?" he repeated as he dropped to the blanket she was sitting on. Sprawling on his side beside her, he seemed oblivious to his nakedness, which made her more conscious of it.

"Anything," she affirmed.

"Well, right now, I want you to take off your T-shirt. Will you do that for me?"

She didn't bother answering. She reached for the hem of her T-shirt, stripped it over her head, and tossed it aside. His quick intake of breath at the sight of her bare breasts sent a thrill of excitement through her. But that thrill was nothing compared to the heat that erupted inside her when he reached out and brushed his fingertips across one nipple and then the other, urging them into taut peaks.

Dropping his hand to the blanket, he said, "Now I want you to take off your jeans."

Shana pulled off her sandals and stood. Slowly, she popped open the snap and lowered the zipper. As she watched him watch her with complete absorption, she let her mind mesh with his until she was feeling what he was feeling. She was so connected with him, that she experienced the hitch in his breathing, the quickening of his pulse, and the further hardening of his penis at her striptease. By the time she finally let her jeans drop to the ground and stepped out of them, he was so overwhelmed by the sensations of his need for her that she could barely stand the assault on her own senses. No one had ever wanted her this badly, and it sent a titillating sense of feminine power coursing through her.

"What do you want me to do now?" she asked, her voice so husky she barely recognized it as her own.

"I want you to come here," he said, extending his hand. She took it and let him pull her toward him. When she stood beside him, he released her hand, rolled to his back, and ordered, "Stand over me."

She moved so that she stood with a leg on either side of his narrow waist. He placed his hands on her ankles, and then stroked upward to the tops of her thighs. He slipped his fingertips beneath the elastic at the legs of her red silk panties and slid his hands toward the apex of her thighs.

As he drew close to the center of her own arousal, Shana caught her breath in anticipation of his intimate caress. Instead of caressing her, however, he withdrew his fingers and slid his hands to her inner thighs.

"Do you want me?" he rasped.

"You know I do," she managed around a gasp as his hands swept down to her knees and then back up. He came so close to the crotch of her panties that she could feel the heat of his hands through the fabric. Again he withdrew without touching her, and she stared down at him in frustration. "Do you want to torture me?"

"Only enough to make you want me as much as I want you," he answered, sliding his hands to the back of her knees and urging her to kneel.

She dropped to her knees so that she was straddling his hips, but as she started to lower herself against his erection, he caught her waist with his hands. "Not yet."

She opened her mouth to object, but he placed his fingers against her lips, reminding, "You said you'd do anything I want, and right now I want you to kneel upright. I'm going to touch you, and while I'm doing it, I want you to hold as still as a statue until I tell you you can move. Will you do that for me, Shana?"

The image his words evoked was so sexy that Shana couldn't speak, so she answered him with a nod. When she did, he removed his fingers from her lips and said, "Good. Now, just kneel right where you are and don't move a muscle."

As he issued the order, he raised his hands to her breasts and fondled her nipples. Then he began to circle them, first in a clockwise motion, and then in a counterclockwise motion. Suddenly, he pinched them lightly. The action was so unexpected that she jumped, though it wasn't from pain. It was from a hot shiver of excitement that shot from her breasts to her womb.

"Ah, Shana, shame on you," he scolded with a seductive chuckle. "You're supposed to hold still, remember?"

"I can't," she gasped, jumping again when he cupped her breasts in his hands and began kneading them.

"Sure you can," he murmured. "All you have to do is concentrate. Maybe it would work better if you closed your eyes."

Shana knew that closing her eyes would make it harder to hold still. Without her being able to see what he was doing, he'd be more apt to catch her off-guard. As she stared into the lambent depths of his dark eyes, she suddenly realized that that was the purpose of his game. He wanted to see her involuntary reaction to his unexpected touches. What startled her was that this was not a fantasy she'd played out before. That could only mean one thing. Somehow, Ryan had taken over her fantasy and was making it his own.

That means you've broken Moira's hold on him. There's no reason for you to continue with the dream lovemaking. It's time for you to pull away.

Just as she reached that conclusion, Ryan slid a hand between her thighs. She gasped, robbed of all thought as he cupped her, his thumb stroking insistently against her silk-covered clitoris.

With a groan she leaned her head back and closed her eyes. Though she had agreed to hold still for him, she couldn't stop herself from rocking against his hand. Never had dream lovemaking been so *real,* nor had she ever been sent hurling toward climax so swiftly.

Just as she hit the crest of fulfillment, Moira's voice declared triumphantly, *The future is mine, and now yours will be mine!*

Shana's eyes flew open at Moira's untimely intrusion, and her mouth dropped open in shock. She and Ryan were no longer in the fantasy setting along the stream. She was straddling his sheet-covered hips on the bed, and she was wearing nothing but her red silk panties and his very capable hands.

That was impossible! Fantasy could *not* turn into reality without her knowing it. But it *had* happened without her knowledge, and it was apparent that this was Moira's handiwork. Resting on the pillow beside Ryan's head was another Tarot card. This one was The Star, reversed. The face of the naked woman pouring the Waters of Life from two ewers was hers, but the meaning of the card—stubbornness, pessimism, and doubt confused her.

Before she could analyze what the card was predicting, Ryan suddenly jerked his hands away from her body and bellowed, "What the hell do you think you're doing?"

Shana arched a brow at his angry tone. "I think that's obvious, Ryan. I'm making love with you."

Ryan blinked, startled by Shana's response, though he didn't know why. It *was* obvious what was going on. The trouble was, he didn't know how they had ended up in bed. The last thing he remembered was Shana placing her hands against his temples and her eyes taking on a strange glow. He'd tried to escape her, but he hadn't been able to move, and then . . .

No matter how hard he tried, he couldn't recall what happened after that. His instincts, however, were screaming at him to get away from Shana Morland as fast as he could. Unfortunately, she was straddling his hips, and outside of pushing her away from him, he was trapped. For some reason, he was averse to touching her. It was as if some inner alarm was warning him that if he did touch her, he would lose control over . . .

Lose control over what? he wondered in confusion, when the thought refused to complete itself.

Involuntarily, he dropped his gaze to her full, rose-tipped breasts and then lower to the sexy scrap of red silk clinging to her slender hips. Suddenly, the memory of caressing her intimately, of feeling the hot, damp heat of her through the silk, came rushing back. When it did, desire erupted inside him with an intensity that he'd never experienced before. He wanted to grab her and throw her to the bed. He wanted to rip those panties off her and torment her with his hands and mouth until she was screaming for him to make love to her. Then he'd ruthlessly take her, bringing her to climax after climax until she was begging him to stop. He wouldn't heed her request. He'd continue to make her climax until she could no longer move, no longer think. Only when she was so weak she was defenseless against him would he be satisfied.

As the fantasy ended, Ryan shuddered. He hadn't just envisioned a healthy bout of uncontrolled passion. There had been an undercurrent of savagery—a primitive need to conquer. Instinct told him that if he ever made love to Shana Morland, there was a possibility he might physically harm her, because the emotions she stirred up inside him bordered on violence.

Knowing that he had to get away from her, and the sooner the better, he glanced up and rasped, "Get away from me, lady, and do it right now!"

Her eyes widened in surprise at his order, and she opened her mouth, as if to object. Evidently, she changed her mind, because she closed it and moved to the edge of the bed.

The moment she did, Ryan bolted upright. He gasped as excruciating pain exploded in his knee. It hurt so badly that he couldn't breathe, and he gritted his teeth as he fought his way through the wave of pain.

"Ryan, you need to lie still. It's going to take awhile for the pain potion to work," Shana said, laying her hand on his forearm.

"Don't touch me!" he yelled, jerking away from her.

She frowned at him. "I just want to help you."

"If you want to help me, then get my clothes so I can get the hell out of here."

"We've already discussed this, Ryan," she said as she climbed off the bed. Grabbing her T-shirt off the floor, she pulled it over her head. Then she retrieved her jeans and stepped into them. As she pulled them on, she continued, "You can't leave because your motorcycle is damaged and you can't walk."

At the mention of his bike, an image of the Harley lying broken and dying on the side of the road flooded into Ryan's mind. He closed his eyes as panic welled up inside him. How was he going to outrun the eyes without his bike?

Now you've found Sanctuary. Your journey is at its end.

His eyes flew open and he glared at Shana. "How do you do that?"

"Do what?" she asked, looking bewildered.

"Dammit, lady! Don't play games with me."

"My name is Shana, not lady, and I'm not playing games with you."

"The hell you aren't! You've been haunting my nightmares for the past six months, and now you've started babbling in my head. Well, I want you to stop it and leave me alone!"

"You've been having nightmares for the past six months?" she gasped. "When exactly did they start, Ryan? Was it on Samhain?"

"Samhain?" he repeated in confusion. The word sounded familiar, but he couldn't quite place it.

"Yes, Samhain, although I think you probably call it Halloween."

Halloween. The word sent Ryan tumbling back in time.

"What have we got?" Ryan asked George Raines, the middle-aged surgical nurse on the night shift, as he burst through the doors of the hospital's surgical unit.

"Five-year-old girl with multiple trauma," George answered, following him into the doctors' dressing room. "We're still waiting for the X rays, but initial examination revealed an open fracture of the right leg, which severed an artery. The paramedics stopped the bleeding, but her blood pressure is still dropping, despite transfusion."

"Then we've got internal bleeding," Ryan noted as he began to strip off his clothes.

"Considering the distension of the abdomen, it looks like a ruptured spleen," George concurred. "She also has major head trauma and possible spinal damage. We've called both orthopedics and neurosurgery, and they have people on the way. The girl's entire right rib cage is caved in, and there's every indication that we're dealing with a punctured lung. These are just the preliminary diagnoses. I suspect that once we get the X rays we're going to find a lot more wrong with her."

Ryan cursed as he reached for the pants to his scrub suit and began to step into them. "What the hell happened to her?"

"Her father caught her sneaking candy out of her trick-or-treat bag after he told her she couldn't have any more."

Ryan stopped dressing and stared at George in disbelief. He didn't know why he felt so stunned. After five years as a pediatric trauma surgeon, he should be inured to this scenario. More than half of his patients were victims of child abuse. But he hadn't become accustomed to adults beating helpless children, and he knew he never would.

"Happy Halloween," he muttered grimly as he resumed dressing.

"Yeah, it's getting to be almost as much fun as Christmas," George responded dryly as he walked out of the dressing room.

His sarcasm wasn't lost on Ryan. It seemed that they got more child abuse victims during the Christmas holiday season than at any other time of the year.

When Ryan entered the surgical suite and got his first look at the child, a white-hot anger enveloped him. Her face was so badly beaten that if George hadn't told him her sex, he wouldn't have been able to determine her gender. He was also startled to see the child was awake. He knew that they couldn't anesthetize her until they had the X rays and were able to determine the extent of her head injuries. However, the agonizing pain she had to be suffering should have rendered her unconscious.

Ryan muttered a violent curse beneath his breath as her gaze latched onto his. Her eyes were nearly swollen shut, but he could see the confusion and fear in their pain-glazed depths. His heart contracted. He wanted to brush his hand across her brow to reassure her, but there wasn't a spot on her face that wasn't bruised. He was afraid that even the gentlest touch might cause her more pain.

He leaned down so that his mouth was close to her ear. "I know it hurts, sweetheart, but I promise that in just a few minutes all the pain will go away. Then I'm going to fix you up as good as new."

Her lips moved, and his heart broke at the realization that she was trying to smile. He also felt humbled at the look of trust that entered her eyes. He smiled and gave her a thumbs-up sign.

He no more than lowered his hand than the heart monitor went crazy. One glance toward it, and Ryan knew the child was going into cardiac arrest.

No! he screamed inwardly as he began to issue CPR instructions by rote. *I just told her I'm going to make her better. I will not let her die!*

Even as he made the vow, a flat line registered on

the monitor. Frantically, he worked to save the child. When she didn't respond to traditional CPR methods, he yelled, "Give me a scalpel! We'll do open-heart massage!"

"It's too late," George said, placing his hand on Ryan's arm. "It's been nearly fifteen minutes. She's gone, Doc. There's nothing we can do."

Turning away from the nurse, Ryan looked down at the child's battered, swollen face. Her eyes were open, staring up at him, and he could swear he could still see trust glimmering in them. He'd told her he'd fix her up as good as new, and she had believed him—trusted him—to make that happen. How could he have let her die?

Blinking against the sting of tears, he gently brushed his hand over her face, closing her eyelids. Then he reached for the sheet to cover her. As he drew it up her broken body, he noticed her clenched fist. Releasing the sheet, he lifted her hand. It wasn't even large enough to fill his palm.

Carefully, he eased her fingers open, and when he did he caught his breath in a painful gasp. She was clutching a piece of pumpkin-shaped candy.

"The staff should have found this when they prepped you," he mumured. "They should have never let you come in here with it, but I guess they were too worried about getting you into surgery to catch everything."

He folded her fingers back over it and glanced up at her face, whispering, "You died for it, sweetheart. It's only fair that you take it with you."

After placing her hand back on the table, he finished covering her. Then he turned and walked out, unable to get the image of her trusting eyes out of his mind.

That night she came to haunt him in his dreams, and she brought all the other dozen or so children he'd lost with her. As their eyes surrounded him, accusing

him for failing them, he woke up screaming. It was
then that he knew that he would never be able to escape them—that they would never let him rest. He had
promised to save them, and then he had stood by and
let them slip into the clutches of that old bastard, Father Death. The children would never forgive him for
that. He couldn't blame them, because he'd never be
able to forgive himself.

"Ryan, this is very important," Shana said, breaking
into his tortured reverie. "Did your nightmares start
on Samhain?"

"When they started doesn't matter," he stated, furious with her for making him relive the horror of Halloween. "What matters is that you get the hell out
of them."

"I am not in your nightmares, Ryan, but I think I
know who is. Now, would you please answer my question? Did your nightmares start on Samhain?"

"I'll make you a deal," he said. "You bring me my
clothes so I can get the hell out of here, and I'll answer
your question."

"If what I suspect is true, you can't leave, Ryan."

"Are you implying that you intend to keep me here
against my will? That's called kidnapping, lady, and it's
against the law!"

"I am not trying to kidnap you," she denied impatiently, "and if you want to leave, I can't stop you. I
am not allowed to interfere with your free will. Moira,
however, is a different matter. As a spirit-witch she is
not bound by the covenant of my race. If, as I believe,
she somehow managed to cast a spell over you on Samhain, then you'll be able to leave only if she wants
you to leave. Since she's the one who brought you to
Sanctuary, I'm afraid you're stuck here until I've either
defeated her or she's claimed my soul."

"I think I just figured this out," Ryan said, regarding her narrowly. "Sanctuary is a mental institution, and you're the head fruitcake, right?"

"I am not crazy, Ryan. I'm a witch."

"Yeah, well, don't worry about it, honey. I have yet to meet a woman who wasn't. Now, why don't you go round up your keeper for me so I can get dressed and leave?"

"You aren't going to believe me until I prove to you what I am, are you?"

"Look, lady, I don't want you to prove anything to me," Ryan responded in exasperation. "All I want to do is get out of here. Now, are you going to go get whomever I have to talk to to make that happen? Or am I going to have to go running around this joint buck naked to get some help?"

"You don't have to go anywhere," she answered. "If you want your clothes, I'll get them for you right now."

"Great. We're finally making some progress."

"Yes, I think we finally are," she said, raising her arms over her head. "Watch carefully, Ryan, because I'm not only going to get you your clothes, I'm going to give you your first lesson in witchcraft."

Shana knew that what she was about to do was melodramatic, but she didn't have time for subtlety. Until Ryan was willing to accept that she was a witch, he would continue to fight her. If her premise was right and Moira had cast some kind of enchantment over him during Samhain, it was imperative that he cooperate with her.

She crossed her arms over her head and murmured a short incantation. An inch-tall whirlwind immediately formed at her feet. She uncrossed her arms and dropped them to her sides. Then she extended her hands in front of her and held them at waist level. The whirlwind began to grow in size until it stood as high as her waist and its top was a good two feet in diameter. She looked down into the funnel and then up at Ryan, who was staring at her in openmouthed amazement.

"What piece of clothing would you like first? Your underwear?"

Before he could respond, she waved a hand over the top of the funnel, and his shorts rose into the air. She flicked her fingers toward them, and they flew across the room, hitting Ryan directly in the face.

"Sorry about that. I haven't done this in a long time, so my aim is off." As she spoke, she again waved her hand over the top. This time, both his jeans and his black T-shirt rose. "Look at this. Two for the price of one."

She left them suspended in the air and glanced back into the funnel, "Oops. I forgot your socks and boots, and of course, you'll need your jacket. I've always liked black leather. There's something so . . . dangerous about it."

When all the items were hanging in the air, she again flicked her fingers. The clothing floated to the bed and dropped to the mattress, and his boots landed on the floor beside the bed.

"Let's see what else we have in here," she murmured, making a show of looking into the funnel. "Ah, yes, your personal items."

With another wave, his wallet, a handful of change, a pack of cigarettes, and a cigarette lighter appeared. She circled her hand in a clockwise motion, and then closed it into a fist. The items disappeared. When she opened her hand, they reappeared on the nightstand.

Again, she extended her hands at waist level and began to lower them. The funnel shrank back to an inch-tall whirlwind. Raising her arms above her head, she crossed them and murmured the appropriate chant. The whirlwind disappeared.

Lowering her arms, she gave Ryan a smug smile. "Now do you believe that I'm a witch?"

Instead of answering, he reached for the cigarette package and the lighter. After tapping out a cigarette, he lit it and tossed the pack and lighter back to the nightstand.

He inhaled deeply on the cigarette and blew a stream of smoke toward the ceiling, before saying, "You're a good magician, but you're not as good as the one who made the Statue of Liberty disappear a few years ago. Now, *that* was a hell of a trick."

Shana's jaw dropped in disbelief. When she realized her mouth was open, she closed it and said, "I am not a magician. I'm a witch."

"In that case, how about conjuring up an ashtray for me? Or aren't you able to do tricks on demand?"

Shana was still so flabbergasted by his refusal to believe her that she could only shake her head. How could he *not* believe after what she'd done? Of course! That's what the Tarot card had meant. Ryan was going to stubbornly refuse to listen to her. But he *had* to listen to her, or she'd never figure out Moira's plan.

"You can conjure up my clothes, but you can't come up with a simple ashtray?" he taunted, apparently considering her head shake a denial.

"Of course I can come up with an ashtray," she said, flicking her wrist. A small, clear glass ashtray immediately appeared on the bed. "Are you now satisfied that I'm a witch?' '

He tapped ashes into the dish and then took a drag on his cigarette. Blowing another column of smoke toward the ceiling, he said, "I'm not that gullible, lady."

"How can you say that after everything I've done?" she gasped, incredulous.

"Look, you don't need to get upset about this," he replied. "If you want to believe you're a witch, that's fine with me. Everyone is entitled to their delusions."

"You're impossible!" she declared in exasperation. "What do I have to do to make you believe me?"

He shrugged. "Turn me into a frog?"

"That's the most ridiculous thing I have ever heard," she replied, propping her hands on her hips and frowning at him. "In the first place, it's a physical impossibility. You don't share the same physiology as a frog. But even if it were possible, why would you want to be a frog?"

"It works in the fairy tales. Of course, if some princess comes along and kisses me, she'll be disappointed. Even at my best, no one would ever call me a prince."

Shanna felt as if she'd been transported to some alien world. What in the world were fairy tales, and why would a princess want to kiss a frog? She started to ask, but realized that it had nothing to do with the matter at hand. How was she going to prove to him she was a witch?

"What?" she said, realizing he'd been talking, and she'd been so lost in thought she hadn't heard a word.

"I said I would like some privacy so I can get dressed."

"I cast a spell over your knee to protect it from further injury," she told him. "You won't be able to bend it, and if you start moving around, you're going to experience a lot of pain. I'll have to help you dress."

Scowling at her, he grabbed the edge of the sheet and pulled it further up his body. "I don't know what kind of trick you're trying to pull now, lady, but whatever it is, you can forget it. I don't expose myself to strange women."

"I am not a strange woman. I'm a—"

"I know, you're a witch," he interrupted irritably.

"And for the record, I don't expose myself to strange witches, either."

"There's no reason for you to be modest, Ryan," she said. "I've already seen your body, and I have to say that it is as magnificent as any warlock's. You're going to make a fabulous mate, assuming of course that I can defeat Moira, which I have every intention of doing.

"So, tell me, are male or female offspring dominant in your family line?" she asked, curious. "They run fifty-fifty in mine, so your genetic background will be the deciding factor in whether or not we have a son or a daughter."

Ryan blinked at Shana several times in rapid succession, deciding that this must have been what Alice felt like when she tumbled down the rabbit hole. He also concluded that his earlier premise was right. Sanctuary had to be a mental institution, and if Shana Morland wasn't their star patient, he'd eat his boots.

Since she was staring at him expectantly, he knew he had to say something, so he muttered, "You are the craziest woman I have ever met."

She shook her head. "Insanity does not run in my race. Unless, of course, you count the occasional megalomaniac," she amended. "They're rare, but they do pop up every now and then. I'm afraid that that's what happened to our previous high priest, Galen Morgan. But he's being rehabilitated and he's much better now."

"I'm glad to hear that," Ryan stated dryly. "And as fascinating as I find this discussion, I'd appreciate it if you'd leave so I can get dressed."

"You really will need my help, Ryan," she reasserted. "I wasn't kidding when I said you'll experience a lot of pain if you start moving your leg around."

Ryan closed his eyes and counted to ten, determined to hold onto his temper. She couldn't help it if she was a few bricks short of a full load, but she'd already managed to crawl into bed with him without him even knowing it. With her now spouting nonsense about them having a child together, he wasn't going to let her get near him. He had many faults, but taking sexual advantage of mentally ill women was not one of them, even if they were gorgeous enough to pose as a *Playboy* centerfold.

Opening his eyes, he said, "I appreciate the offer, but I'd rather do this myself." When she looked as if she was going to continue arguing with him, he quickly added, "If I run into trouble, I'll call for you. Now, will you *please* leave?"

"If you insist," she agreed, although her expression said she was doing so reluctantly. "I'll be waiting outside the door, but you must be careful, Ryan."

"I'll be careful," he assured. "Now, go."

"All right, but if you need me—"

"I'll call." When she finally walked out and closed the door behind her, Ryan muttered, "Thank God."

He tossed back the sheet and cursed when he saw his injured knee. It was swollen to twice its normal size, and the bruise forming around it assured him it was going to be a long time before it was back to normal.

Leaning forward, he gently probed the patella, flinching at the pain the touch provoked. Gritting his teeth, he continued his examination, relieved to discover that though the injury hurt like hell, it appeared to be nothing more than a bad sprain. Once he got away from this loony bin and its witchery nut, he'd pick up an elastic bandage. And the sooner he got dressed, the sooner he could leave, he reminded himself, preparing to move to the edge of the bed.

"What the hell?" he suddenly exclaimed when his knee wouldn't bend.

Quickly, he leaned forward and examined it again,

confirming that there didn't appear to be anything seriously wrong with it. But when he tried to bend it, it still wouldn't give.

As he stared down at it in confusion, Shana's voice suddenly reverberated in his mind. *I cast a spell over your knee to protect it from further injury. You won't be able to bend it.*

"That's impossible!" Ryan declared vehemently. "There is no such thing as a witch!"

But even as he made the declaration, an inner voice whispered, *If that's true, then why can't you bend your knee?*

It's just hypnotism, he told himself. She's a magician, and some magicians are also hypnotists.

But even as he offered himself the explanation, he knew it wasn't true. When he was in medical school, he'd volunteered for a study involving the use of hypnosis to stop smoking. He hadn't been accepted into the study, because he was one of the few people who could not be hypnotized.

Slowly, he turned his head toward the door. When his gaze finally landed on it, he knew that no matter how much he wanted to deny it, Shana Morland had told him the truth. She was a witch. What in hell was he going to do?

CHAPTER FOUR

The Moon
Unforseen Perils, Deception and Psychic Influence

"There is no such thing as a witch. It has to be some form of hypnotism, and what you're going to do is get dressed. Then you're going to get out of here," Ryan told himself firmly.

As he spoke, he scooted to the edge of the bed and swung his good leg over it. Using his hands for support, he began to ease his bad leg over the side. Pain zipped up his leg like an angry lightning bolt, and he mentally chanted a litany of curses until his heel was finally resting on the hardwood floor. Though his every instinct was telling him to hurry, his stiff leg impeded his progress, and it seemed to take forever for him to dress.

"Okay, you're on the downhill slide now," he told himself when he'd finally gotten his clothes on and reached for his boots.

He grabbed the one for his bad leg and started to pull it on. At the first tug, his injured muscles rebelled at the abuse, and he sucked in a harsh breath. Gritting his teeth, he continued to tug until the boot finally slipped on. Then he stamped on the other boot.

After pulling on his jacket, he grabbed his personal items off the nightstand and stored them in his pockets. Bracing his hands on the mattress, he tried to lever himself to his feet. It was only then that he realized that his arms wouldn't lift him high enough for him to pull his stiff leg beneath him.

"Well, hell!" he angrily mumbled, glancing around for something to use to pull himself to his feet. A headboard would have been perfect, but there wasn't a headboard.

He switched his gaze to the chair. Its back was tall enough for him to pull himself up, but he had to get it close enough to use it. Stretching out his leg, he tried to catch the chair with the toe of his boot. He cursed when it remained an elusive few inches out of reach.

"I'm not giving up," he declared, surveying the nightstand. It looked sturdy enough to hold his weight, and he was sure that if he could sit on it, he could reach the chair.

Carefully, so as to jolt his knee as little as possible, he scooted to the top of the mattress. Then he tried to figure out the best way to maneuver himself onto the nightstand. He shook his head in disgust when he realized it wasn't going to be easy. He would have to lean forward and brace his hand on its far edge. Then he would have to lever himself high enough to swing his body onto it. It was going to take concentration to maintain his balance.

Leaning forward, he took hold of the nightstand and heaved himself up. Too late he realized that the nightstand wasn't as stable as it looked. As he felt it tipping over, he made a frantic grab for the bed, but it was too late. The nightstand turned over, and he landed on the floor on his butt. Immediately, pain erupted in his knee, and it was so agonizing that stars exploded in front of his eyes and he began to gasp for breath.

Suddenly, Shana's voice taunted, *Now you've found Sanctuary. Your journey is at its end.*

The hell it is! As soon as I catch my breath, I'm getting out of here!

Never!

It wasn't the implication of her threat that horrified Ryan. It was a card that suddenly fluttered past his face and landed in his lap. At first, it was solid black, but then a picture began to form on its surface. Before the picture was complete, he knew he was looking at a Tarot card, and he shuddered in revulsion. Even as a child, he had loathed Tarot cards with an aversion so strong it was almost primeval.

When the picture was complete, he saw a wolf and a dog standing at the edge of a body of water and howling at the moon. Some type of shellfish were climbing out of the water and taking a path between the canines. He shuddered again. The rendering of the picture was so real that he felt as if the animals would come right off the card. Instinct told him that if they did, they would attack.

He wanted to grab the card and rip it into a million pieces, but he couldn't bring himself to pick it up. Instead he batted it off his lap.

As he watched it fall to the floor, the door flew open and Shana burst into the room, gasping, "What happened?"

Ryan jerked his head up. As his gaze swept over her slender body, he was hit with a jolt of lust so powerful that he was instantly and fully aroused. His involuntary physical reaction to her infuriated him, because she was standing there looking at him through eyes that were wide and guileless. He wasn't fooled. He could see through the veneer of her senusal innocence to the malevolence that lurked beneath it. She was the personification of the Tarot—the embodiment of all that was inherently evil—and she intended to lay claim to his soul.

"You'll never defeat me!" he vowed harshly. *"Never!"*

Oh, no! It's happening again! Shana wailed inwardly.

The moment she entered the room, Ryan's features became subtly blurred. It was as if the visage claiming to be Aric was trying to superimpose itself over his face, but couldn't quite make the transition.

Why did Moira want him to portray Aric? she wondered in bewilderment. It didn't make sense. Aric had killed her, for pity's sake!

As she watched him warily, she said, "I have no desire to defeat you, Ryan. I am, however, concerned about your knee. Your fall must have caused you a lot of pain. Do you want me to help you back to bed?"

He blinked at her words. When he did, the wavering Aric image disappeared, and Shana let out a sigh of relief.

"What I *want* is for you to undo whatever the hell it is you did to my leg, and then I'm going to get out of here," he angrily stated.

"How are you going to leave? You can't walk."

He glared at her. "I'll manage. You just fix my knee."

"Ryan, the purpose of the spell is to protect your knee from further injury. If you'll just go back to bed—"

"Dammit, lady!" he yelled. "What does it take to get through to you? I am *not* going to stay here. Now, fix my knee so I can leave!"

"My name is Shana, not lady, and removing the spell will not fix your knee," she responded impatiently. "You will still be injured, which means you still won't be able to walk."

"Then I'll crawl."

"That's absurd. If you can't walk, you can't crawl."

"I said I'll *crawl*."

She let out an exasperated breath. "Why are you being so stubborn about this? All I want to do is help you."

"Then fix my knee so I can get out of here."

Shana wanted to throw her arms into the air in frustration. This was worse than dealing with a warlock! How was she going to make him listen to her? One look at his belligerent expression told her that the only way to reach him was to give him what he wanted.

"If you want the spell gone, then I'll remove it," she said, giving a resigned flick of her wrist.

He regarded her suspiciously. "That's it?"

"That's it."

Tentatively, he bent his knee, and his soft curse assured Shana that the action hurt. His expression, however, was triumphant, and she gave a confounded shake of her head. How could he be happy about being in pain?

"What are you doing?" she asked in confusion, when he leaned over, grabbed the chair by its leg and pulled it to his side.

"I'm getting out of here," he answered determinedly.

As she watched him maneuver himself into a kneeling position and brace his hands on the chair seat, she realized that he was going to try to stand. When he shifted his weight to his injured knee, he grimaced and muttered another curse. However, his desire to stand was obviously stronger than the pain, because he bent his good leg so that his foot was braced against the floor. Then he pushed himself upright. Turning the chair around, he propped his hands on the back and gave her another triumphant look.

"Very impressive. So what's next?" Shana asked dryly.

"I'm leaving."

"And how are you going to do that? You still can't walk, and your motorcycle is broken."

"I'll call a cab."

She shook her head. "We don't have a taxi service in Sanctuary."

"Then I'll take a bus."

"We don't have bus service, either."

He scowled at her. "Look, lady, I *am* getting out of here, and you can't stop me."

"I am not trying to stop you from leaving, and I've already told you that I couldn't do that if I wanted to," she said, her temper beginning to stir. Why was he being so darned unreasonable? "I'm merely pointing out that your options are . . . limited."

"According to you, they're limited."

Her temper rose another notch. "Are you insinuating that I'm lying?"

"I'm insinuating that where there's a will, there's a way, and I have a hell of a will," he answered with a combative lift of his chin.

"Even a 'hell of a will' can't overcome the impossible," she pointed out. "And as far as I can see, outside of sprouting wings and flying out of here, you're stuck."

"Well, we'll just see about that," he muttered, glancing around the room.

"What are you looking for?" she asked suspiciously.

"Something I can use as a crutch."

"Well, there's nothing in here that could possibly be used as a crutch, so outside of breaking up the furniture, you're out of luck."

The moment the words left her mouth, she regretted them. He began to eye the chair critically, and she suspected that he would tear it apart to make a crutch.

"You don't need to resort to destroying the furniture," she said with an irritable sigh. "If you want a crutch, I'll go find something that you can use as one."

She turned toward the door, but stopped when he drawled, "You have five minutes, lady. If you aren't back by then, the chair is mine."

Shana stiffened at his words. Up to this point, she had managed to hold onto her temper. His threat, however, shattered her control.

Glaring over her shoulder, she stated tightly, "As I have told you frequently tonight, my name is Shana, not lady, and before you start issuing ultimatums, you'd better consider who you're challenging. I am a witch, Ryan, which makes me a hundred times more powerful than you'll ever be, and you are starting to try my patience. Believe me, you would not like it if I lost my temper, and if you damage my chair, I can guarantee that will happen. It may not look like much to you, but that chair has been in my family for nearly three hundred years, and it holds a great deal of sentimental value for me.

"Now, if you will excuse me," she went on before he could respond, "I am going to go find you your crutch. I expect you to remain right where you are, and I will be back when I am damn good and ready."

With that, she stalked out, slamming the door behind her. As she headed for the kitchen, she grumbled, "Why did I ever think I wanted a mortal mate? They're as bad as—no *worse* than—warlocks, because at least with a warlock, I can throw something at his stubborn head and know he has enough common sense to duck!"

Ryan glared at the door as he muttered, "If anyone has a reason to be mad, *lady*, it's me. You not only ran me off the road and caused me to tear up my knee, but you had me stripped, and then tried to have sex with me without my knowledge or my permission. You've been haunting my nightmares for the past six months and jabbering in my head all night. Now you've started throwing Tarot cards at me, and you have the nerve to say I'm trying *your* patience? just who the hell do you think you are?"

A witch.

He closed his eye and shook his head. The logical part of him wanted to refute her claim—to reinforce his lifelong belief that there was no such thing as a witch. But if there wasn't such a thing as a witch, then how had she immobolized his knee by no visible means, and then released it with nothing more than a flick of her wrist?

Unfortunately, he couldn't explain it, which irritated the hell out of him. Compared to the flamboyant stunt she'd pulled with his clothes, his knee was such an insignificant accomplishment. That's what made it so profound. He could dismiss flamboyance as sleight of hand, but he simply couldn't dismiss his knee.

But worrying about whether she really was a witch was a waste of time, he determined as he opened his eyes. What he needed to do was figure out how he was going to get out of here. If this Sanctuary place didn't have a taxi or bus service, then he doubted they'd have a rental car agency or an airport. If he was in California, he could call his family or a friend to come get him. But he was in Pennsylvania, and he didn't know a soul in the entire state.

He considered calling the police. After all, he had had an accident, and they'd have to come and investigate. The trouble was they'd probably be local police. Since Shana had referred to a high priest, they might also be witches. Even if they weren't, they might be afraid of her. Since she'd made it clear she wanted him to stay, they would probably make sure he did what she wanted.

Raking a hand through his hair, he grudgingly admitted that Shana was right. Outside of sprouting wings and flying out of here, he was stuck. *Dammit!* If his bike wasn't totalled, he could just hop on it and be gone, but it wasn't going anywhere without a tow truck, and . . .

That was it! he realized as sudden inspiration hit. He could call the auto club for help. If a town was too small for a bus, it had to be too small to support a local auto club office. He wouldn't have to worry about them being witches or having them fear Shana if they weren't. All he had to do was get to a phone and help would be on the way.

He smiled smugly at the door and said, "I was right, lady. Where there's a will, there's a way, and in a few minutes I'll prove to you that I have a hell of a will."

Shana studied the contents of the broom closet, determining that the best item for a makeshift crutch was the sponge mop. It not only had the right design, but the sponge would serve as an underarm cushion.

Pulling it out, she checked the metal bindings to make sure it wouldn't cause Ryan another injury. Considering how determined he was to be on his feet, he'd probably use it even if it was sharp enough to cut off his arm.

Though the metal appeared safe, she took an extra few minutes to wrap the sponge with some towels for more cushioning. Then she headed back to the bedroom. She knew she'd been gone longer than five minutes, and she wondered if Ryan had ignored her warning and started ripping her chair apart.

As she approached the door, she gave a wry shake of her head. Now that her temper had cooled, she had to admit to a grudging admiration for Ryan. He was not only hurt and basically helpless because of the injury, but he'd just learned that she was a witch. Yet he refused to accept that he wasn't in control. As irritating as his stubbornness was, she acknowledged that it was a laudable trait, because it denoted an innate instinct for survival. If she could just persuade him to work with her instead of against her, she was sure that Moira wouldn't stand a chance against them.

"And the first step in persuading him is to soothe his ego by giving him his 'crutch' and letting him feel in control. Surely then he'll be open to reason," she murmured as she rapped on the door twice and then opened it.

She hesitated in the doorway, surprised to see him standing right where she'd left him. She really had expected him to be up to something, if for no other reason than to defy her.

That he hadn't tried anything made her wary, but it was his equable expression that made her truly suspicious. She might not be an expert on mortals, but she had enough experience to know his abrupt switch in moods was downright suspect. What was he up to? Unfortunately, the only way to find out was to ask, and she doubted he'd tell her the truth. She was just going to have to go along with him for now and see what happened.

"Here's your crutch," she said, walking toward him.

"Thank you," he said when she reached him and extended the mop. He immediately slipped it under his arm. After taking an experimental step, he glanced up at her and smiled. "I'm sorry I was so rude earlier."

"Yes, well, I suppose I should also apologize," she replied, still wary of his sudden change of demeanor, though she had to admit that she liked his smile. It was wide and generous and conjured up a host of delicious little fantasies about his lips. She forced her gaze from his mouth to his eyes, knowing that now was not the time to be indulging in fantasies. "I was a bit rude myself."

"Only because I provoked you," he refuted. "As you said, you were only trying to help me."

Not sure how to respond, she glanced down at his leg and asked, "How's your knee?"

"It hurts like hell," he admitted.

"It would hurt less if you'd lie down."

"You're right, of course, but before I do that, I need to make a call."

Shana jerked her head up and frowned at him. "A call?"

"Yes. You do have a telephone, don't you?"

She considered saying no, but under coven law, the only time lying was acceptable was if it was necessary to protect the coven from harm. Since she didn't know whom he wanted to call or why, she couldn't make that determination.

"It's not going to cost you anything, Shana. It's a toll-free call."

It was the first time he'd called her by name, and every inner alarm she possessed went off. "It's the middle of the night, Ryan. Don't you think it would be better if you waited until morning?"

A brief flash of frustration lit his eyes. It came and went so quickly, however, that if she hadn't been watching for some sign of deceit, she would have missed it.

"No, it can't wait until morning," he replied, an edge creeping into his voice. He must have heard it, too, because he paused for a moment, and the edge was gone when he concluded, "I need to make this call now."

"Whom do you want to call?"

"The auto club."

"The auto club?" When he nodded, she shook her head in confusion. "Why would you want to call the automobile club in the middle of the night?"

"I need to arrange for them to pick up my bike."

"I still don't see why it can't wait until morning."

"I don't want to take a chance that someone will steal my bike."

"I already told you that people don't steal in Sanctuary."

He gave her an exasperated look. "Maybe they don't, but for my own peace of mind, I want my bike taken care of. Now, are you going to let me use your phone?"

Shana gnawed on her bottom lip uncertainly. The purpose of his call sounded innocent enough, but her intuition said there was more going on than he'd revealed.

Suddenly, he shifted on his makeshift crutch. Automatically, Shana glanced down, and when she did, her eyes widened in disbelief. The Tarot card of The Moon was lying at his feet. Since it was lying sideways, she couldn't determine what position it was supposed to be in.

When she saw the faint outline of a footprint across the card, she shook her head, not wanting to accept the implications but unable to deny them. If Ryan had been standing on the card, then it had to have been there for a while. That could only mean that Moira had delivered it to him, and by doing so, she was letting Shana know that he was under her psychic influence.

But did that mean Moira had spellbound him? The only way to find out was to touch his mind, and now she understood that was extremely dangerous.

"Do you know where that came from?" she asked him, pointing at the card.

He glanced down and then hopped backward so fast

that if Shana hadn't moved quickly to his side, he would have fallen.

As she tried to help him regain his balance, he jerked his arm away from her and bellowed, "Don't touch me!"

Shana instantly released him. As he steadied himself, he glared down at the card. When he finally glanced up at her, his voice was low and sibilant like a whiplash as he rasped, "Get that filthy thing away from me!"

She was so stunned by his violent reaction to the card that she automatically bent and picked it up. As she tucked it into her back pocket, she covertly glanced toward the bed, reaffirming that The Star was still lying on the pillow. Sensing that if he saw it, he'd become even more agitated, she mentally chanted an incantation. The card disappeared, and a moment later she felt it settling into her pocket with the other cards she'd gathered tonight.

Turning her attention to Ryan, she said, "I'm sorry if the card upset you, but I need to know where it came from."

The glare he centered on her was so full of malice that it made her shiver. "You know damn well where it came from. You dropped it in my lap right after I fell."

"I didn't drop the card in your lap, Ryan," she denied, her stomach knotting at his response. She'd been right. Moira had delivered it to him. "But I need to know if it was right side up or upside down when you got it."

"I don't want to talk about a damn Tarot card," he snapped. "What I want to do is use the telephone!"

"If you'll answer my question, I'll take you to the telephone. Now, please, Ryan, this is very important. When you got the card was it right side up or upside down?"

He clenched his jaw and unclenched it before he said, "Right side up. Now, take me to the telephone."

Shana nodded, too upset to speak. In the upright position The Moon not only meant psychic influence, but unforeseen perils and deception. But did those warnings apply to Moira, or was it telling her that she couldn't trust Ryan?

Unfortunately, she knew that only time would give her the answer, because each card alone didn't really tell her anything. It was the connection between the cards that told the real story. Only when Moira had given her all the cards and she could look at the spread in its entirety would she be able to do an accurate reading.

With a resigned sigh, she said, "The telephone's this way."

CHAPTER FIVE

The Wheel of Fortune (Reversed)
A Turn for the Worse

As Ryan followed Shana out of the bedroom and down a long, dimly lit hallway, he decided that she could make a fortune renting her house to horror film directors. The walls were made of stone and there were no windows. It was also uncommonly quiet, which enhanced the gloomy atmosphere. Indeed, the only noise he heard was the thump of the mop handle and his own shuffled footsteps against the hardwood floor. He could not even hear Shana. She moved so quietly that if he hadn't been looking at her back, he would not have known she was there. The sensation unsettled him.

Her family crest is probably the same as Count Dracula's, he silently grumbled.

When they reached the end of the corridor, she turned down another hallway. Minutes later, she entered a room on the left and switched on a light. As Ryan entered, he arched a brow. They were in the kitchen. The entire room, as well as the cabinets, was painted white and trimmed in blue. The major appliances included everything from an upright freezer to a microwave oven. There was a butcher block island, with open shelves below it, that housed every type of small appliance imaginable.

Taking in the rest of the room, he noted that instead of a table and chairs, there was a white, triangular-shaped booth built into a corner. There were also a half-dozen garden windows filled with plants, many of which he suspected were herbs.

He wasn't sure why he was surprised by the kitchen's modernity. In part, because it was in such contrast to the rest of the house. Primarily, however, it was because when he looked at Shana, cooking was the last thing to come to mind, and obviously this room belonged to a gourmet cook.

"The telephone's over there," she told him, gesturing toward a wall phone by the booth. It was also white and blended in so well with the wall that if she hadn't pointed it out, he probably wouldn't have seen it.

He moved toward it, carefully testing the mop handle's stability before each step. The white linoleum was so highly polished it sparkled, and he didn't want to slip and fall when he was only a phone call away from getting out of here.

When he arrived at the phone, he pulled out his wallet and retrieved his auto club membership card. Then he lifted the telephone receiver and dialed the number. When it was answered on the other end, he frowned. Instead of reaching a person, he'd gotten one of those maddening computer messages that gave a half-dozen obscure options. Finally, he heard a choice that sounded like what he wanted, and he pushed the button. When he got another message saying all the operators were busy and he should remain on the line, he mumbled a curse. How was he supposed to get out of here if he couldn't even get a person on the line?

He didn't realize Shana had joined him, and he started when she asked, "Is there a problem?"

"I'm on hold," he answered, turning his head toward her.

As their eyes met, desire hit him with such unexpected force that he could barely breathe. Shaken by how easily she could rouse his lust, he tried to excuse his reaction as a healthy libido responding to a beautiful woman. He knew, however, that there was nothing healthy about his response to her. It was primitive and dark. She could become a dangerous obsession.

He tried to look away from her, but his gaze automatically drifted to her chest. Her T-shirt clung to her full breasts, reminding him that she was braless. As he stared at the faint outline of her nipples, his pulse began to pound. He wanted to touch them, to coax them into aroused life, and then he would . . .

"Ryan, are you ill?" Shana asked worriedly, interrupting his fantasy.

"Mm?" he murmured, reluctantly dragging his gaze toward her face. When it landed on her lips, he could only stare at them in awe. They were so perfectly formed, so soft and alluring. What would it be like to kiss them?

"Ryan, what's wrong?" she demanded, sounding even more concerned.

He knew he should answer her, but as he watched her lips form his name, he couldn't stop himself from touching them with his fingertips. At the contact, she let out a tiny, feminine gasp of pleasure that was so seductive he felt it all the way to his groin.

Leaning back against the edge of the booth, he propped his arm on top of the mop. Then slowly, deliberately, he traced the contours of her lips with the tip of his fingernail. When he finished, he smoothed the pad of his finger across them, mesmerized by the feel of their warmth and their firmness, their softness and their suppleness.

Vaguely, he heard a disembodied voice speaking in his ear. Before he could focus on it, the tip of Shana's tongue crept from between her lips and stroked his fingertip. At the action, he released a guttural groan and reached for her, ignoring the clatter of both the telephone receiver and the mop as he released them. He didn't want to think about anything but holding her in his arms. He had to taste her lips and explore the secrets of her mouth. He had to lay claim to her.

Grasping her upper arms, he hauled her up against him and sealed his mouth over hers. Her lips immediately parted, and he thrust his tongue between them. Although every nerve in his body was urging him to hurry, he explored the damp warmth of her mouth with the same slow deliberation that he'd traced her lips. It was like drowning in rich, dark honey, he decided as his tongue began to mimic a more intimate pursuit that made his penis pulse in eager approval.

Touch me! Shana suddenly cried, pressing her body against his so that they were molded together from chest to knee. *Let me show you what your touch does to me.*

Ryan knew she hadn't spoken, but he wasn't surprised to hear her demands in his mind. Their passion was too profound to be voiced aloud. He dropped his hands to her waist and slid them beneath her T-shirt.

As he stroked his hands up her sides toward her breasts, he was overwhelmed by a dichotomy of sensations. Her skin was soft against his palms, and her muscles quivered as he moved upward. He felt the passionate rush of anticipation that raced through her as she waited for him to reach his goal.

When he arrived at the bottom of her breasts and cradled their weight in his palms, she drew in a ragged breath. He felt the soft scrape of her T-shirt against her nipples—felt them begin to harden from both the grazing of the fabric and her craving for his own touch. Her need was so strong, so palpable, that his hands were trembling as he stroked his thumbs upward so that they brushed her nipples.

Immediately, they sprang to erectness, and as the impact of his caress resonated low in her abdomen, he closed his eyes. The feeling was indescribably beautiful, and yet it was almost painful in its force. He also recognized that it wasn't a localized need like his. It was a consuming yearning that radiated from her womb to her mind. At that moment, he understood that physical release would not be enough to please her. To give her complete satisfaction, he also would have to join with her soul.

As the revelation swept over him, she ordered, *Look at me.*

His eyes instantly flew open, and he found himself gazing into hers. They had again taken on an almost blinding luminescent glow, and she mentally whispered, *Now you've found Sanctuary. Your journey is at its end.*

Her declaration was like a douse of ice water, snapping him back to reality. Pushing her away from him, he yelled, "What the hell do you think you're trying to pull? Just get away from me and stay away from me!"

She blinked, and the glow in her eyes disappeared. Then she gave him a confused frown. "What's wrong?"

"You know damn good and well what's wrong," he snapped, glancing toward the wall. The telephone receiver was dangling from the cord, and its shrill beeping told him that he'd been disconnected.

With a violent curse, he grabbed the cord and pulled it up until the receiver was in his hands. Then he reached over and pressed down the button on the phone.

"This is the second time you've somehow managed

to get me into a compromising position," he told her. "I don't know what your game is, but stop playing it with me! I am not interested in having a fling with a . . . a . . ."

"A witch," she provided. "And I did not have you in a compromising position, Ryan. I was trying to help you. You were ill. I think you may have even lost consciousness for a moment."

He released the button and began to redial as he rasped, "The hell I did! *Dammit!* What did you do to the phone?"

"I didn't do anything to the phone."

"Then why is it dead?" he countered, so furious he wanted to grab her and shake her. He refrained, because he sensed that if he touched her, he might lose complete control. The problem was, he wasn't sure if he'd strangle her or throw her to the floor and make love to her.

"That's what that seduction scene was all about, wasn't it?" he angrily accused. "While you distracted me, you did something to the phone so I couldn't arrange for the auto club to pick me up and get me the hell out of here."

"You were going to leave with them?" she gasped.

"Of course I was going to leave with them. Why did you think I was calling them?"

"You told me you were going to have them pick up your motorcycle," she said, propping her hands on her hips and giving him an affronted look. "You lied to me!"

"I did not lie to you," he snapped. "I was—*am*—going to have them pick up my motorcycle. I figured you were smart enough to realize I was—*am*—also going to leave with them. And why the hell am I explaining myself? You *did* know, or you wouldn't have broken the damn phone!"

"I didn't know you were leaving, and I didn't break the phone."

"Well, you sure as hell did something to it, and I want you to fix it right now!"

She stared at him for a long moment, and then she shook her head. "I'm sorry, Ryan, but I won't make the phone operational. If I do, you'll try to leave, and I can't let you do that."

He regarded her through narrowed eyes. "I thought you said that if I wanted to leave, you couldn't stop me."

She gave an uneasy shrug. "I can't stop you, but there's nothing that says I have to help you."

"So, you're going to keep me here against my will? Why, lady? Because you're horny and need a stud?" he drawled disparagingly. "If that's your plan, forget it, because I do *not* perform under captive conditions!"

"I am not trying to keep you here for sex!" she declared in exasperation. "What I am trying to do is divert disaster, and that's exactly what we're going to be facing if you try to leave. I know you don't understand what is going on, and if you'll sit down and let me explain—"

"I don't want explanations! What I want is to get the hell out of here!"

"But Moira isn't going to let you leave, Ryan. That's why she made the phone malfunction."

"Who the hell is Moira?" he asked in angry perplexity.

"I explained that to you already. She's a spirit-witch."

"You're trying to tell me that a *ghost* won't let me use the phone?" he replied incredulously.

She shook her head. "She's not a ghost. At least not the type of ghost your're referring to, and if you try to leave, she will stop you. Unfortunately, she'll probably do it in a dramatic way that will attract Lucien's attention, and I can't let that happen. Once Lucien learns that she's on the loose, not only will his soul be at risk, but it could endanger everyone in the coven. And that's what Moira is after, Ryan. The more recognition she has, the more souls she'll have access to, and that will almost guarantee that she can fulfill the curse and regain existence in this world. So, as you can see, that's why I can't fix the phone."

Ryan gaped at her, trying to decide which amazed him the most—her crazy, convoluted story, or that she'd managed to tell it all in one breath.

When he realized she was regarding him expectantly, he said, "You know, lady, whoever told you that insanity doesn't run in your race must have had a loose screw of their own. You're not only nuts, but a psychiatrist could spend the next decade trying to diagnose all your psychoses."

"I am not crazy!" she declared indignantly. "And if you would sit down and let me explain all of this properly, you'd realize that I am telling you the truth."

"There's only one truth I care about," he shot back as he gingerly eased himself around the corner to the booth's seat and sat down on its edge. He bent to retrieve the mop off the floor before asking, "Can you stop me from leaving here?"

"I've told you several times that I can't."

"You just won't help me," he said as he used the mop to lever himself back to his feet.

"That's right," she agreed, eying him warily.

He nodded. "So, if I walk out the back door right now, there's nothing you can do about it."

"Ryan, I just explained why you can't leave."

"That doesn't answer my question. If I walk out that door, can you stop me?"

She let out an exasperated moan. "I can't stop you, but it would be ridiculous for you to try to leave. Even if Moira decided to let you go, it's nearly thirty miles to the next town. There is no way you can walk that far on a mop."

He arched a brow. "Lady, I already told you that where there's a will, there's a way, and I have a hell of a will."

"Ryan, you can't do this!" she cried in frustration when he started for the door.

He waited until he reached it and pulled it open before he glanced back at her and drawled, "You just watch me."

With that, he hobbled out, slamming the door behind him.

Shana stared at the closed door in shock. He was really going to try to walk thirty miles on a mop! And he had the audacity to say *she* was crazy?

The future is mine, and now yours will be mine!

As Moira's refrain echoed in Shana's mind, a card appeared in front of her face. She had just enough time to recognize it as The Wheel of Fortune—in the reverse position, of course—before it drifted to the floor.

"You know, Moira, you are becoming irritatingly redundant," she snapped as she bent to retrieve the card. "Can't you come up with a new line? And why do you keep giving me superfluous cards? I sure didn't need this one to know that matters have taken a turn for the worse."

As she spoke, she studied the card. The face of the Sphinx perched atop the wheel was Ryan's, and she gave a rueful shake of her head. Normally, she considered the Sphinx an equilibratory force, but so far Ryan had proved to be anything but stabilizing.

Adding the card to the growing collection in her back pocket, she scowled at the door, trying to decide what to do about his departure. She couldn't stop him from leaving, but she knew Moira would. She was also sure it was going to be in a manner that would attract Lucien's attention.

But if she's trying to get to Lucien, why didn't she just let Ryan make his call? her conscience nagged.

Shana frowned. Moira would have attracted far more attention if she had let him try to leave with another person. Two mortals in trouble would have definitely had Lucien running to the rescue.

She began to pace around the room uneasily. So why *had* Moira stopped Ryan from making the call? Unfortunately, only Moira had the answer, and Shana knew she couldn't waste time trying to second-guess her. Whatever Moira's plans, she wasn't Ryan's only risk at the moment. He was wandering around in the dark with a mop for a crutch. If he didn't end up getting lost in the woods, he was sure to fall and break something.

With an irritable shake of her head, she headed for the door, deciding that she had never met a more obstinate person than Ryan Alden. Even worse, she could end up spending the rest of her life with him.

"He's right," she muttered as she pulled the door open and stepped outside. "I *am* crazy. Why else would I have decided I wanted a mortal for a mate?"

As Ryan rounded the corner of Shana's house, the mop handle slipped for what seemed like the hundredth time. To keep from falling, he was forced to stand on his bad leg. When he did, he muttered a curse that was as much a reflection of his frustration as it was due to pain.

Although there was a full moon, the trees surrounding the house were so thick he could barely see his hand in front of his face, let alone where he was walking. The ground was damp, and if the mop handle wasn't slipping, it was sinking into the dirt. He tried to tell himself that once he found a road out of here, the going would get easier. He knew, however, that he was fooling himself. If the nearest town was thirty miles away, he was never going to make it there on foot.

"So I'll find a rock and sit and wait for a car," he grumbled.

But it would be a long wait. Because of his daredevil race on his bike, he didn't remember much about the road leading to Sanctuary. He did recall that it had been a desolate area. Shana was sure to find him long before a car passed by, and he knew she would come after him. She was too determined to let him walk away.

Glancing toward the trees, he wondered if he should try to hide in them until daylight. He dismissed the thought. If he tried to maneuver his way through the woods in the dark, he'd end up breaking his neck for sure.

With another curse, he continued walking, gingerly testing the mop for stability before each step. It seemed to take forever before he finally came to the front of the house. When he did, he let out a relieved sigh. Clearly visible in the moonlight was a dirt road. He was finally on his way to getting out of here.

"Don't you think you should take along some food and water?" Shana suddenly said behind him. "After all, you have a long journey ahead of you. At the rate you're traveling, I'd say about a week."

Her voice was so unexpected that he jumped and nearly lost his grip on the mop. He wasn't surprised that she had managed to sneak up on him. However, it irked him that she had.

After assuring himself that the mop was still firmly

planted, he glanced over his shoulder. Because of the darkness, it took him a moment to find her. He finally saw her leaning against the house about six feet away from him.

He opened his mouth to issue a retort to her gibe, but closed it when he realized she was baiting him. Instinct told him that his best line of defense was to ignore her. So instead of responding, he headed for the road. Just as he reached it, she appeared at his side, moving as quietly as a shadow. After they'd walked several feet, he glanced surreptitiously toward her. The moment he did, he cursed himself for doing so, because she was watching him.

"I have never met a more ... determined person than you," she said as he quickly looked away. When he didn't answer, she sighed and said, "Look Ryan, I know you're unhappy with me, but there is no reason for you to sulk."

Her taunt hit its mark. Despite his resolve not to talk to her, he shot her a glare and said, "I am *not* sulking. What I *am* doing is ignoring you, and I was hoping that by doing so you'd get the message that I don't want you near me. It appears, however, that you're too dense for subtlety, so I guess I need to take a more direct approach. *I want you to leave me the hell alone!*"

"I'm sorry, Ryan, but I can't do that. There are things going on that you don't understand, and if you would let me explain—"

"I don't want your explanations!" he broke in angrily. Coming to a stop, he turned to face her, concluding that he had never met a more infuriating woman in his life. "What does it take to get through to you that I don't care what's going on? Your problems have nothing to do with me!"

"You're wrong, Ryan," she responded, propping her

hands on her hips and scowling at him. "They have a lot to do with you, and if you would stop being so stubborn and listen to me, you would understand that."

He gave an exasperated shake of his head. It was evident that the only way he was going to get rid of her was to hear her out. Grudgingly, he said, "Look, lady, if you promise that you'll leave me alone after telling me your story, I'll give you five minutes. Is it a deal?"

"But—"

"No, buts. I want a simple yes or no."

She regarded him for a long moment before saying, "All right, but you really should be off your feet. Why don't you come back to the house? Then you can sit down while I tell you everything."

He automatically glanced toward the house. If he'd found the interior eerie, it was nothing compared to the exterior. There was enough moonlight for him to see that it was a huge, three-story stone house with pointed arches and slender turrets. It looked like something out of the Middle Ages, and in other surroundings, it probably would have been aesthetically pleasing. But cast in night shadow with huge trees crowding in on it, it had a sinister appearance. He knew it was absurd, but he had the feeling that the house itself was alive—that if he reentered it, it would never let him go.

"No way, lady," he said, irritated with his flight into whimsy, but unable to dismiss the ominous feeling the house gave him. "I have no intention of going back in there so you can figure out some way to keep me prisoner. Either you tell me here, or you can forget it."

Her expression said she wanted to object, but she must have realized he was serious, because she nodded and said, "I'm not sure where to begin."

"The beginning is usually the best place," he stated dryly.

"Yes, well, that was in Europe more than five hundred years ago when Moira was still alive," she said. "You see, she was the most powerful witch who ever lived, and she became the first and only high priestess of a coven. It was then that she created an enchanted Tarot deck that would accurately predict the future."

"Oh, come on. You can't really believe that a bunch of Tarot cards can foretell the future," Ryan scoffed. "Common sense says that it doesn't work, because if you do know the future, you can change it. Therefore, it's impossible to predict it, and that's the fallacy of fortune-telling."

"But that's exactly what gives validity to the Tarot," Shana rebutted. "It's not supposed to be used as a fortune-telling device per se, because when a normal deck is used, it is fallible. It is, however, a good tool for personal growth and insight. Employed properly, it can help guide and direct you to live a better and more productive life. And that's how Moira used her enchanted deck for the first ten years she was high priestess—as a tool to guide and direct the members of her coven to lead better lives."

"Ah ha! Now we're getting to the juicy part of the story," Ryan drawled derisively. "Let me guess. After the first ten years, she got a little power hungry, right?"

"In a manner of speaking," Shana agreed. "She fell in love with Aric, a warlock who didn't return her love. She became obsessed with him, and when he fell in love with another witch, Moira wasn't willing to give him up. The night he was to mate with the other witch, Moira surrendered her soul to the dark forces of nature. In exchange, they gave her the power to manipulate the future through the Tarot. Using her enchanted deck, she caused the other witch to fall off a cliff to

her death. Then she cast a spell over herself that made
her look like the witch and took her place in the mating
ceremony. She was convinced that once she and Aric
mated, he'd love her forever, because that is the way
of the mating spell.

"But when Aric awoke the next morning, he wasn't
in love with her," Shana continued. "When he learned
Moira had killed his true love, he went into a rage and
killed Moira. As she died, she vowed to use the Tarot
to return and claim a soul so that she could regain
existence in this world."

"And you think this Moira is now here to fulfill that
vow," Ryan stated.

"I know she is," Shana answerd, "because I acci-
dently released her from the spirit-world on Samhain."

"You *accidentally* released her?" Ryan repeated dubiously. "Even if I believed that such a thing as a spirit-
witch existed—which, for the record, I don't—how do
you accidentally release one?"

"I broke coven law and used her Tarot deck," she
answered. "I knew something was wrong almost immediately, because Moira arrived without a summons.
Then she took the cards and disappeared. I thought
she'd been forced back to the spirit-world, but then
she reappeared tonight."

"Why would she reappear tonight?" Ryan asked,
while telling himself that he was crazy for even engaging in this conversation. Enchantments? Curses?
Spirit-witches? But as insane as her story was, his curiosity was aroused. She might be a lunatic, but she was
an inventive one.

"That's what I wondered at first," she said, "but I
think it's because its Beltane Eve. Not only is the veil
between this world and the spirit world thin, which
makes it easier for her to cross over, but tomorrow is
Beltane—the celebration of new life and new begin-

nings. Since Moira is intent on achieving both, it makes sense that she'd choose this sabbat to put her plans into motion."

"Yes, well, as . . . interesting as I find this story, it still doesn't explain why you think I'm involved," Ryan noted.

"I don't suppose you'd be willing to just take my word on the matter," she said, rubbing her hands against her thighs.

At her nervous gesture, Ryan's self-protective instincts began to buzz. "You suppose right. Come on, lady. What does all this mumbo jumbo have to do with me?"

She tucked her hands into the front pockets of her jeans and shrugged. "According to legend, Moira can claim only the soul of a person in love. That's why I ignored the curse and used the Tarot. I figured it was safe, because I wasn't in love."

"And?" Ryan prompted when she fell silent, although he had a sinking feeling about where this was going.

She didn't answer for a long moment, and then she said, "I didn't take into account that the Tarot accurately predicts the future. When Moira took the cards, she learned that . . ."

"Learned what?" Ryan prodded when she glanced away from him.

She released a heavy sigh and glanced back at him. "She learned that you were to be my mate, which meant that it was only a matter of time before I fell in love. Evidently, she was able to cast an enchantment over you during Samhain, and now she plans to use you against me. It's an ingenious plan, really, because she knows that I'll be compelled to protect you, even at the risk of my own soul."

Ryan stared at her, dumbfounded. The moment she'd started talking about love, he'd suspected this was where her logic—or rather, illogic—was leading. Still, it shocked him to hear her say it aloud.

"Yeah, well, don't worry about losing your soul over me, lady, because I won't be around for you to protect. In fact, I'm getting out of here right now."

As he spoke, he readjusted the mop under his arm. He resumed his trek down the road, more determined than ever to get away from Shana Morland. She wasn't just crazy. She was bats-in-the-belfry certifiable!

As Shana watched Ryan walk away, she shook her head in stunned disbelief. She had just told him that she was to be his mate. How could he possibly walk away from her?

"After everything I told you, you're still going to try to leave?" she asked as she hurried to catch up with him.

"You're damn right," he replied.

"Moira won't let you leave, Ryan. The moment you try to step off coven land, she will stop you."

He shot an impatient glare in her direction. "Well, I'll worry about Moira when the time comes. In the meantime, why don't you run along home? I'm sure that there's some new ghost or goblin hanging around in your attic that's just dying to haunt you. No pun intended, of course."

"You still think I'm crazy," she said, feeling both dismayed and amazed.

"Let me put it this way. I've heard of women taking desperate measures to find a man, but summoning up a spirit-witch and a curse belongs in the record books. If you're really that lonely, why don't you try the personal column in the newspaper? Who knows? You might hook up with some nice spiritual medium, and the two of you can while away your time, playing with all the spirits you want. If that doesn't appeal to you, you can always check yourself into the nearest mental institution. I can guarantee that you will find a soul mate there."

"Ryan, I know that this has to sound fantastic to you, but it is true. If you would just spend the night, I'll find a way to prove it to you."

"You just don't get it, do you?" he snapped as he again stopped and turned to face her. "Even if it is true, I don't want to know about it. I have enough problems of my own, so if you're looking for a ghost-buster to help you slay the big, bad spirit-witch, you're talking to the wrong person. I am not interested!"

"Well, you may not be interested, but you're involved whether or not you like it," Shana shot back, her own temper beginning to flare. "And if you think I'm going to stand by and let you jeopardize the entire coven because you're too stubborn to listen to reason, you are in for a big surprise."

He opened his mouth to respond, but she held up her hand and continued, "In case you haven't figured out the seriousness of this situation, I'm going to explain it again. Moira wants a soul. Right now, the only soul at her disposal is mine, because I am the only person who has acknowledged her existence. However, if you try to leave Sanctuary and she tries to stop you, you're going to attract Lucien's attention. He's the high priest, Ryan, and that means that he is connected to every member of the coven. Once he knows about Moira, she may be able to connect with the other members through him. If that happens, I'll never be able to stop her, and you have no idea what kind of danger we'll be facing if she regains her existence. She's not only powerful; she's evil. So if you think you have problems, believe me they're nothing compared to mine. And I'm not asking you to fight her for me, because, quite frankly, you wouldn't stand a chance against her. All I want is your cooperation. Now, are you going to give it to me, or am I going to have to find a way to stop you, too?"

"How dare you stand there and threaten me as if I'm the one to blame here," he responded furiously. "If what you're saying is true, you're the one who summoned up this blasted spirit-witch. If you knew she was so dangerous, then you shouldn't have been messing with her in the first place."

"You're right," she said, her temper deflating under his justifiable attack. "I should never have touched the Tarot. All I can say in my defense is that at the time I thought it was safe. However, I was wrong. Now Moira is on the loose and, unfortunately, she has involved you.

"Will you at least stay until morning so I can try to figure out a way to make her release her hold over you?" she asked plaintively. "If you won't do it for me, then think about the other coven members. They're innocent of any wrongdoing, and if you try to leave now, you'll be putting all of them at risk. Don't jeopardize them because I did something stupid. Please, Ryan."

She watched a series of emotions fly across his face at her plea, but they came and went so swiftly that she coudn't identify any of them. *Damn!* If she could connect with his mind, she would not only know what he was thinking, she could mentally reinforce the graveness of the situation. Instead, all she could do was pray that she had reached him.

It seemed that an eternity passed before he finally opened his mouth to respond. Before he could speak, however, a car's headlights suddenly appeared in the road behind him. As Shana's mind automatically brushed against the driver's, she could only stare into the oncoming lights in horror. The driver of the car was Ariel, Lucien's mortal—and *very* pregnant—mate.

Suddenly, Shana understood why Moira had stopped Ryan from making his telephone call. If he asked Ariel to take him away from Sanctuary, she would do so. Moira couldn't come up with a better bait to attract Lucien's attention than to threaten his mate and their unborn twins.

Shana wanted to scream. She'd accused Moira of delivering a superfluous Tarot card, a total understatement. Matters hadn't taken a turn for the worse. They'd become downright catastrophic!

CHAPTER SIX

Death
Transformation and Change

Since Ryan was standing in the middle of the road with his back to the car, Ariel had to stop behind him. The moment she did, Shana hurried toward the automobile, determined to divert disaster.

"Ariel! What are you doing out here all alone in your condition?" she asked when she reached the car and noted that the window was down. "You should be at the festival with Lucien, so he can keep an eye on you."

"Good heavens, Shana, I don't need anyone to keep an eye on me just because I'm pregnant. And I'm here because Lucien asked me to check with you and see how things are going with your guest." She looked toward Ryan before asking, "Why are the two of you out here? And why is he using a mop as a crutch?"

"He's using a mop because I don't have a crutch, and he insisted on having one immediately. It would have taken too much time to conjure one up," Shana replied, casting a glance toward Ryan. He had turned toward the car. His eyes were narrowed against the light, and his expression was wary.

Since he was so intent upon leaving, she knew she

had to get Ariel out of here before he could ask her for help. But she couldn't resist taking a moment to confide, "He is the most stubborn person I've ever met, Ariel. Even though I performed some of my best magic for him, he refuses to believe I'm a witch. He thinks I'm crazy!"

"You told him you were a witch?" Ariel asked in disbelief. When Shana nodded, she said, "No wonder he thinks you're crazy! It's a good thing Lucien sent me over here."

"What are you doing?" Shana asked in alarm when Ariel started opening her door.

"I'm going to introduce myself to him."

"No!" When Ariel arched a brow, she realized she'd responded too vehemently and quickly added, "He's upset with me. I'm afraid that if he meets you, he'll ask you to take him away from Sanctuary, and he can't leave. He's supposed to be my mate."

"Shana, even if he is supposed to be your mate, you can't stop him if he wants to leave."

"I know that," Shana grumbled, perturbed that her friend was beginning to sound exactly like Lucien. Didn't anyone in Sanctuary take her seriously? "And I'm not trying to stop him. I'm trying to make him listen to reason."

"Well, if your methods of persuasion are anything like Lucien's, I have a feeling that you're walking a fine line between reason and coercion," Ariel muttered as she climbed out and shut the door. "I'm going to meet him, Shana, and then we'll decide whether he stays or he leaves."

"But he can't leave! I just told you that he's supposed to be my mate!"

"That may be true, but I'm going to have to go back and tell Lucien what I found out. You know that I'll have to tell him the truth. Now, would you rather have *me* deal with this situation? Or would you rather I turn it over to Lucien?"

Shana frowned at Ariel in frustration. She wanted to argue with her, but she recognized that her friend wasn't being unreasonable. She was simply stating fact. Even if she wanted to lie to Lucien, she couldn't. The mating spell made it impossible for mates to lie to one another. Once Ariel told Lucien what was going on, he'd be here in an instant. He wouldn't think twice about reading Ryan's mind, and he'd find out about Moira. At least with Ariel, she had a chance of keeping her nemesis a secret. She'd just have to make sure that her friend wasn't put in jeopardy.

"I'd rather you dealt with it," she finally said, albeit reluctantly.

"Fine, then introduce me to your guest," Ariel said as she started walking toward Ryan. "And let me do the talking, Shana. I want to find out what is really going on, not what you want me to believe is happening."

"Ariel! Are you suggesting that I'd lie to you?"

"Only if telling me the truth would put the coven at risk," she replied. "However, I know how much you want a mortal mate so you can leave Sanctuary. You might be tempted to bend the truth to get what you want."

Shana wanted to deny Ariel's assertion, but to keep Moira from being discovered, she would not only bend the truth, she would tell an outright lie. It would be justifiable, because she would be protecting the coven, but the thought of deceiving her friend, even for a good reason, made her uncomfortable. She decided to maintain her peace and concentrate on keeping Ariel safe.

*   *   *

Ryan was trying to decide whether or not he should approach the car when the door opened and he saw someone get out. He warily watched Shana and another woman step out of the shadows and into the glow of the headlights.

As he surveyed the stranger, he noted that she was as tall as Shana, but there the similarities ended. With her dark hair and dark eyes, Shana was an exotic beauty. The other woman had a wholesome, girl-next-door-prettiness that was emphasized by extraordinarily long, blond hair. She was also pregnant, and considering her size, probably near her due date.

"Ariel, this is Ryan Alden. Ryan, I'd like you to meet my good friend, Ariel Morgret," Shana said as they came to a stop in front of him. "She's Lucien's—"

"Wife," the woman interrupted, smiling at him as she extended her hand. "It's nice to meet you, Mr. Alden."

"Likewise," Ryan said, accepting her hand, but releasing it quickly. After his encounters with Shana, he was distrustful of touching anyone associated with her.

"I heard about your accident. How are you feeling?" she asked.

"I've had better days," he replied. "Are you supposedly a witch, too?"

She laughed. "Well, I can see you're a direct man, and, no, I am not a witch. I'm a mortal, just like you."

"A mortal?"

"It's the term Shana's race uses when they refer to us," she explained. "It doesn't mean that they're immortal, but their life span is longer than ours. It isn't unusual for them to live well into their hundreds."

"You've really bought into this witch story?" he queried skeptically.

She shrugged. "I know it's difficult to believe, Mr. Alden, but Shana and her people really are witches and warlocks. They aren't, however, Satanists, and they certainly aren't dangerous. So, if you're worried about your safety, you can put your mind at ease. They do have a fascinating history, and I'm sure Shana would be happy to tell it to you."

"I'm afraid I won't be around long enough to hear it," he declared, deciding that if she didn't think Shana was dangerous, she didn't know her very well. "I'm on my way out of here."

"Shana mentioned that you wanted to leave, but do you think that's wise? You are injured, and my husband said that your motorcycle is damaged beyond repair. Maybe you should take a couple of days to recuperate before you go."

He started to tell her that he had no intention of recuperating within a hundred miles of Shana Morland. Before he could, Ariel Morgret suddenly let out a gasp and pressed her hands against her swollen abdomen.

"Are you all right?" he asked in concern.

She drew in a couple of deep breaths before smiling and saying, "I'm fine. I'm afraid these two are already engaged in sibling rivalry. If one kicks, the other tries to kick harder."

"Ariel's carrying twins, and she should be with Lucien so he can keep an eye on her," Shana inserted. "He'll be very unhappy if *anything* happens to her."

"Oh, for heaven's sake, Shana. Nothing is going to happen to me," Ariel said impatiently. "The babies are just extremely active tonight."

"How far along are you?" Ryan questioned, feeling a prickle of unease as his gaze automatically dropped to her stomach. He hadn't done any obstetrical work since his internship, and that had been nearly ten years ago. The last thing he needed was to be stuck out in the middle of nowhere with a woman who might be going into premature labor. And "extremely active" babies did not sound like a good omen.

"Eight months," she answered.

"Is this your first pregnancy?" When she nodded, he said, "Shana's right. You should be with your husband. Twins tend to come early, and often the labor moves quickly. Are you experiencing lower back pain?"

"No more than usual," she answered.

"Unusual cramping?"

"No."

"What about indigestion? Sometimes what seems like indigestion can actually be the beginning stages of labor. Since this is your first pregnancy, you don't know how your labor will present itself, so you need to consider all possibilities."

"Are you a doctor, Mr. Alden?"

Caught off guard by the question, Ryan blinked. How had she known? By the way he'd been talking, he realized disgruntled. *Damn!* He couldn't believe that he'd fallen so naturally into his old medical persona.

His first impulse was to deny his profession, but for some odd reason, he couldn't bring himself to lie to her. He compromised with, "Not any more."

"I see." She was regarding him curiously, and he expected her to pursue the matter. Instead she said, "Well, you don't need to worry about me. My husband is a warlock, and they have a unique bond with their unborn children. They are acutely aware of every stage of their development, and if I was in labor, he would know it, even if I didn't. Believe me, he would be here to haul me off to the hospital before either of us could blink."

Ryan arched a brow at her words. Evidently, Shana wasn't the only crazy on the loose in Sanctuary, although he had to admit that the bond she was talking about was an intriguing delusion. "That's very . . . interesting, Mrs. Morgret."

"Please, call me Ariel."

"Yes, well, Ariel, it's been nice meeting you, but I really need to be going."

"Are you sure? I know that Shana has probably come across as a bit . . . eccentric, but that's because she's lived a very sheltered life. If staying with her makes you uneasy, you could stay with my husband and me."

No! It's too dangerous! Remember Moira!

Shana's voice reverberated with such force in Ryan's mind that he shook his head, feeling dazed. Then he glanced toward her. Her eyes had taken on a faint glow, and she was staring at him intently. He found it damned unnerving, and that irritated him. It also reminded him that the sooner he got away from her, the better.

"Thanks for your offer," he told Ariel, "but I really must leave."

"Mr. Alden, it's more than thirty miles to the nearest town. Would you at least let me give you a ride?"

No! It's too dangerous!

If Shana's voice had been forceful before, this time he felt as if she was screaming through a megaphone full blast. Indeed, it was so loud that his ears began to buzz. When he again looked at her, her eyes had become brighter, and they were beginning to pulse in a rhythm so mesmerizing he could only stare at them.

She's trying to hypnotize me into doing what she wants!

His temper erupted at the realization. He jerked his head toward Ariel, saying, "I would appreciate a ride, and would it be possible to stop by my bike so I can pick up my belongings?"

"Of course," Ariel replied.

"But you can't leave!" Shana objected.

He shot a glare in her direction. "Lady, I said it before, but I'll say it again so that you finally get the message. *You just watch me.*"

Switching his attention back to Ariel, he said, "I'll meet you at the car."

With that, he headed purposefully toward the automobile, and Shana stared after his retreating back in horror. She had risked connecting with his mind to keep this from happening! How could he ignore her warning and put Ariel and himself in jeopardy? She had to do something to stop them, but what?

When Ariel turned to follow Ryan, she caught her friend's arm. "Ariel, you can't drive all that distance by yourself!"

"Thirty miles is not very far in a car. I can drive it in about forty or forty-five minutes. Depending on where Mr. Alden wants to go, I probably won't be gone more than a couple of hours."

"But what if you go into labor or have an accident? People are killed in automobiles all the time. I think you should at least wait until morning, and then Lucien can go with you and keep you safe."

Ariel regarded her suspiciously. "What's going on, Shana?"

"Nothing's going on," she said, glancing guiltily toward the car as she told the lie. As she watched Ryan open the passenger door and start to climb inside, she frowned. He should be getting into the backseat where he could put his leg up. But if she handled this right, he wouldn't be leaving, and where he was sitting wouldn't make a difference.

She switched her attention back to her friend. "I'm just worried about you. Every time I read one of those newspapers that you get in the mail, I see where someone has been hurt in an automobile. They are *not* safe, Ariel."

"It's true that people have accidents, but most of them are what we call fender benders. The car gets dented, but no one gets hurt. You have an irrational fear about cars, and you need to get over it. Why don't you come with me?"

"You want me to get in your automobile?" Shana gasped, staring at her in horror.

"The best way to overcome a fear is to face it," Ariel replied. "I'm sure that after a few rides, you'll wonder why you were ever afraid. Besides, you can keep me company on the way back, and then you won't have to worry about my being alone."

Shana looked fearfully toward the car. Just the thought of getting into it turned her stomach into a knot, but at least she'd have a chance of safeguarding Ariel and Ryan. She might even be able to cast a protective spell that would let them leave Sanctuary without interference from Moira. And she was coming to the conclusion that it would be best for Ryan to leave. He was too stubborn, which made him the perfect foil for Moira's manipulations.

Glancing back at Ariel, she said, "You know I can't leave Sanctuary without Lucien's permission."

"That's easy enough to resolve," Ariel said. I'll just ask him for permission."

Grabbing the silver chain around her neck, she pulled a long, slender crystal from beneath her blouse. Shana knew that it matched Lucien's crystal and mentally linked them. Not only could they communicate with one another, but Ariel could summon him in an instant by simply touching hers.

As Ariel contacted Lucien, Shana again looked toward the car and shuddered. Although her race was long-lived, they were not immune to accidents. No matter what Ariel said, she was convinced that automobiles were death traps. Maybe she wouldn't have to get into it. Maybe Lucien would tell Ariel to wait until morning when he could go along. That would give her a chance to break Moira's hold over Ryan, and . . .

"You've been given a temporary reprieve from Sanctuary," Ariel said, grinning as she grabbed Shana's arm and gave it a tug to get her moving. "You're about to get your first look at the mortal world, Shana. Lucien expects us back in three hours, which will give me time to introduce you to fast food. I've been dying for a burger and fries, but we'll have to hurry to make it there before the restaurants close."

"Hurry?" Shana repeated, her voice abnormally high-pitched. "I don't like the sound of that at all."

"It's just a figure of speech," Ariel assured her as they reached the car and she opened the driver's door. "Just hop into the backseat. Everything will be fine, Shana. I promise."

Before Shana could reply, Ariel climbed into the car and said, "I hope you don't mind Shana coming along with us, Mr. Alden, but she'll be company for me on the drive back."

Ryan grunted something in response, but Shana didn't hear what it was. She was too busy trying to dredge up the courage to get inside.

I have to protect them from Moira, and this is the only way to do it, she told herself firmly when Ariel closed her door.

As she opened the back door, her hands began to shake. By the time she climbed inside, her entire body was trembling. She knew that to keep a step ahead of Moira, she had to get a grip on her fear. But when Ariel turned the car around on the road and stepped on the gas, her heart began to pound so hard she sure it was going to burst.

Pressing a hand against her chest, she closed her eyes and began to breathe deeply against the overwhelming panic surging through her. She had to get herself under control! But the more Ariel increased their speed, the more Shana's fear escalated. She was so frightened that she couldn't even open her eyes.

I can't let myself overreact like this, she mentally chastised herself. I have to be composed and in control. If I'm not, Moira could hurt Ariel, the babies, and Ryan. I can't let anything happen to them. I have to protect them. I . . .

The future is mine, and now yours will be mine!

Her eyes flew open in terror at Moira's voice. Suspended in front of her face was another Tarot card. Although she had acute night vision, the card itself was so dark that she had to squint to make it out. When she did, her racing heart screeched to a halt. She was looking at the macabre, skeletal image of Death!

It doesn't literally mean death, she told herself frantically. It means transformation and change!

She no more than reminded herself of the meaning of the card, when Ariel let out a startled yelp and the car went out of control. As Shana watched a tree loom in front of the windshield, she began to chant frantically.

Damn! Why had she let herself panic instead of casting a protective spell over the automobile? Now, she didn't have time to save it, but hoped she would be able to take care of Ariel and Ryan.

She completed the incantation and propelled it toward the front seat just as they went into a ditch and collided with the tree that was growing at its edge. She saw a brief flash of spell-lightning, but she didn't have a chance to see if the spell had taken hold. As the car hit the ditch, she was thrown into the door and excruciating pain exploded inside her head. Then everything went black.

Ryan stared through the cracked windshield, feeling stunned. The accident had taken place so quickly that it took him a moment to absorb what had happened. The instant he did, he turned toward Ariel, gasping, "Are you okay?"

"Yes," she said, her face pale and her hands shaking as she pressed them to her abdomen. Tears suddenly filled her eyes. "The babies kicked so hard they startled me, and I lost control of the car."

"It's okay," he soothed as he reached out and patted her arm. "You have to calm down, so we can make sure that you and those little ones are okay."

"We're fine," she said, wiping the tears from her eyes. "The spell protected us."

"The spell?"

"Yes. Didn't you see the spell-lightning? Thank heaven, Shana was with us. Oh, my God! Shana, are you okay?"

Ryan twisted around to look into the backseat at the same time she did, and he let out a horrified gasp. Shanna lay crumpled against the door behind Ariel's seat.

"Shana!" Ariel screamed as Ryan unbuckled his seat belt and threw open his door. As he tried to swing his legs out, his knee immediately revolted. He let out a string of scathing curses against the agonizing pain coursing up his leg. Ignoring his discomfort, he grabbed hold of the door and stood. Then he limped to the back door.

"Shana? Are you all right?" he asked as he pulled it open.

When she didn't answer, he sat down on the seat and slid across it to her side. Her face was so pale she looked ghostly, and his hand shook has he pressed his fingers to the side of her neck. It took him a moment to find her pulse, but when he did, he heaved a sigh of relief. She had a strong, if slightly rapid, heartbeat. He knew that didn't mean she wasn't seriously injured, but at least she was alive.

"What's wrong with her?" Ariel asked worriedly as she arrived at the open door.

"She appears to be unconscious, but her heartbeat is strong," he answered. "Do you have a flashlight? The overhead light isn't bright enough, and I can't see a damn thing."

"There's one in the glove compartment. I'll get it."

While she foraged for the flashlight, Ryan had to bite his lip to keep from yelling at her to hurry. He knew that his impatience would only upset her more, and the way his luck was running, she'd go into labor. As it was, he didn't know how they were going to get help. It would take him forever to get anywhere on that damn mop, and Ariel wasn't in any condition for a long walk. He hoped there was someone living close by so they could get to a telephone.

Suddenly, Shana groaned and started to move. Realizing she was regaining consciousness, he quickly caught her shoulders to hold her still. When her eyelashes fluttered and then lifted, he said, "Don't move, Shana. We need to find out what your injuries are."

"Ryan?" she murmured groggily.

"Yeah, it's me. Just sit still until I can find out if you're okay."

"I told you she wouldn't let you leave," she whispered so softly he could barely hear her.

Ryan felt a chill crawl up his spine. Was she right? Had he caused this by trying to leave? He gave a firm shake of his head. Their accident had *not* been caused

by some spirit-witch. It had occurred because of two
extremely active unborn babies.

"We'll talk about that later," he muttered gruffly.
"Right now, I want you to tell me where you hurt."

"Sleepy," she said, closing her eyes again.

"Dammit, Shana! You have to stay awake!" he ordered, but she didn't even twitch a muscle.

"Here's the flashlight," Ariel said, extending it over
the seat. As he grabbed it, she anxiously asked, "Isn't
it a good sign that she woke up?"

"Yeah," he answered as he lifted one of Shana's eyelids and flashed the light into her eye. Then he did the
same to the other, cursing inwardly when her dilated
pupils were slow to respond. Laying the flashlight in
the back window, he began to explore her scalp with
his fingers. When he found the lump he was looking
for, he grimaced. It was already close to the size of a
small egg, and it was dangerously close to her temple.

"We need to get help," he said, looking at Ariel. "Are
we close to a phone?"

"Lucien knew about the accident the moment it happened," she said. "He's already on his way."

She made the statement so confidently that for a
moment, Ryan believed her. Then the absurdity of it
struck him. "Look, Ariel," he said, "I don't want you
to take offense, but just in case you're wrong about
your husband, I think that we should make an effort
to get to a phone."

"I'm not wrong, Mr. Alden. Lucien is on his way."

Ryan frowned impatiently. "And how do you know
that for sure?"

"We're linked through our crystals," she answered,
lifting a hand to a long, slender crystal suspended from
a chain around her neck. The moment she touched it,
it began to glow.

Ryan stared at it in wary bewilderment. It had to

be a trick of the light. People could *not* communicate through crystals!

"Lucien will be here in a few minutes," she said, dropping her hand and smiling at him. "And he said that we shouldn't worry about Shana. He's already touched her mind, and she only has a minor head injury. She's going to be fine."

If Ryan had felt bewildered before, he was now so dumbfounded it took him a second to find his voice. "Excuse me, Ariel, but I *am* a doctor. People with minor head injuries are not unconscious for several minutes. Shana needs to be transported to a hospital as soon as possible."

She shook her head. "I know you find what I'm saying difficult to believe, Mr. Alden, but Lucien is not only a warlock, he's the high priest. He's connected to all the members of the coven. If he says Shana is fine, then she's fine."

"Dammit, lady!" he exploded. "If you think I'm going to sit here and watch a woman possibly die because you're all engaged in some communal fantasy of witches and warlocks, you're crazy. She's going to go to a hospital, if I have to carry her to one."

"And how are you going to do that, Ryan?" Shana suddenly questioned weakly. "You can't even walk."

"Thank God, you're awake!" he said, swinging his head toward her. "Tell me where you hurt."

"Why, Ryan, you sound almost as if you care, but why would you care about a crazy woman?"

"Shana, this is no time to be playing games," he said impatiently. "Tell me where you hurt."

"My head," she said, raising a hand and gingerly touching the bump he'd already discovered. She winced and looked toward Ariel. "Are you and the babies okay?"

"We're fine, thanks to you, but you should have included yourself in the spell."

"I didn't have time," Shana mumbled as she started to sit upright.

"Shana, you need to sit still until I can determine if anything else is wrong with you," Ryan stated, again catching her shoulders to hold her in place.

"You heard Ariel. Lucien says I'm fine."

"You are *not* fine," he said, barely refraining from shaking her in her angry frustration. How could they believe that a man who wasn't even present could determine her medical condition? "At the very least, you have a concussion. At the worst, you may have a hematoma, and that can kill you. You need to be in a hospital for observation."

"Shana is in no need of a hospital," a man stated behind him. "She's got a hell of a headache, but she's fine."

"Lucien!" Ariel cried, scrambling out of the car as Ryan jerked around on the seat.

When his gaze landed on the man, his jaw dropped. If anyone had ever asked him what a warlock looked like, Ariel's husband would have fit the description. He was dressed all in black, and he was huge, both in height and breadth. There was a crystal like Ariel's hanging around his neck, and he wore a small, drawstring pouch at his waist. His shoulder-length black hair was shaggy, and he wasn't by any means handsome. His features were too sharp and angular, but it was his eyes that gave him a menacing presence. They were so pale in color that they appeared silver in the moonlight, and they didn't look at you. They pierced you.

As Ariel arrived at his side, he wrapped an arm around her shoulders and pulled her protectively against him, before saying, "Welcome to Sanctuary, Mr. Alden. I'm Lucien Morgret."

All of Ryan's self-preservation instincts began to blare. Although both Morgret's words and his tone were polite, Ryan knew that he had just been issued a threat.

Evidently, Ariel also considered her husband's words more than polite conversation, because she immediately said, "Lucien! Be nice."

Outside of giving his wife a slight squeeze, he didn't acknowledge her chastisement. Ryan wasn't surprised. He suspected that telling Morgret to be "nice" was about as effective as telling a pit bull to behave when he was faced with a plate of raw meat. Ryan opened his mouth to respond to Morgret's introduction, but the man looked past him to Shana.

Glowering at her, he said, "Why didn't you cast a protective spell over the car? Now it's wrecked, and—"

"Excuse me, but we don't have time to worry about the damn car!" Ryan interrupted, his temper flaring. When Morgret's menacing gaze flew back to his face, he realized the folly of confronting him when he couldn't even stand. However, he was too concerned about Shana's medical condition to back down.

"Shana has a head injury that could be extremely serious, Mr. Morgret," he explained. "She needs to go to a hospital. Since you're the only fit person here, you need to get to a telephone and call an ambulance, and you need to do it *now*."

"Ryan, I'm okay! Really!" Shana gasped, bolting upright beside him. Immediately, she groaned and fell back agains the seat, cradling her head in her hands.

"You are *not* okay," Ryan reiterated, turning toward her. "And I want you to sit still until an ambulance gets here."

"There will be no ambulance, Mr. Alden," Lucien

stated. "As I said, Shana has a hell of a headache, but she's fine."

"*Dammit!* What is wrong with you people?" Ryan railed, looking back at Lucien. "I am not only a doctor, I'm a trauma surgeon. That means I'm well-versed in head injuries, and Shana needs to go to the hospital. So unless you can show me your medical degree, I don't want to hear any arguments from you. What I want to see is your butt headed down the road for help."

Anger flared into Lucien's eyes. He started to raise his hand toward the crystal around his neck, but Ariel caught his hand and said, "Lucien, remember, he's a mortal. He doesn't understand."

"Ariel's right, Lucien. He doesn't understand," Shana repeated urgently as she again sat upright. Her words tumbled over each other as she continued, "And I'm sorry about the automobile. I should have cast a protective spell around it the moment I got in, but you know I'm afraid of them. I was trying to deal with my fear, and then everything happened so fast."

"Yes, it happened so fast I'm surprised she had a chance to protect me and Ryan," Ariel confirmed. "There was no way she could have protected the car."

"I can't believe this!" Ryan gasped in astonishment. "Why are you trying to pacify him over the damn car instead of getting Shana the help she needs?"

"Ryan, *please*," Shana cried, placing her hand against his arm.

He shook her hand off and glared at Lucien. "Look, Morgret, I am not going to stand by and watch something happen to Shana, just because you get a charge out of playing warlock. Now, I expect you to get an ambulance for her, and I expect you to do it *now*."

"Ryan, that is *enough!*" Shana declared, sounding aghast.

"That is not enough," he responded furiously as he again turned to face her. "Your eyes aren't dilating properly, and you have a hell of a lump on the side of your head that's dangerously close to your temple. That's the thinnest part of your skull, which means you have a greater chance for a hematoma. You need to go to the hospital, and the sooner, the better."

She glanced toward Ariel and Lucien. "Could I have a couple of minutes privacy with Ryan?"

"Of course," Ariel said quickly, tugging on Lucien's arm. "Lucien and I need to look at the car to see how much damage there is. It may not be as bad as we think."

"I can't believe they're so damn worried about the car, when they should be worried about you!" Ryan raged as he watched them walk to the front of the vehicle.

"If there was something to worry about, they would be worried about me," Shana said. "And the reason they're so concerned about the car is because it's the only one in Sanctuary. If Ariel goes into labor, Lucien won't be able to drive her to the hospital."

"So, he can call an ambulance for her, just as he should be calling one for you."

She raked a hand through her hair, wincing as she brushed against the lump on her head. "Ryan, I know you think you're doing what's right, but you can't keep ordering Lucien around. He's the high priest, and you have to treat him with respect."

"I don't care if he's the pope! You need medical attention. Why is it so hard for you to understand that if you don't go to the hospital, you might *die*."

"And why do you care if I live or die?" she snapped. "As you'll recall, you were so eager to get away from me that you were willing to walk thirty miles on a mop."

"That has nothing to do with this situation."

"It has *everything* to do with it!" After glancing out the windshield at Lucien and Ariel, she looked back at him and lowered her voice to a whisper. "I told you that if you tried to leave, Moira would stop you, and I was right."

"Dammit, Shana! This accident was caused by two extremely active unborn babies, not a spirit-witch," he argued, automatically whispering, too.

"It was caused by Moira, and I can prove it."

"What are you doing?" he asked as she leaned down and began to search the floor.

"I'm looking for the card."

"What card?"

"The one that Moira delivered a second before the accident. It has to be here. Scoot over," she ordered, sitting up and pushing against his arm. "Maybe you're sitting on it."

"Shana, you shouldn't be moving around like this. You should be sitting still," he said impatiently.

"I'll sit still after I find the card. Now scoot over!"

Ryan opened his mouth to argue, but decided to save his breath. Obviously, she wasn't going to listen to anything he said, so he slid across the seat.

"Where is it?" she mumbled, running her hands over the seat where he'd been sitting, and then bending to search the floor again. "It has to be here."

"Maybe you imagined it."

Her head shot up, and she frowned at him. "I did not imagine it. She delivered the card."

"Well, maybe she took it back."

"Don't be ridiculous. Why would she take it back after delivering it?"

"How the hell would I know? I am not intimately acquainted with the motives of spirit—"

"Lucien! How is the automobile?" Shana broke in as

she caught Ryan's hand and gave it a warning squeeze when Morgret appeared at the open door.

"I think I can get it to run long enough to get everyone home," he answered, "but I need you to help me get it out of the ditch."

"Absolutely not!" Ryan roared. "How many times do I have to tell you that she has a head injury? The kind of physical exertion involved in pushing a car could kill her."

Again, anger leapt into Morgret's eyes. Ryan shuddered when they began to pulse with the same, strange inner glow that he had seen in Shana's eyes. Even more unnerving, however, was that a strong breeze began to blow inside the car. He told himself that it was coming in through the open door, but he had the oddest feeling that it was emanating from Morgret.

"Mr. Alden, I am trying to be patient with you, but I am not going to put up with your harassment any longer," Lucien stated tautly. "I know you don't want to believe in my powers, but I assure you that Shana is in no danger. Even if she was, I still wouldn't call an ambulance. Shana is a witch, not a mortal, and we take care of our own kind in Sanctuary.

"Now, I suggest you get out of the car, while we move it out of the ditch. And don't worry about Shana doing anything physically taxing. The only thing she will have to use is her brain, although I will admit that at times that does appear to be an exhausting task for her."

Looking toward Shana with a stern expression, he finished, "I need your help, Shana. Now."

"Yes, Lucien," she said, reaching for the doorknob as he strode away. Tossing open the door, she climbed out. Then she ducked back inside. "Stop making Lucien mad, Ryan. He'll end up reading your mind and find out about Moira, and I can't let that happen. It's too dangerous."

"They're all lunatics!" Ryan muttered as she slammed the door and hurried toward the front of the car. But he couldn't help noting that the breeze had stopped the moment Morgret had walked away.

"It was just coincidence," he told himself firmly as he began to slide toward the other door. Out of the corner of his eye, he saw something drift toward the floor. He glanced down, and his heart screeched to a halt. Then it began to beat in a frantic rhythm. He was looking at another Tarot card, and he didn't have to read the writing at the bottom to know it was the card known as Death.

Fear shot through him, because at that moment he knew his concerns about Shana were valid. Something was terribly wrong with her, and he was going to have to get her to the hospital. If he didn't—

He wouldn't let himself finish the thought. Instead, he grabbed the card off the floor and hastily stuffed it into his jacket pocket. Just touching it made his skin crawl. But instinct told him that if Morgret saw the card, they would have to waste time explaining it instead of getting Shana the help she needed.

"I'll get the mop for you," Ariel said, suddenly appearing and leaning into the front seat to retrieve it. "And as soon as Lucien finishes moving the car, I'll have him conjure you up a proper crutch. We have one at home, so it will only take him a second or two to retrieve it."

"How . . . considerate of you," Ryan said, forcing himself to be polite. If he hoped to get Morgret to cooperate with him, he couldn't offend his wife. Indeed, he might be able to convince Ariel to side with him. After all, she claimed to be a mortal. Since she apparently didn't have witchcraft delusions of her own,

he might be able make her see that Shana's health was
at risk. In the meantime, he'd just keep an eye on
Morgret. If it looked like he was going to make Shana
do something Ryan felt was dangerous, he'd interfere.
Otherwise, he'd maintain his peace until the opportunity presented itself to make another pitch for an
ambulance.

Accepting the mop from Ariel, he got out and followed her a short distance away from the car. When
they stopped, he saw that Shana and Lucien were
standing on either side of the vehicle and facing each
other. Shana had both arms extended over the hood,
and Lucien held one over it, while gripping the crystal
around his neck with the other hand. They weren't
speaking, and Ryan couldn't figure out what they were
up to.

"What are they doing?" he asked Ariel, his curiosity aroused.

"They're going to levitate the car out of the ditch,"
she answered.

"You're joking!"

She gave him a wry smile. "Just watch, Mr. Alden.
We'll make a believer out of you yet."

Ryan didn't know how to respond, so he didn't even
try. Instead, he focused on Shana and Lucien, determined to interrupt at the first sign of anything that he
felt would be injurious to Shana's health.

Suddenly, Lucien's crystal began to glow. At the
same time, Shana's eyes took on that strange, pulsing
light. Ryan couldn't see Lucien's eyes, but he knew
instinctively that they were also lit with that seemingly
inner force. It was one of the eeriest sights he'd ever
seen. It also scared the hell out of him, and yet it held
him enthralled.

Suddenly, Lucien dropped his arm and stated impatiently, "Shana, I know your head hurts, but you have to concentrate."

"I know I have to concentrate, Lucien, but it isn't as easy as it sounds," she told him. "Can't you draw on the powers of the others?"

"They're at the festival, Shana. I don't want to interrupt the festivities to move a car. Now, please, try to concentrate."

"Just give me a second," she said as she pressed her hands against her eyes.

Ryan frowned. Obviously, she was in pain, and he wanted to order her back into the car. He quelled the impulse, reminding himself that if he wanted Morgret to listen to him, he couldn't interfere unless it appeared the man was putting her in jeopardy. Even if their eyes were glowing, looking at each other across the hood was not harmful.

"Okay, let's try it again," she said, removing her hands from her face and extending her arms over the hood.

Lucien nodded, gripped his crystal and extended his arm. Again, the crystal began to glow, and, again, Shana's eyes began to shine. For several seconds nothing happened, and then suddenly the car began to rise. When it was a few inches off the ground, it began to float backward until it was out of the ditch.

Ryan's jaw dropped, and he shook his head. It's impossible! People cannot levitate cars! But as much as he wanted to intellectually deny it, he couldn't discount what he was seeing.

"Well, Mr. Alden, what do you think?" Ariel asked, amusement tingeing her words.

"It's . . . incredible," he allowed, looking down at her.

"Believe me, it's nothing compared to some of the things they can do. If you hang around for a few days, you'll discover—"

She was interrupted by a sudden, agonized scream that made Ryan's blood run cold. He jerked his head up in time to see Shana's hands fly to her head. The car dropped to the ground with a heavy thud, and she disappeared behind it as she crumpled to the ground.

"Shana!" he yelled, instinctively starting to run toward her and forgetting about his knee. He almost fell to the ground at the tearing pain that ripped through it. But his physical distress was nothing compared to his emotional upheaval. By not forcing his hand with Morgret, he was sure he'd just lost another battle with that old bastard, Father Death. Now, Shana's strangely glowing eyes would join the others that would forever haunt him.

CHAPTER SEVEN

The Magician
Will, Mastery and Power

Shana felt as if her head was ready to explode. The pain was so excruciating that she couldn't see or hear or speak. All she could do was clutch her head and moan in agony. What had happened? Why was she in such horrible pain?

Let me help you, Shana, Lucien's voice murmured in her mind. *Let me link with you and ease the pain.*

No! she replied frantically, knowing that she couldn't let him mentally join with her. If he did, he might find out about Moira. *I can do it myself!*

Shana, now is not the time to be stubborn. Let me help you.

I can do it myself! she reiterated, growing even more frantic at the realization that he might not listen to her. As the high priest, he was obligated to help a coven member in physical distress.

She had never realized that an exasperated sigh could be mentally communicated, but she heard his before he said, *Fine. When you stop being stubborn and decide you're ready to accept my help, just ask for it.*

She was both relieved and infuriated by his response. He was patronizing her, and she was so tired of being

treated like a recalcitrant child. Her anger at him gave
her the extra impetus she needed to handle this on her
own. Forcing herself to breathe deeply and evenly, she
began to concentrate inwardly, trying to reach a medi-
tative state. She wanted to curse when the pain ham-
pered her attempt.

I have to do this, she lectured herself. If I don't
Lucien will take control. I can't let that happen. I can't!

It seemed to take forever, but she finally managed
to go into a self-hypnotic trance. Then she began to
carefully construct the mental barriers that would ease
the pain into a manageable ache. It was a slow, ardu-
ous process, and the drain on her physical strength
became apparent when she let herself begin to surface
from the trance. Her entire body was trembling, and
she felt light-headed and queasy. But her maladies
were overshadowed by her feeling of triumph. Not only
had she kept Moira a secret, but she'd worked her way
through the pain without any assistance from Lucien.
He was going to have to acknowledge that, and maybe
he'd finally start treating her like an adult.

As she became peripherally aware of her surroundings, she was horrified to hear Ryan bellow, "If you
don't get out of my way and let me see to Shana, I
swear I'll beat you to a bloody pulp, Morgret!"

Shana's eyes flew open. She was lying on the ground
and looking at the sky. Quickly, she pushed herself up
on her elbows and stared at the scene in front of her
in horror. Ryan and Lucien were facing each other,
and for the first time she realized how comparable they
were in size. There was no doubt that they were a
physical match; however, Ryan was not only injured,
but Lucien had the advantage of magic on his side.

Instinct told Shana that Ryan wasn't issuing an idle
threat. His expression was so livid that she was sure
the only thing stopping him from hitting Lucien was

Ariel, who was trying to get between them. She couldn't see Lucien's face, but she didn't need to see it to know he was enraged. The wind that accompanied a warlock's temper was swirling around the trio with the force of a small tornado.

"Ryan, stop yelling at Lucien!" she demanded.

His head instantly pivoted toward her, and his furious expression altered to one of relief. As Lucien turned to look at her, the wind died, and Shana felt damned relieved herself. She was sure that if the argument had gone on much longer, she would have been facing disaster.

"Shana, are you all right?" Ariel gasped as she rushed to her.

"I'm a little weak, but I'm fine," Shana assured, as she sat up.

"You are *not* fine," Ryan stated tightly. "And you're getting to a hospital as soon as possible."

"I have already told you that we take care of our own, Mr. Alden," Lucien said just as tightly. "Shana is not going anywhere."

As they glared at each other, Shana recognized that a new confrontation was imminent. To prevent it, she said, "Lucien, what happened to me? Why did I suddenly have so much pain?"

"Before I answer that you need to try to perform some magic," he replied grimly.

"Why?" she asked, alarmed.

"Just try it, Shana, and then I'll answer your questions."

"What kind of magic should I do?" she questioned next, understanding what he was intimating and terrified at the prospect.

"Something simple. Try turning off the car's headlights," he suggested.

Shana glanced toward the automobile in dread.

Wanting to put off the inevitable, she started to tell him that she didn't know how the headlights functioned. She knew, however, that it didn't matter how they worked. Magic could make them behave in whatever manner she wanted.

"Don't be frightened, Shana. Just try it," Lucien urged.

I can do this, Shana told herself firmly, focusing on the headlights. It's so simple, it's child's play.

When she propelled her energy toward the vehicle, however, nothing happened. She looked up at Lucien, stricken, as she cried, "My power is gone!"

"It isn't gone," he soothed as he dropped to a knee beside her. "It's just short-circuiting because of your head injury."

"But it was working fine when we were levitating the car."

"I know," he said, frowning. "Evidently it was too much effort, and that's probably why this happened. But don't worry. When I was a boy, I saw another case like this. The warlock regained his powers in a few days."

"A few days? I can't go without my power for a few days!" she gasped, petrified at the thought of what Moira could accomplish in that much time. How was she going to defeat her if she couldn't fight her with magic?

"Shana, don't get yourself all upset," Ariel said. "You can stay with us until you're feeling better."

"The only place Shana is going is to a hospital!" Ryan said angrily.

Lucien leaped to his feet, his legs spread apart and his arms akimbo. "I have heard enough from you! Shana is our responsibility, and the only thing you need to worry about is how you're going to get out of Sanctuary."

"I am not going anywhere until Shana is on her way to a hospital."

"Then you will have a hell of a long wait, because the only place she's going is home with Ariel and me."

"Dammit, Morgret! What does it take to get through that thick head of yours? Shana has been unconscious *twice*, and the way she was clutching at her head a little while ago tells me that there's something drastically wrong with her. She needs medical attention."

"Stop arguing about me as if I'm not even here!" Shana interjected as she climbed unsteadily to her feet. When both men turned their attention on her, she perched her hands on her hips and glared at them. "I am not a child for you to bicker over. I am an adult."

"What you are in an injured woman," Ryan contradicted.

"What she is is an injured *witch*," Lucien shot back.

"What I am is *very* angry," she supplied, knowing she had to diffuse their argument before Lucien lost complete control over his temper and ended up delving into Ryan's mind. "And if both of you don't shut up, I'm going to . . . to . . ."

She wanted to scream when she realized that without her magic, she couldn't even issue a good threat. "I don't know what I'll do," she admitted grudgingly, "but I can guarantee that it won't be what either of you want me to do. So stop fighting over me."

"Shana, you have to listen to me on this," Ryan said, raking a hand through his hair. "I am a doctor, and I know what I'm talking about."

He looked so distraught that Shana's heart went out to him. "I'm sure you do, Ryan, and if we were discussing Ariel, I would listen to every word you're saying. But we're talking about me, and as much as you want to deny it, I am a witch. Your medicine doesn't apply to me."

"That's absurd," he said. "Even if you are a witch, you're still a human being."

"Yes, I am a human being," she agreed. "But there are physiological differences between us. Granted, they aren't big differences, but they are significant."

"So, you're saying that you refuse to go to the hospital?"

"What I'm saying is that there is no *need* for me to go to a hospital," she corrected. "And even if there was, I couldn't go. If mortal doctors started working on me, they might find those differences I'm talking about. Once they learned about them, it would only be a matter of time before they discovered us. We can't let that happen, Ryan, because your race is not ready to accept ours. The witch hunts could begin again, and we're dangerously close to extinction."

"Witch hunts?" he repeated in disbelief. "For God's sake, this isn't the Middle Ages. People don't engage in witch hunts!"

"Ryan, your people engaged in witch hunts a mere three centuries ago in this very country," she said, pressing her hand against her forehead. The pain was becoming more difficult to control. All she wanted to do was lie down, but she knew she had to make him understand so he'd stop fighting Lucien. "That may seem like a long time to you. For us, it seems like yesterday, because we've been persecuted for more than a thousand years."

He opened his mouth to respond, but she went on before he could speak. "I know that you don't want to believe that any harm would come to me if I went to a mortal hospital, and maybe it wouldn't. I can't, however, take that chance. I can't put the coven at risk."

"So what are you saying? That you would rather die?"

"Of course I wouldn't rather die," she responded impatiently, "but I don't have a choice. My life is insignificant if saving it could destroy the coven."

"That's insane, Shana."

"No, Ryan. It's realistic," she said with a weary sigh, again pressing her hand to her forehead. "We're a race fighting for survival, just as so many endangered animals around the world are fighting for survival. The difference between us and them is that man does not consider an animal a threat, because he is their ultimate predator. We, however, are superior to you in many ways, which means that we would be perceived as your predator. It would be a wrong perception, but when people realize how powerful we are, they aren't going to believe that. Historically, mankind kills what he fears, and, historically, he's feared us. And then there will be those who covet our power and will try to make us their slaves. Either way, it is simply too dangerous for anyone to know about us."

Ryan wanted to argue with her, but he knew that what she was saying was philosophically true. To accept that philosophy, however, he would also have to accept that she was a witch. He wasn't ready to do that, but after everything he'd seen tonight, he couldn't deny that something was going on here that defied all logic.

What if they really were witches and warlocks? Could his society accept them? Unfortunately, the answer came too easily. Mankind couldn't even deal with a difference in skin color. He didn't want to consider how they'd react to a more powerful race. Assuming, of course, that one really did exist.

"So, what are our options here?" he asked, realizing that they'd reached a seeming impasse. He couldn't force her to go to the hospital, but he wasn't ready to give up on her either.

"I think Shana has made that perfectly clear," Lucien answered. "We take care of our own."

"And how many of your *own* die from injuries that might not be life-threatening if they received proper medical care?" Ryan challenged.

"That, Mr. Alden, is none of your concern," Lucien replied with a dismissive shrug.

"Well, Mr. Morgret, you're wrong. I am a doctor, and I took an oath to preserve life. So, as of this moment, consider me your resident physician, and Shana is going to be my first patient."

"You're going to stay?" Shana gasped.

"On one condition," Ryan answered, deciding that insanity had to be contagious. When he'd ridden his motorcycle out of California, he'd vowed that he'd never practice medicine again. But that was before he'd met Shana Morland, and as crazy as she was, there was no way he could stand by and let her die. "You will do exactly what I say. And I mean *exactly*, Shana. Are you willing to do that?"

Shana caught her bottom lip between her teeth uncertainly. She wanted Ryan to stay, but she also recognized the dangers. Without her powers, there was no way she could protect him. Then, again, Moira had made it clear that she wasn't going to let him leave.

"I'm willing," she agreed, promising herself that she would find a way to protect him from Moira, even if it meant sacrificing her soul.

"Morgret?" Ryan then said, looking at Lucien.

Lucien stared at him for a long moment before finally saying, "Welcome to Sanctuary, *Dr.* Alden. Since you're going to be our resident physician, we'd better get rid of that ridiculous mop and get you a proper crutch."

Before Ryan could respond, Lucien grabbed the crystal around his neck. Both it and his eyes began to glow. As he muttered some unintelligible words, Ryan regarded him warily.

Suddenly, Lucien raised his free hand toward him, and lightning shot from his fingertips to the mop beneath Ryan's arm. Ryan let out a frightened yelp, sure that he was about to be electrocuted. Outside of a small surge of warmth coursing up his arm, however, he didn't feel a thing.

As the lightning disappeared, his jaw dropped in shock. The mop was gone, and in its place was a crutch. It had happened so quickly that he hadn't even seen the transfer take place.

"Now, do you believe in witches and warlocks, Mr. Alden?" Ariel asked, again sounding amused.

Looking first at her, and then at Shana and Lucien, he shook his head, still wanting to deny their assertion. He had a sinking feeling, however, that they were telling him the truth. What had he gotten himself into?

Returning his gaze to Shana's exquisitely beautiful face, he suspected the answer was a hell of a lot of trouble.

"Ryan, I am not some fragile flower that has to be hovered over," Shana grumbled as he settled her into the backseat of the car and made her lean against it. "All I have is a headache."

"Well, humor me anyway," he said. "And I don't want you to move a muscle while I help Lucien and Ariel check out the car to make sure it's safe enough to get us all home."

"Get us *all* home?" she repeated in horror, as she bolted upright. "I am not riding anywhere in this automobile."

"Of course you're riding in it. You are not in any condition to walk home."

"I won't have to walk. I'll summon Portent . . . Oh,

damn! I can't summon Portent, because I don't have any powers!"

"Who the hell is Portent?" Ryan asked, frowning at her in confusion.

"My familiar—my horse."

"Your familiar is that white monstrosity who ran me off the road?"

"Yes. Why do you sound so surprised?"

"I thought . . . familiars were supposed to be cats."

"Any animal can be a familiar, Ryan."

"Yeah, well, you can enlighten me on the subject another time. I need to go help Lucien and Ariel, so we can get you home and into bed. You sit back and be still until we're ready to leave."

"Ryan, I am not going to ride in this automobile," she repeated firmly. "They are not safe, and I just learned that firsthand."

"Shana, the chances of us having another accident are a million to one."

"Someone has to be that one, and what if we're it?"

"We aren't going to have another accident, and even if we do, you're going to be wearing a seat belt this time. So sit back and be still until we're ready to leave," he repeated impatiently as he shut the door.

Shana sank back against the seat in frustation. She wanted to continue arguing with him, but as much as she hated to admit it, she had to allow that worrying about another accident was silly. Lucien would be in the car, and he'd cast a protective spell over it. Nothing would happen during the short drive to her house.

Unless Moira decides to interfere.

She again bolted upright in terrified dismay. That had to be why Moira had delivered the Death card just before the accident! It meant transformation and change. Without her powers, she had definitely been transformed, and the change would be the addition of

Lucien to the automobile. Even if Moira couldn't contact him, he would be aware that there was magic going on. Since he knew she was powerless, all hell would break loose.

"I have to find the card and get out of here!" she said as she bent down to search the floor.

She cursed when she couldn't find the card. Had Ryan been right earlier? Had Moira, for some inexplicable reason, taken it back? It didn't make sense that she would, but Shana knew that she didn't have time to worry about it now. If the card was here, it was so well hidden that Lucien wouldn't spot it, and that was all that mattered.

Sitting up, she looked out the windshield. The hood was up, and she couldn't see Lucien and Ryan. Ariel was standing on the passenger side of the car and looking in at the engine. Shana knew that even if there was something wrong with the car, Lucien would simply cast a spell to make it run long enough to get everyone home. Thankfully, it took longer to cast an enchantment over mechanical devices, particularly ones that weren't working properly. She should have enough time to sneak away.

She grabbed the door handle and pulled it up. When she eased the door open, it let out squeak that sounded like a wailing shriek to her. She immediately glanced out the windshield, praying that the noise wasn't as loud as she thought. Evidently, it wasn't, because Ariel was still looking in at the engine, and Lucien and Ryan remained out of sight.

With a relieved sigh, she swung her legs out. As she started to stand, she let out a startled cry when Ryan suddenly demanded, "Just what do you think you're doing?"

"Ryan! What are you doing back here?" she gasped

when she realized that he was standing by the back fender.

"I came to check on my patient, whom I gave specific instructions to sit still, and guess what I saw?" he muttered grimly. "She wasn't sitting still, but rummaging around on the floor. I decided I'd wait and see what she was up to."

"In other words, you were spying on me!" she accused indignantly.

"Yep," he admitted without any sign of remorse. "And it's a good thing that I was, because not only is my patient ignoring my orders to sit still, she's actually getting out of the car. Get back inside, Shana."

Glancing toward the front of the vehicle, she noted that Ariel was looking their way, but Lucien was still out of sight. That did not guarantee, however, that he couldn't hear them.

Lowering her voice to a whisper, she said, "I can't ride in the automobile with Lucien. Moira might try something!"

"We'll worry about that if it happens," he said. "Get back in the car, Shana, and do it right now."

"I can't, and I just told you why."

"Shana, I am going to count to three. If you aren't back in the car by then, I am going to ask Lucien to cast a spell that will put you in it and keep you there."

"You wouldn't dare," she said, aghast that he would even suggest such a thing when she'd just explained her reasoning.

He arched a brow and counted, "One . . ."

"Ryan, you have to listen to me!" she cried in frustration.

"Two . . ."

"Oh, all right, you win," she muttered, realizing that he was serious. She was going to have to go along with him for now and hope that there would be another opportunity to escape. As she swung her legs back into the car, she added irritably, "I just want you to know that if anything happens, it's going to be your fault."

"I will be happy to accept responsibility, as long as you are doing what I tell you," he said, again closing the door. "Now, stay in the car and sit still."

"He is utterly impossible!" she grumbled as she watched him go back to the front of the car. "And if he thinks he's going to order me around, he's in for a big surprise. I may not have my powers, but that does not mean I'm powerless."

The future is mine, and now yours will be mine! Moira taunted as a new card suddenly appeared in Shana's lap.

She stared down at it and gave a disbelieving shake of her head. It was The Magician, and his face was Ryan's. Except for The Emperor, The Magician was the most domineering male figure in Tarot. He achieved what he wanted through will, mastery, and power, or, as Ariel had once so appropriately described him, he was a control freak.

As she saw Ariel approaching, she grabbed the card and swiftly tucked it into her back pocket, cursing the fact that she would not have another opportunity to escape. Damn Ryan, anyway!

"So, how does it feel to have the handsome Dr. Alden caring for you?" Ariel asked as she climbed into the car beside her.

Instead of answering, Shana watched the hood close, revealing Ryan and Lucien. They were engaged in conversation, and suddenly Lucien leaned back his head and laughed. Shana gave an amazed shake of her head. Not more than fifteen minutes ago, they were ready to beat each other up, and now they appeared to be the best of friends. It was too mind-boggling to even contemplate, and damnably worrisome. If they got too friendly, Ryan might blurt out something about Moira. *Damn!* Why didn't she have her powers so she could cast a spell that would keep him silent on the issue? Since she couldn't do that, she'd just have to hope for the best. But once they got home, she was going to find a way to impress upon him the seriousness of her situation.

"I'll tell you how it feels to have him caring for me. I think I finally understand that mortal saying you're always spouting at me," she told Ariel.

"And which saying is that?"

Shana frowned as she murmured, "Be careful of what you wish for, because you just might get it."

Shana stared out the window as Lucien drove the car down the road. She was too nervous to participate in the conversation the others were having. Since she had just received a new Tarot card, she didn't think Moira would bother them, but she wouldn't be able to relax until she was home. At least that was one good thing about the automobile, she decided. It could make the trip in about five minutes.

"Lucien, you just missed the turn to my house!" she declared a few minutes later.

"You're staying with us," Ariel announced.

Shana jerked her head toward her friend, appalled by the suggestion. Where she went, Moira went, and she was not going to take her into Lucien's home. "No, I am not staying with you."

"Yes, you are," Lucien said. "We discussed it while we were checking out the car, and we all felt that since both you and Ryan are injured, it would be best if you stayed with us."

"Well, you should have included me in this discussion, because I am *not* staying with you," she said, angered that they had so blithely excluded her from their talk. "So, turn the automobile around and take me home."

"You said you'd do what I told you to do," Ryan reminded, as he frowned at her over the seat.

"And I will, but I'm going to do it at *my* home," she insisted, glaring at him. How could he have possibly forgotten Moira? For pity's sake, they had just been discussing her when he insisted she stay in the car instead of making her escape!

"Shana, I understand why you're upset, and I'm sorry," Ariel said contritely. "We should have included you in the discussion. But you have to agree that with both you and Ryan injured, it will be easier if you stay with us. For instance, who's going to cook for you?"

"I lost my powers, Ariel. I did not lose my ability to function, and I am not going to impose on you," Shana stated firmly. "I am going home. If Lucien isn't going to take me there, then when I get to your house, I will walk back."

"The hell you will," Ryan said, glowering at her. "You are going to go to Lucien and Ariel's house, and you are going to climb into bed and stay there until I say you can get up."

"You have the last part right, Ryan," she responded, deciding that since she couldn't connect with his mind, she needed to give him some kind of verbal code to remind him of Moira. "It's the first part that needs some work. I suggest you listen to me closely, because I am *not* staying with Lucien and Ariel. They have enough problems without me dragging my *special* problem into their house."

"Dammit, Shana! Now is not the time for you to indulge in a fit of rebellious independence," Lucien snapped. "You know very well that your problems are my problems. Now, you are going to our house, and that is final."

"It is not final!" she declared furiously. "And don't you dare talk to me in that tone. As I keep reminding you, I am not a child, and I am getting sick and tired of your treating me like one!"

"Then stop behaving like one!"

"Lucien, that isn't fair. Shana has a perfect right to be angry," Ariel quickly interceded. "We did make a decision about her without including her in the conversation. If I were in her place, I'd be upset with us, too."

"Fine. She can be as upset as she wants, but she is still going to stay with us," he stated in a manner that indicated the subject was closed.

Shana was so infuriated she wanted to hit him. She knew, however, that would only make matters worse. Instead, she forced herself to speak calmly, as she pointed out, "You said there was nothing seriously wrong with me, Lucien. Were you lying to me?"

He scowled at her in the rearview mirror. "Of course, I wasn't lying to you, but you've lost your powers. The only way I can protect you is to keep you close by."

"Protect me from what? Is there some danger in Sanctuary that I don't know about?" she asked, shooting a warning look at Ryan in case he should choose this inauspicious time to suddenly remember Moira. When his eyes widened, she realized that her precaution had been warranted. It appeared that he was finally getting the point. Too bad he hadn't done so before Lucien had returned to his surrogate father role.

"You know perfectly well that there is no danger here, but—"

"If there isn't any danger, then I am not in need of protection," she broke in. "Besides, Ryan will be with me, and I'm sure that if he thinks there is a problem, he'll contact you right away. So, I would appreciate it if you would take me home."

Lucien released an exasperated sigh and looked at Ryan. "I'll leave the decision up to you."

As she waited for Ryan's answer, Shana caught her breath. If he wouldn't go along with her, she didn't know what she'd do.

He regarded her for a nerve-rackingly long moment before finally saying, "If Shana swears she will obey my every command, we can stay at her house."

If Moira hadn't just delivered The Magician—the control freak—Shana would have eagerly agreed to his terms. Now, every feminine cell she possessed rebelled at the implication inherent in his words.

He can't be that bad, she told herself. After all, he's just a mortal.

That didn't quell the foreboding suspicion that he was going to be big trouble. Unfortunately, she didn't have any other option.

She released her breath and muttered in resignation, "I'll do everything you say."

Silently, she added, As long as it doesn't interfere in my efforts to save us all from Moira.

CHAPTER EIGHT

The High Priestess
Hidden Influences

When Lucien pulled up in front of Shana's house, Ryan stared at its menacing-looking exterior with a sense of foreboding. He knew it was absurd, but he again had the feeling that the house was alive and if he went back inside it would never let him go.

Unfortunately, he didn't have a chance to change his mind about staying. The moment the car stopped Shana jumped out, saying, "Thank you for bringing me home, Lucien, and good night, Ariel."

Then she shut the door and ran toward the house. As Ryan watched her disappear inside, a chill crawled up his spine. He felt as if the house had just swallowed her.

It's just a house, he told himself with an impatient shake of his head. Now, haul your butt out of the car and get in there, so you can put her to bed.

"I guess I'd better get inside," he said, reaching for the door handle.

"Before you go, I want you to have something," Lucien said. He removed the drawstring pouch at his waist. Opening it, he took out a clear, rod-shaped crystal about an inch long and handed it to Ryan.

"I know you're concerned about Shana, but I assure you that she isn't in any physical jeopardy. She can, however, be difficult to deal with, and the loss of her powers may make her more contrary than normal. So if you decide you need help in dealing with her, just hold the crystal and think of me. I'll come immediately."

An hour ago Ryan would have discounted Lucien's declaration as delusional. Now he wasn't sure what to believe. Tucking the crystal into his jacket pocket, he said, "Yeah, well, just in case this doesn't work, how about giving me your phone number."

"Still doubtful?" Lucien asked wryly. Before Ryan could answer, he rattled off a phone number.

"Thanks." Ryan opened the door and swung the crutch out. As he stood, he said, "I guess I'll see you two later."

"We'll be checking in," Ariel said, while getting out of the backseat.

He waited until she climbed into the front before he headed toward the house. When he knocked on the door, it swung open. Obviously, Shana hadn't shut it tightly, but that didn't alleviate the eerie sensation that it was the house itself letting him in.

"You're getting to be as nutty as the rest of the Sanctuary crew," he muttered disparagingly. "You have a patient to worry about, so stop indulging yourself in bump-in-the-night fantasies and get your act together."

The moment he crossed the threshold, however, he came to a stop and stared at his surroundings in confusion. Since he had left by the back door, he hadn't seen this part of the house, and he had expected to be entering a traditional living room. It was apparent, however, that this room, which stretched the entire front of the house, was not used for "living." It had an inlaid hardwood floor and vaulted ceiling. There was a

spiral staircase at the far right end, and a massive stone
fireplace filled the entire left wall. The stones had been
laid so that there was a stone mantelpiece, as well as
dozens of stone shelves running from floor to ceiling.
The mantelpiece and shelves were cluttered with old
bottles filled with what looked like dried plants. The
only furniture consisted of two rough-hewn chairs sitting in front of the fireplace, with a matching table
between them.

Shana wasn't in the room, and he knew he should
go looking for her. Curiosity, however, drew him to the
fireplace, where he studied the jars. Many of them
were layered with dust so thick they couldn't have been
used in years. Suddenly, he had the oddest feeling that
he could take down some of those dusty jars, and he'd
know exactly what to do with the plants inside them.

"You must have landed on your head when you
wrecked your bike. You couldn't distinguish dried oreg-
ano from dried catnip if your life depended upon it,"
he stated dryly, as he turned away from the fireplace
and again surveyed the room.

He wasn't sure what drew his attention to the floor,
but as he studied the intricate inlaid pattern on its
surface, he blinked in astonishment. There was a huge
pentagram built into the center of the floor, and it was
surrounded by two circles. In between the two circles
were strange-looking symbols.

As he studied the pentagram, he was hit with an
overwhelming sense of déjà vu. He could see flashes
of himself sitting cross-legged in its center and performing some type of ritual that had to do with the
plants. The images came and went so quickly that he
couldn't describe them. But, paradoxically, they had
such a realistic quality that it made the hair on the
back of his neck stand on end. What the hell was
going on?

"Nothing's going on. This is familiar because of all those horror films you watched as a kid," he chided himself, irritated when the rationalization didn't alleviate his unease. Deciding it was time he found Shana, he headed toward the hallway, careful to avoid stepping on any of the lines forming the pentagram.

As he proceeded down the hall, he realized that when he'd gone down it before, he'd been too intent on reaching a telephone to pay much attention to the layout of the house. Now, he saw that there were several closed doors on the left and no doors on the right. He was tempted to stop and look behind some of the doors to see what they hid, but he refrained. His first priority was to find Shana and get her into bed. Besides, instinct told him that he was better off remaining ignorant of the goings on in this house.

When he finally reached the kitchen it was empty, and he frowned. Where was Shana? He considered calling for her, but the majority of walls were made of stone, so he knew she probably wouldn't hear him. Returning to the hallway, he saw that it continued around the corner. He suspected that it would lead back to the room with the pentagram, and he decided to follow it. If he still hadn't found her by the time he'd gone full circle, then he'd resort to yelling for her.

As he entered the corridor, he noted that it was darker than the other hallways. He had become so accustomed to all the doors being on the left that he was almost on top of the one on the right before he saw it. Even then it was so heavily shadowed he might have missed it if he hadn't heard a faint thudding sound.

He stopped and eyed the door. If Shana was in there, she either had the lights out, or the door was so well-fitted that not even a glimmer of light showed through the cracks. He listened intently for another sound. When several silent seconds passed, he was convinced he had imagined the thud. Just as he started to turn away, however, he heard it again.

Immediately, he knocked on the door. "Shana, are you in there?"

There was no answer. He was debating whether or not to look into the room, when the door suddenly opened a crack. Shana peered out at him, the light behind her confirming that the door was well-fitted.

"Ryan!" she said breathlessly. "What are you doing here?"

He arched a brow. Obviously, she was up to something, and he wasn't pleased that it involved sufficient exertion to affect her breathing. "You know why I'm here, and you're supposed to be in bed. Is this your room?"

She widened her eyes in a parody of innocence. "Every room in the house is mine, Ryan. This is my home, remember?"

"That wasn't what I meant, Shana, and you know it," he said, regarding her suspiciously. "What are doing in there?"

"I'm looking for something to protect us from Moira," she answered. "Just go to the kitchen and have a snack or something. I'll be with you shortly."

"You're coming with me now. You have a head injury, and you need to go to bed."

"And I'll do that just as soon as I find what I need. Just go to the kitchen and wait for me," she repeated as she shut the door.

Her dismissal was so peremptory that Ryan stared at the door, dumbfounded. Then his temper flared. How dare she ignore his instructions! He'd gone against his better judgment and agreed to let her come home. And he'd only done so because she'd promised to obey his every command.

He raised his hand to knock again, but decided to

hell with the amenities. If she was rude enough to close the door on him, then, by damn, he was rude enough to enter uninvited. He grabbed the doorknob and opened the door.

As he stepped inside, his jaw dropped. The room was built in a circular fashion that was open all the way to the roof. It was a good twenty-five to thirty feet in diameter, and there was a huge brick fireplace on one wall. Another pentagram was built into the center of the floor. Lining the walls were display cases and tables cluttered with objects, most of which seemed to be rocks.

On the wall opposite the fireplace was a staircase. His gaze followed it upward to a balcony on the second-floor level, where there appeared to be hundreds of books in built-in bookcases. From there, another staircase led to a balcony on the third-story level, which had more display cases and tables. The ceiling consisted of a stained glass pentagram mirroring the one on the floor. The lighting was soft, diffused, but he couldn't see any light source.

"What the hell is this place?" he gasped, incredulous.

"Ryan, you shouldn't be in here!" Shana declared in alarm as she suddenly leaned over the balcony railing on the second floor. "I told you to wait for me in the kitchen!"

"You promised to obey me, Shana, not the other way around. Now, I want you to come down here and get into bed," he returned, scowling up at her.

She rolled her eyes. "Lucien said there is nothing seriously wrong with me, so I wish you'd stop worrying."

"Well, Lucien doesn't have a medical degree, and I do. That means I know when to worry, and your condition is serious enough to make me worry. I want you in bed, so get your fanny down here, and do it right now."

"I'm sorry, Ryan, but I can't do that. Since I've lost my powers, I have to find some way to protect us from Moira or she's going to claim my soul. Believe me, that's more serious than a bump on the head. So, you just go to the kitchen. As soon as I find a way to protect us, I'll join you."

Ryan started to argue, but she disappeared. He stood glaring up at the spot where she'd been. When she didn't reappear, he glanced toward the staircase. The steps were dangerously narrow, and the only railing was located on the side where he had to use the crutch.

Damn! If he tried to climb the stairs, he'd probably fall and break his neck. Even if he did make it up them, he didn't know what he'd be able to accomplish. There didn't appear to be a door on that level, and he wasn't in any physical condition to bodily haul Shana down the stairs.

"Shana, I want you to come down here *now*," he stated firmly.

"Ryan, I've already explained that I have to find some way to protect us from Moira." She reappeared at the railing with a huge, tattered-looking book clutched to her chest. "I'm sure there's some type of protective object in here that I can use without my powers, but if you don't stop interrupting me, I'm never going to find it. So, please, go to the kitchen and wait for me. I'll join you as soon as I can."

"Dammit, Shana! I'm not leaving this room without you."

"In that case, sit down and be quiet," she ordered. "I need to concentrate. And don't touch anything. This is a repository, and everything in here is either sacrosanct or has been banned from use."

Again, she disappeared, and Ryan decided that when he got his hands on her, he'd shake her until her teeth rattled. Unfortunately, he wouldn't be able to do that until she came downstairs. Muttering a frustrated curse, he looked around for a place to sit. There was a chair shoved between two display cases, and he limped to it and sat down. He wanted a cigarette, but he couldn't bring himself to light one in here. It was too much like a museum.

Instead, he leaned back in the chair and studied the articles in one of the display cases next to him. There were several old cups that resembled chalices, and so many rocks that he felt like he was in a stone quarry. What could be sacrosanct about a bunch of rocks?

He turned to look at the other display case. When he did, his elbow bumped against the crutch, which was leaning against the chair arm. It slid to the floor with a clatter.

"Ryan, are you okay?" Shana called from somewhere above his head.

"I'm fine. I just dropped my crutch," he answered, leaning over to get it. When he did, he spied what looked like a stick lying on the floor between the chair and the display case. His first impulse was to leave it alone, but the angle at which it was lying made him believe it had fallen. Since Shana had indicated that everything in this room was important, he decided he should retrieve it.

Grabbing the end of the stick, he pulled it out. As he sat up, he examined his find, frowning in puzzlement. It was a gnarled tree branch about eighteen inches long and an inch in diameter. There wasn't anything particularly distinctive about it. What could possibly be special about a piece of misshapen wood that could most likely be found on any tree?

"I sure as hell wish I knew why I had the bad luck to end up in this loony bin," he mumbled, leaning back in the chair and swinging the branch from side to side in front of his face.

Now you've found Sanctuary. Your journey is at its end.

As the voice echoed in his mind, lightning suddenly erupted from the end of the stick. Horrified, he watched it shoot toward the ceiling. It hit the center of the stained-glass pentagram and then spiraled downward. A moment later, it hit the center of the pentagram on the floor. Then it rebounded and shot toward him, hitting the end of the stick. An electrifying surge of energy sped through the wood and up his arm. Then it exploded through the remainder of his body, making his hair stand on end and his nerve endings tingle.

When it was over, Ryan was so stunned, he couldn't move. The energy that had coursed through him was powerful, but it hadn't hurt him. If anything it had left him feeling strangely energized.

"Ryan, what happened?" Shana gasped as she raced down the stairs.

"I don't know," he said, looking at her in bafflement. "I was holding this stick, and—"

"How did you get this?" she cried in horror, grabbing the stick out of his hand.

"It was lying on the floor by the chair."

"That's impossible. This wand has always been on the third floor."

"Well, it wasn't on the third floor tonight. It was lying right there," he said, pointing to the spot where he'd found it.

"What did you wish for?" she suddenly demanded.

"Wish for?" he repeated, confused.

"This is the wishing wand, Ryan. It will grant any wish you want. Unfortunately, it also makes you sacrifice something very important to you in return, which is why it has been banned from use. Now, what did you wish for?"

"I don't know," he said, raking a hand through his hair. "As I said, I was holding it, and then I said—"

"Said what?" she prodded urgently. "This is very important. I must know exactly what you said."

"I think I said something like I wished I knew why I had the bad luck to end up in this loony bin."

"And what was the answer?"

"There wasn't an answer."

"There had to be an answer," she said impatiently. "Otherwise, the wand wouldn't have activated. What did it tell you, Ryan? Why are you here?"

"I'm here to repeat the cycle," he replied automatically, startled by his response. He didn't know where that knowledge had come from, but he knew instinctively that it was true.

"What does that mean?" she asked in bewilderment.

"I have no idea."

"You must have *some* idea."

He shook his head. "That's all I know, and I'm not even sure how I know that."

"You know it because that's what you wished for."

Bending to retrieve the crutch off the floor, he grumbled, "Yeah, well, if I'd known that stupid stick was a genie in disguise, I'd have asked it to transport me the hell out of here. I can't believe I wasted a perfectly good wish."

"That's the least of your worries. What you need to be concerned about is what the wand will demand in return for the wish you did make. What's important to you, Ryan? What will be the most painful thing for you to give up, because whatever it is, that's what the wand is going to demand in return."

He got the crutch and stood before saying, "There was only one thing important to me, and that was my bike. Since it's already gone, I guess your wand is out of luck."

"Oh, come on, Ryan. There has to be something more important to you than a motorcycle."

"There isn't, and I'm tired of this conversation," he snapped. "I'm also going to insist that you come with me so I can put you to bed."

"I can't go to bed," she objected. "I have to find a way to protect us from Moira."

"You don't have to worry about Moira. She isn't any threat to either of us tonight." Again, he was startled by his words, but again, he knew it was the truth.

"And how do you know that?"

He shrugged uncomfortably. "I just know it. Now, come along. I want you in bed, and I don't want an argument. You promised to obey me, and I expect you to uphold that promise."

"But—"

"You're going to bed *now*, Shana."

"All right," she said irritably.

Her capitulation was too easy, and Ryan eyed her suspiciously. He started to ask her what she was up to, but decided to maintain his peace. Whatever it was, she wouldn't get away with it. He was going to be keeping a close watch on her, because he suddenly had another flash of insight that scared the hell out of him. Shana was in mortal danger, and he knew intuitively that he was the only one who could keep her alive.

As Shana led the way toward the kitchen, she gnawed worriedly on her bottom lip. When she first realized that Ryan had used the wishing wand, her biggest concern was the consequences. Now, she was trying to figure out how he had activated the wand. It was specifically designed to respond only to persons with magical abilities. He was a mortal. He didn't have magical skills.

Unless Moira had somehow endowed him with powers.

Shana shook her head. That was impossible. But the last Tarot card Moira delivered was The Magician. Perhaps it didn't mean Ryan was a control freak. Perhaps its meaning was more literal.

The Magician . . . So powerful because he knew how to combine his magical abilities with his earthly knowledge to get what he wanted. If Moira had somehow managed to grant Ryan even a modicum of power, it would make him extremely dangerous. Not only was Lucien sure to pick up on his abilities, but Ryan wasn't trained in magic. As he had with the wand he could inadvertently create situations of potential disaster, and she couldn't intervene. She was powerless.

Don't create catastrophes where none exist, she told herself firmly. It's possible that Ryan's activation of the wand was just a fluke.

But there were no flukes in magic. She knew that. So at least at the moment he'd made his wish, Ryan had had some magical ability. As distressing as that was, some good had come out of it. The wand had given her a clue as to what was going on. Ryan was here to repeat a cycle. Now she had to figure out what that meant. Since the enchanted Tarot had been stored in the repository, she was sure the answer could be found in the reference books on the second story of the room.

She cursed the fact that Ryan was insisting that she go to bed. When he had made the demand, she had considered ignoring him. Then she had realized that if she stayed in the repository, so would he. After the incident with the wishing wand, she knew she had to get him out of there. There were too many objects that carried harsh penalties for their use, and he was already going to suffer the consequences of his wish. Regardless of his claim to the contrary, there was something important to him that would be painful to lose or the wand wouldn't have worked. *Damn!* Why had she let him stay in there in the first place? If she had made him leave, he wouldn't have found the wand.

But that was a fait accompli that she couldn't do anything about, so chastising herself over it was a waste of time. What she had to do was get Ryan out the way so she could get back to the repository and continue her research. Unfortunately, she could think of only one way to guarantee his noninterference. She was going to have to give him a sleeping potion.

"You're supposed to be going to bed, Shana. Why are you coming in here?" Ryan demanded when she enterd the kitchen.

"I'm too keyed up to rest, so I'm going to fix myself some tea," she answered, walking toward the stove. "Would you like some?"

"No. What I'd like is for you to get to bed."

"And I'll do that as soon as I have some tea," she stated, cursing silently as she filled the tea kettle and set it on a burner. How was she going to give him the potion if he didn't have any tea? "Are you sure you won't have some?"

"No, thanks."

"Won't you just try it? It's a special blend I make myself, and I'm sure you'll like it." When he didn't respond, she glanced toward him. He was watching her through narrowed eyes, and his expression was unreadable. Uneasy with his veiled scrutiny, she asked, "Is something wrong?"

"No. I'll try some of your tea," he replied.

"Good," she said, opening a cupboard and getting out the teapot and two tea cups.

"What was that room we were in?" he suddenly asked.

"It's the repository for the coven," she answered, retrieving her tin of tea and the vial containing the sleeping potion from another cupboard. Thankfully, they were stored on the same shelf, and the vial was so small she could easily shield it from him.

Deciding that keeping him talking would be to her advantage, she continued, "Every family within the coven is tasked with a responsibility. Centuries ago, my family became the guardians of items that are either sacred or considered too dangerous for use. These items are stored in the repository, and we maintain a reference library that lists what the item is and what magical capabilities it possesses. This was particularly important when the covens practiced the Old Ways and their magic involved the dark forces."

He pulled out a chair and sat down at the table. "The Old Ways? Dark forces? Are you talking about black magic?"

"Yes, but probably not in the context in which you're referring," she answered while spooning tea leaves into a tea ball. "We are followers of nature, and there are what we call light forces and dark forces. We believe that both must exist for nature to be in perfect balance.

"The dark forces, however, are dangerous and can turn into evil if handled improperly," she explained. "You must be very devout to resist their temptations, and some witches and warlocks were seduced by them and used their powers inappropriately. That's what started the witch hysteria. About two hundred years ago the council of high priests—that's the high priests from all the covens around the world—banned the practice of the Old Ways. After that, not many items were put into the repository, so now I just more or less keep an eye on what's already in there."

"And many of those items are banned from use because they involved the dark forces?"

The tea pot began to whistle. She took it off the burner and poured the water into the teapot. "Yes. During the practice of the Old Ways, an item was often imbued with destructive powers that could only be controlled by the witch or warlock who created it. Thus, when they died, the item had to be put into the repository so that someone else wouldn't use it and bring harm to the coven."

"Why wasn't the item just destroyed?"

"That's one of the complications of working with the dark forces," she replied, surreptitiously popping the cap off the sleeping potion vial. Using the guise of rinsing the cups out at the sink, she poured the clear liquid into one of the cups. Then she began placing everything on a tray while continuing, "Once they've been activated, it's almost impossible to deactivate them. You have to know exactly what spell the creator used, and many spells practiced in the Old Ways can't be undone. Once they're cast, they are in effect forever."

"That sounds pretty damned ominous."

"It is, and that's why we have the repository," she said, carrying the tray to the table. Pouring tea into the cups, she placed the doctored one in front of him. "Would you like anything else?"

"Some sugar."

"Of course. I keep forgetting that mortals like sugar in their tea."

As she walked back to the cupboards, he said, "Moira's Tarot deck was in the repository, wasn't it?"

Caught off-guard by the question, she stopped and glanced warily over her shoulder at him. "How did you know that?"

"That's easy. You told me earlier tonight that you

broke coven law to use it. You also said you ignored the curse. It makes sense that if her cards carried a curse, they would be in the repository. Why did you use the deck?"

She frowned, trying to decide how to answer his question. "Because I felt like my life was going nowhere, and I wanted to know if my future was going to be better."

"And you couldn't wait for the future to unfold like everyone else?"

She resumed her trek to the cupboards. "At the time I didn't think I could. I know that probably sounds . . . immature, and I guess it was. It's just that . . ."

"It's just that what?" he encouraged, when she stopped speaking.

She took the sugar bowl out of the cupboard and got a spoon out of the silverware drawer. Carrying both back to the table, she handed them to him and sat down.

She took a sip of tea before saying, "I've always felt like an outsider in the coven. We have a very strict and structured patriarchal society. There are so many rules to be learned and obeyed, particularly if you're a witch, and I've never been very good at following the rules."

She paused and took a sip of tea. "It wasn't so bad when I was a child and my parents were alive, because I had the security of their love to keep me . . . balanced, I guess. After their deaths, everyone in the coven looked after me. But it seemed that the harder they tried to make me feel a part of them, the more separate I felt from them, and the more I wanted to escape them. I used to read everything I could find on the mortal world, and I'd sit and daydream about going out into it."

"So why didn't you?" he asked as he finished putting sugar in his tea and took a sip.

She shrugged. "Pure, unadulterated fear. A witch cannot leave coven boundaries without permission from the high priest. If I left without permission, then I would never be able to return. So, if I got out into the mortal world and discovered that I hated it, I'd be stuck."

"They why didn't you just ask for permission to leave?"

"Because it wouldn't have been granted. I'm a witch, which makes me one of the most valuable commodities within my race."

He eyed her over the rim of his cup. "How could a person be considered a commodity?"

"One of the reasons we're on the brink of extinction is because we have a serious procreation problem," she answered. "A warlock can sire only one child during his lifetime, and a witch can bear only one child. To make matters worse, there are more warlocks born in every generation than there are witches. The disparity in numbers isn't staggering, but it is sufficient to cause concern. The loss of one witch before she's given birth could be the beginning of the end of our race. Or at least, that's what we thought until the truth about Lucien came out."

"The truth about Lucien?" he repeated curiously.

"Lucien's mother was a mortal, which is why he has to use the crystal to augment his powers," she expounded. "For years we all thought that made him inferior to us. Only recently did we learn that because he's half mortal, he can sire as many children as a man. By mating with Ariel, who is a mortal, they can have as large a family as they want. Since our survival has been in question, that aspect of his breeding makes him superior to us."

"But isn't there a chance that his children won't have powers? And if that's true, won't they be considered inferior?"

"Lucien's mother is a geneticist, and she says that we have an additional gene that is dominant, so all children of mixed blood will have power," she replied. "It's true that they won't be as powerful as a normal witch or warlock, and, like Lucien, they will have to use crystals to augment their magical abilities. When you weigh the pros of having more children against the pros of maintaining a pure race, however, it's pretty obvious which situation is the winner. That's why the council of high priests has decided to let members of our coven seek mortal mates. If we are successful, then other covens will be allowed to do the same."

Ryan gave an amazed shake of his head. "Don't take offense, but all of this sounds like something out of a science fiction novel."

"I suppose that it does," she said with a wry smile. "How do you like your tea?"

"It's great," he said, lifting his cup and draining it. "It's also time that you get into bed, so you'd better drink up."

"You're a worse nag than a familiar," she murmured, wondering how long it would take for the sleeping potion to go into effect. Because she wasn't sure what his constitution could handle, she hadn't given him a full dose. But he should be showing signs of drowsiness shortly.

"Familiars are nags?" he asked.

"The worst," she answered, startled when she found herself yawning. "I'm sorry. I must be more tired than I thought."

"Well, I'm sure the sleeping potion is going to make you sleep like a baby," he said. "And before you fall asleep on the table, we'd better get you to the closest bedroom."

It took a moment for his words to sink in, and when they did, she stared at him in horrified disbelief. "What do you mean you're sure the sleeping potion is going to make me sleep like a baby?"

He grabbed his crutch and stood. Staring down at her, he announced, "I switched teacups with you when you went to get the sugar. You should be ashamed of yourself for trying to drug a guest. I would have thought that a witch would have better manners than that."

Shana shook her head, unable—or perhaps unwilling—to accept what he was insinuating. "How did you know I was giving you a sleeping potion?"

He smiled grimly. "I seem to have developed the ability to read your mind."

"You can read my mind? That's not possible!"

"Well, it must be possible, because not only can I read your mind, I'm in tune with your body." He regarded her thoughtfully. "Lucien was right. You aren't seriously injured, but I'm surprised that you can even walk with that headache. Now, you can sleep it off."

Shana opened her mouth, but closed it when she realized she didn't know what she wanted to say. If what he was claiming was really true . . . It couldn't be true!

The future is mine, and now yours will be mine!

As Moira chanted her familiar litany, Shana felt something brush against her hand. She glanced down and her eyes widened in horror. Lying beside her cup was the card of The High Priestess. The face was a woman's, but it was oddly blurred so that Shana couldn't distinguish the features. She knew instinctively, however, that it was Moira's face, and The High Priestess was the appropriate card in which to make her appearance. It very simply meant that hidden influences were at work.

At that moment, Shana was forced to accept the unacceptable. Somehow Moira had endowed Ryan with powers, and he had just plied her with her own sleeping potion. Soon she would be asleep, and he'd be left unsupervised in a house filled with enough dangerous objects to destroy Sanctuary in the blink of an eye.

CHAPTER NINE

The Hierophant (Reversed)
Unconventionality, Unorthodoxy

I can't go to sleep until I figure out a way to neutralize Ryan! Shana thought frantically, but already a mind-numbing lethargy was seeping through her. Thankfully, she hadn't given him a full dose. With the differences in their bodies, it would take the potion slightly longer to work on her than it would on him. However, she was still looking at probably no more than ten or fifteen minutes, which meant she had to do something fast. But what?

She looked up at Ryan. He was staring down at the Tarot card with an expression that she could only describe as mesmerized.

"My God, she's beautiful!" he suddenly said in awe. "Who is she?"

He reached for the card. When he did, the significance of his words jelled in Shana's already sluggish brain. Moira's image might be blurred to her, but he could see it!

"Don't touch the card!" she yelled, grabbing it off the table a mere second before his fingers reached it.

"What is wrong with you?" he asked, frowning at her.

"Moira is manipulating you, Ryan. You must not touch this card under any circumstances."

She quickly struggled to her feet and stuffed the card into her back pocket with the others, but she knew it was only a stopgap. Once she went to sleep, he could take it and all the other cards, for that matter. She considered hiding them, but then realized that Ryan could read her mind, so he'd know where she put them.

Damn! What am I going to do?

"Shana, you're swaying on your feet. You must get to bed," Ryan said, before she could ponder the question. "And don't worry about the damn cards. I don't want anything to do with them."

"What you want isn't the point," she argued. "It's what Moira *wants*, and she obviously wants you to have the card. Since she does, that means its dangerous for you to have any of them."

"That's ridiculous. I already have . . ."

"It's *not* ridiculous," she interrupted, rubbing her hands across her eyes, which were becoming difficult to keep open. "I have to figure out a way to neutralize your powers."

"What you have to do is go to bed," he rebutted.

"I can't go to bed yet," she replied, stumbling toward the door. With her own powers on the fritz, there was only one way she could make sure he didn't get into trouble while she slept. She had to use something from the repository and pray that it wouldn't backfire on them.

Suddenly, Ryan appeared at her side. "Where are you going?"

She peered up at him through eyes so heavy-lidded she could barely see him. "If a man on a crutch can catch up with me, I really am in bad shape. I can't *believe* that you gave me the sleeping potion."

"I can't believe you were going to give it to me," he countered irritably. "And you can't keep stumbling around. You have to get to bed before you fall flat on your face."

"For months I've dreamed of a mortal wanting to get me into bed," she said around a huge yawn, "but I expected it to be more romantic. I don't want to hurt your feelings, Ryan, but you've turned out to be a big disappointment."

"Yeah, well, don't take it personally. I've been a big disappointment most of my life."

He made the statement with such quiet vehemence that Shana stopped walking and looked at him. She intuited that he had just revealed a critical part of his personality, and she wanted to pursue it. The better she understood him, the better chance she'd have of ascertaining why Moira had a hold on him. To her frustration, however, her eyes began to close the instant she stopped moving.

"I have to keep going," she mumbled, making herself resume walking. "I can't go to sleep."

"Shana, you're fighting a losing battle. You can barely keep your eyes open, so go to bed."

She didn't bother arguing with him. It would take too much energy, and she needed every ounce she had just to walk. Thankfully, she reached the repository's door a few steps later. Opening it, she staggered inside.

As she came to a stop, she had to rub her eyes again to clearly see the tables and display cases. She looked at them in confusion. There were so many items, and she was so tired she could barely remember her name. How was she going to choose what was the safest one to use?

It has to be something he can keep with him.

An amulet would be perfect, she concluded, heading for the display case that held the charms. Not only would he be able to wear it, but it was the least likely object to carry a spell involving the dark forces.

She had narrowed down the field, but when she opened the lid, she groaned. There were at least two hundred amulets, and they were made from every type of crystal, gem, and metal known to man. One of the first things witches and warlocks learned as children were the magical properties each stone possessed. As tired as she was, it wasn't too difficult to recall them.

Her first instinct was to go with something made out of lava, onyx, or sapphire, which were used for defensive magic. But Moira had already done her damage, so Ryan didn't need to be defended. He needed to be restricted.

With a yawn, she began to sift through the charms, finally picking up a glittering emerald and eying it consideringly. Emeralds were good for exorcising an evil entity, and Moira was about as evil as they came. However, Ryan wasn't possessed by her.

Replacing the emerald, she lifted a handful of the charms and sorted through them, eliminating the diamond, the ruby, the tiger's-eye, the amethyst, and the opal. All had potent magic, but none of them could inhibit Ryan's newfound powers.

She started to dismiss a jade pendant, but something about its properties began to nag at the back of her mind. She rubbed a hand over her eyes to help her think. Jade was used for longevity, healing, gardening, prosperity and . . .

What else was it used for? she asked herself in frustration as another yawn escaped. She mentally ticked through the list again. Finally the elusive property came to her. One of jade's strongest attributes was wisdom! It wouldn't inhibit his powers, but it would give him the ability to make safe decisions about anything he did try to do. She was too exhausted to search any further. This would have to do.

Tossing the other amulets back into the case, she

closed the lid. As she turned toward Ryan, he said, "I am not going to wear that, Shana, so you might as well put it away."

She blinked at him, startled. How had he known that she wanted him to wear it? Of course. He could read her mind.

"You have to wear it," she said, holding it out to him. "Moira has given you magical abilities, and you aren't trained to handle them. You might accidentally do something to bring harm to yourself or to the coven. This amulet will give you the wisdom you need to determine what you can and cannot do."

"I am not going to wear it," he repeated staunchly.

"Why not?" she asked impatiently.

"It's a necklace, Shana, and where I come from, men do *not* wear necklaces."

She could barely keep her eyes open, and it was only through sheer willpower that she was managing to do so. *Dammit!* She didn't have time to argue with him. Within minutes she was going to be asleep.

"We are not where you come from, Ryan. We are in Sanctuary, and warlocks wear amulets all the time. And unless you run around with your shirt open, no one will know you're wearing it. It's supposed to rest against your skin."

"Well, I am not a warlock, and I don't wear necklaces, even if people don't know I have them on. So, put the damn thing away and get to bed."

"I am not going to bed until you put this on."

He scowled at her. "You promised to obey my every command."

"And I will, but only after you've put this on."

"Dammit, Shana! You are about to collapse, and I am not in any condition to pick you up and carry you to bed."

"Then I guess you had better put on the amulet,"

she said, around still another yawn. He was right. She was about ready to collapse. "Otherwise, you'll just have to toss a blanket over me when I fall asleep right here on the floor."

"You can't sleep on the floor. This place is as cold as a tomb. You'll catch pneumonia."

"You're a doctor. You can take care of me."

"You are the most infuriatingly stubborn woman I have ever met!"

"I am not a woman. I'm a witch," she said, leaning her hips against the display case and closing her eyes. "I'm also very tired."

"Don't you dare go to sleep."

"I'm afraid I don't have much choice," she murmured, dropping her hand to her side. She heard the amulet clink against the cabinet, but she was too exhausted to care.

"Give me the blasted necklace," he snapped. "I'll put it on, but only if you promise to stay awake long enough to get to a bed."

All Shana wanted to do was sink to the floor and go to sleep, but she knew she couldn't do that until he was wearing the amulet. Somehow, she dredged up enough energy to open her eyes, and she lifted her arm toward him. He snatched the amulet out of her hand and slipped its gold chain over his head.

After dropping the stone down the front of his T-shirt, he said, "Come on. Let's get you to bed."

She was sure she'd never make it out of the room. But he had done what she asked, so she had to at least make an effort. Her body felt boneless, and her head spun when she pushed herself away from the display case.

"Easy," Ryan said, gripping her upper arm to steady her. "Just take it a step at a time."

She nodded and began to shuffle forward. She had

no idea how they reached the bedroom. All she knew was that a bed was suddenly in front of her. With a relieved sigh, she collapsed onto the mattress and closed her eyes.

As she drifted off to sleep, an inner voice whispered, *You forgot an important aspect of jade. It not only grants wisdom, it's an ancient* . . .

The potion took over before the thought could complete itself.

Ryan frowned down at Shana's prone body. She was sprawled sideways across the bed, and her legs were hanging halfway over the edge. He knew he needed to shift her so that her legs were supported. With his bad knee, however, there was no way he could move her.

He considered trying to wake her enough to get her to move on her own. But, as he'd told her earlier, he was somehow attuned to both her mind and her body. Whatever was in that sleeping potion was potent, because she was so sound asleep she might as well be comatose.

"So, what the hell am I going to do? I can't leave you like this," he muttered, frustrated with his infirmity.

Use the wishing wand to heal your knee, an inner voice urged.

He shook his head. One zap from the wand had been enough for him. Besides, it was insane to believe that a piece of gnarled wood could heal.

So, if it doesn't work, what will you have lost? But if it does work, you'll be whole again—in control again.

He raked a hand through his hair. The suggestion was tempting, but it was still insane.

Suddenly, Shana murmured in her sleep, and she shifted her head. When she did, her hair fell away from her face. Ryan sucked in a harsh breath. Her entire left temple was covered with a blue and purple bruise.

She's all right! he told himself. I'm in touch with her body. I can feel what's happening to it, and there's nothing seriously wrong with her.

But even as he offered himself the reassurance, he shoved his hand into his jacket pocket and touched the Tarot card he'd retrieved in Lucien's car. It was the card of Death.

Again he had an intuitive flash that Shana was in mortal danger. He also knew in that instant where the danger was coming from—Moira.

And you're the only one who can save her. How are you going to do that if you can't even walk?

His common sense told him that he wasn't being rational. But what had rationality ever gotten him? It sure as hell hadn't saved the children whose eyes haunted him. They had depended on him—*trusted* him—and he'd let them die.

Use the wand, the voice urged again. *Don't stand by and wait for Shana's eyes to exist only in your nightmares.*

He shuddered at the thought, but still he was torn. If everything Shana had said about Moira was true, then how could he possibly defeat her? He didn't know anything about spirit-witches. He was a doctor, for God's sake, and not a very good one at that. Look how many times he had failed.

Except now you have powers. You're more than a man. You've been transformed.

"I've lost my mind," he muttered, turning toward the door. "And since I have, I might as well play with that stupid stick. With Sleeping Beauty out cold, it's not as if I have anything else to do in this mausoleum."

When he arrived at the repository, however, he began to have second thoughts. Shana had said that the wand would make him sacrifice something important for using it. When he told her that the only important thing to him was his bike, he hadn't been lying. But what if it was a long-range curse? What if something became important to him at a later date?

"The only thing that will be important to you will be another bike," he stated derisively as he made his way purposely toward the chair. Shana had laid the wand on its seat. "So, what if it ends up taking a bike or two away from you? It will play hell with your insurance premiums, but it won't be the end of the world. You may have been a lousy doctor, but you made an obscene amount of money. As the old saying goes, you can't take it with you, and it's not as if you have anyone to leave it to."

When he reached the chair, he grabbed the wand. All he had to do was make a wish, and he'd either end up looking like a fool, or he'd be able to walk.

Make your wish in the pentagram, Shana's voice stated so clearly in his mind that he started.

He jerked his head toward the door, expecting to see her standing there. As he looked for her, his mind automatically connected with hers, confirming that she was still sound asleep. But if she was sleeping, how could she be speaking in his mind?

Even as he asked the question, he knew the answer. It wasn't Shana speaking to him. It was Moira.

Warily, he surveyed the room. He knew Moira was present. He could sense her, and he demanded, "What do you want from me?"

There was no response, not even a rustle, and he raked a hand through his hair in nervous frustration. If Moira wanted him to use the wand, then, logically, he shouldn't use it. But if he didn't use it, what kind of help could he be to Shana?

Without even realizing what he was doing, he raised his hand to his chest and touched the amulet through his T-shirt. When he did, the stone began to vibrate gently. It was an odd sensation, but strangely soothing.

Instinctively, he closed his eyes, murmuring, "Tell me what to do."

Suddenly, he knew the solution. He opened his eyes and smiled in triumph. Then he limped to the center of the pentagram and released the crutch. As it fell to the floor, he balanced his weight on his good leg and gripped the wishing wand with both hands.

Extending his arms upward so that the wand was pointing at the center of the pentagram on the ceiling, he said, "I wish to be physically whole and endowed with the magical skills to save Shana from Moira."

Instantly, lightning shot from the end of the wand to the pentagram above. Then it spiraled toward him. But instead of entering the end of the stick, it struck his chest where the amulet rested. The stone grew red-hot, and the fabric of his T-shirt began to smoke. But, to his amazement, it didn't burn him. Instead, the same electrifying energy he'd experienced before streaked through him.

Now you've found Sanctuary. The battle can begin!

The lightning disappeared. Ryan immediately tested his knee. It was in perfect working order. More important, he knew he was also mentally equipped to fight the war that Moira had just declared. Not only had the wishing wand healed his leg. It had granted him the same powers as a warlock.

"Yes!" he declared, perching his hands on his hips and gazing around the room victoriously. "The battle *can* begin!"

As Shana drifted toward wakefulness, a sense of urgency began nagging at her. There was something she had to do, but what was it?

It's about time you woke up.

When Ryan's voice reverberated in her mind, her eyes flew open in shock. All the events from the night before came flooding back. It was one thing for Ryan to read her mind, but it was an entirely different matter for him to be mentally communicating with her! What was going on?

She bolted upright in bed. Sunlight was pouring through the windows, and a quick glance around the room proved that it was empty. Where was Ryan?

I'm in the repository.

"The repository?" she gasped in horror.

Scrambling out of bed, she raced toward the closed door. As she stopped to open it, she suddenly realized that she was wearing only her T-shirt and panties. Panic surged through her. Ryan had removed her jeans, and the Tarot cards had been in the back pocket. If he had taken the cards . . .

I didn't bother your cards.

His reassurance didn't appease her. She turned to look for her jeans. They were lying across the back of the chair. She ran to it and grabbed the cards out of the pants pocket. Quickly, she counted them. All of them were there, she realized, sighing in relief.

Not all of them are there. I still have the Death card.

His words shocked her so badly that she nearly dropped the cards. What did he mean, he *still* had the Death card?

I found it in Lucien's car. Come to the repository. I'll tell you all about it.

"You're damn right you'll tell me all about it," she muttered, tucking the cards back into the pocket and pulling on her pants.

As she hurried through the house, her mind was racing toward a conclusion she didn't even want to consider. But as much as she wanted to ignore it, she knew she had to analyze it. Death meant transformation. When she received the card, she lost her powers. Had Moira somehow managed to transfer her powers to Ryan?

You're partly right.

Ryan's confirmation rattled her. She wanted to pursue the matter, but she decided to wait until she reached the repository. What was he doing in there anyway? She expected him to provide an answer. When he didn't, she really began to worry.

By the time she reached the repository, she was out of breath. She burst through the door and stopped, panting as she looked around. Ryan's crutch was lying in the middle of the pentagram, but he wasn't there.

"Ryan?"

"I'm up here with the books," he called out.

She glanced upward and frowned. How had he gotten up the stairs without his crutch? Walking to the crutch, she picked it up and headed up the stairs. At least he was on the second level, and he couldn't cause any damage there. All it contained were the journals that listed the objects and their magical properties.

When she reached the top of the stairs, she slid to a stop and her jaw dropped. Ryan was sitting cross-legged on the floor. About a dozen books were piled around him. His hair was mussed, and his jaw covered with a morning beard. She knew instinctively that he'd been up all night, but he didn't look tired. If anything he looked . . .

"Warlocklike?" he provided, grinning at her.

It was exactly what he looked like, and she shook her head in confusion. Before she could think of what to say, he climbed to his feet. Her gaze automatically dropped to his bad leg. "Your knee is okay!"

"Yep," he said, bending his knees slightly, as if to confirm the claim.

"But how?" she asked, glancing up at him in bewilderment.

"The wishing wand," he answered.

"You used the wishing wand again?" she exclaimed in horrified disbelief.

"Hey, don't get so uptight about it. It was necessary."

"Ryan, the wand works only if you have something painful to lose. Now it's going to collect from you *twice!*"

He frowned. "I considered that, Shana, and I came to the conclusion that I'll probably have to lose a couple of bikes. I'll admit that it will be inconvenient, but it isn't any big deal. Besides, as I said, it was necessary."

"What could possibly be so important that you'd risk using the wand again?" she demanded, knowing that the wand would never be satisfied with something as materialistic as a motorcycle.

"You," he answered simply.

"Me?" she said, becoming even more bewildered.

"Moira wants you dead, and there was no way I could help you fight her if I couldn't walk."

"Ryan, that's so . . . touching, but we're dealing with magic. *Evil* magic. Your ability to walk isn't going to help defeat Moira."

"I realize that," he said. "That's why I made the wish twofold."

"Twofold?" she repeated in trepidation.

He nodded. "I not only wished to be physically whole. I also asked to be granted the magical skills needed to save you from Moira. The wand not only healed my knee. It gave me all the powers that a warlock possesses."

Shana stared at him, stunned. Then she shook her head in frantic denial. This couldn't be happening!

"Why are you so upset?" he asked irritably. "I thought you'd be pleased."

"Pleased?" she gasped. "It takes *years* of training to become an accomplished warlock. When you made that wish, did you also think to ask for the knowledge that goes along with those powers?"

"Well, no," he answered uncertainly. "But I did touch the amulet you gave me. You said it would grant me wisdom."

She had forgotten the amulet. When he mentioned it, she recalled that it had been made from jade. He was right. It should have granted him wisdom, and that wisdom should have prevented him from using the wand. So why hadn't it?

"Let me see the amulet," she said, unable to recall exactly what it looked like.

He grabbed the chain and pulled it from beneath his shirt. When he did, she saw the butterflies carved into the stone and knew exactly why it hadn't prevented him from using the wishing wand.

She brought her hand to her mouth and shook her head, too dazed to absorb the ramifications of what she'd done. Why, out of all the amulets, had she chosen that one? Because she'd been in a hurry to curb Ryan's powers before she fell asleep. She'd been concentrating on the properties of the stone, not the meaning of the amulet. Unfortunately, she'd forgotten one of jade's most ancient uses.

The future is mine, and now yours will be mine!

Another Tarot card appeared in front of her. It was The Hierophant, reversed. The Hierophant was a religious figure, and reversed it meant unconventionality and unorthodoxy in religious practices. No card could have been more fitting for the moment.

As the card fell to the floor, Ryan asked, "What's going on?"

Shana slowly raised her eyes to his and said, "Jade not only grants wisdom. It is an ancient love-attracting stone, and that particular amulet is a . . ."

"A what?" he demanded, scowling at her.

"A witch's vow."

"A witch's vow? What the hell is that?"

"It's a jade stone that binds a witch and a warlock together. When a witch gives it to a warlock and he accepts it, they're . . ."

"They're what?"

She closed her eyes and shook her head again. Then she opened her eyes and said, "In mortal terminology, when you accepted that amulet from me, we entered into a common law marriage. Quite simply, Ryan, you and I are mated for life."

· CHAPTER TEN ·

The Tower
Unforeseen Catastrophe

Ryan blinked at Shana several times in rapid succession. Then he yelled, "What the hell do you mean we're mated for life? What kind of insane game are you trying to play with me?"

Shana took a step backward and regarded him nervously. His eyes were beginning to glow, and a strong breeze, just like the one that accompanied a warlock's temper, was starting to emanate from him. Any doubts she had about his claim of having a warlock's power disappeared.

"I am not playing a game with you," she said, hoping to pacify him. He didn't know how to control the breeze, which would grow in direct proportion to his anger. If he got mad enough, it could reach cyclonic force. "I'm sure if you'll just calm down . . ."

The breeze became a wind. "You trick me into a common law marriage, and you want me to *calm down*?"

"I did *not* trick you. It was an honest mistake, and if you want to be mad at someone, you should be mad at yourself. This is your fault," she accused, knowing she had to make him angry with himself. Then he would propel his anger inward, not outward.

"*My* fault?"

"Yes, your fault. You're the one who gave me the sleeping potion. If you hadn't done that, I would not have given you the amulet."

"I gave you the damn sleeping potion, because you were trying to drug me with it!"

The wind grew so strong it began to whip her hair around her face. She suspected he was barely aware of what was happening. He was like a fledgling warlock, who was always oblivious to anything going on around him when he was mad. But why wasn't he reading her mind, so he'd know how devastating his anger could be? A glance toward the stained-glass pentagram overhead gave her the answer. It was nearly noon, and his mental powers were lessening. Unfortunately, that wouldn't curb the side effects of his temper.

Knowing he was too enraged to listen to reason, she rebutted, "If you hadn't kept insisting that I go to bed, I wouldn't have tried to drug you."

"I wanted you in bed because I was concerned about your health!"

The wind increased to the point that the books on the floor were flying open, and Shana stumbled backward beneath its force. If she hadn't come up against the railing, she was sure she would have fallen off the balcony.

"Well, you weren't concerned about my health when you drugged me, because you were able to read my mind by then," she countered. "You knew that there was nothing seriously wrong with me, but did you tell me that? No. You let me use the potion, and then you switched it out of spite."

"I did *not* switch it out of spite!"

A gale erupted around them. Books began to fly through the air, and Shana could hear the rattle of glass both above and below them. The balcony started to sway beneath her feet, and the creaking of wood assured her that it was in danger of collapsing. Obviously, Ryan was not willing to accept his responsibility in this debacle and turn his anger inward. She had to find another way to stop him. But how?

Appeal to his libido.

Even as the thought presented itself, she knew she couldn't do it. He already believed she had tricked him into mating with her. Seduction, even if it didn't progress beyond a kiss, might temporarily allay his temper. In the end, however, it would only make the problem worse. She had to find another way to stop him. Maybe she could appeal to his intellect, and—

Her musing was interrupted by a loud crack. When she felt the railing give way behind her, she let out a scream. Frantically, she flailed her arms for balance, but the wind was too powerful. As she fell backward, she instinctively closed her eyes and screamed again.

But instead of dropping to the floor below, she felt something grab her wrist. Her body jerked to a stop so rapidly that she felt as if her arm had been yanked out of its socket. Pain exploded through her, but she welcomed it. As long as she could hurt, she wasn't dead.

Opening her eyes, she told herself not to look down, but she couldn't seem to stop herself from doing so. She shuddered. Directly below her was a bundle of archaic spears made out of magical steel. They had been tied together and were stored in a tall, narrow urn, with their razor-sharp tips pointing upward. If she had fallen . . .

Shuddering again, she glanced up. Ryan was kneeling above her, one hand gripping the balcony's edge, and the other locked around her wrist. Evidently he had received a warlock's quick reflexes and strength along with the powers, and she heaved a grateful sigh.

She no more than did so, however, than his features began to blur and shift. She let out a terrified gasp. He was reverting to Aric, and the last time he had done so, he wanted to kill her!

"So, we finally meet again," he drawled, when his face completed his metamorphosis. "I told you that you would never defeat me, and this time I will make sure you are destroyed forever."

Shana shook her head, too frightened to speak. To her horror, he said, "You have always underestimated me, Moira, and you should be smarter than that. I am, after all, your creation. My soul is as black as yours."

"I am not Moira! I am Shana!"

"You can't fool me with that deception. I can recognize you, no matter what guise you wear."

"This is *not* a guise! *I am Shana Morland!*" she cried desperately, realizing that he might release his grip on her wrist at any moment. She had to persuade him to pull her onto the balcony.

"Touch my mind, Aric," she urged fervently. "You'll see that I'm powerless. I can't harm you, and I can't run away from you. Pull me onto the balcony. Give yourself a chance to make sure Moira isn't tricking you again. Don't let her make you act rashly, because if you make a mistake, she will have defeated you!"

She saw the confusion in his eyes and could sense the war of wills taking place inside him. She wanted to make another appeal, but instinct told her that if she pushed too hard, he might become more convinced that she was Moira.

Without warning, he began to pull her up. Shana hadn't realized she was holding her breath until she released it in a relieved rush. The instant she was on the balcony, she crawled to the bookcases against the wall. If Ryan's Aric persona changed his mind, she didn't want to make it easy for him to throw her over the side.

Sitting down, she rubbed her aching shoulder and arm. Suddenly, Ryan loomed in front of her. Slowly, fearfully, she glanced up at him, hoping that he had changed back to himself. He hadn't. She shivered beneath his intense, probing gaze, which was so full of hatred it was almost palpable.

Unexpectedly, he grabbed her by the shoulders and dragged her to her feet. His fingers dug into her flesh, making her flinch in pain, and he shook her hard, as he declared furiously, "You *are* Moira!"

"I am *not* Moira. I am Shana Morland, and Moira is making you believe that I'm her in disguise!"

"Do you think I'm a fool?" he roared. "When you tricked me into mating with you before, you pretended to be Terza!"

Suddenly, Shana understood what was happening. Moira had tricked Aric into mating with her by assuming the identity of his true mate. Ryan thought she had purposely tricked him with the amulet. When Ryan assumed Aric's persona, he believed that history was repeating itself. But why was Moira causing him to become Aric? It didn't make sense!

"Listen to me, Aric. Moira is a spirit-witch. If you kill me, she will claim my soul, and you'll be giving her life."

"You're lying! I see her in you!" he bellowed, his eyes beginning to glow.

"She also made you believe that she was Terza. Think about that. She knows how much you hate her. If she wanted you to destroy an innocent person, wouldn't she make you believe that you were killing her?"

Again, she saw confusion enter his eyes. Abruptly, he released his hold on her shoulders and turned away

from her. He strode to the edge of the balcony where
the railing had given way and stared down at the floor.
She knew he couldn't have stood there for more than
a minute or two, but it seemed like hours before he
turned back to face her. When he did, she was startled
to see that he was Ryan again.

His eyes were glazed with shock and his face was
pallid as he whispered hoarsely, "My God, I can't believe that I almost killed you!"

"That wasn't you! It was Moira manipulating you,"
Shana replied, stunned to realize that he remembered
what had happened. With the type of magic Moira
would have to use to change him into Aric, he
shouldn't have remembered anything.

He shook his head, his face growing paler. "It was
me. I am Aric."

"No," she stated firmly. "For some bizarre reason,
Moira is turning you into Aric, but she's doing it
through magic. All you are is the instrument she's
using against me."

"You're wrong, Shana. *You* are Moira's instrument,
and she's using you against me, because she wants
my soul."

"That's absurd," she said, rubbing at her shoulder.
Between the fall and Aric's manhandling, it was now
throbbing. "You're a mortal, and she needs someone
with power. That's why she is trying to make you kill
me. The only thing I can't figure out is why she keeps
turning you into Aric."

"She's turning me into Aric, because that's the only
way she can repeat the cycle."

"What are you talking about?" she asked in bewilderment.

He raked a hand through his hair and frowned. "Aric
was a mortal, Shana. Moira sacrificed part of her pow-

ers to transform him into a warlock. I don't know how or why, but it was his transformation that cursed her."

Shana opened her mouth to object, but Ryan held up a hand. "The only way Moira can regain existence is to repeat what happened between her and Aric. That's why she took away your powers. She had to transfer them to me, so that the past could be re-created. Now that I have the power, she can do battle with me. And she has to fight me, because the only way she can be reborn is to defeat me and claim my soul."

Shana surged to her feet, perched her hands on her hips, and frowned at him. "Moira is feeding you all this garbage so that I'll be confused!"

"It's not garbage. It's the truth."

"And how do you know that for sure?"

"Because I asked the wishing wand for the magical skills I needed to save you from Moira. When I became Aric, I learned what I needed to know from the past."

He paused and studied her thoughtfully. "The only thing I don't understand is how you fit into the puzzle. For some inexplicable reason, Moira wants you dead, and I'm the only one who can save you from her. Whenever I become Aric, however, you appear to me as Moira and I want to kill you.

"In short, you're in danger from both of us," he went on. "I'd suggest that one of us leave Sanctuary, but you were right. Moira won't let either of us go until she and I have fought our battle. That means you must always be on your guard around me, because I can change into Aric without warning."

She shook her head. She didn't want to believe what he was saying, but he had used the wishing wand. A cold wave of fear washed over her.

"If what you're saying is true, there is no way you can fight Moira by yourself," she told him. "She may have empowered you, but you don't know how to use those powers. Are you absolutely sure it's *your* soul she wants?"

"Oh, yeah, I'm sure about that," he stated dryly.

"In that case, she's no threat to Lucien. We can go to him for help."

"No!" When she looked at him in confusion, he said, "You were right in keeping Moira's presence hidden from Lucien. It's my soul she wants, but she can—and *will*—destroy anyone who tries to interfere. No one, and I mean *no one* must know what's going on. We have to do this on our own."

Again, Shana shook her head, but she didn't know what she was denying. Burying her face in her hands, she cried miserably, "I can't believe this is happening. Why did I use the Tarot? Why didn't I just let the future unfold on its own?"

"Don't be so hard on yourself," he said.

She jerked her head up and gaped at him. "A spirit-witch, who just happened to be the most powerful witch who ever lived, wants me dead and wants your soul. I don't see how we can possibly defeat her, because I'm a trained witch without an ounce of power. You're an untrained mortal with power. We can't ask anyone for help, and you're telling me not to be so hard on myself?"

"What's done is done, Shana, and beating yourself up won't change it. All we can do is fight this battle the best we can."

"How can you be so blasé about this?" she asked impatiently. "Don't you understand the seriousness of the situation? You could lose your life, Ryan. You could lose your *soul*!"

"Things could be worse."

"How could they possibly be worse?"

He shrugged. "I might beat Moira. I'm starving. Let's go have some breakfast."

He turned and headed down the stairs, and Shana stared at his retreating back in complete bafflement. How could defeating Moira be worse than losing his soul?

The future is mine, and now yours will be mine!

At Moira's chant, Shana's mind was thrust back in time.

She was leaning over Ryan after his accident, trying to figure out why he was unconscious. Suddenly, she was caught in a whirling vortex, and its emotional emptiness terrified her. She was trapped in a mind that had no soul, and a person who had no soul had nothing to bind them to this world. Their fondest wish—their greatest fantasy—was death.

The memory ended, and Shana felt something slide into her hand. She looked down. When she saw the Tarot card, she let out a frightened whimper. It was The Tower, and the faces of the woman and man tumbling from its crumbling facade were hers and Ryan's.

The card was predicting unforeseen catastrophe, and she suddenly understood the meaning behind Ryan's words. He wasn't upset about fighting Moira, because his greatest fear wasn't death. It was *life*.

Tucking the card into her pocket, she hurried after him. She had to find a way to change his attitude, or Moira was going to destroy them both!

As Ryan strode into Shana's kitchen, he decided he'd never felt more alive. It was as if he'd been waiting all his life for this moment. The feeling was so overpowering that he felt dizzy, and he stopped and shook his head.

"Is something wrong?" Shana said behind him.

He spun toward her in surprise. How had she man-

aged to sneak up on him without him knowing it? It
suddenly dawned on him that he could no longer read
her mind. Panic stirred inside him. Had he lost his
newly acquired powers?

That couldn't be possible, he quickly assured himself. Moira wanted—needed—him to have powers for
them to confront each other. But if he hadn't lost his
powers, then why couldn't he read Shana's mind?

"Have your powers come back?" he asked, concluding that that was the only answer that made sense.

"Unfortunately, no," she stated ruefully. "What
makes you think they might have?"

He frowned. "For hours I've known your every
thought and every move. Now, there's nothing."

"That's because it's almost noon," she said, heading
for the stove. "Our powers peak at midnight and wane
at midday. They will begin to gradually increase between now and sunset."

"You mean I'm powerless?" he gasped, alarmed by
the possibility. "What am I supposed to do if Moira
comes after us?"

"You are not powerless," she replied, turning to the
sink and filling the teakettle with water. "You're weak,
but so is Moira. She can torment us between now and
nightfall, but she can't harm us."

"The hell she can't. Look what she just did in the
repository. She broke the railing on the balcony and
almost killed you!"

She glanced over her shoulder at him. "Moira didn't
break the railing, Ryan. That happened because you
lost your temper. Weren't you even subliminally aware
of the wind in the room?"

"Yes, but I thought it was . . . I don't know what I
thought it was," he stated, frowning in puzzlement.

"That's because you were letting yourself be controlled by anger, so you weren't thinking at all." She

set the kettle on the stove and switched on the burner. Then she turned and leaned her hips against the counter.

Crossing her arms over her chest, she continued, "You now have the powers of a warlock, which means you also have their idiosyncracies. When a warlock gets mad, his anger manifests itself as a breeze. The angrier he gets, the stronger it becomes. If he lets himself become too angry that *breeze* can actually reach hurricane force. A warlock is able to contain it so that it doesn't cause damage, but you aren't trained to do that."

"In other words, when I'm mad, I'm dangerous," he said, shoving his hands into his pants pockets.

"Very dangerous," she agreed.

"How do I learn to contain this . . . breeze?"

"It's a matter of self-control. When you feel yourself getting angry, you should try to calm yourself or turn the anger inward. That will keep the breeze from surfacing. If, however, you can't control your temper, then you must focus entirely on the person with whom you're angry. The breeze will then center around the two of you, and it won't cause any damage to the surrounding area."

He pulled a hand out of his pocket and raked it through his hair. It was difficult to believe what she was saying, but then he recalled that after the car accident, he had experienced the "breeze" phenomenon with Lucien. At the time, he tried to blame it on the open car door, but he'd sensed that Lucien was causing it.

"Are there any other of these . . . idiosyncracies I should know about?"

A strange expression flickered across her face. Before he could figure out what it was, she pushed away from the sink and walked to the refrigerator.

Opening the door, she leaned down to look inside, saying, "There's nothing else that's physically dangerous. Unless you're casting spells, of course. You may have the power to do that, but you don't have the knowledge. So, thankfully, we don't have to worry about that aspect. Would it be okay if I fix French toast? Or would you prefer to have lunch?"

He regarded her narrowly. She was wrong about his ability to cast spells. He had spent the entire night reading the journals in the repository. Though most of them contained nothing more than an inventory of the objects, some of the older journals listed some very interesting spells. He had also obtained some spell-casting knowledge while he'd been masquerading as Aric.

Instinct told him, however, that he should keep that information from her. Besides, he was more interested in knowing why she was avoiding his question. What warlock peculiarities didn't she want him to know about?

"Forget the food, Shana. I'd rather you told me about the quirks of being a warlock."

"One of those 'quirks' is that a warlock must eat regularly to keep his powers in balance. Missing one meal can cause him a lot of problems. So you must eat. Do you want French toast or something else?"

"You don't need to go to a lot of work for me. A bowl of cereal will be fine."

She straightened and shook her head. "Your powers are new, Ryan. You need something more substantial than cereal to align them. And don't worry about the work. I like to cook."

"Then French toast is fine."

While she gathered the necessary ingredients, he sat down at the table. He waited until she was preparing the egg mixture, before saying, "Tell me more about

being a warlock. I need to watch my temper, and I
need to eat regularly. What else?"

She shrugged uneasily. "Warlocks have dozens of
unique characteristics. It would be easier if we address
them as they arise."

"Shana, you're keeping something from me," he said
impatiently. "What is it?"

She looked at him, her eyes widened in innocence.
"I don't know what you're talking about."

He scowled at her. "Don't play games with me. I
might not be able to read your mind at the moment,
but I know when someone is avoiding my questions.
There's something you aren't telling me, and I want to
know what it is."

"It's nothing that can't wait," she said with an exasperated sigh. "You need to eat, and then you need to
rest. You've been up all night. You must be exhausted."

"I'm a doctor. I'm used to going without sleep. Now,
tell me whatever it is that you're hiding from me."

"Let's eat first."

"Dammit, Shana! Tell me!" he exploded.

Instantly a breeze began to blow through the room.
It was strong enough to rattle the dishes on the kitchen
counter where Shana was working. She quickly backed
away and gazed at him in wariness. He cursed inwardly. If he hoped to get her cooperation, he had to
get his temper under control.

He drew in a calming breath. The breeze quieted,
and he drew in another. By the time he released it,
the breeze had stopped.

"I'm sorry. I shouldn't have lost my temper," he said
when she continued to regard him cautiously. "It's just
that I know there's something you aren't telling me,
and your refusal to do so is driving me crazy. So,
please, tell me what it is."

Staring at some unseen spot above his head, she

crossed her arms over her chest and shifted nervously from one foot to the other. It wasn't auspicious body language, and he began to feel damn edgy himself. He wanted to order her to start talking. Instead, he curbed his tension by drumming his fingers against his thigh.

"It's rather complicated," she finally said, glancing toward him and then quickly away. "I'm not sure how to explain it to you so you'll understand."

"I'm a doctor, Shana. I spent years learning to understand complicated subjects."

"But you're talking about the human body. This is more a psychological aberration among my race, although it does present itself in a physical form."

"I've had plenty of psychology courses, too. I'm sure I'll be able to understand what you're saying. If I need something clarified, I'll ask you to explain it in more detail."

"I don't know, Ryan," she murmured, frowning at him uncertainly. "I'm afraid that you're just going to get angry again."

"If I do, then I'll control my temper," he said, again drumming his fingers against his thigh. He was becoming so exasperated with her that he wanted to grab her and shake her. Why wouldn't she just tell him what he wanted to know? "And I just proved I can control it."

She still looked uncertain, but she said, "I guess I might as well tell you, because come nightfall, you're going to find out about it anyway. At least you'll have some time to get used to the idea."

"What's going to happen come nightfall?" he asked, instantly on guard.

She drew her arms tighter across her chest. "Do you remember me telling you about our procreation problems?"

"Yes," he answered hesitantly, deciding that he already didn't like the turn the conversation was taking.

"Well, when a witch and warlock mate, things get a little . . . crazy between them."

"Crazy?" Instinctively, he raised his hand to the spot on his chest where the amulet rested, touching it uneasily. In all the upheaval of turning into Aric, he'd forgotten her claim that the charm had entered them into a common law marriage. Of course, even if she believed it was true, there was no legal basis for such a claim. They hadn't even had intercourse, and as far as he was concerned, they never would. The last thing in the world he wanted was a wife, common law or otherwise.

She nodded. "Once they've mated, they can't keep their hands off each other."

"That sounds normal for a newly married couple."

"Yes, but . . ."

"But?" he prompted, growing more uneasy, as she again began to stare at the unseen spot above his head.

"This is an uncontrollable urge to procreate, Ryan, and it's even stronger for a warlock than it is for a witch. The moment the sun goes down . . ." She glanced toward him, and then quickly away. "Well, you get the picture."

"Are you trying to tell me that when the sun goes down, I'm going to turn into some kind of a sex maniac?" he said incredulously.

She returned her gaze to his and stared at him for a long moment. Then she said, "I'm afraid so, but don't feel bad. So will I."

CHAPTER ELEVEN

The Lovers
Struggle Between Sacred and Profane Love

Ryan leaned back in his chair and eyed Shana skeptically. What she was saying sounded ludicrous. Of course, so had just about everything else she'd told him so far, and all of it had been true.

But uncontrollable sexual urges? Involuntarily, he dropped his gaze to the front of her T-shirt. The fabric clung provocatively to her full breasts. As he stared at the faint outline of her nipples, he was suddenly hit with an overpowering need to strip her clothes off her.

This is nuts! I'm only responding to her because of her stupid prediction.

Unfortunately, that didn't curb the feelings moving within him. He longed to see her naked. He yearned to touch her body—to revel in the softness of her skin. He craved to feel what his touch did to her, and then he would show her what her touch did to him. And now that he had a warlock's power, he could do that and more.

Oh, God, yes. So much more!

He dragged his gaze back to her face. Her expression

told him she was aware of his stirring desire, and the heated look in her eyes said she was willing—and *ready*—to succumb to him.

He might have succumbed himself if she hadn't chosen that moment to say, "See. The urge is already beginning to surface. In a few more hours, you won't be able to think of anything else, and it will happen every night until we've achieved procreation."

"I'll admit that I find you attractive, Shana, but I sure as hell can control myself," he declared, irritated that he had fallen so easily into her trap.

"Maybe you can control yourself as a mortal, but you're now functioning as a warlock—a newly mated warlock," she rebutted.

"You gave me a damn necklace. That does *not* make us married," he said impatiently. "Even if it did, there's a very big hole in your uncontrollable lust theory."

She eyed him dubiously. "A hole?"

He nodded. "You gave me the necklace last night. If what you're saying is true, then why wasn't I hot to trot then? It sure as hell was dark outside."

"You had given me the sleeping potion, Ryan. My libido was dormant, and because it was, so was yours."

"That's absurd. A man's libido is not dictated by a woman's."

"As I keep reminding you, I am a witch, not a woman, and at this point, you are a warlock, not a man. Witches and warlocks function quite differently from your race, particularly when they've mated."

"Oh, come on," he drawled derisively. "Sex is sex, regardless of the race."

She looked as if she would disagree, but then she shrugged and said, "If you say so."

It was such an overt attempt at humoring him that his temper flared. When he realized the breeze was again surfacing, he drew in a frustrated breath. He didn't like having his emotions so readily apparent.

Forcing his temper back into check, he said, "I know that you believe what you're saying, Shana, but you told me your race is in danger of extinction. I'm sure that from childhood it has been stressed that you must procreate or the race will die. This aberration, as you call it, has nothing to do with being a witch or a warlock. It's a simple case of brainwashing, and since I haven't been subjected to it, I won't be affected by it."

"If you say so," she repeated, pushing away from the counter and returning to her food preparations. "But don't get upset if you find out differently."

He wanted to continue arguing with her, but he knew she wouldn't listen to him. Exasperated, he reassured himself that come nightfall she would find out that he was quite capable of controlling himself.

So why did he have the nagging feeling that the moment the sun went down, he should lock himself in a room and throw away the key?

As Shana watched Ryan start on his third helping of French toast, she worriedly mulled over their conversation about the sexual urges that would overwhelm them both come nightfall. Regardless of what he said, she knew they were going to end up in bed. She also knew that when he lost control he was not going to be happy about it. Indeed, he'd probably be furious, and she heaved an inward sigh. This was not how she had expected her mating night to turn out.

But that was the least of her problems, she reminded herself, staring worriedly at her own plate. At some point, Lucien and Ariel would stop by to check on them. How was she going to hide Ryan's transformation from Lucien?

"Why don't you just call them and tell them we're

fine? Then they won't have any reason to stop by," Ryan suggested.

Startled, Shana jerked her head up. "When did your ability to read my mind return?"

"Just this very instant. Why?"

She glanced toward the window. The position of the sun against the windowpane told her it was shortly after one. Though his powers were gradually growing again, he shouldn't have been able to pick up on her thoughts without intense concentration. Since he was, it could only mean . . .

"Mean what?" he demanded suspiciously when she didn't complete the thought.

She returned her attention to him, trying to decide whether or not she should answer.

"You had better answer me," he said, scowling at her.

"And what are you going to do if I don't?" She knew she shouldn't taunt him, but his attitude was becoming as overbearing as a true warlock.

"I'll make you tell me."

"And just how are you going to do that?" she challenged.

He didn't answer. Instead, his eyes began to glow, and as they slowly lowered to her breasts, she watched, transfixed. He was going to try to mentally seduce her into answering him! She wasn't surprised. With their mating night just ahead of them, both their minds were subconsciously focused on sex. That was the first weapon either of them would use in a confrontation.

She opened her mouth to object to his tactics. Before she could utter a word, she felt his hands slip beneath her T-shirt and glide upward.

This isn't happening! she told herself firmly, when she felt him cup her breasts. *It's all a fantasy. I can see him sitting across the table from me, and he hasn't moved a muscle.*

That didn't stop her from gasping as she felt his thumbs stroke over her nipples, causing them to tighten in excitement. She had to make him stop this!

Why, Shana? don't you like my touching you?

He didn't give her an opportunity to respond. As he began to lightly pinch one nipple, he trailed his other hand seductively down her abdomen. When he finally slid his hand between her thighs, cupping her intimately, she automatically stiffened in anticipation.

What do you want me to do, Shana?

I want you to stop this right now!

Liar.

He began to stroke her, and sweet, hot desire swept through her. With a soft groan, she closed her eyes.

Tell me what I want to know, Shana.

No! I won't let you force me to tell you through sex!

As he centered his ministrations on the area surrounding her clitoris, she caught her breath, no longer able to think. All she could do was respond to the explosive passion propelling her toward climax. When she reached the brink of completion, however, his hand stilled.

Ryan! Don't torture me like this! Please! She hated that she was pleading, but she was unable to stop herself.

Tell me what I want to know, he ordered again. Urgently, she rocked against his hand, but she couldn't re-create the magical friction she needed to reach fulfillment. How could he leave her hanging like this when he knew how badly she needed release?

If you tell me what I want to know, I'll give you what you want. He stroked his hand against her once, as if to prove what he was saying.

Desire coiled tightly inside her. When she found herself on the verge of giving in to him, she opened her eyes. He was sitting across from her, his hands folded on the table and his eyes glowing brightly. She knew that without her powers she didn't stand a chance against him. He was making a bid for control, and he would continue to mentally seduce her until she would tell him anything he wanted to know.

Indignation stirred inside her. He was her mate, and he was *not* going to manipulate her with sex—even fantasy sex. If he wanted to play sexual games, he'd met his match, and she was going to prove it to him.

Clearly he was still reading her mind, because when she started to stand, she felt his mouth close over her nipple. When his hand resumed its exquisite torment, every nerve—every *cell*—in her body began to vibrate with need. Somehow, she found the fortitude to climb to her feet, purposely keeping her mind blank. As she walked around the table toward him, he ceased his mental seduction and watched her warily.

When she reached his side, he looked up at her, and she said, "There's an old saying in Sanctuary that applies to this situation. What's good for the warlock is good for the witch."

Before he could respond, she caught his face in her hands and lowered her mouth to his. He kept his lips closed firmly against hers, assuring her that he had no intention of giving her the upper hand. Determined to break through his wall of control, she kissed him with all the desire he had aroused in her.

She had to give him credit. He managed to hold himself in check for a good minute. But when she trailed her hand down his chest and headed unerringly south, he let out a groan, buried his hands in her hair, and thrust his tongue into her mouth.

Shana couldn't decide what she found more thrilling. His ravishment of her mouth or the hard bulge of his erection against his trousers. As she stroked him, she concluded that both were equally stimulating, and she bemoaned the loss of her powers. She wanted to link with his mind and feel what her touch was doing to him.

Apparently, Ryan decided to grant her wish. She no more than completed the thought than her mind was filled with the very feelings she yearned to experience. The desire spiraling through him was dark and primal and seductive, and the throbbing heaviness in his groin made her catch her breath in awe. As her hand neared the sensitive head of his penis, she shivered at the quivering expectation that shot through him. Slowly, she let her fingers glide over the head, and the indescribable sensations that rocked him nearly made her knees buckle.

Frantically, she reached for his zipper, needing to touch more than denim. But Ryan suddenly jerked his head away from the kiss and caught her hand, stopping her. She stared at him in dazed shock. How could he stop her when he wanted—*needed*—her touch so badly?

"I don't *need* your touch, and I sure as hell don't *want* it," he rasped furiously. "So, leave me alone!"

Releasing her hand, he shoved his chair back and climbed to his feet. As he turned and strode away from her, Shana stared at his back in bafflement. "Why are you so angry with me?"

"Because I'm sick and tired of your trying to seduce me," he snapped, stopping halfway across the kitchen and turning to glower at her. "Ever since I've arrived you've been coming on to me. First I wake up from an unconscious stupor and find you in bed with me. Then you pounced on me when I was trying to call the auto club, and—"

"I did not pounce on you when you were making your call," she objected. "I didn't even touch you."

"The hell you didn't! No, I take that back. You didn't

touch me. You somehow enticed me into touching you. Then you tricked me into taking some blasted necklace and claimed it makes us married. Now you're trying to lure me into making love to you so you can add validity to that claim. Well, you can forget it, lady, because I don't want a wife, and I will not be forced into a marriage—common law or otherwise!"

"Excuse me, but I did *not* start what just happened in here, and I will not take responsibility for it," she shot back as she perched her hands on her hips and glared at him. "You decided to engage in a power play, and all I did was turn the tables on you. That's why you're so angry, isn't it? You were bested by a powerless witch, and your pseudo warlock ego can't handle it. Well, you can take that ego and—"

Her tirade was interrupted by a hollow echoing sound. With a gasp, she spun away from him and stared toward the kitchen doorway in dread. Someone was knocking on the front door. It was probably Lucien and Ariel, and she couldn't let Lucien see Ryan like this!

"It's not Lucien and Ariel. It's someone named Sebastian," Ryan informed her tautly.

"Sebastian?" She spun back around to face him, unable to decide what horrified her the most. That Sebastian was at the door, or that Ryan had regained enough power to make the determination. If Sebastian realized that someone was brushing against his mind . . .

"Who is Sebastian?" Ryan asked, interrupting her panicked thoughts.

"He's Lucien's cousin," she answered, wringing her hands together. "He's also the troubleshooter for the council of high priests, which makes him the most powerful warlock alive. We can't let him see you. He'll realize you've been transformed. But if I don't answer the door, he's going to get suspicious. What are we going to do?"

"Considering the options, I'd say the best one is to answer the door."

"Didn't you hear what I just said? We can't let him meet you!"

"So, I won't meet him. Tell him I'm asleep or something."

"It isn't that simple, Ryan. Even at this time of day, Sebastian's mental abilities are acute. If I show the least amount of nervousness, he'll connect with my mind and learn everything.

"*Damn!* Why don't I have my powers?" she railed. "If I did, I could cast a spell that would shield my thoughts and portray whatever image I wanted him to have of you."

"If that's all you have to do, then tell me the spell and I'll cast it over you."

"No! Casting spells is not something to be taken lightly. If you don't know exactly what you're doing, you can really cause trouble."

"Well, I think you've already got trouble," he stated, glancing toward the doorway at the sound of another knock. "And this Sebastian guy is getting damned impatient."

"Stop brushing against his mind! You'll give yourself away!"

"What does it matter?" he countered impatiently. "If I don't cast a spell over you, he's going to find out about me anyway, and what do you think Moira is going to do when that happens? I wasn't kidding when I said she will destroy anyone who tries to interfere between her and me, so you have to be sensible, Shana. The only safe way to deal with the situation is to tell me the spell."

Shana gnawed worriedly on her bottom lip. He

was right, but did she dare give him spell-casting knowledge?

"I already have some spell-casting knowledge," he said.

"What do you mean you have spell-casting knowledge?" she gasped.

"We don't have time to discuss it right now," he replied when there was still another knock. "Time is running out, Shana, and you have to make a decision. Are you going to tell me the spell? Or are you going to jeopardize this guy's life?"

Shana felt torn, but she knew she only had one option. "I'll tell you the spell," she said, albeit reluctantly. "Just repeat what I say, and then circle your left hand clockwise and point your index finger at me."

Ryan nodded, and she quickly murmured the words to the incantation. He repeated them and circled his hand as instructed. Spell-lightning circled around her.

The moment it disappeared, she said, "You stay right here. We'll continue our discussion when I return, and don't, under any circumstances, brush against Sebastian's mind!"

With that, she turned and ran toward the front door, vowing that the moment she got rid of Sebastian, she was going to find out just what spell-casting knowledge Ryan had.

"Sebastian! What are you doing here?" Shana asked breathlessly when she opened the door a crack. She shivered as she peered out at him. She had always found him physically intimidating. He had shoulder-length, dark brown hair, a hooked nose, and fanatically glittering dark eyes that made you feel that he could see right into the depths of your soul. He also had a dark aura of danger surrounding him, and she knew it wasn't her imagination. Even the warlocks gave Sebastian a wide berth.

wasn't her imagination. Even the warlocks gave Sebastian a wide berth.

He hefted a duffel bag toward her. "Lucien had to attend the Beltane festivities, and he asked me to deliver the mortal's belongings and check on you. What took you so long to answer the door? Are you feeling okay?"

"I'm feeling fine. Why?"

"You just look a little . . . flushed and disheveled," he said, settling his soul-seeing eyes on her.

"I was, um, resting," she said, blushing at the reference to her heightened color. If he'd arrived just a few minutes earlier, he'd have caught her more than "flushed." She also suddenly realized that so much had happened since she awakened, she hadn't even had time to comb her hair. She quickly ran her fingers through it and then opened the door wide enough to hold her hand out for Ryan's duffel bag.

Giving it to her, he asked, "How's the mortal doing?"

"He's better. I wouldn't be surprised if he was completely well in a day or two. He seems to have an almost warlocklike ability to heal," she added ruefully.

"Is he close by? I'd like to meet him."

"I'm sorry, but he's resting right now." The moment she made the statement, she wanted to groan. Since she'd said she was resting, she could only imagine what conclusion he was going to reach.

She was right. His gaze swept over her appraisingly as he said, "Lucien says you think he's supposed to be your mate."

"I don't think it. I know it," she stated, dismayed to realize that by tomorrow anyone who saw her or Ryan would also know it. There was a look to new mates that was unmistakable, and Lucien was not going to be pleased when he realized what had happened. He'd demand to know why she had rushed into mating, and she was sure he'd insist on talking to Ryan about his role as a mate. She didn't even want to imagine Ryan's reaction to that. How much more complicated could this mess become?

"I'm sorry, Sebastian. My mind was wandering," she said when she realized he'd spoken. "What did you say?"

He regarded her for a long moment. "I asked if I could come in."

"Come in?" She was stunned by his request. Because of their ability to read each others' thoughts, a coven member's home was their private, inviolable space. For another member to enter other than a relative's home was considered an intrusion, and they would only ask to do so under extraordinary circumstances.

"I know it's an unusual request, Shana, but I'm concerned about how you're dealing with the loss of your powers," he said.

Shana arched a brow. Instinct told her that he sensed something was going on, and he was using her loss of powers as a reason to come in and investigate. He was, after all, the troubleshooter for the high council, and it was his job to check out anything that was out of the ordinary. Ryan and his accident were definitely out of the ordinary. *Damn!*

"You don't have to worry about me, Sebastian. I don't like being without my powers, but I'm fine."

His lips settled into a grim line. "You don't need to put on an act for me, Shana. It's obvious that you're upset, and it isn't healthy to hold all that worry inside. I know how averse you are to asking anyone for help, but you need to talk about what's happened to you. I also want you to know that I'll make sure that you're protected from harm, so if that's been one of your fears, you can put yourself at ease."

"That's very . . . considerate of you," she said, more

convinced than ever that he was suspicious. Warlocks were never this sensitive with anyone but their mate, and they'd never be comfortable discussing a witch's mental state with her. They'd send another witch to deal with such an onerous task. "But Lucien said that my powers will come back in a few days, so you don't need to worry about me."

"And what if they don't come back?"

She frowned at him. "Of course, they'll come back. Lucien said—"

"I've had more experience than Lucien with these types of incidents," he broke in. "It's true that your powers will probably return in a few days. But there is an occasional case where they don't come back. In every instance, it involved a blow to the left temple. According to Lucien, that's where your injury occurred."

A shiver of alarm crawled up Shana's spine, and she automatically raised her hand to her temple. What would she do if her powers never returned?

Of course, they'll return, she immediately assured herself. He's just trying to frighten me so I'll ask him in. And even if he is sincere, I know that my loss of power wasn't caused by the accident. It was caused by . . .

She quickly stopped herself from completing the thought. Ryan may have cast a shielding spell over her, but it was foolish to take any chances around Sebastian. He was powerful enough to sense a shielding spell and bypass it.

"I'm sure that I won't be one of those rare cases," she told him. "And I refuse to believe otherwise. I'll be fine, so you don't have to worry about me."

He looked as if he wanted to object, but then he said, "It's always good to be optimistic. Just remember that I'm around if you need anything, and I'll be keeping an eye on you until we find out for sure what's going on with your powers."

"Thanks," she said, forcing a weak smile. "Now, I'd better go check on Ryan and give him his belongings."

Sebastian nodded and headed down the steps. Shana waited until he was walking down the road before she closed the door. When she did, she sagged against it and let out a dismal groan. Sebastian was going to keep an eye on her? He was definitely suspicious. Matters were going from bad to worse!

But her biggest worry right now was Ryan. Where had he obtained spell-casting knowledge? Unfortunately, she suspected she knew the answer, and it scared the daylights out of her. He'd been reading the journals in the repository. They were filled with old spells, and every one of them involved the use of dark forces. If he invoked any of them, he could be unleashing disaster, because no one within the coven was trained to counteract them.

She burst into the kitchen, determined to confront him. Instead she slid to a stop and stared around the room in confusion. Ryan was gone, and the back door was standing wide open. She rushed to it, but he was nowhere to be seen. She started to yell out for him, but she stopped herself. Sebastian would hear her calling and come running.

Why had he left? she wondered in bewilderment. Whatever the reason, if he couldn't take the time to close the door, it had to be serious.

The future is mine, and now yours will be mine!

Moira's voice didn't come from her mind, but somewhere behind her. Startled, Shana turned quickly. Moira's dark, incorporeal form hovered beside the spot where Ryan had been standing. Moira pointed downward and then disappeared.

Slowly, fearfully, Shana approached the spot. On the

floor lay another Tarot card. The Lovers in the upright position, and the naked couple portrayed on it were she and Ryan. Shana shook her head as she stared down at it. She'd never seen a Lovers card like it. Normally the lovers on the card stood apart, or, occasionally, they held hands. She and Ryan were lying in a meadow and were in an embrace so passionate that it made her blush. Above their entwined bodies were crossed swords. One of the swords was a shining ebony and the other was a glittering gold. The symbolism wasn't lost on Shana. The swords represented the dark forces and the light forces in conflict.

As she bent to retrieve the card, she realized that Moira must have delivered it to Ryan. That was why he had fled. He was fighting against the inevitable mating between them. He probably thought the card was predicting that they would become lovers, and he'd run away to make sure it didn't happen. But Shana knew that the card wasn't predicting lovemaking. Moira was informing them that they were going to face a struggle between sacred and profane love.

After tucking the card into her pocket, Shana bowed her head and released a forlorn sigh. Tonight should have been a glorious celebration between mates. Instinct, however, told her that it would be the beginning of Moira's battle for Ryan's soul.

CHAPTER TWELVE

Temperance (Reversed)
Out of Balance

With a low and vicious curse, Ryan came to a stop at the edge of a small meadow. For the past two or three hours he'd been moving through the forest, determined to get lost. But no matter how far he went, or how many times he aimlessly switched direction, he knew instinctively how to get back to Shana's house.

Was this also a part of being a warlock? he wondered in chagrin. Did they have some built-in compass that prevented them from getting lost? Unfortunately, he knew the answer was more basic. He was incapable of getting lost because of the inescapable mental bond he had with Shana. He could probably parachute blindfolded into the Amazon jungle, and he'd still know how to get back to her.

With another curse, he walked to an outcropping of rock and sat down on it. Closing his eyes, he tried to shut his mind off from hers. It didn't work any better now than it had during a dozen previous efforts. Ever since Shana had returned to the kitchen and found him gone, her worried thoughts had been running around inside his head like a rat trapped in a maze. At least she had finally stopped begging him to tell her he was all right.

He opened his eyes and shrugged guiltily. He shouldn't let her worry like this, but he couldn't bring himself to make contact with her. After seeing that damn Tarot card, he was, quite simply, too afraid.

As the memory of that card insisted on surfacing, he closed his eyes again and shuddered.

He watched Shana race out of the kitchen to answer the front door. When she disappeared, he noticed that the light in the room was beginning to dim. Absently, he glanced toward the windows, thinking that a cloud was passing over the sun. As he gazed outside, he frowned in confusion. The sun was shining brightly, so why had it gotten so dark in here?

Now you've found Sanctuary, and the battle has begun!

Moira's voice came from the darkness—was the darkness—and he felt both terrified and strangely electrified by her presence. A hatred surfaced that came from a place deep inside he had never known existed. It was instinctive. It was primal. It was so violent in intensity it frightened him.

Suddenly, a Tarot card appeared in front of his face. It was a picture of him and Shana lying naked in a night-shrouded meadow, and the embrace they shared was as intimate as a man and woman could get. Suspended above their bodies was a pair of crossed swords. One sword was black, and the other was gold. He had no idea what the swords meant, but he knew intuitively that their presence was something to fear.

"Just look away from the damn card," he ordered himself, as an icy shiver tracked its way up his spine.

Before he could glance away, however, the figures on the card began to move in the timeless rhythm of lovemaking. It wasn't the visual image of him and Shana making love that held his attention. It was the sight of the black sword moving slowly, insidiously, down the card toward them.

It's going to kill me! he thought as it suddenly began to drop swiftly toward his back.

Horrified, he watched the sword hit him. But it didn't kill him. It turned into a mist. A black, evil mist that engulfed him. Became him. His body disappeared, and he rematerialized into the cold, deadly steel of the sword. Then he plunged himself into the center of Shana's heart.

"It's just a fantasy!" Ryan declared desperately as the memory ended. Burying his face in his hands, he muttered, "It's a damn fantasy that Moira cooked up to torture me—to drive me over the edge."

But it wasn't a fantasy. It was a prediction of the future, and the most horrible part was that he wasn't really surprised by what he'd seen. Last night, when he'd awakened and found Shana straddling him on the bed, he'd known that if he ever made love to her there was a good possibility he would harm her. That was the symbolism for what he'd seen. The sword hadn't harmed him, because he *was* the sword. He was going to be the instrument of Shana's death.

"If you had a lick of sense, you'd get the hell away from here," he told himself, raising his head. "You have two good legs now, so hit the road. Between now and nightfall, you can put several miles between you and Shana."

But Moira will never let you leave Sanctuary, and how many innocent people will suffer if you try?

With a heavy sigh, he leaned his head back and looked up at the sky. When he did, he frowned. Above the treetops and stretching toward the sky was a shimmering wall of . . . Energy was the only descriptive term that seemed to fit.

Curious, he shifted on the rock so he could follow the strange wall. It formed a complete circle around what he estimated to be fifteen or twenty miles of the forest. What the hell was it?

"It's the magic circle that protects Sanctuary from the mortal world," a quavering, raspy voice announced. "Our ancestors put it in place nearly three hundred years ago, after they fled the witch hunts in New England."

Startled, Ryan nearly fell off the rock. He quickly twisted around to confront the voice and saw an ancient, withered man and a beautiful young woman standing in the shadows of nearby trees. They were both wearing white robes with hoods trailing down their backs. The old man had long, silver hair that fell well below his shoulders, and a silver beard that hung almost to his waist. His body was stooped with the ravages of arthritis, and he was leaning heavily on a gnarled cane.

He was the oldest-looking man Ryan had ever seen, and his age was emphasized by the youthfulness of the young woman standing beside him. As Ryan switched his gaze to her, he guessed her age to be in the early twenties. Like Shana, she was extraordinarily beautiful, with long brown hair, large brown eyes and a cupid-bow mouth. But where Shana radiated life and vitality, this woman was so ethereal that Ryan felt that if he touched her, his hand would pass right through her. He shivered, because he couldn't help wondering if they were ghosts.

The old man chuckled. "No, we're not ghosts. I am Oran Morovang, and this is my great-granddaughter, Kendra. You are Mr.—excuse me, *Dr.*—Alden, are you not?"

"Yes," Ryan answered, while cursing inwardly. He knew it was dangerous for anyone to see him in his transformed state. Why hadn't he taken better precautions to hide himself from discovery? Because he'd been too concerned about protecting Shana from himself. Now, these people would be suspicious. They'd probably run right back to Lucien, and he didn't even want to consider what Moira would do when Lucien showed up, demanding answers.

Oran suddenly smiled. "Your secret is safe with us, Dr. Alden. Even if we wanted to reveal that you have become a warlock, we couldn't. You see, we are the narrators of our coven."

"Narrators?" Ryan repeated cautiously.

"Yes, though I believe that in the mortal world we would be called historians. Long ago, before the written word, our ancestors began to observe and memorize the historical events of coven life. It was their job to pass the stories down so that future generations would know and understand their past. Thus, the title of narrator," he stated, smiling again.

"I see," Ryan said, fascinated. "But why would being a narrator prevent you from revealing that I have become a warlock?"

"Eons ago, a spell was cast over our family that prohibits us from speaking of anything that might affect the outcome of history in the making. We can only speak of events after they have happened. So, we will only be able to speak of you when your mission here has been completed."

"My mission?" Ryan repeated warily.

"It is good that you're cautious," Oran stated approvingly. "But, again, you have no reason to fear us. As I said, we know the past, and your arrival last night fulfilled the prophecy. It is always gratifying to learn that the histories our ancestors kept were accurate. We do pride ourselves on our attention to detail, which is why we're here. We must be able to accurately describe

what you look like when the prophecy has been carried out."

"Prophecy?" Ryan regarded the old man in bewilderment. "What in hell are you talking about?"

"You mean Moira hasn't revealed everything to you?"
Kendra gasped, speaking for the first time.

The alarm in her voice caused Ryan to jerk his head
toward her. "Revealed everything to me?"

"Oh, this is quite disturbing," Oran murmured, causing Ryan to switch his attention back to him. "Moira
is not following the rules."

"What rules?" Ryan demanded.

The old man opened his mouth, but then closed it
abruptly. "I'm sorry, Dr. Alden, but I cannot tell you."

"What do you mean you can't tell me?" Ryan
snapped as he climbed down off the rock and strode
toward the couple. "Dammit, man, you have to tell
me!"

"Dr. Alden, please. You must understand," Kendra
stated, moving in front of her great-grandfather as if
to protect him.

Ryan came to a stop in front of her. Glaring down
at her, he said, "There's only one thing I understand,
lady. That's that I've landed in a parody of Oz, and I'm
fighting the Wicked Witch of the Tarot. But unlike
Dorothy, I don't even have a damn pair of red slippers
to protect me. If it was just me involved, I wouldn't
give a damn. But in case you don't know it, Moira also
wants to kill Shana Morland. It's up to me to make
sure that doesn't happen. So, if there are some kind
of rules that Moira is supposed to be following, I want
to know what they are. Now, get the hell out of my
way so the old man can tell me what I need to know."

"But you don't understand," Kendra stated, not moving an inch. "Even if we wanted to tell you, we *can't*
do it. The spell won't let us speak."

"How can a spell stop you from telling me if Moira is breaking the rules? That wouldn't be fair!"

"I believe that you mortals have a saying about that," Oran stated, pushing against Kendra's shoulder until she reluctantly moved out of his way. "Isn't it something like, Who said life is supposed to be fair?"

Before Ryan could respond, Oran said, "We cannot help you in the way you want us to help, Dr. Alden."

"Not in the way I want?" Ryan said, staring at the old man thoughtfully. "Okay, you can't *tell* me what I want to know. What can you give me?"

The old man seemed to hesitate, as though trying to make a decision. Finally, he thrust his hand through a side opening in his robe. When he pulled it out, he was holding a small drawstring pouch, much like the one Lucien had used when he'd given Ryan the crystal. Passing his cane to Kendra, Oran opened the pouch and removed a small, wafer-shaped stone.

Handing the stone to Ryan, he said, "This is what we call a witch stone. It is part of an ancient, fossilized sponge, and it is used to travel back in time. That is all I can do for you, Dr. Alden."

Ryan arched a brow as he studied the stone. It was a gray stone about the size and shape of a quarter, with a striated surface. There was a hole through the center of it, and it was such an uneven opening that Ryan was sure it had occurred naturally.

"Are you trying to tell me that this is some kind of a time machine?" Ryan asked skeptically, glancing up at the old man.

Oran smiled enigmatically. "In a manner of speaking. That's all I can tell you, and now, we must go. We will be watching you and praying for your success."

They turned and headed into the trees. As Ryan watched them go, he frowned. It seemed as if every time he turned around, someone was giving him a rock.

First, it was Lucien's crystal that supposedly acted like a call to 911. Then it was Shana's blasted necklace that was not only supposed to give him wisdom but had also supposedly entered them into a common law marriage. Now, he had a fossilized sponge, that would, purportedly, take him back in time. And to think that when he was a kid, he'd been silly enough to collect rocks just because he thought they had an interesting shape or were pretty.

Tucking the stone into his pants pocket, he tried to decide what to do. After what he'd seen in the Tarot card, he knew that if Shana's theory about uncontrollable lust was correct, he didn't dare go near her before morning. Then again, the old man had sounded so upset when he said that Moira wasn't playing by the rules.

If that was the case, then maybe the vision she'd shown him wasn't a prediction of the future. Maybe he wasn't a threat to Shana. Maybe Moira was just trying to get him out of the way tonight so he wouldn't be there to protect Shana.

And maybe the old man and the girl weren't real. Maybe they were merely manifestations of Moira's imagination to persuade him to go back to Shana.

Ryan nervously rubbed a hand across his face. There were so damn many maybes, and if he made the wrong choice, it could cost Shana her life. He wouldn't— *couldn't* let that happen. For once he was going to beat that old bastard, Father Death, at his own game.

Or, at least, he was going to die trying.

As Shana paced from the kitchen doorway to the back door for what seemed like the thousandth time, she couldn't remember ever being so worried. Ryan had been gone nearly three hours, and no matter how many times she had begged him to tell her he was all right, he hadn't made contact with her.

"He is all right," she assured herself. "He's my mate, so if anything had happened to him, I'd know it."

Unfortunately, that didn't appease her anxiety. Physically, Ryan was all right, or she would know it. It was his emotional state, however, that had her concerned. He'd turned himself into a warlock with the wishing wand, and now he was fighting against the very nature of what he'd become. To make matters worse, he'd been up all night, and she suspected that he hadn't spent the last few hours resting. The mating urge made a warlock volatile at best. Without sleep, he'd be at his worst. There was also the complication of Moira, who was sure to take advantage of his weakened state.

"Dammit, Ryan, come home!" Shana whispered miserably as she pivoted at the back door and paced back toward the kitchen doorway. "You have to get some sleep. If you don't—"

"If I don't, what?" Ryan suddenly asked.

With a startled yelp, Shana spun around to face him. He was standing just inside the kitchen door. She was so relieved to see him that she wanted to run across the room and throw herself into his arms.

Instead, she tucked her hands into the front pockets of her jeans and asked, "Why didn't you answer me, Ryan? Why didn't you tell me you were okay?"

He shrugged. "I needed some time alone, Shana, and you know as well as I do that it was ridiculous for you to worry about me. I have the powers of a warlock now."

"I don't care if you have the powers of ten warlocks!" Shana declared, her relief suddenly veering into anger. "In the first place, you don't know how to use your powers. In the second, having a warlock's powers does not make you any less subject to accidents. You could

have fallen out there and broken your neck. You could
have been attacked by a wild animal and torn to shreds.
You could have—"

"That's enough," he broke in, holding up a hand to
halt her tirade. "You've made your point, and I'm sorry
for worrying you. The next time, I'll let you know that
I'm okay. So, let's call a truce, okay?"

Shana opened her mouth to deny his request. He
had worried her needlessly, and she wanted to continue
railing at him. Thankfully, her common sense surfaced,
and she closed her mouth. He was back and he was
safe. That was all that mattered.

She drew in a deep breath and let it out slowly,
before saying, "You need to go to bed and get some
sleep, Ryan. Nightfall is only a few hours away, and
when it arrives, so will Moira. She's a dangerous
enough opponent to face when you're rested. Exhausted . . . Well, let's just say it isn't a good idea."

"Yeah, well, before I hit the sack, there are a few
things we need to talk about," he said.

Shana shook her head. "Those things will have to
wait."

"They can't wait, Shana. They're important."

"Are they more important than our lives? Or the lives
of Lucien and Ariel and everyone else in the coven?"
she countered impatiently. "Maybe you don't care
whether you live or die, Ryan, but you don't have the
right to endanger the rest of us."

The moment the words left her mouth, she wanted
to snatch them back. His eyes suddenly started to glow,
and a breeze began to emanate from him.

"I don't have the right?" he said in a voice as low
and sibilant as a whiplash. "If you're going to start
assigning blame, then you had better start by looking
in the mirror. *You're* the one who used Moira's Tarot
cards. *You're* the one who turned her loose. So, if any-

one dies, it isn't going to be my fault. It's going to be *yours!*"

"You're right," she responded bleakly. "This is my fault, and if I could go back in time and change what I've done, I would. But I can't go back, and the burden of defeating Moira has fallen to you. That isn't fair, and if I could figure out a way to assume that burden for you, I would do it in an instant. But there isn't any way for me to do that."

But there is a way for you to do that, an inner voice suddenly whispered. *All you have to do is use the wishing wand.*

"Don't you even *think* of using the wishing wand!" Ryan declared. "That is not an option."

"It's not only an option; it's the perfect solution to our problems," Shana rebutted. "I can't believe I didn't think of it before. I can use the wand and wish Moira away!"

"Are you crazy?" he yelled. "For God's sake, Shana. Moira is not going to let you wish her away. She will destroy you before you even make it out of this room!"

"Okay. I won't wish her away. I'll just wish for my powers back."

"*No!*" he stated vehemently as he strode quickly across the room. He grabbed her shoulders and gave her a slight shake. "I forbid you to use the wishing wand."

She frowned up at him in exasperation. "I wasn't asking for your permission, Ryan."

"You are *not* going to use the wishing wand, Shana."

"Why not?"

"Because you have to think of the curse that goes along with it. You said that it demands something important from you for its use. I can't let you make that type of a sacrifice."

"You made that type of sacrifice, Ryan. And you did it *twice*."

"But you're forgetting one important element, and that's that Moira is after *my* soul. She's carefully orchestrated events up to this moment. If you start fooling around with the wishing wand, you might screw everything up. And who do you think is going to pay the price for that, Shana? I'll tell you who. The same person who paid the price for you messing with the cards in the first place. *Me*.

"So before you go off half-cocked and do something stupid again," he continued ruthlessly, "you had better take a moment to consider the consequences. In other words, Shana, it's time for you to grow up."

Shana recoiled, as if slapped. Of all the things he could have said, nothing could have hurt her worse.

She raised her chin a notch and said, "I will admit that using the Tarot was immature, but using the wishing wand is an entirely different matter. The wand requires a sacrifice, but it's *my* sacrifice, Ryan. I know for sure that it won't punish anyone but me, and at this point I'm willing to give up almost anything to undo what I've done. In other words, I'm trying to take *responsibility* for my actions, and if that isn't mature, then I don't know what is."

"But don't you see that if you ask for your powers back, the wand might take mine away from me?"

"That's what this is about!" she gasped, wriggling away from his grip on her shoulders. Infuriated, she took a step back and perched her hands on her hips. "You don't want to lose your powers, and you're willing to sacrifice the entire coven to keep them!"

"Dammit! That's not true! If I thought giving up my powers would solve this mess, I'd do it in a minute, but I don't think it will solve it. Moira went to a great deal of trouble to make sure I became a warlock. If you try to change things, she's going to stop you, and she might end up killing you. I've already let too many people die, Shana. I can't stand by and let you make a decision that might make you die, too. Don't use the wishing wand. *Please.* Do this for me."

He looked so tormented that Shana felt torn. She wanted to ask him what people had died, and why he blamed himself for their deaths. She knew, however, that this was not the time. And as much as she hated admitting it, he did have a valid point. Moira had gone to a great deal of trouble to turn him into a warlock, and she might end up killing her to stop her from changing things. If she was dead, then she wouldn't be here to help Ryan, and he was sure to lose his soul.

"All right, Ryan," she said. "I won't use the wishing wand. Or at least I won't use it unless we can determine for certain that it won't make matters worse."

"Thank you," he said.

"Now that that's settled, you had better go to bed and get some sleep," she told him.

"There are some things we need to talk about first. It's important, Shana."

"Okay. Let's talk."

Ryan shrugged uncomfortably. He had returned to the house for the specific purpose of telling her what he'd seen in the Tarot card Moira had shown him. He had hoped that between the two of them, they'd be able to figure out whether it had been an accurate prediction of the future, and if it was, how they could deal with it. But how did you tell a woman that if you slept with her, there was a good chance you would kill her? Very carefully.

He drew in a deep breath and let it out in a rush. Then he asked, "Did you see the movie *Fatal Attraction*?"

She shook her head. "We don't have a movie theater in Sanctuary, and I'm not allowed to leave coven land."

"And you never rented the videotape?"

She smiled wryly. "To watch a videotape, you need a television set. We don't have televisions, because the magic circle interferes with the reception."

"The magic circle? That's the circular barrier outside?"

"Yes. How did you know about it?" Before he could answer, she said, "Of course. You're a warlock now, so you can see it."

"Tell me about the circle," he said, knowing he was stalling for time. He still wasn't quite ready to confess that he might be able to kill her.

"It's a rather long story, Ryan, and I thought that what you wanted to talk about is important."

"It is important, so, give me a condensed version of the story about the circle. I'm curious about it."

She frowned, but said, "The coven originally came to this country with the Pilgrims. They were hoping to escape centuries of persecution, and for more than seventy years they coexisted peacefully among their neighbors. But then the witch hysteria began."

"You're talking about the Salem witch trials?" he asked, fascinated.

"There were other trials, but that's the most famous," she confirmed. "By the time the hysteria ended, our coven was on the brink of extinction. They decided that the only way to ensure their survival was to move into the wilderness and create a sanctuary. They ended up here, and they combined their powers and formed a magic circle that is fifteen miles in diameter and stretches from ground to sky. It protects the coven, and within its confines we are omnipotent. Or at least we are protected from the mortal world. I'm afraid that a situation like Moira is a different matter."

"Amazing," he said.

"You might find it amazing, but I find it confining," she replied dryly. "My entire life has been limited to a fifteen-mile circle of land."

Ryan arched a brow. When she put it in that perspective, he could see why she wanted to escape from here so badly. It had to be damn claustrophobic to be confined to such a small area of land.

"But enough about the magic circle," she said, breaking into his thoughts. "What were you trying to tell me about this movie?"

"Yeah, the movie," he said, realizing that he couldn't put this off any longer. Raking a hand through his hair, he explained, "In the movie, this married man becomes embroiled in a hot and heavy affair with a single woman. Eventually, he tries to end the affair, but the woman is obsessed with him and doesn't want to let him go. She ends up trying to kill both him and his wife. Thus, the term 'fatal attraction'."

"I see," Shana said, regarding him in confusion. She'd never heard a more horrible or macabre story. She also had no idea why he was sharing it with her. "That's a very . . . interesting story. But why are you telling it to me?"

"Because I think we may have a fatal attraction going on here."

"Are you trying to tell me that you're *married* to a mortal?" Shana gasped in disbelief.

"Of course not!"

"Then how could we be involved in a fatal attraction?" she asked, feeling more confused than ever.

"Damn! I'm not handling this well at all," he muttered. He began to pace in front of her. "Look, when you went to answer the door this morning, Moira delivered another Tarot card."

"I know that, Ryan. I found it lying on the floor."

She started to tell him that she also knew that it was the thought of them making love that had made him run, but she decided to hold her peace.

He stopped pacing and stared at her. "Did Moira happen to give you the little preview that went along with it?"

"Preview?" she repeated warily.

He nodded. "Moira gave me what I can only assume was a glimpse of the future. You and I were making love on that card, and then the black sword hanging over us fell on me. At first, I thought it was going to kill me, but it didn't kill me. It absorbed me, Shana. I became that sword, and then I stabbed you in the heart. That's the fatal attraction I'm talking about."

"I see," she said again as the analogy of his movie finally made sense. "You think that Moira was telling you that if we make love, you'll kill me."

"Exactly."

"Well, you're wrong, Ryan. We're mates now, and you couldn't kill me if you wanted to. We're compelled to protect each other."

"Then how do you explain what I saw in the card?" he asked in frustration as he began to pace again.

"It was some kind of symbolism, Ryan. Since I didn't see it, I don't know what it meant, but I do know that it didn't mean actual death. I'm serious when I say you couldn't kill me if you wanted to. That would be against the rules."

He came to an abrupt halt and stared at her, but it was a strange stare. She felt as if he were looking through her. She shivered at the eerie sensation.

"Do you know some old man by the name of Morovang?" he suddenly asked.

"Of course," she said, relieved to see that his gaze was now focused on her. "He's one of the coven's narrators. How do you know about Oran?"

"When I was out in the woods, I met him and his great-granddaughter, Kendra."

"They approached you?" Shana said in disbelief.

"Yes, and the old man had some interesting things to say."

"Like what?"

"He said that I was fulfilling some prophecy."

"A prophecy?" Shana repeated in bewilderment. "What kind of prophecy?"

"That's what I asked him, but he said he couldn't tell me. He was horrified, however, to discover that Moira hadn't, and I quote, 'revealed everything to me.' He then said that Moira isn't playing by the rules. Unfortunately, he couldn't tell me what the rules were, either. He did, however, give me something that he implied would help me."

"And what was it he gave you?" Shana asked in trepidation. The narrator's job was to observe and nothing more. If Oran had actually become involved, then something was seriously wrong.

She watched Ryan reach into his pocket. When he removed his hand, it was closed in a fist. He extended it toward her and uncurled his fingers.

When Shana saw the witch stone cradled in his palm, her hands flew to her mouth. They didn't get there in time to muffle her gasp of horrified disbelief.

Oran's wrong! she told herself, as she gave a desperate shake of her head. He has to be wrong!

The future is mine, and now yours will be mine! Moira crowed triumphantly, as a Tarot card suddenly appeared in Ryan's open hand. It was Temperance, reversed, and the mystical warlock clothed in pentagrams from the crown on his head to the sandals on his feet bore Ryan's face.

As Shana stared at the card, she saw the mystical

warlock's visage begin to waver and change. A moment later, he resembled Aric.

Shana gave a desperate shake of her head, refusing to accept what she was seeing. It wasn't true! It *couldn't* be true! If it was, then nothing would be as it should be!

Unfortunately, she knew it had to be true, because that's exactly what Temperance in the reverse position meant. Everything was out of balance, and Moira's delivering the card with the stone clearly told Shana that Ryan wasn't who he appeared to be. He was . . .

She closed her eyes and shook her head again, unable to make herself finish the thought.

CHAPTER THIRTEEN

Justice (Reversed)
Unfairness

Caught off guard by Shana's distressed reaction to the stone, it took Ryan a moment to realize that a Tarot card had suddenly appeared in his hand. Before he had a chance to see what the card looked like, Shana grabbed both it and the stone.

"What's going on?" he demanded, dropping his arm back to his side as he watched her tuck the card into her back pocket.

She closed her hand over the stone and looked up at him, her eyes wide and frightened. "I . . . You're . . . Oh, I don't believe this is happening. It *can't* be happening. It isn't fair!"

Ryan took a deep breath against the alarm coiling inside him. He had said the same thing to Oran Morovang. He couldn't believe it when he heard himself mimic the old man with, "Who said life is supposed to be fair?"

She gaped at him before railing, "How can you stand there and be so calm at a time like this?"

"Believe me, I'm anything but calm, Shana. Right now, my gut feels like an atomic bomb has been detonated inside it. The problem is, I don't know what set it off, so how about answering my question. What's going on?"

She stared at him, her eyes filled with so much torment that they made his heart ache. He wanted to reach out and draw her into his arms. He wanted to croon nonsensical words of comfort in her ear. He wanted to be the rock she could cling to in her distress, but how could he be her rock when he was floundering himself?

"Shana, please tell me what's going on. Whatever it is, we'll figure out a way to deal with it," he encouraged.

She opened her hand and looked down at the rock. Then she looked back up at him, her expression resigned. "Did Oran tell you anything about this stone?"

"He said it's called a witch stone, and that it's a piece of ancient, fossilized sponge that's used to travel back in time." He paused and glanced down at the rock. Returning his gaze to hers, he said, "I'll admit that I've had to come to terms with a lot of unbelievable things in the past couple of days, but a rock that acts like a time travel machine? You might be able to sell it to H. G. Wells, but I'm sorry, Shana. I can't buy this one."

"What if Oran wasn't talking about time travel, Ryan? What if he was talking about . . . reincarnation?" she suggested hesitantly.

Ryan blinked at her, sure he'd misunderstood her. "Reincarnation?"

She nodded, her expression so solemn that he knew she was serious.

"That's absurd. Everyone knows that there is no such thing as reincarnation."

"I'm not very familiar with the mortal world, Ryan, but Sanctuary has an excellent library. From what I have read, a good portion of the world's mortal population does believe in reincarnation."

"But you don't believe in it, do you?" he challenged.

She shrugged. "We don't believe that everyone is reincarnated. But we do believe that the soul is eternal, and if a soul's need is great enough, then, yes, reincarnation does occur."

Ryan let out a brittle laugh. "So, who in hell am I supposed to be?"

"Aric."

His jaw dropped in shock. When he realized his mouth was hanging open, he closed it and said, "Oh, come on. You can't really believe I'm Aric!"

"When you consider everything that's happened, I think that's the only logical answer," she said. "I couldn't figure out why Moira kept turning you into Aric. Aric killed her, so it didn't make sense that she would want to use his personification."

"And from the fact that she's turned me into Aric, you've reached the conclusion that I *am* him?" Ryan stated skeptically. "That's one hell of a leap, Shana, especially when you don't have one fact to support your theory."

"But I do have facts to support it," she countered. "You told me yourself that you are here to repeat a cycle, and Oran told you that you're fulfilling a prophecy. There's also the fact that if Moira's only desire was to be released from her curse, then any soul should suit her purposes. But she doesn't want *any* soul, Ryan. She wants *your* soul specifically. She wants it so badly that she connected with you on Samhain, and she drew you here on Beltane Eve. She's also made it clear that this battle is between you and her, and she'll destroy anyone who gets in the way.

"I don't know what you call behavior like that in the mortal world," she went on, "but in my world, we call it revenge. And the only person I can think of that Moira would hate that badly is Aric. Like your fatal attraction story, she was obsessed with him, and she sold her soul to the dark forces to get him. But Aric not only rejected her. He killed her and condemned her to an eternity of unrest. Now, if you were in Moira's place, and you had a chance to condemn him to the hell you've suffered through for five hundred years, would you pass it up?"

Ryan began to pace as he argued, "Okay, let's look at your premise. It's true that Moira has every reason to hate Aric. But you said that a soul has to have a great enough need to reincarnate. What's Aric's need? Moira killed the woman he loved, and when he killed Moira, he got his revenge by balancing the scales. An eye for an eye, so to speak. Why would he come back and give Moira a chance to get even?"

"That's what the witch stone can tell us," Shana answered. "Until we know the true story of what happened between Aric and Moira, then everything is merely conjecture."

Ryan stopped pacing and looked at her. "And what if you're wrong? What if I'm not Aric? What will the witch stone tell us then?"

"That depends on whether or not you're a reincarnated soul. If you are, then whoever you were will come out. If you aren't, then nothing will happen."

"And it's that simple?"

She shook her head. "There is nothing simple about past life regression, Ryan. It is a serious undertaking and should not be taken lightly. A soul can choose to reincarnate for many different reasons, but it's often because it wants to atone for some terrible misdeed it performed in its previous life. If you are not emotionally prepared to handle that type of knowledge, it can be devastating to your psyche."

"Do you think that's the case with Aric? Do you believe he did something terrible to Moira—besides the obvious act of killing her, of course—that made him reincarnate?"

"What I believe is that if you decide to use the witch stone, then you must be prepared for the worst and hope for the best."

"What do you mean *if* I use it? You're making it sound as if I have a choice."

"You do have a choice. You don't have to use the stone."

"Of course I have to use it," he grumbled. "Oran Morovang said that Moira isn't playing by the rules. My gut instinct says that if she's breaking them, then she has an Achilles' heel she doesn't want us to know about. If we know the rules, then maybe we can figure out what that weakness is. And the only way for us to find out what's going on is for me to use the stone."

"So, you accept that it's possible you are Aric's reincarnation?"

"Hell, I don't know what I think anymore," he muttered, raking a hand through his hair. "All I know for sure is that—pardon the pun—we cannot leave any stone unturned. So how do I make that damn thing work? We might as well get this over with," he finished, nodding toward the rock.

"You won't be able to use the stone until your powers are stronger, and that won't be until nightfall," she replied.

"Nightfall?" he repeated warily. When she nodded, he said, "I can't wait until nightfall."

"You don't have a choice, Ryan. Until your powers are stronger, you won't be able to make the stone work."

"There has to be *some* way to make it work before then," he argued.

She frowned at him. "Why are you being so insistent about this?"

"Because I have to be gone by nightfall."

"Gone? To where?"

"To anywhere that isn't near you!" When she regarded him in confusion, he sighed in frustration. "Shana, I told you what I saw in that damn Tarot card of Moira's. If we make love, I'm going to harm you, maybe even kill you. If what you've said about this uncontrollable mating urge is true, then I have to make sure that I'm so far away from you that I can't act on it."

She released an exasperated sigh. "I explained that it's impossible for you to harm me, Ryan. And I really hate to break this to you, but you can't leave coven land. I don't think that's enough space for you to get so far away from me that you can't act on the mating urge."

"You don't know how determined I can be."

"Well, you can be as determined as you want, but it isn't going to change the fact that you can't use the witch stone until nightfall. So, what I suggest is that you get some sleep, and we'll worry about everything else when the time comes."

"I'm not tired."

"That's because you're operating at a warlock's energy level, but even a warlock needs a few hours rest to function at his peak," she said impatiently. "And you need to be in top form come nightfall, because Moira's going to be back with all her powers intact. If you're exhausted, you'll be more likely to make a mistake when dealing with her, and a mistake with Moira could be fatal for both of us."

"And if we end up making love that could prove to be fatal to *you*," he rebutted.

"Well, at least I'll die with a smile on my face," she said wryly.

"I wouldn't be so sure about that," he muttered.

"Oh, but I am sure about that," she said, her gaze moving over him suggestively.

"Stop that," he ordered gruffly as he stuffed his hands into his pockets. It was the only way he could keep from grabbing her and kissing her, and he knew he didn't dare do that.

"Only if you promise to go get some rest," she said, giving him a cheeky grin.

"I'll get some sleep if you promise that you'll get me up before nightfall so I can get away from you," he said irritably.

"I'll get you up before nightfall," she said.

"Fine. Where should I sleep?"

"There's only one bedroom set up in the house, and you know where that is."

"Yeah," he said. "I should probably take a shower."

"The bathroom's right next door to the bedroom."

"I know. I found it last night."

"Well, have a nice rest. I'll wake you up just before nightfall."

"Yeah."

Unable to think of anything else to say, he headed for the bedroom. When he walked in, he took one look at the bed and groaned. It was still rumpled from Shana's drugged sleep of the night before, and just the thought of climbing into the bed where she'd been sleeping made him aroused. The sheets still probably carried her unique, and very sexy, scent. He groaned again when his mind suddenly conjured up the image of her straddling his hips, wearing nothing more than a sexy scrap of red lace.

"I am not going to make love to her. *Ever!*" he told himself firmly.

When an inner voice began to laugh at his claim, he angrily snatched his duffel bag off the floor and stormed toward the bathroom. A few minutes later, he got his revenge. He drowned that damned voice in a *very* cold shower.

After Ryan left the kitchen, Shana walked over to the table. She laid the witch stone on the tabletop, pulled out a chair, and sat down.

As she stared at the stone, she released a sigh and muttered, "All I ever wanted out of life was a nice, mortal mate who would take me away from Sanctuary and build a wonderful, happy life with me. So what do I get? The reincarnation of the mortal enemy of the most powerful witch who ever lived. Why did this happen to me? It just isn't fair!"

But what else is new? she thought morosely, as she propped her elbows on the table and cradled her chin in her hands. Nothing in my life has ever been fair.

The future is mine, and now yours will be mine!

Shana frowned at the Tarot card that suddenly appeared on the table. It was Justice, reversed, and her face was the same blurred image that had appeared on The High Priestess card. Shana wasn't sure what confused her the most. That Moira would portray herself as Justice, or that the card was mirroring the thoughts that she, herself, had just expressed—that all of this was unfair.

She looked around the room in search of Moira, but she wasn't there. "So why *are* you protraying Justice, Moira? Are you saying that you are meting out your own form of justice? Or are you telling me that all of this is happening because of some injustice done to you? Or, perhaps, this is nothing more than an ego trip?"

Of course, Moira didn't respond to her taunt, and

Shana heaved a frustrated sigh. Instinct told her that there was a significant clue in the card, but for the life of her, she couldn't figure out what it was.

"Don't worry about it," she mumbled, again cradling her chin in her hands. "Once Ryan uses the witch stone, everything should be clear."

Unfortunately, that didn't reassure her. Once Ryan used the witch stone, she knew they would have an entirely new set of problems to face. Although she had sidestepped Ryan's question, she was sure that Aric had to have done something really horrible to Moira before her death. Other than an intense need for atonement, Shana couldn't think of any other logical reason for him to reincarnate and risk his eternal soul. She was afraid that when Ryan learned whatever Aric had done, he was going to have a difficult time dealing with it.

"I should just throw you away," she mumbled, picking up the ancient fossil and rubbing her thumb across its lined surface. "The sins of one lifetime are a heavy enough burden to carry. No person should be asked to lug around two lifetime's worth."

But as tempting as the thought was, she knew she didn't dare get rid of the stone. By giving it to Ryan, Oran had come uncomfortably close to breaking the rules, and the spell that ruled his family was an ancient and ruthless one. If Oran had miscalculated that fine line between observance and interference, the spell would have killed him instantly.

"No, if Oran was willing to risk his life over you, I can't throw you away," she said, laying the stone back on the table.

She scooted back her chair and stood. Grabbing the newest Tarot card off the table, she continued, "What I can try to do is a reading with the cards Moira has already given us. Maybe it will give me a clue as to what she's up to."

Knowing that once she had the cards laid out, she would want to leave them in position, she decided to do the reading in the repository. When she entered the room and saw the broken balcony railing, she shuddered. So much had happened that she had forgotten the accident that almost cost her her life.

Involuntarily, her gaze moved to the bundle of spears she'd been hanging over, and she shuddered again. If Ryan hadn't caught her . . .

"But he did catch you." She walked over to the spears. "And I think it's time I moved you guys to a safer place."

Luckily, neither the spears nor the urn were very heavy, so she was able to lift the urn and carry it to the other side of the room. After she had stored them well beneath another section of balcony, she turned around and looked for any other objects that might prove deadly.

When she found herself actually considering moving some of the display cases, she gave a chastising shake of her head. "You're looking for reasons to keep from doing what you came here to do. Stop wasting time and get to the cards.

She walked over to one of the least cluttered tables. Carefully, she removed all the objects and crowded them onto other tables. Then she retrieved the chair from between the two display cases. Pulling the cards from her pocket, she sat down and began to sort through them to make sure they were in the order she had received them.

When she reached the point where the Death card should have been, she suddenly recalled that Ryan had said he had that card. Uneasiness stirred inside her. She had already determined that it was dangerous for him to have any of the cards. Instinct was insisting that it was particularly dangerous for him to have that one.

"So, I'll go get it from him," she said.

When she stood, however, she changed her mind. He had just gone to bed, and he needed his rest. She considered substituting a Death card from another deck, but decided it would be better to do the spread without the original card than bringing outside energy to it from another deck.

"I'll just have to make sure I get it from him as soon as he wakes up."

Sitting back down, she finished sorting the cards. When she was done, she closed her eyes, trying to recall exactly how she'd laid out the unfamiliar spread on Samhain. She remembered that The Fool had been in the center. Then she had positioned the next card below it and moved counterclockwise, until she'd laid out five cards that resembled an inverted pentagram. That night she had repeated the pattern until the last card, which she had placed in the center with The Fool. Opening her eyes, she knew it was time for her to begin the spread.

"Now, this has to be an objective reading," she lectured herself. "I have to keep all emotion out of it and stick to the facts. Otherwise, I'll be trying to bring in interpretations that might not even apply to this deck."

She laid The Fool on the table in the reverse position. "Well, I don't need a full spread to know what this card means," she said dryly. "I foolishly took an irrevocable step that turned Moira loose and put this entire mess into motion."

Beneath that card, she placed The Chariot, also in the reverse position. "This is Ryan traveling into Sanctuary. I run him off the road, and he loses control. Moira left the card on his chest, telling me that he's to be my downfall.

"Next came the Devil card, and this was right after Ryan turned into Aric the first time. Moira was telling me that black magic is at work here," she went on as she placed it to the right and slightly above the first card.

She placed the Star card, which was also reversed, at the top right position. "Here's all of Ryan's doubts and pessimism. He simply refused to believe I was a witch."

She positioned the Moon card in the top left position. "Moira delivered this card to Ryan, and she was telling me that there are psychic influences at work. That news was a little late. By this time, I already knew that. And here's The Wheel of Fortune—reversed—a turn for the worse. This was where Ariel showed up and screwed up everything," she said, placing that card in the lower left position.

Holding the remainder of the cards in her hand, she rested her forearms against the table edge and studied what she had so far. Since it completed the spread's pattern, she had to assume that it was a "set" of cards, and that together they meant something.

"But how do I interpret them?" she murmured in frustration. "In a regular spread I have four sets of cards representing past, present, future, and outcome. Even if I discount The Fool, I still have five sets here.

"Maybe if I lay out the rest of the cards, I'll figure out what's going on," she finally said. She tapped her index finger against The Chariot. "Okay, once I get the Death card from Ryan, it will go here. It came during my transformation and loss of powers.

"Next comes The Magician," she said, placing it beside The Devil. "I thought it was showing me that Ryan was a control freak, but what it was really alerting me to was that Moira had given him powers. That's when he read my mind and gave me the sleeping potion.

"And here's The High Priestess." She put it with The Star. "She's a woman with power and intuition and a hidden agenda, and this is the first time Moira actually represented herself in the cards.

"Now we have The Hierophant, reversed, telling me that everything that is going on is nontraditional and unconventional," she stated wryly as she dropped it next to The Moon. "That's when I discovered that I'd accidentally mated with Ryan.

"And here comes The Tower, showing complete change from one structure to another—complete loss of control and unforeseen catastrophe. This is where I found out that Ryan had used the wishing wand to become a warlock, and that he's more afraid of life than death. Definitely a disaster of the first order," she noted, placing that card with The Wheel of Fortune.

Again, she had laid out a complete set, and again, she studied them. She still couldn't figure out a pattern to help her do a reading, so she took the next card out of her hand.

"The Lovers," she said with a sigh, placing it with The Chariot and reminding herself that this was also where the Death card would go. "Moira delivered it to Ryan with a special preview that convinced him that if he makes love to me, he'll kill me. But I know that it's symbolic of a struggle between sacred and profane love. It's also a card that means decisions, so what Moira may have been showing him was that he might make a decision that could kill me. Not a pleasant thought at all, and one I have every intention of ensuring doesn't come true," she said with a delicate shudder.

"Now we have Temperance in reverse. Moira delivered it with the witch stone, and then she makes Ryan's image on the card turn into Aric. That pretty well assures me that Ryan is Aric's reincarnation, which puts everything out of balance."

She placed that card with The Devil and The Magician, and then she looked at the final card in her hand. *Justice.* And Moira was portraying her in the reverse position, letting Shana know that things are unfair.

"As if I didn't already know it's unfair," she muttered, depositing it with The Star and The High Priestess. "I don't have any power. My mate is probably some tortured, reincarnated soul with a death wish, and the most powerful witch who ever lived has eternal revenge on her mind. Yes, I've definitely had better days."

As she spoke, she again surveyed the cards. Suddenly, what she was seeing registered, and she shook her head in disbelief that she hadn't realized it before.

"All of the cards are from The Major Arcana, which I should have figured out on Samhain. There were only twenty-two cards in the enchanted Tarot deck, which is the exact number of cards in The Major Arcana. But what does it mean? Why does the deck only consist of these cards?"

She quickly took a tally of the cards she had. Counting the Death card, Moira had delivered thirteen. That left eight to go.

"So, which cards are missing?" she mused, running the list of cards through her mind. "We haven't received The Empress or The Emperor. Strength and The Hermit are also missing. There's The Sun and The Hanged Man. And finally, Judgment and The World. Now, if I can just figure out how to read this spread, I might be able to figure out her next move. If we can stay one step ahead of her, we might have a good chance of beating her."

But no matter how many times she looked at the cards, she couldn't get a fix on them. If there had been the traditional four sets of cards, she could have played with different combinations until she found a pattern that fit their circumstances, but the fifth set of cards completely baffled her.

"All I'm doing is going around the pentagram; going around in a circle," she mumbled, slumping back in the chair and raking a hand through her hair in defeat. "Just round, and round, and . . .

"That's it!" she gasped bolting upright and staring down at the cards in excitement. "I'm going around in a circle, so each set of cards is a cycle. If I can figure out how the cycle works, then I'll have the key."

Unfortunately, that wasn't as easy as it sounded. After she'd gone through each cycle for what seemed like the hundredth time, she wasn't any closer to a solution than she had been before.

"Maybe if I had the Death card, it would help me see things more clearly," she said with a discouraged sigh. "But I can't get it until Ryan wakes up."

You could sneak into the bedroom and get it.

The thought had come from out of nowhere, and she shifted uncomfortably. It was the word "sneak" that made her uneasy. It sounded so . . . wrong.

It would only be wrong if you were trying to hurt Ryan. You're trying to help him, and if you can figure out how to read the spread, you may be able to save the day. Go get the card.

She was still uncomfortable with the idea. When she looked back down at the cards, however, she frowned in frustration at her inability to read them.

"So, I won't *sneak* in," she said, pushing back her chair and standing. "I'll go in *quietly* and get the card. As soon as Ryan wakes up, I'll tell him what I did, and he'll agree that it was the right thing to do. After all, figuring out how to interpret these cards could save his soul and my life."

She headed for the bedroom. The door was closed. Before her conscience could get another chance to wrangle with her, she quickly opened the door and slipped into the room.

She blinked in surprise at the darkness that greeted her, and she glanced toward the window in confusion. When she did, her heart skipped a beat. She'd been so involved with the Tarot cards that she'd lost track of time. It was . . .

"Nightfall," Ryan suddenly murmured huskily from the bed. "And you were supposed to get me up before nightfall so I could get far away from you. But you didn't get me up, so now you'll have to pay the price."

At the unexpected sound of his voice, Shana let out a startled gasp. She jerked her head in his direction just in time to see spell-lightning zipping toward her. It circled around her, and she let out another gasp as unseen hands began to peel her clothes off her. It took place so quickly that she was stripped down to her panties before she even truly realized what was happening.

"Come to me, Shana," Ryan rasped. Though she could see he was sitting up in bed, his body was no more than a shadow in the waning light. But his eyes were glowing so brightly that she could see his face. His expression was taut with lust, and she felt a reverberating chord of sensual longing come to life deep within herself.

She couldn't have denied his summons if she'd wanted to, and she didn't want to. Desire was suddenly coiling inside her with such force, that she was sure that all he'd have to do was touch her and she'd explode.

With an awed shake of her head, she started toward the bed. She had been waiting for this moment all her life. In just a few minutes, she'd find out if her mating night would be everything that she had dreamed it would be.

· CHAPTER FOURTEEN ·

The Sun
Rebirth

Uncontrollable lust. Ryan had scoffed at Shana's theory, but as he watched her walk toward the bed, he knew it was true. How else could he explain what had been happening to him during the last few minutes?

As his gaze took in her high, firm breasts and her lithe body, he recalled that he'd been lying here, hovering somewhere in that netherworld between wakefulness and sleep. Then, abruptly, he'd been fully awake. It hadn't been a noise that had awakened him. It had been Shana's scent, so faint but so heady it was intoxicating.

When he opened his eyes, his gaze had homed in on her as quickly and as accurately as a heat-seeking missile. At the sight of her creeping stealthily into the room, every nerve, every muscle in his body had come alive. He'd recognized that nightfall was here, and it was time to make Shana his.

The undressing spell had been instinctive. He'd cast it without thinking, just as he now instinctively threw back the covers and climbed out of bed. He had summoned her to him, and she was responding to his bidding. But he knew she wouldn't succumb to him until they had engaged in the mating rite that witches and warlocks had been performing since the beginning of time.

As he continued to watch her walk toward him, his breathing became fast and shallow. He was so in tune with her body that he could feel her pulse racing and her nipples tightening into sensitive peaks. But what held him spellbound was the passion he could feel mushrooming low in her abdomen. It was hot and tight and urgent, and his penis began to swell in direct proportion to the lustful demands of her body.

It's true, he thought in shocked wonder. My libido is being dictated by hers.

"Open your mind to me, Ryan," she ordered as she drew near him. "Let me feel what you're feeling."

He couldn't have ignored her request if he'd wanted to. And, God help him, he didn't want to, because he knew intuitively what was going to happen. Her passion would feed on his response to her, and his passion would feed on her reaction to him, until they both were so turned on they'd be frenzied.

When she came to a stop in front of him, he drew in a deep breath and did as she asked. He opened his mind to her and let her feel what he was feeling. She gasped softly and dropped her head back, exposing the elegant column of her throat and thrusting her breasts toward him.

He stared at her roseate nipples. They were taut, and he wanted to lean forward and draw one into his mouth. He wanted to taste it and tease it. He wanted to nuzzle it and lave it. And then he would move to the other breast. When he was through tormenting it, he'd move lower, and . . .

Suddenly, desire exploded inside Shana. It ricocheted immediately to his own groin, and he became so hard that he groaned from the ardent pressure. He wanted to grab Shana and throw her to the bed. He wanted to take her fast and hard until they were both screaming in climax.

Instead, he balled his hands into fists and kept his arms at his sides. He instinctively knew the rules, and they were very simple. Shana got to explore him first. Only when she was done would he be allowed to touch her.

It was as if she'd been waiting for that acknowledgment. The instant he completed the thought, she raised a hand and placed it against the center of his chest. She fingered the amulet, and then slowly, torturously, she smoothed her hand across his skin until she came to one of his nipples. She let her palm rest against it, and then she stroked her thumb across it. He stiffened and barely suppressed another groan as a new explosion of desire hit them both. It was like being on a sexual roller coaster. Her passion making him hot; his passion making her hotter.

Before he could even catch his breath, she leaned forward and licked his nipple, while trailing her hand down his abdomen. As impossible as it seemed, his penis grew even harder. He couldn't remember ever being this aroused, and he knew he wouldn't be able to take much more.

"Of course you can take more," Shana assured throatily. "Much, much more." And then she stroked him through the fabric of his shorts.

Ryan's knees nearly buckled, and he cursed. He was so near ejaculation that it took every ounce of his willpower to regain control. His precarious condition didn't slow Shana down. She dropped to her knees in front of him and slipped her fingers beneath the elastic of his waistband.

As she slowly stripped them down his legs, he leaned

his head back and rasped, "Dear God, Shana! You're killing me!"

"This isn't death, Ryan. This is life, and this is the way it will always be between us."

As she took him in her hand and began to stroke him, he cursed again, and then kept on cursing. It was the only way he could keep from coming. He was sure she couldn't torture him any worse than this, but then she took him into her mouth.

Ryan knew he had hit his limit, and he tangled his hands in her hair and held her head still. Then he slowly extricated himself, reached down and pulled her to her feet. Lifting her into his arms, he laid her on the bed and lowered himself over her.

Staring into her eyes, he declared gruffly, "Now it's my turn."

Shana opened her mouth to object to Ryan's arbitrary takeover of their lovemaking. But when his lips sealed over hers and his tongue thrust into her mouth, she forgot everything but sensation. She had never experienced anything like this. She felt as if he were devouring her.

When he suddenly pulled away from the kiss, she moaned a protest. But he lowered his head to her breast, and her moan turned into a gasp of pleasure. She could feel the passion spiraling through him, and it was so intense that his entire body was shaking with the need for release. Knowing that she, and only she, could push him to this degree of passion made her own body tremble.

She wouldn't have believed that anything could make her more aroused than she already was, but as he honored her breast, his hand glided down her abdomen and slid beneath the fabric of her panties. When he reached the juncture of her thighs, she felt as if her body was going to explode. As he began to lightly tease her clitoris with his fingers, she urgently rocked against his hand, barely able to breathe as he quickly propelled her toward climax.

"No! Not yet!" he ordered harshly when she neared the edge of the precipice. He quickly sat up and stripped her panties off her. Then his mouth replaced his fingers, and Shana's entire body arched toward him in a frenzy. As his tongue teased and laved her, she tangled her hands in his hair and began to move against him, frenzied and panting for release. Just when she was teetering on the edge of the precipice, he suddenly stopped.

"Ryan! No!" she cried out in disbelief.

"Yes, Shana!" he responded as he rose above her and positioned himself between her thighs. "Yes!" he repeated as he flexed his hips and thrust into her.

Shana was so close to climax that the sharp, tearing pain barely registered. What did register, however, was that Ryan suddenly froze.

"Ryan, please!" she gasped, wrapping her legs around his waist and arching up against him. "Don't torment me like this!"

His only response was a muffled curse, and then he began to move against her so slowly it was an exquisite torture. When she was sure she was going to die if he didn't move faster, he began to pick up his pace. She eagerly matched him thrust for thrust, until she was again poised on the precipice. But no matter how hard she tried to fall over the edge, she couldn't seem to make it.

"Come with me, Shana," Ryan urged, lengthening his strokes. "Come with me. Now!" he demanded as he withdrew completely, and then plunged back into her.

As her climax hit and pleasure engulfed her, Shana closed her eyes and cried out in joy and relief. She heard Ryan's harsh cry of satisfaction a moment later, and she clung to him as he shuddered with his own release. When he collapsed against her, she could only hug him in wonder. Lovemaking had never been better for her. Her mating night was definitely living up to her dreams.

"What do you mean lovemaking has never been better for you?" Ryan growled as he suddenly raised up on his forearms and glared down at her. "You were a virgin!"

She blinked at him, startled by his anger. "I was not a virgin, Ryan. I have engaged in dream lovemaking for years."

This time, he blinked. "Dream lovemaking? In other words, you fantasize a lot. You *pretend* to make love."

She shook her head. "It's more involved that that, Ryan. It is as real to the participants as what you and I just shared."

"But it isn't physical sex," he qualified.

"No."

He scowled at her. "So, I was right. Technically, you were a virgin."

"If you want to get technical, yes."

"*Damn!* I don't believe this," he railed, as he rolled off her and sat up.

"Why are you so upset?" she asked in confusion, sitting up beside him.

He swung his head toward her and scowled again. "Because, I just took your virginity!"

"You didn't *take* anything. I gave myself to you."

"Well, you should have saved yourself for someone worthwhile," he snapped, climbing off the bed.

Shana frowned as she watched him walk to his duffel bag. He pulled a pair of jeans out of it and tugged them on. She waited until he turned to face her before saying, "I don't understand why you're so angry, Ryan."

"Don't you realize what we've done?" he asked in exasperation.

"Yes, we've consummated our mating."

"Dammit, Shana! We are not married!"

"We may not have gone through the traditional rites, but we are mated, Ryan. I'm sorry if that upsets you, but it's done and there's nothing we can do to change it."

"We are *not* mates," he reiterated furiously. "We will *never* be mates. I don't *want* a mate. All I want is . . ."

"All you want is what?" she prodded when he fell abruptly silent.

Instead of answering, he shook his head. Then he slipped his bare feet into his boots, grabbed his duffel bag off the floor and headed for the door.

"Where are you going?" she asked, more confused than ever.

He pulled the door open and then glanced back at her. "As far away from you as I can get."

Before she could respond, he walked out, slamming the door behind him. What was going on? she wondered in bewilderment. Why was he so angry with her?

The future is mine, and now yours will be mine!

As she saw the card drift to the bed, she cursed. She had enough problems without another of Moira's troublesome interruptions. She grabbed the card, but even with her keen night vision she couldn't make it out. She cursed again. If she had her powers, all she would have to do is flick her wrist to turn on the lights. Instead, she would have to go all the way to the door to hit the switch.

As she grabbed the card and climbed out of bed, she suddenly realized just how much she had taken her powers for granted. She missed them, and she wanted them back.

And what if they never come back?

"Of course, they'll come back," she grumbled. "Just as soon as we defeat Moira, everything will be back to normal."

But what if the transfer to Ryan is permanent?

Like so many of her thoughts lately, this one had come out of the blue. Panic fluttered in her stomach, because she suddenly realized where all those inappropriate thoughts were coming from. *Moira.*

"She couldn't possibly be right," Shana whispered frantically as she raced to the wall and hit the light switch. When the lights came on, she glanced down at the card, and her world seemed to tilt. It was The Sun—rebirth—and the warlock grinning joyously up at the benevolently smiling sun had Ryan's face. What Moira was suggesting was true! Ryan would remain a warlock, and she would stay as powerless as a mortal.

"It's *not* true!" she declared hoarsely, her panic veering toward alarm. "Moira is only toying with me. My powers will come back. *They will!*"

A cold wind suddenly swirled around her, and Moira's unearthly cackle filled the air as she repeated, *The future is mine, and now yours will be mine!*

"The hell it will!" Shana yelled angrily. "You had your chance for a future, and you blew it. This future is *mine,* and I am *not* going to let you steal it away from me."

She looked around the room, expecting Moira to respond. But, as usual, Moira had hung around just long enough to deliver her bad news.

"I am going to beat you," Shana said, continuing to search the room for some sign of her nemesis, even though she knew that Moira was gone. How could she disappear so quickly? For that matter, where did she go?

"I *will* beat you," she repeated. But she recognized that to do that, she had to know what had happened in the past. "I have to find Ryan so we can use the witch stone."

She ran across the room to the small closet and jerked open the door. Grabbing one of her white ceremonial robes, she pulled it on. In just a couple of hours, everyone would be gathering for the nightly ritual, so there was a chance she might run into someone. If she was wearing the robe, they wouldn't think twice about seeing her in the woods. They'd simply think she was going to the nightly services. Also, the robe's hood would shield her face, which was essential. She couldn't let anyone see her, because they would realize she had mated, and they would mention it to Lucien.

After slipping on her sandals and grabbing her charm bag, which she stuffed into the robe's pocket, she headed for the kitchen to get the witch stone. She had to find Ryan. The sooner she could take him into the past, the sooner she'd know how to send Moira back to the spirit world where she belonged.

But when she stepped onto the back stoop, she frowned at the woods. Ryan could be anywhere out there, and she couldn't stumble around in the dark looking for him. *Damn!* If she just had her powers . . . But she didn't have her powers, and if Moira had her way, she never would.

Closing her eyes tightly, she said, "Ryan, please tell me where you are. We need to talk about Moira. It's important. Just tell me where you are, and I'll come to you."

When he didn't respond, she heaved a disheartened sigh. He was her mate now, and he should feel compelled to respond to her. The fact that he was refusing to answer both hurt her and frightened her. On the surface, he was a warlock, but beneath that facade he was still a mortal. What if the mating spell wasn't enough to bind him to her? What if he really could walk away from her?

The questions were too frightening to think about, so she pushed them aside and concentrated on Moira. After all, if they didn't defeat her, whether or not he could leave her wouldn't matter.

"Please tell me where you are, Ryan. We have to talk about Moira. It's important."

When he still didn't respond, she continued to repeat the request over and over until it became a frantic litany.

As Ryan struggled through the dense undergrowth, some brambly bushes tore at his bare chest. He muttered a vicious curse. He knew he should stop and finish dressing before he went any farther into the woods. He feared, however, that if he stopped, he'd heed Shana's frantic summons. She was insisting that it was important they talk about Moira, but he knew that it wasn't only Moira she wanted to talk about. She wanted to talk about them. Didn't she remember that he could read her mind? That she couldn't hide anything from him? Evidently not.

When her pleas continued to torment him, he muttered another curse. Why couldn't he shut her out of his mind? For that matter, why wouldn't she leave him the hell alone? Why wouldn't she just accept that he didn't want anything to do with her?

Liar. You aren't running because you don't want anything to do with her. You're running because you want everything to do with her, and it scares the hell out of you.

His conscience was right, he admitted, as panic surged through him. He had to get away from Shana and stay away from her. She wanted more from him than he had to offer. More than he could possibly give. All he wanted to do was challenge death until it finally claimed him, and, damn Shana to hell, she was so vibrant, so *alive*, that she made him want to live!

He began to run, ignoring the bushes that continued to tear at his flesh. Suddenly, the bushes gave way to a small meadow. Panting, he came to a stop, trying to decide which direction to go from here. As long as he kept moving away from her, he could stay away from her.

Keep running, and I'll kill her!

He shivered as the words echoed through his mind. But it was the dark, shrouded figure that suddenly materialized in the center of the meadow that made his blood run cold. *Moira.*

"Dammit, what do you want from me?" he yelled at her.

Keep running, and I'll kill her! she repeated, and then she disappeared.

He shuddered. Though her voice was only in his mind, he had heard the malice in her words. She hadn't been kidding. But why did she care if he ran away from Shana? It was his soul Moira was after, so why was she insisting on involving Shana in the battle between them?

Unfortunately, only Moira knew the answer. He dropped his duffel bag to the ground in defeat. He had no choice but to connect with Shana. Then he closed his eyes and let his mind meld with Shana's, promising himself that he'd find a way to keep his distance from her if it killed him.

I'm in the woods, Shana, but I don't know exactly where.

"Finally!" Shana gasped, leaping to her feet as Ryan's words flooded into her mind. "Just look around and let me see what you're seeing, Ryan. I'll be able to find you."

When the image of the small meadow sprang into

her mind, she knew exactly where he was. Thankfully, he hadn't gone that far from the house. Of course, even if he had gone to the farthest border of coven land, she could have found him. She supposed that was one of the perks of spending your life in a confined space. You became intimately acquainted with every square inch of it.

She hurried down the steps and into the woods. It took her less than five minutes to reach the meadow. When she arrived, however, Ryan was nowhere to be seen. Where was he?

"I'm right here," he muttered disgruntledly.

She jerked her head toward the sound of his voice, but it still took her a moment to locate him. He was sitting in the shadows across the meadow with his back against a tree trunk.

"What are you doing?" she asked warily, as she walked hesitantly toward him.

"I'm sitting here wondering what the hell's wrong with me," he answered. "I've been a smoker for nearly fifteen years, and I've spent a fortune trying to kick the habit, but nothing ever worked. Right now, I want a cigarette so bad I can't stand it, but just the thought of lighting up makes me ill."

"That's one of those warlock idiosyncracies," she said. "A warlock's psyche is conditioned to keep him in top physical shape so he can protect his family. His mind won't let him develop habits that might damage his body."

"Well, hell, I guess that's why the thought of a good, stiff drink also makes me sick to my stomach," he muttered irritably.

"Alcohol is also taboo," she agreed. "If you can't think clearly, you can't be a good protector."

"Yeah, well, don't take this personally, but warlocks sound like a damn stodgy bunch."

"Why would I take it personally? I'm not a warlock," she said as she drew close enough to see that he still hadn't put on a shirt.

"Yeah, I know. You're a witch, but I bet you don't have any bad habits either."

"Believe me, Ryan, I have tons of bad habits, and . . . Oh, my word! Look what you've done to yourself!" she gasped when she got close enough to see the scratches all over his upper body.

He glanced down at himself and shrugged. "It's just a few scratches. Nothing to worry about."

"Of course, it's something to worry about," she said in exasperation as she came to a stop in front of him and frowned. "Scratches can become infected. We need to get you home so we can put something on them."

"I said it's nothing to worry about," he repeated, scowling at her. "I am a doctor, and I know what the hell I'm talking about. So stop trying to play nursemaid. I can take care of myself."

"I wasn't suggesting that you can't take care of yourself, Ryan. I was merely expressing my concern."

"Well, I don't want your concern, so don't waste it on me. Save it for someone who cares."

Shana arched a brow at his belligerent tone. "I'm your mate, Ryan. I couldn't stop being concerned about you if I wanted to, which, I assure you, I don't."

"Damn you!" he bellowed as he suddenly leaped to his feet. He grabbed her shoulders in a painful grip and shook her hard. "How many times do I have to tell you. *We are not married!*"

Stunned by his volatile reaction, Shana stared up at him in disbelief. A gale force wind was emanating from him, and his expression was so furious that it truly frightened her. What had she done to make him so enraged?

"I'm not sure why you're so angry with me," she said,

unable to keep the quaver out of her voice. "But I would appreciate it if you would let me go. You're hurting me."

He blinked at her words, and then he released her with a violent curse. The wind disappeared as quickly as it had arisen, and Shana didn't need powers to realize he'd turned his anger inward. His expression was still furious and his body had gone rigid.

"Ryan, what is wrong with you?" she asked, raising her hand to his arm.

"Don't touch me!" he stated in a voice so low and taut that it sounded like the crack of a whip.

Hurt, she quickly pulled her hand away. "I just want to help."

"Then leave me the hell alone."

"I'm sorry, Ryan, but I can't do that. You're my—"

"Don't say it!" he broke in curtly. "I never again want to hear the word 'mate' in relation to me."

"Well, what would you like me to call you?" she asked impatiently. His refusal to accept their relationship was beginning to make her own temper stir.

"I would just as soon you didn't call me at all," he snapped. "Unfortunately, Moira has different ideas. So until I can get her off my ass and blow out of this hellhole, I guess I'm stuck with you."

Shana sucked in a harsh breath at his gibe. Unable to decide if she should be offended or angry, she decided to ignore both reactions. They could deal with this problem later. Right now, they had a more pressing one—Moira.

"Look, Ryan, I don't know why you're so upset, and obviously, you don't want to explain it. What I do know is that if we hope to beat Moira, then we need to get some answers."

She paused to retrieve the witch stone from the pocket in her robe. Extending it toward him, she said,

"If you're still willing to use this, then I think we'd better get started."

Ryan stared down at the rock, his pulse picking up speed and his mouth going dry. He didn't know why he was suddenly so nervous about using the stone. He knew that Shana was right. They needed answers, and after his little tête-à-tête with Moira, he was convinced they needed them fast. Otherwise, he was sure to do something that would inadvertently tick Moira off, and it would probably cost Shana her life. And he had to save her. He'd lost too many souls to death. He couldn't let her be another.

So, why, instead of agreeing with Shana, did he hear himself say, "I don't think I can use the stone, Shana. I can't be hypnotized."

"There is no hypnosis involved, Ryan. The stone will do everything for you. But if you're . . . uncertain about this, just say so, and we'll find another way."

"You know as well as I do that there isn't any other way," he stated dryly. "And you don't have to couch your words with me by saying things like, 'if you're uncertain,' when you really mean 'if you're afraid.'

"And in case you're wondering," he went on, "yes, I am afraid, but not in the way you think. What scares the hell out of me is that I might find out reincarnation is a reality."

"And why would that frighten you?" Shana asked in confusion.

"Because if it's true that you have to pay for the sins you commit in this life in your next life, then I'm in a hell of a lot of trouble."

Before she could respond, he grabbed the stone out of her hand and said, "Let's get this show on the road before I lose my nerve."

CHAPTER FIFTEEN

The Empress
Fertility

Ryan had suspected for a long time that he'd gone off his rocker. As he stared down at the stone in his hand and realized he was about to use a rock to attempt a past life regression, he knew it was time for a serious mental health checkup. He jerked his head up when Shana said, "Having second thoughts?"

"More like fourth or fifth thoughts, but what the hell. Nothing ventured, nothing gained." When she frowned worriedly, he gave her a rueful smile and said, "Quit worrying about me, Shana. I can handle this. So, like I said before, let's get this show on the road."

Picking up on her thoughts, he knew she was still worried, but she said, "We need to sit in the center of the meadow."

"You want to do this out here?"

"It's the perfect environment," she explained, as she started walking.

He fell into step beside her. "Why is it perfect?"

"The witch stone is the fossil of an ancient sponge, so it was once alive. That connects it to the wellspring of life. Out here, you are surrounded by living things, which creates a natural bridge between nature's energy of the present and nature's energy of the past. It's that energy that will allow you to connect with the memories of the past. Let's sit here," she said.

"So what now?" he asked, when they were seated cross-legged on the grass.

"Before you do anything, you need to put on a special charm."

She reached into her robe's pocket and pulled out a small, drawstring pouch. It was just like the ones that Oran and Lucien carried.

"What is that bag?" Ryan asked, curious.

"It's my charm bag. It holds protective charms, as well as some potions that are used in protective spells." She withdrew a fine, gold chain, from which a round, clear crystal was suspended.

"You don't expect me to wear another necklace!" Ryan objected, touching the witch's vow already around his neck.

She held it out to him. "This is not a necklace, Ryan. It's a special crystal that will protect you from undue disturbances, such as an animal walking by. It will also keep you from being magically harmed during your psychic state."

"In other words, it will keep Moira away." He reluctantly took it and slipped it over his head. "If you ever tell anyone I've resorted to wearing jewelry, I'll make you rue the day."

"Your secrets are safe with me."

She made the statement so softly, so solemnly, that Ryan knew she wasn't just talking about the necklaces. He shifted uncomfortably and muttered, "Yeah, well, I'm properly adorned. What should I do now?"

Even if he hadn't been able to read her mind, her expression told him that by not responding to her comment, he had hurt her feelings. He expected her to say something about it, and he was surprised when she chose to ignore it. That made him feel like an even bigger heel.

"You're left-handed, right?" she said. He nodded. "That means you need to hold the stone in your right hand, which is your receptive hand."

"Receptive hand?"

"Yes. The dominate hand is your projective hand. Through it you release your personal energy—your mental power and your physical strength. Your receptive hand is the calm, spiritual side of your energy. That's the power you use for meditation, and such."

"What happens if you're ambidextrous?"

"Then you're in perfect balance, so you can use either hand."

Ryan transferred the stone to his right hand and looked down at it. "Now, what?"

"When you're ready to start, you need to close your eyes, clear your mind, and breathe deeply," she instructed. "Let yourself get in touch with nature, become one with it. When you've finally reached that stage, you'll feel the energy vibrating in the witch stone. At that point, you should let your energy connect with it. It will let your subconscious open to the memories of the past. Once you've done that, I want you to say my name. When you do, I'll start asking you questions. If you find yourself reliving a scene that's too upsetting for you to deal with, all you have to do is release the stone. The moment you do, you'll be back in the present."

"It doesn't sound like a complicated process," Ryan told her.

"It isn't complicated. It's just a matter of concentration. Don't fight it. Flow with it, and it will happen naturally and quickly."

"Assuming that I really am Aric's reincarnation, when I open up the memories, will I be me or will I be Aric? I guess what I'm asking is, will I know what's going on?"

"You'll be Aric during the regression, but when you return, you will remember everything you learned."

"Okay," he said. "I guess it's time."

"Not quite," she said, nervously fingering the fabric of her robe. "Before we begin, you need to cast a spell over me that will shield my thoughts from you."

"Why do I need to do that?" Ryan asked, frowning. A short time ago, he would have given anything to be able to shut her out of his mind. Now that she was suggesting it, however, he found the thought intolerable.

"Because you need to be completely focused within yourself. Now that we're ... friends, we're too intimately connected, and my thoughts and emotions could interfere with that process."

Ryan's frown deepened. He wasn't disturbed by what she was saying, because it made perfect sense. What bothered him was her use of the word "friends," and that was ridiculous. He had ordered her not to refer to them as mates, and that was what she had been about to say. But she could have come up with a better description of their relationship than "friends." It was so ... innocuous, and what they had shared tonight had *not* been innocuous.

He started to correct her, to declare that they were more than friends, when his common sense surfaced. After all, he didn't want to encourage her.

"Do I use the same spell that I used to shield you from Sebastian?" he asked instead.

"The hand gesture is the same, but the spell's a bit different," she answered. "The one you used before allowed me to portray what I wanted Sebastian to believe. This spell will cut me completely off from you."

Again, Ryan experienced a strange aversion to the

thought of being closed off from her mind. He quickly tamped it down. "Okay, give me the words to the spell."

She said them. He repeated them, circled his wrist in a clockwise motion and pointed his index finger at her. He watched spell-lightning erupt from his finger and circle her. Before he could even blink, he was disconnected from her mind.

Ryan felt as if he'd just been kicked in the gut. Losing contact with her gave him a strange feeling of . . . emptiness. He didn't like the feeling at all, and he wanted to undo the spell immediately. But to do that, he'd have to ask her for the reverse spell. That would let her know that it bothered him to be separated from her. Instinct said that was a weapon too dangerous to give her.

"Whenever you're ready, you can start the regression," she said, interrupting his brooding.

"Yeah." He glanced down at the stone and folded his fingers over it. Then he glanced back up at her. "Well, as they say, there is no time like the present—although, in this case, I guess that should be the past."

He didn't give her a chance to respond. He closed his eyes and began to breathe deeply, telling himself to concentrate. He forced his mind to empty of everything but the sounds surrounding him. He heard the sigh of a soft breeze and the rustling of leaves. There was the distant hoot of an owl and the low croaks of frogs. There were other sounds he couldn't identify, but he didn't need to identify them. All he had to do was feel them, and doing so seemed as natural to him as breathing.

He had no idea how much time passed before he felt the soft vibration of the witch stone, and he didn't care. Time seemed unimportant, insignificant. He just let the vibrations of the stone absorb him into the continuum of all that was, of all that had ever been.

His mind seemed to slip away from this body, from this time, this place. And then he was settling into another body. One that, remarkably, seemed more familiar to him than the one he'd just left. He knew at that moment that he had come home.

"Shana?"

As Ryan's eyes suddenly flew open and he spoke her name, Shana started. He was looking at her, but his eyes were unfocused. She knew instinctively that he'd done it. He'd gone back in time, so he was a reincarnated soul. But was he Aric?

She swallowed against the sudden lump in her throat. Though she had been schooled in the techniques of past life regression, this was the first time she had been involved with one. She reminded herself that the key to a successful interview was to keep the questions straightforward, businesslike. That way you didn't color the regressed person's responses by asking them leading questions. With that in mind, she said, "I'm Shana. May I ask your name?"

"I am Aric."

"I'm glad to meet you, Aric," she said, shivering. It was one thing to believe he was Aric. It was quite another to have him confirm it. She was also surprised that he was speaking in modern English. Then she realized that it was really Ryan answering the questions, so it wasn't so surprising after all. "May I ask what you do for a living?"

"I am a healer."

"A healer," she repeated. She found it interesting that he'd chosen the same profession in this incarnation. Normally, a reincarnated soul chose a different line of work. "That's a very noble profession. You must be greatly admired among your people."

"Yes," he said with a frown.

"You're frowning, Aric. Is there something wrong with being admired?"

"They expect miracles from me. I try, but . . ."

"I understand," Shana murmured sympathetically when his voice trailed off. "It must be terribly hard when you've done all that you can do, and it just isn't enough."

"Yes," he said with a heavy sigh.

"Aric, you have knowledge that is very important to me. May I ask you some questions?"

"I am very busy. I am a healer," he said, frowning again.

"I know you're very busy, Aric, and I promise that I won't take up much of your time. Will you answer my questions?"

He hesitated, but then he nodded. "I will answer them."

"Good," Shana said, smothering a relieved sigh. For a moment she thought he might deny her request, and she didn't know what she would have done. She couldn't force him to cooperate with her.

"Aric, you know a witch named Moira. Can you tell me how you met her?"

His expression became alarmed. "No one must know about Moira! You must leave! At once!"

Shana blinked, startled by his obvious fear. "Aric, there is no reason for you to be afraid of me. I promise you that I won't tell anyone about Moira."

He shook his head adamantly. "You must leave. I will not talk to you."

Shana opened her mouth, but closed it when she realized she didn't know what to say. *Damn!* She was so close to getting the answers they needed. Why was he so frightened?

She regarded him for a moment and then said, "Aric,

I already know about Moira, and I have brought no harm to you. You can trust me."

He shook his head again. "No. Moira said I must trust no one. If I tell, she will kill her."

"She will kill whom?" Shana asked, gaping at him. Murder was against every principle that governed her race. They were not allowed to bring harm to another human being, not even to protect themselves, which was why they had been so devastated by the witch hunts.

He glanced around furtively, as though trying to assure himself that they were alone. Then he leaned toward her and whispered, "Terza."

"Why will she kill Terza if you tell?" Shana asked in bafflement. Terza was a witch, and had been a part of Moira's coven. As the high priestess, Moira was compelled to protect Terza, even if it cost her her own life.

"I cannot tell you," Aric said, nervously glancing around again.

"Aric, please. You must trust me. Moira is also threatening someone I love. I can't help him if you don't answer my questions. I swear to you that I mean you no harm. I just need to know about you and Moira. Your story might help me save him."

He stared at her belligerently for a long moment, and she was sure he was going to refuse her request. Then he suddenly said, "Terza was very ill. I could not help her."

He paused and raked a hand through his hair. His expression was tormented when he finally continued, "I know it was wrong, but I love Terza. I went to the witch and asked for her help. She agreed to cure Terza, but only if I promised to never tell that she had cured a mortal."

"Terza is a mortal?" Shana gasped in shock.

His eyes widened, and his expression became fearful

again. "Of course, she is a mortal! Has someone accused her of being a . . . witch?"

"No!" Shana quickly assured, realizing that Aric had lived in the fifteenth century. An accusation of being a witch usually resulted in torture and death. "No one has accused Terza of being a witch."

Just my entire race, she silently added. Obviously, the history behind Moira's and Aric's fatal attraction was completely fabricated. But why would the narrators tell such a blatant lie?

"So, that's how you met Moira," she said, when he sat back with a relieved sigh. "You asked her to cure Terza."

He nodded, his expression becoming pensive. "It was wrong, but I love Terza."

"I understand," Shana murmured, putting her hand over his and giving it a squeeze. She was amazed by Aric's meekness. Since her only encounters with him had been when he was trying to kill her, she'd thought he would be more forceful. More like Ryan. But Aric appeared to be a gentle, uncomplicated man. Ryan, on the other hand, was the most complex male Shana had ever met. At that moment, she realized that even though Ryan was Aric's reincarnation, they were not the same person. Ryan was his own man, and on some basic level that reassured her that they truly belonged together. "When we love someone, we will do anything for them. That is not wrong, Aric."

"She will not leave me alone," he said so quietly, so softly, that Shana knew he was talking to himself. "I told her I love Terza, but she will not leave me alone."

"Moira is bothering you?"

"Yes." He glanced away guiltily. "She comes to me in my dreams and we . . . do what a man should do only with his wife. I try to resist her, but I cannot."

He glanced back at her, his expression again alarmed. "You will not tell Terza?"

"Of course not," Shana said, realizing that he was describing dream lovemaking. "You have done nothing wrong, Aric. What is happening to you is Moira's fault, and I would never hurt Terza by telling her."

"Moira is tempting me," he suddenly announced. "She tells me that if I will mate with her, she will give me powers. I cannot mate with her. I love Terza. But . . ."

"But?" Shana prodded when he fell silent.

He shook his head wearily. "I am a healer. If I had powers, I could touch people and know what is wrong. I could save lives. I know it is wrong, but it is tempting."

"I understand," Shana said, squeezing his hand again. "Aric, I want you to do me a favor now. I want you to close your eyes and let Ryan surface. He's going to lead you into the future so we can learn more about Moira. There is no reason for you to be frightened. So when you get to the spot that Ryan thinks is important, I want you to open your eyes and we'll talk some more."

He closed his eyes. Shana knew that no more than a few seconds passed, but it seemed like an eternity before he opened them again. When he did, she stared at him, stunned. His eyes were glittering with rage, and his expression was furious. Now, this was more like Ryan!

"Aric, what's wrong?" she asked.

"Moira has given me powers. I told her I did not want them, but she gave them to me anyway. Now Terza is afraid of me. She says I am evil. I am not evil!"

"Of course, you aren't evil," Shana quickly soothed. "And I'm sure that when Terza has a chance to calm down, she will realize that you're the same man you always were. So, I want you to take a deep breath and tell me why Moira did this to you."

He inhaled deeply and let the breath out slowly. Then he said, "Moira is tempting me. She says when I have a taste of the powers, I will accept the bargain she has made."

"What bargain is that?" Shana asked in confusion.

"The one she made with the dark forces for my soul."

"She made a deal with the dark forces for *your* soul?" Shana asked, concluding that he had to be wrong. It was impossible to bargain another's soul, because they had to be willing to fulfill the bargain. Obviously, Aric wasn't willing.

He nodded vehemently. "She says it is a good bargain. The dark forces gave me some of her powers. Now, I must surrender my soul to them for five centuries. Then they will release me. I told her I will not accept the bargain. I do not want her powers. I want her to take them back. She says she cannot do that."

"Did she say why she can't do that?"

He nodded again. "She says that the bargain is already made and cannot be undone."

"Are you sure that she said the bargain is already made?" Shana asked, positive that he must have misunderstood.

"Yes," he said. "She says that if I do not agree to fulfill it, the dark forces will take her soul and they will not release her until I surrender mine. She says that if they take her, she will spend eternity in unrest. I told her I do not care. I do not want her powers. They make Terza frightened of me. *I want Moira to take the powers back!*"

"I know you do," Shana comforted. "Aric, I want you to close your eyes again and let Ryan take you farther into the future. When you get there, open your eyes and we'll talk some more."

His eyes fluttered closed, and then they flew open a moment later. He sighed heavily and said, "I am tired. My journey was long, and I am glad to be home."

"Your journey? Where did you go, Aric?"

"You must not tell anyone," he whispered, leaning toward her. "Moira must not learn what I have done."

"I won't tell anyone, Aric. I promise. Where did you go?"

"Far away to see the warlock."

"The warlock?" Shana repeated in confusion.

He nodded. "He is the protector of all the witches and warlocks. The most powerful warlock alive."

"I see," Shana said, realizing that he must be talking about a warlock who had been a troubleshooter like Sebastian. "How did you find out about this warlock?"

"Moira's father. He came to me and said that he knew what Moira was doing and it was wrong. He told me to go to the warlock and he would help me defeat her." His expression suddenly grew sad. "Moira found out that her father had spoken with me, and she killed him. I was on my journey, so I was not here to help him."

"Moira killed her father?" Shana asked incredulously. For Moira to commit the crime was serious enough, but for her to kill her own father was inconceivable.

He nodded again. "I feel bad. He was a good man. He wanted to help me. Moira is evil. I must make her leave me alone. Now, I know how. The warlock told me what to do."

"And what is it that you're supposed to do, Aric?"

"I cannot tell. Moira must not find out. I cannot tell."

"You can tell me, Aric. I promise that your secret is safe with me."

He gave such an adamant shake of his head that

Shana knew instinctively that he wouldn't answer any more questions. "Okay, Aric, we need to move forward in the future again. You know what to do."

He closed his eyes, and when he opened them this time he was smiling triumphantly. "I have done it! Tonight I will defeat Moira."

"How will you defeat her?"

"You will not tell?"

"I won't tell anyone. I swear."

"Tonight I marry Terza. Once I am married to her, then I will no longer be free to mate with Moira. She must take her powers back. I will be free of her forever."

"I see," Shana said, realizing that the marriage solution made perfect sense. "So you were able to persuade Terza that you are not evil, and she has agreed to marry you?"

He frowned worriedly. "I had to tell Terza everything. It is dangerous. If Moira finds out what we are doing . . ."

He shuddered as his voice trailed off. Then he shook his head. "Moira will not find out. Terza and I will marry. I love her," he finished with a joyous smile.

"I know you do," Shana said, saddened as she recalled the tragic end to his story. She wished that she didn't have to make him relive it, but she knew she didn't have a choice. "We need to make another trip into the future, Aric."

He instantly closed his eyes. When he opened them, he was breathing stridently, and his eyes were wide and filled with horror. "It is Moira in my bed! But it cannot be Moira. I married Terza. This is not happening. It is a dream!"

Before Shana could respond, he shook his head frantically. "No! I am not mated with you. I married Terza."

Suddenly his expression changed and a forceful wind

began emanating from his body. It was so strong, Shana almost fell backward from its force.

"Aric! You must calm down!" she yelled.

If he heard her, he ignored her as he bellowed, "Where is Terza?" Suddenly the wind died, and he screamed, "*Noooo!* She cannot be dead. She cannot. *I love Terza!*"

He fell silent and began to pant, as though he'd been running fast. Suddenly, tears appeared in his eyes and began to roll down his cheeks. "It is not true. Please, it is not true. Terza, where are you? I love you, Terza! Where are you?"

Again, he fell silent. His head fell forward so that his chin was resting on his chest. Then he began to rock back and forth and sob. "It is true. She has killed you. It is my fault. *It is my fault!*"

There was so much torment in voice that Shana's heart broke. She touched his hand. "It is not your fault, Aric. Moira did this. It is not your fault."

His head suddenly jerked up, and he stared at Shana with so much hatred in his eyes that she shivered. "Do not touch me. You killed Terza, and now I will kill you!"

"Aric, it's time for you to close your eyes again," Shana stated, trying to keep the alarm out of her voice. Apparently, he thought she was Moira, and she knew how dangerous that was. "Close your eyes and let Ryan surface."

He shook his head. "You cannot fool me again. You will never fool me again."

"Aric—"

"You did what?" he bellowed as he suddenly lunged forward and grabbed Shana's upper arms in a grip so painful she was sure she'd be bruised.

"Aric, please close your eyes," Shana stated, her voice hoarse with terror. For him to grip her with both

hands, he had to have released the stone. That should
have brought Ryan immediately back to the present.
So why hadn't it? "It is time for you to let Ryan surface,
Aric. You must let Ryan surface."

His lips curved into a sinister smile. "I do not care
if killing the child will damn me. You should not have
taken the potion. I do not want your child. It is the
spawn of evil, just as you are the spawn of evil. I will
kill you both!"

That's why he has reincarnated, Shana realized in
horror. Moira must have taken a potion to ensure she'd
get pregnant, and when he killed her, he killed their
child. There is no greater sin a warlock can commit,
and because he had powers, he was the same as a
warlock!

"Aric, it is time to let Ryan surface," Shana repeated
urgently. "We know your story now, and we will find
a way to defeat Moira. You can leave now and rest.
We will take care of Moira. I promise. Now, let Ryan
surface. You cannot refuse him, because he is your
future, and that is where we are. In the future. You
are the past. You must let Ryan surface."

He let out a laugh that Shana could only describe
as maniacal, and she gasped in terror when his hands
suddenly flew up to encircle her neck. Her first impulse
was to struggle, but then she realized that though his
grip was tight, he wasn't hurting her.

Ryan won't let him hurt me, she told herself, fighting
against the panic threatening to overwhelm her. He's
my mate now, and he won't let Aric hurt me. All I
have to do is remain calm and let Aric finish reliving
his story.

"You dare curse me, witch?" he said, letting out another maniacal laugh. "Do you think I care? We can
fight this battle throughout eternity, and I will win. I
will always win, because I know you now. I will recog-

nize you, and I will kill you again and again and again. You will spend eternity trapped within the cards!"

With those words, he thrust her away from him with such force that Shana fell backward onto the ground. She lay there, gasping in shock as his words reverberated through her mind. *You will spend eternity trapped within the cards.*

That was why, when she had first touched the cards on Samhain, she had thought she felt a heartbeat. It was also how Moira had materialized without a summons. She hadn't been in the spirit world. She had been in the cards!

The future is mine, and now yours will be mine!

At Moira's voice Shana bolted upright, and she gasped at what she saw. Ryan was lying on the ground, and it appeared that he was unconscious. Moira was standing over his body. Suddenly, she dropped a card, and she let out a spine-chilling laugh as it fell to his chest. Then she disappeared.

"Ryan?" Shana cried as she quickly crawled the short distance separating them.

"Ryan?" she repeated desperately when he didn't move. It was then that she realized he didn't seem to be breathing. She glanced down at the card. It was The Empress. She impatiently brushed it off his chest, too concerned about his condition to worry about Moira's damn Tarot card and what it meant.

Pressing her hand over his heart, she released a relieved sigh. His heart was beating. She bent close to his mouth. When she felt his breath against her cheek, she sighed again. He was breathing shallowly, but he was breathing.

"Ryan, please wake up," she said, patting his cheeks. He didn't even twitch a muscle. She sat back on her heels and worriedly dragged both hands through her hair.

"The past was too much for you to handle, wasn't it?" she whispered miserably. "You don't want to remember it, so you've decided to just go away and stay away. But you know you can't do that. You have to finish fighting Moira. If you give up now, you'll be surrendering, and she will win. You have to fight her, so, please wake up. *Please.*"

When he still remained motionless, she cursed. If she hadn't made him cast the shielding spell over her, his mind would be connected with hers and she could mentally appeal to him. How was she going to reach him?

Instinctively, she bent over him and murmured, "You're my mate, Ryan, and you can't ignore me. I love you and I need you. You have to fight this battle for me—for us."

Then she sealed her lips over his and kissed him, praying that her love would be enough to bring him back to her.

CHAPTER SIXTEEN

The Hermit
Guidance

When Ryan found himself surrounded by darkness, he gave a frantic shake of his head. He was in the world of the eyes, and he watched them soaring out of the darkness, closing in on him with such speed that he knew he couldn't escape them. He also knew what they were doing. They were bringing the new pair of eyes to him.

"I'm not going to look!" he yelled at them, covering his face with his hands. "I will not look!"

But no matter how hard he fought against them, his hands pulled away on their own accord. As his arms dropped to his sides, he groaned. The new eyes were there, but they weren't open. Pale, translucent lids covered them. This was the way they would always be, because to be able to see, you first had to live.

Frantically, he glanced around at the other eyes. They were staring at him in condemnation. Suddenly, he understood why they were there. He had done the unforgivable. When he had killed Moira, he had unfairly condemned the child—*his* child—for the sins of its mother. He had stolen its life before it even had a chance to live. He would spend eternity trying to make up for that wicked act.

That's why I came back, he suddenly realized. To atone, I have to save the lives of children.

But as his gaze was drawn back to those closed eyes, he knew that no matter how many children he saved, it would never make up for what he had done. That's why every failure haunted him. Why he would always be trapped in the silent world of the eyes. They were his punishment—his torture—and they would be there always and forever to remind him of the horrible, unforgivable crime he had committed.

"Come to me, Ryan. I love you. Let me help you."

He spun toward the sound of Shana's voice. She was standing in the distance, her white robe billowing around her and her arms outstretched to him. Hope surged through him. If he went to her, she would enfold him in her arms. She would let her love wash over him, and she would give him sanctuary from the eyes.

He took a step toward her, but stopped and shook his head. He couldn't go to Shana. No matter how much he wanted it, he could not accept what she had to offer, because his sin was too great. This was the world in which he belonged—the world in which he had to stay.

"Ryan, please! I love you. You must come to me. You are my mate!"

He frowned at her. Why was she saying that? He had told her he didn't want her to call him that. He *couldn't* be her mate. A mate protected the ones he loved from harm. He had already proved that he couldn't do that. Look what had happened to Terza, and it was his fault. If only he hadn't asked Moira to cure Terza. If only he had been able to resist Moira when she came to him in his dreams. If only he had truly rejected the powers Moira had given him, then she would have never been able to harm Terza.

That was the secret. The terrible secret he carried

inside. Though he had wanted Moira to take her powers back, there was a part of him that had wanted to keep them. And in the end, it was that desire to keep them that gave Moira the power to destroy Terza.

And it is that same desire that will give me the power to destroy Shana!

At Moira's voice, Ryan shuddered, feeling chilled to the depths of his soul. "I no longer want the power!" he declared passionately as he searched for her. He knew she was there. He could feel her presence.

Of course, you want the power. Why else would you have used the wishing wand?

Ryan shuddered again, recalling that Moira had been the one to encourage him to use the wand. "I used the wand to save Shana from you."

Then why did you ask for the magical skills to save her from me? Why did you not just wish her safe? Because I gave you a taste of the powers after the accident by giving you the ability to read her mind. And once you had that taste, you wanted the powers back!

"That is not true!" Ryan declared, shaking his head frantically.

Just as it is not true that you want me? That you have always wanted me? she taunted. *When you make love with Shana, it is not her you see. It is me. It has always been me. That is why I could assume Terza's identity. It is why I can now exist inside Shana. Love is not enough for you. You want the power and the excitement I can give you. You want me!*

"No!" Ryan yelled. "I don't want you. I *never* wanted you."

Then prove it. Resist me.

There was a flash of blinding light, and when it disappeared, Ryan caught his breath. Moira was standing in front of him, dressed in a white robe just like Sha-

na's. He told himself to turn away from her. He had
to resist her. He had to!

But she was so beautiful he couldn't pull his gaze
away from her. As he stared at her face, he suddenly
realized that he couldn't describe her. She seemed to
change from moment to moment, which had always
been a part of her allure. Whenever he looked at her,
he felt as if he was looking at all of womankind in her
many and varied appearances, and God save his soul,
she was right. He wanted her.

Resist me, she ordered, as she walked to him.

She wrapped her arms around his neck and pressed
her body against his. He mumbled a curse, but it came
out as a groan of need. He knew he shouldn't—
couldn't—touch her, but he couldn't stop himself from
doing so. As his hands skimmed over her, he groaned
again. Beneath the robe, her body was full and ripe
and soft. But it was her scent—a heady aphrodisiac—
that sent his senses spinning.

"Damn you!" he declared hoarsely as he tumbled her
to the ground and came over her. "Damn you. Damn
you. Damn you."

Her only response was to cup his face between her
hands and seal her lips over his.

It's working! Shana thought in relief, when Ryan
suddenly began to return her kiss. He's regaining consciousness. He's coming back to me!

She cupped his face in her hands and kissed him
more passionately. Suddenly, he groaned and wrapped
his arms around her. Then he rolled so that she was
beneath him. As he pressed his hips against hers, she
wanted to gasp at the hard evidence of his arousal. To
do that, however, she would have had to release him
from the kiss, and it was too wonderful to let it end.
Instead, she contented herself with a moan of approval.

When she did, he thrust his tongue into her mouth and began to slide it in and out in the ardent rhythm of lovemaking. Desire exploded inside Shana, and she began to arch her hips up against him in urgent appeal. The intensity of her passion frightened her, because it was almost as if these emotions were not her own. It was as if someone else were using her body. Even more terrifying was that she didn't care. All she wanted was Ryan deep inside her, and she eagerly reached for the zipper on his pants.

At her touch, Ryan jerked away from her with a cruel, vindictive curse. Alarm again stirred inside her, but when he grabbed the hem of her robe and began pulling it over her head, it quickly died. He might be cursing her, but it was clear he wanted her as badly as she wanted him.

When her robe was discarded, he quickly shed his boots and pants. He then positioned himself between her thighs, and, with a guttural groan, dropped a hand to the ground on either side of her head.

As he lowered his lips to hers, Shana experienced another wave of alarm. This was the same scene she'd seen in his mind when she had connected with him after his motorcycle accident. But as his mouth branded hers with his passion, her alarm was replaced with a need so strong she thought she might die from its intensity. When he suddenly flexed his hips and sheathed himself inside her with one quick, hard thrust, she cried out in wonder at the glorious feel of him.

"Damn you," he cursed softly as he began to ride her urgently. "Damn you, damn you, damn you."

"I love you!" she cried, closing her eyes as her climax hit with such pleasurable force that she felt as if she were flying.

She was still hovering in that euphoric state when

she felt Ryan shift above her. Suddenly, his hands
closed around her throat, and her eyes flew open, startled. As she stared up at Ryan, terror flooded through
her. He had metamorphosed into Aric.

Again, her first reaction was to struggle against him.
Then she realized that, as during the regression, he
was gripping her tightly, but he was not hurting her.
That assured her Ryan was in control. All she had to
do was remain calm and draw him out.

"Where is Ryan, Aric?" she asked, unable to keep a
quaver out of her voice despite her determination to
be calm. "You shouldn't be here. This is Ryan's life.
Your life is in the past."

As he stared down at her, his brow furrowed into a
puzzled frown. Then he scowled at her. "You will not
confuse me, witch! I know it is you, and I am going
to kill you."

"You can't kill me, Aric, because I do not belong to
you. I belong to Ryan," Shana stated, trying to keep
the panic out of her voice as his hands squeezed a little
tighter. She sensed that if he recognized the extent of
her fear, it would incite him. "So, you must leave now
and let Ryan come forward."

"You killed Terza, and for that you must die!" he
yelled furiously, his grip tightening even more.

"I did not kill Terza!" she said, her voice no more
than a quavering rasp. If he squeezed much harder,
she was sure she wouldn't be able to talk at all. Why
wasn't Ryan surfacing? Why was he letting Aric do this
to her? "I am not Moira. I am Shana Morland."

"You lie! You told me yourself that you exist inside
this body. It is you!"

Suddenly, some of the missing pieces of the puzzle
started dropping into place, and Shana's heart began
to beat in a fearful cadence. When she released Moira
from the cards, Moira had to have gone some place. If

what Aric was saying was right, then Moira was existing inside her. It explained how Moira was able to introduce her insidious thoughts into Shana's mind. It was how she had managed to turn Shana's fantasy lovemaking with Ryan into reality without her knowledge. It also explained why, whenever Aric appeared, he believed she was Moira, because that was the image Moira was presenting to him. And it was that image that would push him into killing her!

"If Moira is inside me, she's using me. Just as she used you when she came to you in your dreams," Shana told him frantically. "She's also threatening the man I love—the man you have become in this lifetime. You have to let Ryan surface. Then we can fight Moira together, and I know that we can defeat her. You'll finally find peace, Aric. Don't let Moira destroy that chance for you."

He shook his head in violent denial. "No. I will never find peace. My sin is too great, and it is your fault. I must kill you. I must!"

Again, his hands tightened around her throat, and she began to have difficulty breathing. Panic flooded through her. Every cell in her body was screaming at her to fight him, but she forced herself to remain passive as she managed to gasp. "You can't do this, Aric. It is not your right to kill me. It is Ryan's right. You have to let him surface!"

Again, he frowned in puzzlement, and she felt his fingers twitch reflexively. At that moment, she knew that if she didn't reach Ryan now, it was going to be too late.

She stared deeply into Aric's eyes and managed to find enough breath to whisper, "I love you, Ryan. Come forward. Please. Do it now. Before it's too late!"

"No! You must die!" Aric bellowed, but even as he spoke, his hands flew away from her neck. She let out a sob of relief when she saw that his face was changing back to Ryan's.

Oh, dear God, I almost killed her! Ryan thought in shock, as he stared down at Shana. Though her expression was one of relief, he could see the remnants of terror reflected in the depths of her eyes. But it was the marks on her neck that filled him with true panic.

He was straddling her hips, and he quickly moved to kneel beside her. Then he gathered her up into his arms, hoarsely asking, "Did I hurt you?"

"Of course you didn't hurt me," she answered just as hoarsely. She wrapped her arms tightly around him and buried her face in the crook of his neck. "I told you that it was impossible. You're my . . . friend."

"Yeah, well, with a friend like me, you'd be better off with a few dozen enemies," he muttered gruffly. "Are you sure you're okay?"

"Yes," she said, pulling away from his embrace and gazing up at him worriedly. "Are you?"

He blinked at her is disbelief. "For God's sake, Shana. I almost *killed* you, and you're asking if *I'm* okay? What the hell is the matter with you? Don't you have any survival instincts?"

"You didn't try to kill me, Ryan. That was Aric," she said, shivering as she rubbed at her neck.

"Shana, I *am* Aric, so I am responsible for his actions."

She shook her head. "You and Aric share the same soul, but you are also separate. That became clear to me during the regression. Aric is nothing like you, and you're nothing like him."

"How can we be the same and be separate?" he asked impatiently. "That isn't logical."

"Of course it's logical," she argued. "It's true that his life experiences have an effect on you, but you are not Aric. You're an evolution of him—a conduit for his memories. If it wasn't for Moira, nothing more than portions of those memories would surface. You might have unexplained nightmares or particularly vivid dreams. You might dislike something he disliked, or find extreme pleasure in something that he did like. Your intuition would be affected by his experiences, and you might have moments of déjà vu. But you would live your life, making your own mistakes and having your own triumphs."

"I'll concede that we're different on one level," Ryan said as he rose agitatedly to his feet. He grabbed his pants and began to tug them on. "But, again, that doesn't change the fact that when Aric surfaces, I become him."

"No," she said again. "When he surfaces, his *memories* dispossess your consciousness. He psychically takes over your body, but you're in control. If you weren't, you wouldn't have been able to stop him from hurting me.

"I think that's Moira's Achilles' heel," she went on. "She keeps drawing Aric out, because she knows his strengths and his weaknesses. As you mortals say, she knows what buttons to push to get him to react the way she wants. I think that's what Oran meant when he said she wasn't playing by the rules. She isn't supposed to be fighting Aric. She's supposed to be fighting you."

Ryan wearily dragged his hands over his face. "I'm not sure how you reached your conclusions, and I also don't see what difference they make. The simple fact is, Moira is drawing Aric out, and every time he makes an appearance, he becomes more dangerous to you. She wants him to kill you, and I don't know why."

"I don't either," Shana admitted, watching the moonlight play over his face. He looked so distraught, so lost, that her heart went out to him. "But I think Oran can tell me."

Ryan looked down at her askance. "Shana, Oran made it clear that he can't interfere, so asking him anything would be a waste of time."

"Oran can't give me information that I don't already have," she corrected. "He can, however, confirm if what I do know is correct."

"And you really think that getting confirmation is going to help us fight Moira?"

She shrugged. "It's all we have at this point."

"Well, I think that the best thing I can do right now is to stay away from you. If I'm not around you, then Aric can't harm you."

She frowned at him. "I disagree. The only real strength we have is each other. We're . . . friends, Ryan. That means we have a bond that Moira is going to have trouble breaching. The stronger we make that bond, the more trouble she's going to have."

He frowned back at her. "And what if you're wrong, Shana? What if your being around me costs you your life?"

"I will do anything to save you from Moira or anyone else who threatens you. I love you," she said simply.

"That is the most ridiculous thing you've said to date!" he declared, glaring down at her. When she simply stared back at him, he began to pace. "You can't possibly love me. We've only known each other for a few days. Love can't evolve in that short a time."

"I was destined to love you from the moment I was born," she stated quietly as she also rose. "And it was the same for you, Ryan. If it wasn't, you could have never accepted the witch's vow from me."

"Dammit, Shana!" he said, coming to a stop and scowling at her. "I know you believe in all this mystical junk, but you're talking about a piece of rock on a chain. It doesn't mean anything. You don't love me, and I sure as hell don't love you!"

"If you don't love me, then you should be able to take off the witch's vow. Try it, Ryan. Try to take it off," she challenged.

Angrily, Ryan brought his hand up to his neck. The first thing he grasped was the quartz crystal, and he jerked on it, breaking the chain. He threw it to the ground and reached for the jade stone. He curled his fingers around it, but no matter how much he wanted to jerk it off, he couldn't make himself do it.

"See," Shana said. "You can't take it off, and the reason you can't is because you love me."

"You're crazy," he snapped, bending down to get his boots. He set them upright and stomped his feet into them. "And I'm getting the hell away from you."

"You can run from me, Ryan, but you can't run from yourself. You love me, and, eventually, you're going to have to accept that fact."

Ryan opened his mouth to issue a retort, but he couldn't think of a decent comeback. With a curse, he stalked over to his duffel bag and grabbed it off the ground.

He glanced toward Shana, stating curtly, "I'll be at your house in the morning."

With that, he headed into the trees.

As Shana watched Ryan disappear into the darkness, she shook her head and sighed heavily. She knew he'd be back long before morning. He was her mate, and he couldn't stay away from her any more than he could remove the witch's vow. Why was he fighting against their love? Why wouldn't he just accept it?

Unfortunately, only he knew that answer, and she couldn't afford to waste time stewing about it. She needed to go talk to Oran about what she'd learned from Ryan's regression.

She walked over to where her robe lay. When she picked it up, she was startled to see two Tarot cards lying beneath it. She pulled on the robe and then bent to pick up the cards. As she examined the top one, her heart skipped a beat. It was The Empress—the card Moira had left on Ryan's chest when he had been unconscious. In her concern for him, Shana had dismissed the card. Now, she wondered how she could have possibly ignored its ramifications.

The woman on the card had her face, and Shana gave an awed shake of her head as her gaze drifted down to the figure's swollen abdomen. The Empress represented fertility. Was Moira trying to tell her that she was pregnant? Her first impulse was to deny the possibility, but she knew that it was common for a witch to conceive on her mating night.

As a mixture of excitement and fear rushed through her, she caught her breath and held it. If she was pregnant, then it proved that Ryan did love her. A witch could only conceive with the warlock, or in this case man, who was destined to be her lifetime mate. It also added more urgency to their predicament with Moira, because now she and Ryan wouldn't be just fighting for their own lives. They'd be fighting for the life of their child.

Letting her breath out in a rush, she began to examine the other card and she arched a brow in surprise. It was The Hermit, a solitary figure holding a lantern and leaning on a staff. The Hermit provided guidance, and the old man portrayed on the card had Oran Morovang's face.

"So, going to Oran is the right thing to do," she murmured thoughtfully. "But why did you deliver the card without your usual taunt, Moira? Up until now, I thought it was no more than your way of telling me that you're in charge of the future. Now, I have to wonder if it's possible that you aren't as in control as you want us to think. Could it be that you aren't predicting the future, but reporting on events as they happen?"

Of course, Moira didn't answer, but Shana would have sworn she felt an uneasy stirring within her. It was so subtle that she might not have noticed it if Aric hadn't accused Moira of existing inside her.

Instinct told Shana that her premise was true, and she tucked the cards into her pocket. She had to find Oran fast, because time was running out. Moira had only five cards left to deliver.

CHAPTER SEVENTEEN

Strength
Courage and Confidence

While walking along the wooded path to Oran's house, Shana tried to put her thoughts into cohesive order. As she'd told Ryan, Oran could verify what she did know, but he couldn't offer any information. She needed to make sure that she didn't overlook anything that might be important.

She was so concentrated on her thoughts that she let out a startled yelp when a voice said, "Hello, Shana. I've been expecting you."

"Oran!" she gasped, her hand flying up to her chest. He was standing directly ahead of her on the path, and she was surprised to see he was alone. Kendra was always with him. As the youngest member of her family, she had the most to learn from him. Shana suddenly felt a pang of sympathy for Kendra. All of them inherited coven responsibilities from their family. She was responsible for protecting the repository, but her job seemed like child's play compared to Kendra's work. The young witch had not only spent her entire life memorizing literally thousands of stories about their race, but she also would have to observe and memorize the events during her own lifetime. It sounded like an overwhelming task to Shana.

"I'm sorry, Shana," Oran said. "I didn't mean to frighten you. I thought you had seen me."

"I know you didn't mean to frighten me," she replied. "And it's my fault. I should have been paying attention to my surroundings."

"It's understandable that you're preoccupied right now, Shana. You have many important thoughts to sort through."

"You can say that again," she said with a sigh. "Where's Kendra?"

"At the nightly ritual. As I said, I was expecting you, and I left early. I felt it best if we spoke alone."

He turned and headed down the narrow path. Shana followed him, uneasy with his comment. Why would it be best if they spoke alone? She wanted to ask, but she knew that now was not the time.

When the trees gave way to the clearing surrounding his house, he walked toward a rough-hewn bench sitting close to the front stoop. At the sight of the bench, memories from Shana's childhood began to surface. Fondly, she recalled the many times that her school class had sat on the ground around it, while Oran told them about the past. He had such a gift for words that his recitations had created vivid images for her. While listening to him, she had always felt transported back in time.

When they reached the bench, he sat down slowly. Shana saw the flash of pain that crossed his face, and she knew his arthritis must be bothering him. She waited until he was safely settled before she sat on the ground in front of him.

Gazing up at him, she said, "Thank you for giving Ryan the witch stone, Oran. I know that by doing so, you were taking a risk."

He smiled ruefully. "At my age, getting out of bed is a risk, Shana, and you don't need to thank me. I was being rather selfish when I gave the stone to the mortal."

"Selfish?" she repeated dubiously. She'd never known a kinder person than Oran, and she doubted he had a selfish bone in his body. "How could giving him the stone be selfish?"

"Being a narrator is an honored position within our society, but it also has its drawbacks," he replied. "I've spent my life observing the lives of the others, but I have never been able to actively participate in any of the excitement. I can't tell you how many times I've wished I could have been a part of events. Or, for that matter, how many times I've wanted to impart my knowledge to stop what I considered a needless tragedy."

Shana took a moment to absorb his confession before asking, "Is that why you gave Ryan the witch stone? Because you feel that what is happening with him is a needless tragedy?"

"I gave him the stone because he was astute enough to realize that though I couldn't tell him what he wanted to know, I did know a means through which he could find it. As to whether or not it will be a needless tragedy, only time will tell us that."

She frowned in confusion. "Then, why do you say that giving the stone to Ryan was selfish on your part?"

"Because people will know that Oran Morovang gave the witch stone to Aric's reincarnation. I will be an active participant in this historical moment."

"Historical moment? You make this sound like a very important event."

"It *is* a very important event, because it is the fulfillment of a very old prophecy."

"I don't suppose you can tell me just what this prophecy is." He shook his head, and she sighed in resignation. "But you can verify any knowledge I do have, right?"

"Of course. What would you like to know?"

"Well, when Ryan did the regression, he said that Aric and Terza were mortals. Is that true?"

"Yes."

"Then why have we always been told they were a witch and a warlock? I know that our people love to embellish the stories about our past. I also know that the narrators don't always correct their inaccuracies, particularly if they feel the exact details are immaterial to the moral of the story. But it seems that this is an important detail that the narrators should have corrected. So why didn't they?"

As though uncomfortable with the question, Oran shifted slightly on the bench. "You must remember the time in which Moira and Aric lived, Shana. The Inquisition had turned their attention on us. Witches were being declared heretics and devil worshippers. They were being tortured and put to death. Our people were in extreme danger, and they were afraid. Many coven members felt it was wrong for the council of high priests to forbid them to use their powers in self-defense against the witch hunters."

"I know all of that Oran, but I still don't understand why we were not told that Aric and Terza were mortals," Shana replied.

Again, he shifted uncomfortably. "As I said, it was a time of great upheaval in our society. It was difficult enough to keep our people calm. You can imagine what would have happened within the covens had it been learned that Moira, the most powerful witch who ever lived—the witch who was more powerful than any warlock who had ever lived—was destroyed by a mere mortal."

"So when Aric killed Moira, the narrators decided to

lie and say that Aric and Terza were a warlock and a witch?" Shana asked in disbelief.

He shook his head. "The council of high priests made that decision. They cast a spell over all the people, both coven members and mortals, who knew the truth, so that was the story they believed. The members of the council and the narrators, of course, were exempt from the spell."

Shana shook her head in amazement. "I guess I can understand their decision, but we are no longer living in immediate danger of persecution. Why hasn't the truth been revealed?"

"Because the story of Moira and Aric is too ingrained within our society," he said with a pensive frown. "If the truth was told now, coven members would begin to wonder what other lies they've been told, which I assure you are very few. However, there are many young coven members around the world who are becoming as restless as you have become. They're tired of being confined within coven boundaries, and they're looking for reasons to dissolve the barriers that restrict them."

He paused and sighed heavily, before continuing, "That's why the experiment of intermarriage within our coven is so critical. The council recognizes that changes must be made, but they also understand that these changes must come about with great deliberation if we hope for our race to survive."

"You don't sound as if you approve of the changes," Shana noted, not surprised to learn that Oran was privy to the inner workings of the high council. For years, it had been rumored that he was the narrator who observed their actions. She was also sure that the moment she walked away from him, he would cast a spell and she would forget most of this information.

"I don't disapprove of the changes, because I know

that they are necessary for our survival," he replied, giving her another rueful smile. "But I also recognize that when that happens much of what we are—*who* we are—will begin to disappear. At some point, our descendents will grow up never learning the story of Moira and Aric, or a thousand other stories that have been passed down for several millennia. Eventually, there will be no need for my family, because we will be absorbed into the mortal society. No matter how hard we fight to keep our history and our traditions alive, much of it will be lost. It may be necessary for that to happen, but it saddens me."

"It saddens me, too," Shana said, and it was the truth. Though she'd spent her life yearning to flee the coven and its restrictions, she had always believed that the coven would be there—a haven to which she could always return if she wanted. Now, she truly understood the losses involved. As more and more members left, the entire fabric of the coven would begin to disintegrate. There would no longer be the strong sense of community and unity. Jobs, such as Oran's, would eventually become irrelevant, and, thus, die out. Shana found it ironic that in order to save the race from extinction, a society that had existed for thousands of years would have to die. She thought it was not only sad, but tragic.

"I'm afraid I've been rambling," Oran said, interrupting her musing. "And I apologize. You have more important matters to discuss than the reflective thoughts of an old warlock. What else would you like to know?"

"You haven't been rambling, Oran," Shana quickly assured. "I've enjoyed listening to what you've had to say, and when this matter with Moira is over, I will give it more thought."

"If that's true, then I'm glad I've rambled," he said,

giving her a pleased smile. "Now, what else would you like to know?"

Shana took a moment to gather her thoughts, then said, "Ryan, or rather Aric, claimed that Moira made a bargain with the dark forces for his soul. Is that true?"

"It's true that she negotiated a bargain," he replied.

Shana quickly picked up on the nuance of his answer. Negotiation was not the same as actually making a bargain.

She took a moment to consider that before saying, "According to Aric, the agreement with the dark forces was that he would surrender his soul for five centuries. Why five centuries? Why not two or ten or eternity, for that matter?"

"I'm sorry, Shana, but I can't answer that question," he said, shaking his head.

Shana frowned in frustration. "Can you tell me if this is important? Will I be wasting my time trying to figure it out?"

"You will *not* be wasting your time."

Shana arched a brow. So there was something important about the terms of the bargain. But what?

Knowing she couldn't waste Oran's time thinking about it, she continued, "You told Ryan that Moira wasn't playing by the rules. Is it because she's forcing Aric to the surface instead of fighting Ryan for his soul?"

"I'm impressed with your deductive abilities," Oran said, giving a pleased nod of his head.

"Is there any way to use that against Moira?"

"There is always power in knowledge, Shana."

Shana frowned at his ambiguous answer, but she knew that pursuing the matter would be useless, so she asked, "Can you tell me why Moira became so obsessed with Aric? She was, after all, the most powerful witch who had ever lived. Why would she want a mortal mate?"

"I'm sorry, Shana, but I can't answer that question."

She drew in a frustrated breath. "Can you tell me if it's important? If so, is there a clue in the knowledge I *do* have?"

"It is important, and a part of the answer is available to you."

"Can you tell me what knowledge I should examine for the answer?"

He stared at her for a long moment, and Shana realized she'd just asked him to again walk that fine line between observance and interference.

Suddenly, he replied, "Why do all the coven members' last names begin with the letters M-o-r?"

She recited what every witch and warlock was taught before they even entered school. "It's because the letter 'M' is the thirteenth letter in the alphabet, and symbolizes the original thirteen covens, from which our coven is descended. The letter 'O' is the fifteenth letter, and 'R' is the eighteenth letter. When you add thirteen, fifteen, and eighteen together, you come up with a total of forty-six. Add the four and the six together, and you come up with ten. The zero is automatically canceled out, which leaves you with the number one. That is symbolic, because it means that everyone in the coven is united as one."

He nodded. "Do you have any other questions?"

Shana gaped at him. What did the meaning behind coven members' last names have to do with Moira? She wanted to ask, but she knew he wouldn't—or, rather, couldn't—answer her, or he would have done so. So what was he trying to tell her by making her go through that exercise?

"Actually, I have two more questions," she replied, raking her hand through her hair in an effort to clarify

her thoughts. "I know that Moira is using the enchanted Tarot deck to direct whatever is happening. If
I figure out the key to reading the cards, will that help
us defeat her?"

"Again, knowledge is power," he answered. "Whether
that knowledge can be used to defeat her will depend
upon the mortal. What is your final question?"

"I know that you have touched my mind, so you are
aware of everything I have learned about Aric and
Moira. Am I overlooking anything that could help us,
and if so, can you provide me with any guidance toward
finding out what it is?"

"I believe that is two questions," he said, smiling
indulgently, "but I will answer them both. Yes, there
is something important you are overlooking. The only
guidance I can give you is that you should closely examine everything you learned during the regression."

Shana opened her mouth to ask another question,
but Oran held up his hand. "I'm sorry, Shana, but
those are all the questions I can answer. It's up to
you now."

Shana heaved a heavy sigh. "Thank you for taking
the time to talk with me, Oran."

"You don't need to thank me, Shana. I'm simply
doing my job, and again I'm being selfish, because our
conversation will again make me part of history. I just
hope that I'm portrayed as the narrator who helped
you to succeed," he said, bending forward so he could
catch her chin in his hand.

He lifted her face up and stared deeply into her eyes.
"There is something I want you to remember. You may
be powerless, but you are still a witch, Shana. Remember the doctrines you've been taught and use them
accordingly. In the meantime, I will pray for your success, but know that regardless of the outcome, you will
be portrayed as a very brave witch."

"Thank you, Oran," she said, touched by his statement. Then she smiled wryly. "I have to say, however, that I would have rather been portrayed as a smart witch. If I had obeyed the rules, I wouldn't have created this mess."

"You didn't create this situation, Shana. Moira and Aric created it five hundred years ago. So don't waste your time worrying about matters beyond your control. Concentrate on the facts. As I've said, knowledge is power.

"Now, I must retire," he said, releasing her chin and reaching for his cane, which was resting against his knee. Shana quickly stood and helped him to his feet.

"Good night, Oran," she said as he began to walk toward the stoop.

He nodded. "Good night, Shana, and my prayers will be with you."

Shana waited until he was in the house before she turned to go. As she did so, she caught her breath. Another Tarot card was lying on the bench where Oran had been seated.

Quickly, she grabbed it. It was Strength, and Shana shook her head in awe. She'd never seen such a sensual portrayal of Strength. The witch, who had her face and body, was naked. She was kneeling on the ground, her arms wrapped around the neck of a ferocious lion, and her cheek resting against his head. His mouth was open, and his teeth were glistening menacingly just inches from her throat, but there was no fear in her expression. She looked serene and all-powerful—a woman supremely in control of the world around her.

And, of course, that's exactly what the card meant, Shana realized. Courage and strength.

But do I have enough courage and strength to win this battle? she asked herself uncertainly, still staring at the card. The symbolism was clear. Her nakedness meant that she would have to bring nothing into that battle but herself—who she was, what she was inside. She would have no weapons, no clothes, no friends. She also knew instinctively that the lion was a portrayal of Ryan and the threat he presented to her through Moira. If she hoped to survive, she would have to have enough faith to lie down with the lion—to turn herself over to Ryan—and believe that she would come through the battle unscathed.

And do I have that much faith? That much courage and strength?

Suddenly, Oran's words slipped into her mind, *Regardless of the outcome, you will be portrayed as a very brave witch.*

Tucking the card into her pocket, she headed for home, saying, "Oran's right. I am brave, and you've met your match in me, Moira. But you already know that, don't you? Why else would you deliver two cards without your usual gloating declaration about my future being yours? It means that I've done the unexpected, and now that I know that you aren't completely in control of the future, you're in serious trouble. You've also given me three more cards, and I'm going to figure out how to read your spread if it kills me."

She shuddered at the unintentional pun, but then she shrugged off the fearful feelings stirring within. She could beat Moira. She was, after all, Strength, and she would fight tooth and nail for her mate and her child.

Go back to Shana, or I'll kill her!

When Moira issued her threat, Ryan had been wandering through the woods for more than an hour. He stopped instantly and glanced warily around the heavily wooded area, scrutinizing every shadow. He knew Moira was here. He not only sensed her presence, but he could smell her intoxicating scent. It was so provocative, so seductive, and yet it was so strong it was almost cloying. So why did he find it so sexy?

Because you have always wanted me.

"That's not true!" he declared angrily as he continued to search for her. "I wanted Terza. I never wanted you. You forced yourself on me."

You could have resisted me back then, but you didn't want to resist me. Just as you don't want to resist me now.

Suddenly, an invisible hand trailed down Ryan's chest and over his abdomen. He stumbled back a step in horror. But it wasn't her unseen contact that distressed him. It was that her touch had made him instantly and fully aroused. How could she do this to him when he hated her so badly? And it was hate rising inside him. Hate so strong he could almost taste it.

"Dammit! Leave me alone!" he yelled.

You want me, mortal. Even if you deny it, you want me. You can't hide the evidence from me anymore now than you could the first time you saw me. Do you remember that day when you came begging for me to cure Terza? You told me you loved her, but I saw that you really desired me. That is your weakness, mortal, and it is that weakness that will be your downfall.

Again, the invisible hand touched his abdomen. When it began to move lower, he swatted at it, but his hand only struck air.

Gritting his teeth, he growled, "Leave me alone, Moira, or I swear I'll . . ."

You'll what? Kill me? she taunted.

When he realized there was no good retort for that one, he said, "If I'm no threat to you, then why are you hiding from me? Why don't you come out and face me? Why don't we get this damn battle over with right now?"

Soon, mortal. Go back to Shana, or I'll do to her what I did to Terza.

As a cold wind suddenly swirled around him, Ryan shivered. An instant later, he felt the invisible hand stroke seductively against the front of his pants. Before he could move away from it, the wind disappeared.

"Dammit! Why do you insist on involving Shana in this? Why do you want me to kill her?" he asked furiously, even though he knew Moira was gone. And instinct told him that that was Shana's role in this conflict. For some unknown reason, Moira wanted him to kill Shana—that his doing so was a critical part of their battle.

If that's true, then she's bluffing when she says that if you don't go back to Shana, she'll kill her.

"God, I want to believe that," he stated hoarsely. However, as much as he wanted to believe it, he knew he didn't dare risk calling her bluff.

But there had to be *something* he could do to protect Shana from himself until morning, he thought in frustration as he reluctantly headed for her house. By then both his and Moira's powers would begin to wane. He was sure Moira wouldn't risk a confrontation unless she was in full possession of her powers. That would give him and Shana tomorrow to try to come up with a solution for this mess. And he knew in his heart that that was all the time they had. By this time tomorrow, the battle would be over. He just had to make sure that when it was, Shana was still alive.

CHAPTER EIGHTEEN

The Emperor
Advisor and Authority

As Shana frowned down at the Tarot cards, she drummed her fingers against the tabletop. For nearly an hour, she'd been trying to figure out how to read the spread. The only conclusion she had reached so far was that each cycle had five cards, and there would be four complete cycles. The first card, The Fool, was in the center of the spread. The last card Moira delivered would also go into the center. But no matter how many times Shana studied the other cards, she couldn't figure out how to read them.

"But I have to figure it out!" she declared in frustration.

Leaning back in the chair, she looked up at the stained-glass pentagram overhead. The moon had disappeared from sight, so it wouldn't be too many hours before dawn arrived. Where was Ryan? It had been more than two hours since he'd stormed away from her at the meadow. Although he was determined to stay away from her, the mating bond should have brought him back to her by now.

Worriedly, she raked a hand through her hair, wishing she had made him release her from the shielding spell. If she had, she could make a mental appeal for him to reassure her that he was okay.

"He's fine," she told herself firmly, returning her attention to the cards. "He's your mate now. If he were in immediate danger, you'd know it, so stop wasting time by needlessly worrying about him. He'll be back soon, and the moment he does return, you need to get the Death card from him. If you can see it lying here with the other cards, maybe you'll finally figure out the key to reading this spread."

Maybe it isn't the missing Death card that's the problem. Maybe it's because Moira is existing inside you, and she isn't letting you find the solution.

Shana shook her head in denial of the thought, but even as she did so, she had to admit that it made sense. If Moira could take over her mind and turn fantasy lovemaking into reality, then it stood to reason she could stop Shana from reading the cards. On the other hand, maybe Moira was afraid that she would be able to read them. If so, she would try to make her think she couldn't read them, so she'd stop trying to figure them out.

"Everything is so damn complicated!" She leaned forward and studied the cards again. When she still couldn't find the pattern, she said, "Maybe if I put it down on paper, I can see what's going on."

Rising, she headed for the kitchen. There she retrieved some paper and a pen from a cupboard drawer. Sitting at the kitchen table, she began to make a chart. She put the beginning card at the top. Then she listed each cycle and began to record the cards in the order received. When she was done, she propped her elbows on the table and rested her chin in her hands as she studied her efforts.

Beginning: The Fool, Reversed

Cycle One	Cycle Two	Cycle Three	Cycle Four
The Chariot Reversed	Death	The Lovers	The Hermit
The Devil	The Magician	Temperance Reversed	Strength
The Star Reversed	The High Priestess	Justice Reversed	???
The Moon	The Hierophant Reversed	The Sun	???
Wheel of Fortune Reversed	The Tower	The Empress	???

Ending: ???

"Okay, what does the chart show me?" she mused as she looked at each column.

She couldn't see any pattern there, so she looked at the top row. The Chariot, reversed; Death; The Lovers; and The Hermit. Other than the fact that each of them was the beginning card of a cycle, what else did they have in common?

For what seemed like the thousandth time, she went through the circumstances surrounding the delivery of each card. The Chariot came at Ryan's motorcycle accident. Death came when she lost her powers. The Lovers card had frightened Ryan. He'd run away and met Oran, who gave him the witch stone. The Hermit came when she went to Oran for help. They were all events, but . . ."

"That's it!" she gasped, bolting upright. "They are all *events*."

She quickly added a new column to the left and wrote the word events. Then she switched her attention to the second row of cards.

Comparing them to the first group of cards, she murmured, "The Chariot was Ryan's arrival, which was brought about by black magic, thus the Devil card. Death was my loss of powers and Ryan's transformation into a warlock, which is represented by The Magician. The Lovers are struggling between sacred and profane love because of Temperance being reversed. That was the card that told me Ryan was Aric's reincarnation. And, of course, Strength represents my determination to save Ryan and our child from Moira, which sent me to Oran, The Hermit, for guidance. So what does all that mean?"

She quickly reviewed the comparison again, and then she frowned in confusion. These cards seemed more like *causes* of the events, but why would causes come after the events? That didn't make sense.

She closed her eyes and visualized the spread. The first group of cards was at the bottom. Then she moved counterclockwise to the next set of cards, and . . .

"Of course!" she gasped, opening her eyes and staring down at the chart. I'm going counterclockwise, so everything is backward. The event will take place, and then I'll find out what caused it!"

Excitedly, she wrote causes next to the second row and moved to the third one. Now that she finally understood the pattern, their meaning came almost instantly. "They're the *influences* over the events! The Star represents Ryan's stubbornness, pessimism, and doubt, which allowed Moira to work her black magic to bring him to Sanctuary and to continually turn him into Aric. The High Priestess was the hidden influence—Moira—stripping my powers from me and giving them to Ryan. Justice, reversed, is Moira's unfair means of drawing Aric out instead of fighting Ryan for his soul."

She moved on to the fourth row. Again, the solution came quickly, and she shook her head in disbelief.

"They're *clues!* The Moon—unforeseen perils, deception, and psychic influences—was Moira's way of telling us that she is playing games with us. The Hierophant, reversed, was to let us know she'd use unconventional and unorthodox means to get us to do what she wants. The Sun, of course, was telling us that all of this is happening because Ryan is Aric's reincarnation."

After adding clues next to that column, she moved on to the last row. It took her a little longer to figure out what they represented, but then it came to her like a thunderbolt.

"Complications!" she declared in excitement. "The Wheel of Fortune, reversed, was Ariel's unexpected arrival, which prevented me from stopping Ryan from trying to leave. Unforeseen catastrophe in The Tower was my giving Ryan the witch's vow. That mated us and drew Aric out, because he thought Moira was trying to trick him again. That's also where Ryan confessed that he's not afraid of death, but life."

Pausing, she gave a rueful shake of her head. "And finally, there's The Empress. If Moira's right, I'm pregnant, which makes matters even more urgent and precarious. A definite complication."

Adding the word "complications" to the chart, she again studied it. Now that she understood the pattern, all she had to do was look at the last four cards and decide how they could fall into the empty categories. She wrote the names of the missing cards at the bottom of the paper, and then she lifted it and studied her efforts.

Beginning: The Fool, Reversed

	Cycle One	Cycle Two	Cycle Three	Cycle Four
Events	The Chariot Reversed	Death	The Lovers	The Hermit
Causes	The Devil	The Magician	Temperance Reversed	Strength
Influences	The Star Reversed	The High Priestess	Justice Reversed	???
Clues	The Moon	The Hierophant Reversed	The Sun	???
Complications	Wheel of Fortune Reversed	The Tower	The Empress	???

Ending: ???

MISSING CARDS: The World; The Hanged Man;
The Emperor; and Judgment

"I can't believe it was so simple," she said, shaking her head in amazement. "If I can figure out the clues that Oran gave me and apply them to the cards, I should be able to figure out what Moira has planned."

She laid the chart back on the table and leaned back in her chair. Going over the points of her conversation with Oran, she held up her index finger. First, he told her that this is the fulfillment of a very old prophecy.

Raising her middle finger, she noted that Moira had *negotiated* a bargain with the dark forces for Aric's soul. According to the terms of the bargain, he would surrender his soul to them for five hundred years. Though Oran couldn't tell her why it was specifically for five centuries, he had indicated that the terms of the bargain were important.

Her ring finger came up. When she asked him why Moira had been obsessed with Aric, he had told her the answer was important and that there was a clue in the knowledge she had. When she tried to get him to elaborate, he made her recite the meaning behind the spelling of the coven members' names. She frowned, still bewildered by that exercise. What did the names have to do with Moira?

The answer was as elusive now as it had been then, so she ignored it and raised her little finger. When she asked if figuring out the key to reading the cards would help defeat Moira, Oran said that knowledge was power, and whether or not that knowledge would help would be up to Ryan. So figuring out how to read the cards wasn't as important as what Ryan would do with the information.

She raised her thumb, recalling that when she asked Oran if she was overlooking something important, he said she was. He then told her to examine closely everything she'd learned during the regression. What had she overlooked? she wondered, frowning again.

She began to sort through the events that had occurred during the regression. The first thing Aric told her was that he'd gone to Moira and asked her to cure Terza. Moira had done so, but threatened to kill Terza if he told anyone what Moira had done. Evidently that was when Moira first became obsessed with him, Shana realized, because he said she'd started coming to him for dream-lovemaking. That's when she had also started tempting him with the offer of powers.

"Okay, let's figure this out," Shana said, leaning forward and grabbing a new piece of paper. She quickly jotted down: Threatens to kill Terza; begins dream-lovemaking; makes first offer of powers.

Putting the end of the pen in her mouth, she gnawed on it as she recalled the next scene with Aric. He was furious that Moira had given him powers by making a deal with the dark forces for his soul. Moira told him it was a good bargain, because he'd have to surrender it for only five centuries. He told Moira to take the powers back. She refused, saying the deal had already been made, and if he refused it the dark forces would take her soul until he surrendered his.

"Well, that's simple enough," Shana murmured as she began to add to the list: Negotiates bargain and gives Aric powers. He refuses bargain. Why five hundred years?

Circling the question, she moved on to the next scene. Aric had just returned from seeing the powerful warlock, who must have been a troubleshooter like Sebastian. He had told Aric how to defeat Moira, and . . .

"That's what I overlooked!" Shana gasped, quickly pushing aside the paper she was writing on and grabbing the Tarot chart.

She looked down at the bottom where she had listed the missing cards. When she saw The Emperor, she grinned triumphantly. The Emperor was an advisor and authority figure. What Oran had been trying to tell her was that she and Ryan needed to go to Sebastian for advice!

"Oh, Ryan, where are you?" she asked, surging to her feet. Still clutching the chart, she began to pace. "Please come back. We don't have much time."

It was as if her plea summoned him, because the door suddenly swung open and Ryan stepped into the room. Immediately, Shana started running toward him, but she stumbled to a stop when she realized he was glaring at her.

Eying him warily, she said, "What's wrong?"

"You're what's wrong," he said in a low, furious voice. "I'm here only because Moira insists that I be with you. I don't want you to look at me, talk to me, or come near me until morning. Have you got that?"

"Moira's been in touch with you?" she asked in horror. "Did she give you another card?"

"Dammit, Shana! Didn't you just hear what I said? I don't want to have *anything* to do with you until morning, and that includes conversation."

"I heard you, Ryan, but this is important. Did Moira give you another card?"

He glared at her. "No. Now, leave me alone."

"I'm sorry, Ryan, but I can't do that. Moira has only four cards left to deliver, and morning might be too late. We have to find Sebastian. I want you to contact him with your mind and tell him we have to see him. Ask him where we can meet with him."

Ryan gaped at Shana, certain he'd misunderstood her. She couldn't have really said that she wanted him to contact Sebastian. But even as he tried to deny it, he knew that was exactly what she had said.

"Have you completely lost your mind?" he asked. "If I make contact with Sebastian, he's going to know I've become a warlock. He'll try to get involved, and Moira will destroy him."

She shook her head. "You're wrong. During the regression, Aric said he had gone to see the most powerful warlock alive—the protector of all the witches and warlocks. That had to be a troubleshooter like Sebastian. That warlock told Aric how to defeat Moira, and I think Sebastian can tell us what to do. We have to go to him and ask his advice."

"You're willing to risk this guy's life because Aric went to see a warlock?" he said incredulously. "That's almost as stupid as your using Moira's damn cards in the first place!"

"I've already admitted that using the cards was wrong," she said as she stared at him with a wounded expression. "But this is not stupid. When I went to see Oran, he told me that I was missing something important—something that could help us. He said that the key was in the information we got from the regression. That's the only point I didn't discuss with him, Ryan.

"The Emperor is one of the cards that Moira hasn't given us," she went on before he could argue the point. "The Emperor is an authority figure. He advises people, and that's part of Sebastian's job as the troubleshooter. Another part of his job is to protect our race from harm. Can't you see that going to him is the only smart thing to do?"

"What I *see* is that you want to go to a man whose job it is to protect your race," he snapped. "What do you think he's going to do if he thinks that Moira has a chance of getting loose? I'll tell you exactly what he's going to do. He's going to jump in with both feet and probably get us all killed."

"Sebastian is a warlock," she replied. "I would suggest you remember that when you're dealing with him. I'm afraid he has a bit of an ego problem, and he wouldn't take kindly to being referred to as a man. I can also guarantee that he isn't going to get in the middle of our battle with Moira. Oran says that we're fulfilling a very old prophecy. That prohibits Sebastian from getting involved with Moira."

"Then you've just made my case," Ryan stated smugly. "If he can't get involved, he can't help us. So there's no reason for us to go to him."

"You're purposely misunderstanding me!" she declared in exasperation. "You know very well that when I say he can't get involved, it's that he can't, as you said, 'jump in with both feet.' He can, however, give us the benefit of his knowledge. And several times, Oran told me that knowledge is power. We have to go see Sebastian."

Ryan gave an adamant shake of his head. He understood what she was saying, but he also recognized the threat Moira had just issued to him out in the woods.

For whatever reason, Moira wanted them in the house, and she wanted them to stay there. He wasn't about to risk Shana's safety on a theory that might prove to be fatal.

"It's too dangerous, Shana, and if you'll give yourself some time to think about it, you'll see that I'm right. Moira is not going to stand by and let us run to Sebastian for help."

"We don't have time to think, Ryan. I just told you that Moira has only four cards left to deliver, and she could deliver them at any time," she said, shaking a piece of paper at him. She pointed to it as she reiterated, "One of those missing cards is The Emperor, and I know that it represents Sebastian."

"I don't care what the damn card is. Common sense says that your reasoning is not only convoluted, but suicidal."

"My reasoning is not convoluted or suicidal," she asserted. "It's a compilation of the facts. I've finally figured out the key to reading the cards, and Oran said that it's how you deal with that knowledge that will make a difference. So stop arguing with me and listen to what I'm saying. The Emperor card is the key, and combined with what Aric told us, it makes perfect sense for us to go see Sebastian.

"So, we're going to go see Sebastian," she reiterated, "and we're going to go see him right now. Now, contact him and ask him where we can meet him."

"I am *not* going to contact Sebastian, and we are *not* going to go see him," Ryan said, crossing his arms over his chest and glaring at her. "And if you try to go on your own, you'll have to step over my dead body first."

She perched her hands on her hips and glared right back. "And if you don't do this, that is exactly what I'll be doing—stepping over your dead body. Assuming, of course, that you don't have to step over *my* dead body first!"

Ryan sucked in a harsh breath, feeling as if she had just delivered a punch to his gut. Suddenly, his mind filled with a vision of Shana lying at the bottom of a ravine, her body bruised and broken and lifeless. It was such a clear image—so *real*—that it terrified him. He closed his eyes tightly, trying to shut out the vision, but the attempt only made it more vivid.

With a vicious curse, he opened his eyes, and said, "Shana, you can't . . ."

His voice trailed off when he realized he was alone in the room. It didn't take a genius to figure out that she was headed to see Sebastian.

Stop her!

As Moira's furious voice erupted in his mind, a card floated past his face to the floor. Without even thinking, Ryan bent to pick it up. He quickly examined it. It had to be the Emperor card Shana had been talking about. It showed a man sitting on a throne with a crown on his head. His face was unfamiliar, but Ryan was sure it was this Sebastian character.

I said, stop her! Now!

The threat was apparent in Moira's voice, and Ryan started running for the front of the house. Since Shana hadn't gone past him, she had to have used the front door. At least she'd be on the road, so he should be able to catch up with her. When he threw open the door a minute later, however, it was to see Shana turning into the woods from a spot several feet down the road.

"Shana! Stop!" he yelled, but she ignored him.

Wishing he had never cast the shielding spell over her, he ran after her. If he had contact with her mind, he'd at least be able to keep track of her. And he knew that keeping track of her was going to be a problem.

He might be faster, but she had the advantage of knowing the woods. She could probably lose him in a heartbeat.

By the time he reached the spot where he'd seen her disappear, he couldn't even hear a rustle in the underbrush. She was already gone.

A new wave of terror washed over him. If he didn't stop her, Moira would. That's why he had had that vision of her lying dead. Moira had been showing him what she planned to do to her if he didn't stop her.

He leaned his head back and screamed, "Shana! Please! Come back! You can't do this!"

The only answer was the echo of his own frantic voice.

As Ryan screamed for her to come back, Shana slid to a stop and turned to look back along the path she was traveling. His voice was filled with so much torment and fear that she felt as if a knife were being plunged into her heart.

She wrung her hands together, feeling torn. He was her mate, and he was suffering. All of her instincts were clamoring at her, compelling her to go to him and comfort him. Yet she knew that if she went back, he wouldn't change his mind about seeing Sebastian. Intuitively, she knew that it was imperative that she see him, even if it meant letting Ryan suffer for a while.

Suddenly, a bitter cold wind swirled around her, and she shivered violently. But it wasn't the cold that chilled her to the depths of her soul. It was the dark figure that began materializing on the path. *Moira!*

When the specter fully took shape, it pointed a shrouded arm down the path. *Go back or I'll kill him!*

Again, Shana shivered violently. Though she knew Moira's voice was only in her mind, she could hear the malevolence in her threat. But even as terror mushroomed inside her, urging her to run back to Ryan before Moira carried out her threat, her common sense surfaced. In the first place, Moira hadn't delivered all the cards. Shana was sure that Moira couldn't harm Ryan until she had. Secondly, this was the first time Moira had said anything to her other than "The future is mine, and now yours will be mine." The only reason Shana could come up with for Moira to suddenly change her infamous line was because she was afraid.

Afraid? Of you? Moira let out a scornful laugh. *You are nothing but a vessel for me. Like Terza, you have foolishly given your heart to a man who does not love you. Will never love you. It is me he wants. It has always been me.*

"That is *not* true!" Shana declared furiously. "Ryan loves me, or he wouldn't have been able to accept the witch's vow from me."

When he looks at you, he sees me. When he touches you, he is touching me. When he makes love to you, he is making love to me. When he took the witch's vow from you, he thought he was accepting it from me!

Shana shook her head in adamant denial. But even as she did so, she could feel doubt creeping in. Could it be true? Was it possible that when Ryan was dealing with her, he thought he was dealing with Moira? If she was existing inside her, then . . .

Confused, she glanced down at the chart in her hand. It was dark, and she shouldn't have been able to see more than a white blur of paper. But a shaft of moonlight was angled across the bottom right corner, and the words "The Empress" stood out in bold relief. She was pregnant, and the only way that could happen was if Ryan truly loved her.

"You're lying!" Shana declared angrily as she jerked her head up and glared at Moira. "You're only trying to confuse me so I won't go to Sebastian. Ryan does love me, and that's why you keep bringing Aric out, isn't it? He knows his true love is dead, so he has nothing to lose. And a man who has nothing to lose is reckless. Ryan, however, has me to fight for, and that makes him a dangerous adversary. You're afraid that his love for me will make him strong enough to defeat you. You're afraid he'll force you back into the cards, and you'll be trapped there forever."

Fool! Moira raged as her image began to fade, and then, in the blink of an eye she was gone.

"I may be a fool about many things," Shana said, "but love is not one of them."

With that, she turned and hurried down the path. She had to find Sebastian, because instinct told her that the final battle was near.

CHAPTER NINETEEN

Justice
Release

When Shana arrived at the campsite where Sebastian lived, she saw him sitting in a classic meditation pose in front of a small fire. Though he seemed oblivious to what was going on around her, she knew he was aware of her presence.

She forced herself to stand at the edge of the trees and wait for him to surface from his trance, concluding that it was just as well that she was powerless. Otherwise, she might be tempted to connect with his mind and urge him to acknowledge her immediately. That would definitely be a breach of protocol, and not a good thing to do to the most powerful warlock alive.

Shifting impatiently from one foot to the other, she surveyed the area. She had never had a reason to visit Sebastian before, and she was surprised by the setting. There was a lean-to, and that slight protection against the elements appeared to be the only indulgence he'd permitted himself.

Why did he choose to live such an austere and secluded lifestyle? And she knew it was by choice. Sebastian was from one of the covens in Europe, so he didn't have a home of his own in Sanctuary. However, Lucien was his cousin, and because of their family bond, Sebastian could have lived with him and Ariel. But Sebastian had refused their offer to stay with them, saying that he preferred living in the woods.

Shana knew some coven members felt Sebastian chose this lifestyle because it made him closer to the forces of nature, and that made him stronger, more powerful. She suspected, however, it was because Sebastian liked the air of mystery—of separateness—it gave him.

Her musing was interrupted when Sebastian suddenly took a deep breath and began to let it out slowly. Realizing he was coming out of his trance, she nervously clutched the chart between her hands.

"Hello, Shana," he said as his eyes finally opened.

"Sebastian," she said, taking a tentative step toward him. "I hope I'm not interrupting anything important, but I need to talk to you."

"Actually, you saved me a trip," he said, gesturing toward a spot on the other side of the fire. "I was about to pay you a visit."

She approached the circle and sat down. When she did, he eyed her critically. Frowning, he said, "You've mated since I saw you this afternoon."

"Umm, yes," Shana said, glancing nervously away from his probing gaze.

"Lucien didn't announce it at tonight's service."

"Well, Lucien doesn't know about it yet, and I'd appreciate it if you didn't tell him," she said, fingering the chart, which she had placed in her lap. "In fact, I'd appreciate it if you don't tell him about this visit until . . ."

"Until?" he prodded. When she didn't answer right away, he frowned again. "What's going on, Shana? When I brush against your mind, all I get are pleasant images and thoughts. Yet it's obvious that something's

wrong. If I didn't know you were powerless, I'd swear
you have a shielding spell in place."

"I do have a shielding spell in place," Shana replied,
"and that's sort of the reason I'm here. I need your
advice, but so much has happened, I'm not sure where
to start."

Sebastian regarded her for a long, nerve-racking moment, and Shana couldn't help shifting uncomfortably
beneath his assessing gaze. Finally, he said, "I suggest
you start at the beginning."

"Yes, well, that would have been Samhain. You see,
that night I was feeling particularly lonely, and . . ."
She paused and sighed heavily, then confessed, "On
Samhain, I used the enchanted Tarot deck and released Moira from the cards."

He glanced at some unseen spot over her head, and
then returned his gaze to her, his expression grim. "I
see. The prophecy."

Shana had braced herself for an explosion of temper,
and she shivered at his unemotional response. His lack
of feeling alarmed her, because she sensed that beneath the surface he was anything but calm.

"You know about the prophecy?" she asked.

"Of course, I know about the prophecy," he said, his
tone suddenly tense. "Why do you think I've stayed in
Sanctuary all this time? If Moira regains existence, she
becomes my problem. We're talking about the most
powerful witch who ever lived, and she's not only evil
but fully trained in the use of the dark forces. You can
imagine the disastrous consequences to our race if she
isn't neutralized quickly."

Again, Shana shivered. Though she had already recognized the inherent problems of Moira regaining existence, hearing Sebastian verify her conclusions made
them more substantial—more frightening.

"You're afraid of Moira, aren't you?" she questioned

softly, tentatively, hoping he'd deny her statement. If the most powerful warlock alive was afraid of Moira, how could she ever hope to defeat her?

"Only a fool wouldn't be afraid of her, Shana."

Shana nodded in fateful resignation. "So, you've known all along that I had released her?"

He shook his head. "I knew that she was due to be released. I didn't know it had already happened."

"But you must have had some suspicions that I had done it, or you wouldn't have visited me this afternoon," she noted.

"Shana, I'm the troubleshooter. I'm suspicious of anything that's unusual and your mortal definitely falls into that category. When I stopped by, I was trying to check him out. It didn't occur to me that Moira had entered the picture."

"Well, unfortunately, he entered the picture because of Moira."

He eyed her assessingly. "I see. What's his connection to Moira?"

She shook her head. "It's a very long and involved story, and I intend to tell you every detail. But before I do that, can you tell me your version of the prophecy?"

He gave her another one of those soul-probing stares. She had to force herself to breathe normally. A spell had restricted Oran from telling her the details of the prophecy, but Sebastian wasn't under that restraint. However, she was taking a big chance by leading him to believe that she knew more than she did. If he figured out what she was doing . . .

"Since it has already come true, I don't see why not," he finally said. "At the end of five hundred years, Moira will be released from the enchanted Tarot deck. At dawn 183 days later, she must claim a soul to replace her, or go back into the Tarot deck forever." He glanced toward the sky for a moment, and then returned his gaze to her. "If you loosed her on Samhain, then, she only has—"

"A couple more hours," Shana completed, having just done some quick calculations of her own. Urgently, she asked, "Why was she given that specific amount of time?"

"I don't know," he answered, frowning thoughtfully. "I'll have to think about it. How did you know about the prophecy?"

"Oran told me. You see, he gave Ryan the witch stone, and . . ."

Sebastian stiffened and his expression became dangerous. "He gave the mortal a witch stone?"

Shana gulped and wondered if she had made the right decision coming here. But even as she felt her confidence wavering, she reminded herself that she was Strength. She could handle anyone, even the most powerful warlock alive, if it meant saving her mate and her child.

"As I said, it's a long story." Over the next several minutes, she told him everything, excluding only the intimate details between her and Ryan.

When she was done, she said, "So, can you help me?"

"That depends on what you mean by help," he answered guardedly. "Because this is the fulfillment of a prophecy, I can't become involved in your battle with Moira. That stage was set by the dark forces, and only the three of you can carry it to a conclusion. However, if you want me to give you my opinion on information you have, yes, I can do that."

"That's all I'm asking for," Shana assured. "Your opinion."

He nodded curtly and gestured toward the piece of paper in her lap. "Is that the chart of the Tarot cards you've received so far?"

"Yes," she said, handing it over.

He quickly glanced over it, and then looked up at her. "Congratulations."

"Congratulations?" she repeated skeptically.

"On The Empress," he said. "It appears your mating night was successful."

"Oh," she said, blushing. "Yes. Thanks."

He nodded and returned his attention to the chart. It seemed as if he had been looking at it forever when he finally handed it back to her.

"Well?" Shana prodded as she took it.

"You said that after using the wishing wand the first time, Ryan told you he was here to repeat a cycle. When you look at your chart, it appears that you and Ryan are reliving a parody of Moira's and Aric's relationship."

"What are you talking about?" Shana asked, glancing down at the chart in puzzlement.

"In the first cycle, Ryan shows up unexpectedly in your life, just as Aric showed up unexpectedly in Moira's life. I don't know if any of the other cards in that cycle are significant. The regression didn't give you that many details.

"Now, move on to the second cycle," he instructed. "You lose your powers and Ryan becomes powerful. Just as Moira gave up some of her powers so that Aric could become powerful. We know that Moira negotiated a deal with the dark forces, thus The High Priestess—a conniving witch—is significant in both your lives. We also know that she tricked Aric into mating with her by pretending to be Terza. You inadvertently gave Ryan the witch's vow, so your mating was also done on the sly, so to speak."

"And the third cycle?" Shana questioned, staring at the chart with feelings of both fear and excitement. What he was saying made sense, but would it help her?

"There are only two cards in that cycle that appear to involve the past," he noted. "The first is The Lovers—a struggle between sacred and profane love. Aric loved Terza, but he must have had some feelings for Moira. If he hadn't, she wouldn't have been able to insinuate herself into his life. Then there's the last card in the cycle—The Empress. Moira had every reason to believe she was pregnant when Aric killed her. You also have every reason to believe you're pregnant."

"And the last cycle?" Shana asked reluctantly, fearfully, because she suspected what he was going to say. She wasn't wrong.

"If it truly is a parody of their lives, then it has to end with Ryan trying to destroy Moira, just as Aric destroyed her. And, of course, you have to die."

"Why do I have to die?" Shana asked, an involuntary shiver of fear racing through her. Before the feeling could take root, she forced it back down. If she was to beat Moira, she had to be strong. Fear would make her weak. "Ryan is sure it's his soul Moira's after, so my death would be pointless."

"It wouldn't be pointless at all," he replied. "Remember, you're repeating a parody of their lives, and Moira killed Terza, Aric's true love. You're Ryan's true love, and the cycle can't complete itself if you don't die."

"Of course!" Shana declared in chagrin. "I should have seen that all along. But why are we repeating the cycle in the first place?"

"The key is in The Lovers card—a struggle between sacred and profane love," he answered. "As I said, Aric must have had some feelings for Moira. I suspect she felt his feelings were strong enough to make him choose her over Terza. Since mating with mortals was forbidden, she evidently decided to bargain with the dark forces and have him transformed into a warlock.

"However, when Moira negotiated with the dark

forces to change him, she had to make a deal of her own," he continued, stopping to look at her. "Remember, during the regression, Aric said that if he did not accept the bargain, the dark forces would claim her soul and she'd spend eternity in unrest. But Moira was too smart to endanger her soul for eternity, so I think she made sure she had a loophole."

"What kind of a loophole?" Shana asked.

Staring toward the trees, he rubbed a hand against his jaw. "I suspect that she agreed that if Aric chose Terza over her, she would surrender her soul. But only if she would be given another chance to make him choose her over the woman—or, in your case, the witch—he loves in the future."

"In other words," Shana said, "to be freed from eternal unrest, she has to persuade him to choose profane love—her—over sacred love—me. Since the deal she negotiated for Aric was for five hundred years, we can assume that the dark forces agreed to give her that chance, but only after she had served Aric's time. That's why the cycle is repeating itself now."

"Exactly," Sebastian said with a nod.

"There's only one thing that bothers me," Shana said. "I assumed that Aric had reincarnated because when he killed Moira, she was pregnant with their child. Since killing his child is the greatest sin a warlock can commit, and Aric was essentially a warlock at the time, then it makes sense that he would return to atone. However, if your theory about Moira's bargain with the dark forces is correct, then Aric didn't have a choice in the reincarnation. He would have come back, even without the child's death. Could the dark forces do that? Could they force him to reincarnate just so Moira would have a chance to release her soul?"

"Yes and no," he replied. "The death of the child would, of course, guarantee that he would come back to atone. But if that was his only sin, he could have come back at any time, settled his karmic debt and moved on. That he returned now—the end of the five hundred years he would have served if he had accepted the bargain—suggests that there was some element in his relationship with Moira that condemned him. My guess is that it's because he took the powers she gave him."

"But he didn't want the powers," Shana objected. "During the regression, he kept saying that he wanted her to take the powers back."

"You're overlooking one of the fundamental doctrines of our race, Shana. What is given must be given back. Moira couldn't *take* the powers back. He had to *give* them back."

"Are you saying that because he didn't say something like, 'I don't want your powers, here they are,' the dark forces sentenced him to giving Moira another chance?"

"Basically, yes."

Shana shook her head in bewilderment. "That sounds so unjust, because it was really just a matter of semantics. Aric didn't want the powers, and the dark forces should have accepted his demand that Moira take them back as proof of that."

"Ah, but are you sure that deep down he didn't want the powers?" Sebastian countered. "Remember, Aric told you he was tempted by Moira's offer to give him powers, because it would make him a better healer. When he told Moira to take them back, it wasn't because he felt it was wrong for him to have them. It was because the powers frightened Terza. If he did have an inner desire to keep the powers, then that would have been enough for the dark forces to uphold their bargain with Moira."

"This is all so complicated," Shana said with a heavy sigh. "But if I'm understanding you correctly, to defeat

Moira, Ryan has to choose me over her. If he does that, then the cycle will be broken, and his soul will be free?"

"Maybe not," Sebastian hedged with a troubled frown. "I think Moira may have managed to give herself another loophole, so that the cycle has a chance to repeat again, even if Ryan does everything right."

"What loophole is that?" Shana asked in alarm.

"The wishing wand," he answered. "You said that it was normally on the third floor of the repository, and you didn't know how it got to the first floor. Logic says Moira made sure he had access to the wand. Since he was set up by Moira, the wand won't punish him for the first wish, because he didn't consciously choose to use it. However, he did choose to use it the second time, and the wand will make him pay for that wish.

"But how would that give Moira a loophole?" Shana asked, completely baffled.

"The wand will only grant a wish if a person has something important to lose. In Ryan's case, I can see two important things he can lose. His eternal freedom from Moira and you."

"And?" Shana whispered hoarsely, not liking the turn of this conversation at all.

"And Ryan's only saving grace is that when he used the wand, he wished for the knowledge and magical skills to save you from Moira," Sebastian noted. "That was not a selfish wish, so the wand will probably give him a choice between what he is going to lose, rather than arbitrarily take something away from him."

"You're saying that he'll be given a choice between eternal freedom from Moira or a life with me?" Shana gasped in disbelief.

"I'm afraid so," he answered. "I'm sure Moira thinks he'll choose to stay with you, and she'll have a chance to claim his soul in another lifetime."

Shana stared at him aghast. Then she surged to her feet and glared at him. "You're wrong. It wouldn't be fair for him to fight Moira and win, only to have love taken away from him."

"He won't necessarily have it taken away," Sebastian pointed out, with a shrug. "He can choose to stay with you and have this lifetime of happiness."

"But if he does that, he will have to fight Moira again. Next time, he might lose and condemn his soul to eternal unrest. That wouldn't be fair!" she reiterated, as panic began to take life inside her. Could she and Ryan come this far, only to lose each other? *No!* She wouldn't—*couldn't*—believe that.

"To you, it doesn't seem fair. But we're talking about the dark forces, and they have a very exacting scale of balance," he said with a heavy sigh. "Ryan chose to use the wand, even though he knew the penalty for doing so. Now, he'll have to pay the price."

"You're wrong!" she insisted again, hating the frantic pitch in her voice. "As you said, it wasn't a selfish wish, so that *can't* be the price he'll have to pay!"

"Our debating the issue is moot, Shana," he said tensely. "We'll only know who's right after Ryan has fought Moira. If he's successful, you'll have your answer the moment the last card drops. If the images on the cards remain visible, then you'll know that Ryan has defeated Moira forever."

"And what will happen to the cards if he hasn't defeated her forever?"

"They'll fade back to black. Then Ryan will have to make a choice. You, or the eternal freedom of his soul."

As the ramifications of what he was saying hit her, Shana felt her world tilt. Ryan was her mate, and she would love him until the day she died. But if what Sebastian was saying was true, there was no way she could stay with Ryan if it would endanger his soul. But she was pregnant with his child. Could she deny him his right to fatherhood? Could she deny their child its right of a father? Could she—

She forced herself to cut off the questions surfacing, reminding herself that Sebastian was right. Until it was over, neither of them would know what payment the wand would exact. She also knew she didn't dare dwell on the matter. It would distract her, and she had to focus all her attention on beating Moira.

"Why is Moira delivering the cards?" she asked instead. "When I first started receiving them, I thought she was just deviling me by letting me know that she was in control of my future. But now I've received two cards without any taunt from her. That tells me that she must be compelled to deliver them. Why?"

Sebastian stood and stuffed his hands into his back pockets. "My guess is that's her punishment for masquerading as Terza to mate with Aric. As I said, the dark forces have a very exacting balance. She had agreed to surrender her soul if he chose Terza over her, and she tried to finagle her way out of it by tricking Aric into mating with her. That upset the balance, and now she must allow you and Ryan to have a certain amount of equal footing in this cycle."

Shana considered his answer before asking, "Can you tell me why the coven members' names would be important in all of this?"

"The coven members' names?"

She nodded. "When I asked Oran why Moira became obsessed with Aric, he told me he couldn't answer the question. I asked him if the answer was important, and he made me recite the meaning behind why all our names begin with M-o-r."

"Why would he think that's important?" Sebastian murmured. Then he began to recite the reason behind the names, just as she had done with Oran. Shana absently listened, and she gasped when he said, "When you add thirteen, fifteen, and eighteen together, you come up with a total of forty-six—"

"That's it!" she interrupted excitedly. "Oran wasn't talking about the names. He was talking about the premise behind them—the numerology. But how does it apply to Moira and Aric?"

"That's simple," Sebastian answered. "Moira has to claim a soul at dawn 183 days after she's released. Add those numbers together, and you come up with twelve. Add the one and two together, and you come up with—"

"Three!" Shana finished triumphantly. "And that's symbolic, because all things consist of three parts—a beginning, a middle, and an end. Her beginning was her obsession with Aric. Her middle is her revenge with Ryan. And the end will be the fate of her soul. But why was she given 183 days? Why not just three days?"

"The dark forces were rich in ritual and symbolism, Shana. They had you release her on Samhain—the beginning of our New Year—and the battle is culminating during Beltane, two of our Greater Sabbats."

"That explains her time frame, but why did she wait until the last minute to start the battle? Oh, don't even bother answering that," she said, waving her hand dismissively before he could respond. "If Moira had taken more time, Ryan and I would have had more time to figure out what was going on, and we would have had a greater chance of beating her."

"Right," Sebastian said.

"But why did the dark forces want Aric's soul for 500 years? That's the numerology equivalent of the primary number five and has to do with male sexuality," she said, frowning.

"Oran said it had to do with her obsession with Aric. Aric told you that Moira was engaging in dream-lovemaking with him. He said that he tried to resist her, but he couldn't."

"Of course!" Shana said. "When we find our lifetime mate, we never have sexual feelings toward any other person. I'd forgotten that mortal relationships have not yet reached that sanctified state. So even though Aric loved Terza, he desired Moira, and the dark forces would have considered that his downfall. Thus, the number five, with a couple of zeroes added for good measure."

Sebastian nodded. "Do you have any more questions? If not, I think you had better get back to Ryan. He's been brushing against my mind for the past several minutes, trying to get a fix on us. Moira delivered a card to him, and he's convinced that your talk with me is going to get you killed. He's becoming extremely agitated."

"She gave him a card?" Shana gasped. "Was it The Emperor in the upright position?"

"Yes."

"So, I was right to come see you," she said, glancing down at the list of cards that were still missing—The Hanged Man, Judgment, and The World. Sacrifice, release, and success. But whose sacrifice? Whose release? And whose success? Would the cards be upright, or would they be delivered in the reverse position, creating different meanings? The World, reversed, would mean only partial success. That brought her right back to the question of *whose* success?

"Thank you, Sebastian," she said, hurrying toward the trees. "Would you mind connecting with Ryan and telling him I'll meet him at the house?"

"I'll take care of that. And good luck, Shana. I'll be praying for your success."

"Thanks," she called, not bothering to look back. "I have a feeling I'm going to need all the help I can get."

*   *   *

"*Dammit!* Where is she?" Ryan raged as he slammed his hand against the frame of Shana's open front door.

He stared out at the woods, quelling the impulse to go out and search for her. Even if she wasn't trying to elude him, he had no idea which direction she had gone. Why had he let her talk him into casting the shielding spell? If he just had contact with her mind, he could find her and bring her back before Moira could get to her.

For what seemed like the hundredth time, he closed his eyes and tried to connect with this Sebastian guy. If he could get a fix on him, he could then track Shana. But, as had happened with all his other efforts, he no more than touched the warlock's mind than some kind of a mental wall came between them. Was Sebastian keeping him out, or was it Moira? Not that it mattered, because both answers were equally disastrous. If anything happened to Shana . . .

Unable to complete the thought, he pulled from his T-shirt pocket the Tarot card Moira had delivered. Maybe if he stared at the image of Sebastian—The Emperor—while trying to reach him, it would help him connect. He concentrated on the card while projecting his mind, but it didn't make any difference. As soon as he touched the warlock's mind, the wall went up.

With a violent curse, Ryan spun toward the room, crushed the card into a ball, and threw it to the floor. It hit, bounced once, and began to open. By the time it fell back to the floor, it was in its original state.

"What the hell?" Ryan muttered, bending to pick it up. As he examined it both front and back, he shook his head in disbelief. It had no folds or crinkles on its surface. It was as if he had never crushed it.

"Well, I'll fix you," he stated angrily, ripping the card in half and then into fourths. He tossed the pieces to the floor, but even as they fell, he watched them come back together. When it landed, it was in perfect condition.

Swallowing against the fear stirring inside him, Ryan again picked up the card. He wasn't sure why he found his inability to destroy it so frightening. It was, after all, from Moira's enchanted Tarot deck. It made sense that it was indestructible.

But if the cards are indestructible, then what chance do you have of defeating Moira? This is where she exists, and if you can't destroy where she exists, then how can you possbily destroy her?

As doubt began to overwhelm him, he shook his head. He could defeat Moira. He *had* to defeat Moira. If he didn't, then Shana would die, and he couldn't—*wouldn't*—let that happen.

Frantically, he dug his cigarette lighter out of his shirt pocket and flicked it. As a flame shot up, he held it to the bottom of the card. He sighed in relief as it caught fire. Then he realized that although the flame was creeping toward his fingers, the card remained unscathed.

Stunned, he automatically dropped the card. By the time it hit the floor, the fire was out and the card was still in perfect condition.

He was so focused on the ramifications of what he was seeing that he started when a voice suddenly echoed in his mind, *This is Sebastian. Shana is on her way home. She said she'll meet you at the house. She's fine.*

Where is she! Ryan demanded, latching onto Sebastian's mind before he could break off.

She's on her way. Just wait for her.

I am not going to wait for her! Tell me where she is!

For a moment there was no response. Then his mind was flooded with an image of a path that began at the section of woods where Shana had disappeared. It ended at the top of a hilly ridge that overlooked a steep, rocky ravine. Ryan's heart skipped a beat, and then resumed in a terrified cadence. He knew that ravine. It was the same one in the vision he'd had of Shana lying at the bottom of it, bruised, broken, and dead.

Stop her! he mentally screamed, even though he knew that Sebastian had already severed the connection between them.

It is too late, mortal, Moira's insidious voice replied instead. *You did not stop her, and now it is the time for Judgment. The time for my release!*

A new Tarot card appeared in front of his face, and Ryan gave a frantic shake of his head. At the top of the card, the sun and moon seemed to be colliding and sparks were flying off them, filling the sky with burning balls of fire. Superimposed over those celestial bodies was the black sword that had been on the Lovers card. He could see the image of himself caught within the gleaming steel, and he was looking down at Shana, who, naked and vulnerable, was rising up from an earthen grave. Her arms were raised toward the sword—him—as though in joyous welcome. Then the sword began to drop toward her so swiftly that she had no time to move. As the sword struck her, she fell back into the grave. A moment later, Moira arose in her place.

Stunned, Ryan stared down at the card and shook his head, refusing to believe what he'd just seen. However, no amount of denial could wipe the images from his mind. Shana was going to die, and Moira was going to take her place.

Instinctively, he raised his hand to the witch's vow around his neck. As he curled his fingers around it, he felt the jade stone grow as cold as death. Panic erupted inside him, but it was the lancing pain that shot

through him that made him almost double over. It
wasn't a physical pain. It was a soul-wrenching pain
so terrible that he wanted to scream at the agony it
caused him.

At that moment he knew that Shana was right. As
impossible as it seemed, he loved her—was born to
love her—mind, body, and soul. Just the thought that
Moira might destroy her was more than he could endure, and if anything happened to her . . .

"No!" he yelled, as he ran out the door and toward
the woods. He had to find her. He had to save her.
"Oh, God, please. You can't let Shana die. If anyone
has to die, let it be me. *Please, God, let it be me!*"

CHAPTER TWENTY

The World (Reversed)
Partial Success

The future is mine, and now yours will be mine!

At the taunt, Shana slid to a stop on the path and looked around warily. "The future is *not* yours, Moira," she stated with more bravado than she felt, her gaze darting from shadow to shadow. Something was wrong with this scene, but she couldn't quite figure out what it was. "I know your limitations, and Ryan and I are going to destroy you forever."

Now is the time for judgment. The time for my release!

Shana's heart began to pound. *Judgment and release.* Moira had to be talking about the Judgment card. That's what was wrong here! Moira had made the taunt, but she hadn't delivered the card.

"Where's the card, Moira?" she demanded, again searching the shadows. The sense of Moira's presence was stronger than it had ever been. "I know you are compelled to deliver it, and I want to have it. Now!"

Fool! The card is not yours. It is the mortal's.

Shana's throat went dry. Moira must have given the Judgment card to Ryan. If it was supposed to be release, then it had to have been in the upright position. But whose face had been depicted on it? Who was to be released?

The future is mine, and now yours will be mine!

As Moira crowed the refrain in triumph, there was a blinding flash of light. Shana instinctively closed her eyes against it. When she opened them, she gaped in astonishment. The path was no longer ahead of her. It had been replaced by a huge, kaleidoscopic circle. The circle's colors were so brilliant and swirling so fast that Shana pressed her hands to her temples to avoid dizziness.

Realizing what she was looking at, Shana began to tremble uncontrollably. She knew she had to squelch the terror stirring inside her. Fear was her worst enemy, but how could she be brave when she finally understood the meaning behind Moira's taunt: *The future is mine, and now yours will be mine.*

Shana had assumed that Moira meant she was planning on taking over Shana's future and making it her own. Now, she understood that Moira had been telling her that Ryan was Shana's future, and Moira was going to take him away from her. That she was going to take him back into the past to her own future, because that's what the circle was—a psychic time portal.

Shana shook her head in numb disbelief. Moira hadn't been drawing Aric out because she feared Ryan's love for Shana. Moira had been drawing him out in preparation for this moment. Once Ryan stepped through the portal, he would automatically become Aric, and Shana knew that Moira couldn't have chosen a safer battle plan. Since Moira already knew Aric would kill her when he first found out about Terza, she would merely stay away from him until he had some time to calm down. Then she would begin to work her magic on him until he chose her over his revenge for Terza's death. She would trick him into choosing profane love over sacred love, just as she'd tricked him into mating with her in the first place!

But if that is her plan, then why did she open a portal for me? Shana wondered in confusion. She should want to keep me out, so I can't interfere with her plans. It doesn't make sense.

But there has to be a reason, she told herself, quickly reviewing what she had discussed with Sebastian.

Then the answer hit her. Moira was required to deliver the cards to give Ryan and Shana equal footing. It made sense that she would have to do the same thing with the portal. But she probably thought Shana wouldn't enter it. After all, she was powerless, which, in Moira's mind, would make her no better than a mortal. Also, there was the fact that every time Aric looked at her, he saw Moira. How could she possibly persuade him to choose her over Moira, when he thought she was the witch he hated? The witch who had killed the woman he loved?

"There has to be a way for me to get past Aric and reach Ryan!" she said, running to the portal.

As she stepped into the whirling colors, she reminded herself that she was Strength. She could lie down with the lion, and she'd come through unscathed. It would have been easier to believe that was true if she hadn't known that the lion she'd be lying down with was Aric.

"Shana's okay. I know she's okay." Ryan told himself as he raced along the path toward the ravine. "I'm her mate. If anything had happened to her, I'd know it in my heart. I'd feel it in my *soul*. She is okay!"

Unfortunately, that didn't curb the desperation clutching at her insides. Even if Shana was okay, it didn't remove Moira from their lives. And as long as Moira was around, he knew that Shana's life was at risk. There was only one thing he could do to save her. He had to find Moira and make a bargain with her. If she'd agree to leave Shana alone, he would forfeit the battle and give her his soul.

Your soul already belongs to me. It always has. It always will!

"Moira!" he gasped, skidding to a stop and glancing around frantically. "Where is Shana? I swear to God, if you have harmed her in any way, I'll make you pay!"

Make me pay? And how will you do that, mortal? Condemn my soul to eternal unrest?

She let out a laugh so malicious, so evil, that Ryan shuddered. "All right, Moira. You've made your point. My threats are worthless, but I can give you what you want."

He paused and glanced around again. Moira's presence was stronger than it had ever been, and he couldn't believe she hadn't materialized. "Promise me that you'll leave Shana alone, and you can have my soul without a fight. You'll be free again. You can live again. And that's what you want, isn't it? To regain existence?"

Fool!

Before Ryan could respond, there was a blinding flash of light. He instinctively brought his forearm up to shield his eyes. When he dropped his arm a moment later, his jaw dropped open in disbelief. He was staring at a huge, swirling circle about six feet in diameter that resembled a brightly colored pinwheel.

Suddenly a dark form began to materialize in front of it. As the black, robed figure took shape, the hair on the back of Ryan's neck stood on end. He knew this was Moira, but she didn't resemble the beautiful woman who'd been haunting his nightmares. She was the spitting image of that old bastard, Father Death.

She's in there, mortal. The battle can begin! she said, pointing a shrouded arm at the circle. Then she stepped through it.

Ryan hesitated only a moment before running after her. He figured the worst that could happen was that he'd die. With any luck, he might be able to save Shana before he did.

With that thought in mind, he plunged through the circle.

"*Terza!* Where are you?" Aric yelled frantically, as he raced up the steep, mountainous path to the cliff where Moira said she had—

He cut off the thought, refusing to finish it. Terza was all right. She had to be all right. He loved her with all his heart. With all his *soul.* It wasn't Moira in his bed this morning. He had married Terza last night, and now Moira had to leave him alone! But it was Moira in his bed. She said they were now mated forever.

"No! It is not true! It is not! It is just a dream," he told himself as he increased his speed. "Nothing more than a horrible nightmare. In a few minutes I will wake up and find myself in bed with Terza. Moira must have found out about our marriage, and this is her way of punishing me."

When he reached the top of the cliff, he stopped and nervously stared at the horizon. Though dawn was only a short time away, it would still be several minutes before the sun rose. That fact reassured him that this was nothing more than a dream.

"So do not even look over the edge," he told himself firmly. "Close your eyes. When you open them, you will be in your bed, and Terza will be beside you."

But even as he said the words, he couldn't stop himself from walking to the ledge. Slowly, fearfully, he lowered his gaze. It was so dark in the ravine that even with the powers Moira had given him, he had trouble seeing. Frustrated, he raked a hand through his hair. All he had to do was use one of the spells Moira had taught him, and it would fill the ravine with light. But he had promised Terza that he would never again use the powers.

But this is only a dream, so you will not be breaking your vow by using the powers, he told himself. Cast the spell, so you can wake up!

Uneasily, he raised his hand and chanted the spell. When he circled his wrist and flicked his fingers, a small, golden ball appeared in the sky. As it grew larger, chasing away the shadows, Aric held his breath and stared down into the ravine. When it had lit all but the narrowest strip at the bottom, he began to smile. Terza wasn't there.

He started to turn away, but then a small swatch of white appeared from the last of the shadows. Fear surged through him, and his heart began to thump so wildly that he feared he might die. Then, as the remainder of the shadows disappeared, he wanted to die. Lying at the bottom of the ravine was Terza, her long red hair framing her head like a fiery halo, and her body as broken as the kindling sticks he placed on his fire.

"Noooo! It is not true! It cannot be true!" Aric screamed as he threw back his head and looked up at the sky. *"Terza, I love you! Where are you? Come back to me!"*

When Shana heard Ryan's anguished scream, she started running up an unfamiliar path that led to the top of an equally unfamiliar cliff. His words alone assured her she'd been right. When he'd entered the portal, he'd become Aric. Worse, if she was interpreting what she was hearing correctly, Moira must have brought them back at the time of Terza's death. So not only would he see her as Moira, but all his hatred toward Moira would be fresh. She couldn't think of a more volatile or dangerous situation to be in when trying to deal with him. Unfortunately, she didn't have a choice, because the longer she waited, the more time Moira would have to work her magic on him.

When she reached the top of the cliff, she came to a stop and stared at the scene in horror. Ryan, who looked like Aric, was standing precariously on a ledge, and even though she was several feet away from him, she could see the devastation on his face. She also sensed that he was getting ready to jump. It was the same scene she'd seen in his mind following his motorcycle accident! And following that scene, he'd thrown her off the cliff!

Suddenly, he took a tentative step forward. She tried to cry out to him, to tell him to stop, but as had happened in the vision, no sound came out. With a frustrated sob, she began running toward him. If he heard her coming, he didn't acknowledge it, so when she drew near, she stopped and said, "Aric?"

He started and spun around to face her. His foot slipped on loose rock. As he teetered on the ledge, Shana let out a gasp of fear.

Before she could leap to his assistance, he righted himself and bellowed, "You dare follow me after what you have done? I will kill you!"

He lunged for her, but she darted out of his way, saying, "Aric, please. I am *not* Moira! My name is Shana. Shana Morland, and I am here to help you destroy Moira forever. You must listen to me. You *must!*"

"You killed Terza!" he repeated, lunging for her again.

This time, she wasn't fast enough to escape his reach. As he grabbed her upper arms, she said, "Please, Aric. You have to listen to me. I am *not* Moira. If you just touch my mind, you'll know that I'm telling you the truth!"

Even as the words left her mouth, Shana wanted to snatch them back. She had forgotten about the shielding spell Ryan had put over her. As Aric stared into her face and his eyes began to glow, she knew she was doomed. The moment he touched her mind and realized he couldn't get through, he'd be more convinced than ever that she was Moira.

"You lie!" he yelled a moment later as he dragged her toward the cliff. "You lie, and now you will die!"

"Ryan, please! I know you're in there. I know you can take control," Shana gasped while struggling frantically against his iron hold. "You love me, Ryan. I am your mate. You can't let Aric do this to me. Please, Ryan. *Please!*"

"Why?" she screamed at him when he had her dangerously perched on the ledge. "Why won't you come out, Ryan? *I love you!*"

Instead of answering, he released his hold on her and pushed. As she felt herself falling into space, her eyes locked with his. She would have sworn she saw a flicker of triumph flash through them, and then there was nothing reflected in their depths. She was falling to her death, but she recognized that he was already dead, and she'd been the one to kill him. She should have never left him alone at the house. She should have made him come with her to see Sebastian. She should have . . .

She let out a gasp of surprise when spell-lightning suddenly flashed around her and she stopped falling. Cautiously, she glanced down and let out another gasp. She was sitting in midair on what appeared to be a huge hand. Only, it didn't have corporeal substance. It appeared to be some type of mist.

Stunned, she glanced up to find herself looking at

Ryan. Aric's image was gone. Where in the world had he learned this spell? The answer, of course, was obvious—in the journals in the repository. Fear shot through her. He was using the dark forces, and no one knew how to counteract them. Then it occurred to her that they weren't in Sanctuary. They were in the past, and here the dark forces were used frequently. If a spell got out of hand, someone would know how to control it.

With a relieved sigh, she opened her mouth to thank him for saving her. But before she could speak, she saw the dark figure materializing behind him.

"Ryan! Behind you," she screamed.

At Shana's warning, Ryan spun around just in time to see Moira take full form. He narrowed his eyes and said, "It's over, Moira. I offered you the chance to take my soul, but you turned it down. Now, you have to go back into the cards, because I will not leave Shana. She's my mate, and I love her. I plan on living a long and happy life with her. You killed Terza, but you are *not* going to take Shana away from me."

"Fool!" she hissed, and Ryan determined that was exactly what her voice sounded like—a hiss. "The battle is over. You lost."

"That is not true!" Shana yelled from behind him. "If it was over, you would have delivered the card. Where is the card, Moira?"

"Silence!" Moira ordered imperiously, pointing her finger at her. "The battle is over. He claims to love you, but he threw you off the cliff. That is not love!"

"He threw me off the cliff because you turned him into Aric. Then you made me look like you at a time when he was consumed by grief," Shana argued. "But even as I fell, he saw through your trick and recognized his love for me. That's why he saved me. He chose me over you!"

"That is not true! He threw you off the cliff. The battle is over, and I have won!"

"Then, where's the card, Moira?" Ryan asked, picking up on Shana's original premise.

She jerked her head toward him and smiled maliciously. Then she flicked her wrist, and a card appeared in her hand. "The card is here, mortal. Do you wish me to deliver it now, or would you like to make a bargain with me?"

"Ryan, don't make any bargains with her!" Shana cried frantically. "She's trying to trick you."

"Is Shana right, Moira? Is this another one of your tricks?" Ryan asked, surveying the distance between them. If he could catch her by surprise, he might be able to throw her off the cliff. Then all of this would truly be over.

"Ah, mortal, you disappoint me," she stated derisively as she took several steps back. "I gave you the powers, but you do not even bother to shield your thoughts from me. The battle is over, and you cannot kill me. Now, do you wish to bargain with me? Or should I deliver the card?"

"What kind of bargain are we talking about?" Ryan questioned warily.

"Give me the card you possess, and I will let her live," Moira answered. "Keep the card, and she dies."

"The card I possess?" Ryan repeated in confusion.

"She's talking about the Death card!" Shana gasped. "Don't give it to her, Ryan. It's the transformation card. It must contain the power she needs to transmute from a spirit. Without it, she can't regain existence!"

"Silence!" Moira screeched, turning her attention back on Shana. "The battle is over, and the card is mine. I can take it whenever I wish!"

"You're lying, Moira," Shana replied. "You *gave* the card to Ryan. The only way you can get it is if he *gives* it back to you. And without the card, you lose!"

"Is that true, Moira?" Ryan demanded. "If I refuse to give you the card, do you lose?"

"You won't refuse—can't refuse me, mortal," Moira said, her voice suddenly turning into a seductive croon. "It's me you want. It always has been, and it always will be."

She didn't move, but as had happened before, Ryan felt her invisible hand stroke his chest. When he felt it begin to move unerringly lower, he cursed and stumbled back a step.

"Leave me alone, Moira," he ordered harshly.

She released a throaty laugh. "You don't want me to stop, mortal. You crave my touch, and you know it. You've never been able to turn away from me."

"*Aric* couldn't turn away from you," Ryan responded, swatting at empty air as he felt her invisible fingers trace the length of his zipper. "But I am not Aric. I am Ryan, and your touch sickens me."

"Liar!" she hissed, but at least she stopped touching him.

"If I'm lying, then why am I not aroused, Moira?" he asked. Before she could respond, he relentlessly continued, "I'll tell you why, because it's Shana I love. It will always be Shana until the day I die, and no other woman will ever appeal to me. So, answer my question. If I refuse to give you the card, do you lose?"

"The only one who will lose is you!" she replied furiously, "If you do not give me the card, she will die. I will kill her, just as I killed Terza."

"And if you kill her, what reason would I have to give you the card? Revenge alone would make me keep it from you," he countered. "You've painted yourself into a corner, Moira, and there's no way out. I am not going to give you the card, so go back into the Tarot deck where you belong."

"Do you think you can beat me so easily?" she shrieked, raising her arms over her hand. "Shana is under my spell now. In order to save her, you must give her the card. But will you be able to recognize her? Will you make the right choice? I think not, mortal, for I am Moira. The most powerful witch who ever lived. You cannot defeat me, and your Shana will die!"

Before Ryan could begin to assimilate what she was saying, a lightning bolt shot from the sky and struck the ground between them. As the crack of thunder reverberated through the air, he heard Shana scream. With a gasp, he spun around in time to see her falling.

"Shana!" he bellowed in terror, as he raced to the cliff ledge.

Fearfully, he glanced down, expecting to see her body lying broken and lifeless in the ravine below. But she wasn't there. Frantically, he searched the area for her, and when he finally spied her, he caught his breath in horror. She was standing on a small ledge several feet beneath him, and he could see it beginning to crumble beneath her feet. If he didn't get to her quickly, she would fall to her death for sure. There was only one problem with rescuing her. There were two Shanas standing on the ledge!

That's right mortal, Moira's voice whispered insidiously in his mind. *To save her, you must give the card to the right Shana. But she will not be able to speak to you. You must make the choice with your heart. Do you love her enough to do that mortal? Can you recognize her without her words? Without access to her mind?*

Even as Moira tormented him with the questions, he began to climb down the cliff. When he reached the small overhang above the ledge, he dug the Death card out of his pocket and stared down at the two women beneath him.

He searched their faces, looking for something—*any-thing*—that would help him distinguish Shana from Moira. But they were identical, right down to their pleading eyes that were widened in fear. How could he possibly choose the right Shana?

What's the matter, mortal? Moira taunted. *Isn't your love strong enough that you can see beneath the surface to her soul?*

At her words, Ryan closed his eyes and gave a desperate shake of his head. This was worse than the nightmare that had haunted him for months! To save Shana, he was going to have to go with his instincts. But was his love deep enough, profound enough, to trust his instincts? If he made a mistake, Shana would die!

Time has run out, mortal. You must make the decision now. Who will you save? The one you claim to love, or me, whom you truly love!

"I do not love you!" Ryan yelled, opening his eyes and glaring down at the two women. "I never loved you. I love Shana!"

Then prove it. Save her. Now!

There was a loud cracking noise, and he realized that the ledge was giving way. He had to make the choice, and he had to make it now!

He lay down on his stomach and extended the card, glancing frantically between the two of them. Suddenly, one of them raised her hand for the card. The other one merely stared up at him sorrowfully, her eyes filled with love and resignation.

That has to be Shana! he thought, quickly shifting to extend the card toward her. *Only she would look at me with love in her eyes when she knew she was condemned to die.*

But would Shana give up that easily? an inner voice prodded. *She loves you, and she knows that if she dies, you will be condemned for eternity. She wouldn't give up. She'd fight to live so you'd be saved!*

The resigned Shana had just begun to reach for the card, and he snatched it back, returning his attention to the other one. Was his conscience right? Was this the real Shana?

Unfortunately, there was another loud crack, and he knew he didn't have time to contemplate the issue. He had to deliver the card now, or the question would be moot.

"God help me, I hope I'm making the right decision!" he declared hoarsely as he handed the card to the Shana who was frantically reaching for it. She snatched it out of his hand just as the ledge broke and both women began to fall.

"Nooo!" he screamed in agony, closing his eyes at the realization that he'd waited too long. "Shana, I love you!"

"I love you, too, Ryan!" she yelled joyously. "And it's over. We've defeated Moira!"

His eyes flew open, and he stared in disbelief. Shana was again perched on the hand he'd conjured up to save her when he had thrown her off the cliff.

"Shana?" he gasped, scrambling to his feet as the hand moved to gently deposit her beside him.

"Yes, Ryan, it's me," she replied, throwing her arms around him and hugging him tightly. "It's me."

"Oh, thank God!" he murmured, crushing her to him and burying his face in her hair. "Thank God."

Suddenly, she pulled away from him, stating urgently, "We have to find the card, Ryan."

"The card?" he repeated in confusion.

"Yes, the card," she answered, eying the ground. "It's

the end of the cycle, and Moira has to deliver the card. It will determine—"

"Determine what?" he asked, when she suddenly bent to scoop a Tarot card off the ground.

She stared at it for a long moment, and then glanced up at him, her face so pale she looked ghostly. "What is it? What's wrong?" he gasped, grabbing her shoulders, as fear stirred inside him.

"It's The World, reversed," she answered, holding the card up so he could see it.

He shuddered as he looked at it. Moira was naked and standing with her feet braced apart on top of a globe of the world. Her hands were outstretched, and she held the sun in one hand and the moon in the other. A dark mist curled around her like a sinuous snake. Suddenly, the card faded to black.

"What does it mean?" he asked, glancing back at Shana.

"It means that Moira has given herself a loophole," Shana answered, gazing up at him with so much misery in her eyes that fear shot through him.

"What kind of loophole?"

"The wishing wand."

"The wishing wand?" he repeated as a sense of doom began to mushroom inside him.

She nodded. "Moira is the one who introduced you to the wand. She was counting on you using it, and now . . ."

"Now?" he prodded, grabbing her shoulders again and giving her a slight shake.

She sighed heavily and looked down at the ground. "Now you have to pay the price for using the wand, and that price is the choice between eternal freedom of your soul or me."

"What the hell does that mean?" he demanded, giving her another shake.

"It means you have to leave me," she said, raising her tormented gaze to his. "If you don't, you'll have to fight Moira again in another five hundred years."

"You're wrong!" Ryan said, shaking his head frantically.

"I'm afraid she's right," a man's voice drawled from above them.

Ryan jerked his head toward the voice just as Shana cried, "Sebastian! You were right!"

Before Ryan knew what was happening, she broke away from him and scrambled up the cliff. A bolt of jealousy shot through him as she threw herself into the man's arms and buried her face against his chest.

"There is no need for jealousy," Sebastian told him, his lips twisting into a grim smile. "It is you she loves, and it will always be that way. Now, come, Dr. Alden. The past is over, and you're back in the present. You and Shana have much to work out before you can determine your future."

"I am *not* going to leave her," Ryan stated staunchly as he climbed the cliff to join them. "And if anyone, including her, thinks otherwise, they're crazy."

Sebastian merely gave him another grim smile, and then turned, leading Shana down the path. Ryan quickly followed, fighting against the panic threatening to overwhelm him.

I will not leave her, he silently vowed.

So why did he have the horrible sensation that he was not going to have any other choice?

CHAPTER TWENTY-ONE

The Hanged Man
Self-sacrifice

"You *don't* need to borrow Lucien's car," Ryan stated angrily as he glared at Sebastian. "I told you, I'm not leaving."

A moment before, Shana had run into the house after asking Sebastian to get the car so he could drive Ryan away from Sanctuary. They were standing in her front yard, and instead of responding, Sebastian bent to pick up a rock. He studied it for a long moment, as if he found something particularly interesting in its unremarkable appearance.

"Ignoring me is not going to change my mind," Ryan snapped.

"I'm not ignoring you," Sebastian replied, tossing the rock to the ground and raising his disturbingly probing gaze to Ryan. "I'm merely giving you some time to think."

"I don't need time to think. I know exactly what I'm going to do, and that's stay here with Shana."

"And if she doesn't want you to stay?"

"Of course, she wants me to stay. She loves me."

"Exactly," Sebastian said. "And that's why I'm going to go get the car."

"Dammit, man! What does it take to get through to you? I am *not* leaving here, or at least I'm not leaving without Shana."

"If that turns out to be your choice, then I can always return the car," Sebastian said, turning away from him.

Ryan opened his mouth to argue further. Realizing that Sebastian was not the one he should be arguing with, he closed it and headed for the house. If Shana thought she was going to send him away after all they'd been through, she was nuts!

I am not crazy, Ryan. Come to the repository, so I can explain.

As Shana's voice echoed in his mind, Ryan staggered to a halt and shook his head in shock. He'd been so focused on Shana's determination to send him away that he hadn't realized he was now powerless. When had that happened?

When you gave me the Death card—the transformation card. Come to the repository, and I will explain everything.

Reluctantly, he did as she instructed. Was that why she wanted to send him away? Because he was now no more than a mortal?

Don't be ridiculous! she chided. *I love you, and I will love you until the day I die. Your being a mortal doesn't change that.*

"Then why do you want to send me away?" he questioned hoarsely. When she didn't answer, he felt his stomach twist into a knot.

By the time he reached the repository, the knot had become the size of a boulder. Drawing in a deep breath, he forced himself to open the door and step inside.

Shana was standing beside one of the tables, and she glanced up at him, giving him a smile that didn't reach her eyes. "Come and look at this, Ryan."

He unwillingly walked to the table and looked down. He saw a bunch of black cards scattered around it in various piles.

"Obviously, these are Moira's Tarot cards," he said.

She nodded. "This is the spread Moira had me lay out the night I released her. All of the cards are here but one."

"There's a card missing?"

She nodded again. "The Hanged Man."

He curled his lip in distaste. "Sounds like a disgusting card."

"It's not disgusting at all. He's hanging upside down, with a rope around his ankle, and he's done this by choice. It takes great courage for him to put himself in that position, but he is a man of self-sacrifice. A man who will do what must be done, even at the risk of losing what he wants the most."

"Dammit, Shana! Don't play this game with me. I couldn't leave you if I wanted to, and I sure as hell don't want to!"

"Don't you understand the seriousness of this situation?" she asked impatiently, gesturing toward the cards. "If you don't leave me, then Moira will have another chance at your soul. This way it's over. You'll be free."

Ryan stared at her in disbelief. "*Free?* My God, Shana. I *love* you. If I leave you, I won't be free. I'll spend the rest of my life grieving for you!"

She gave an adamant shake of her head. "You're wrong, Ryan. When you first arrived, Lucien made me cast a spell over you. For a while, I wasn't sure it had worked. Then, you were able to pick up on my thoughts yesterday afternoon when your weakened powers should have prohibited you from doing so without great concentration. Do you remember that, Ryan?"

"Of course, I remember it," he said gruffly, his gaze

automatically dropping to her breasts. "I tried to mentally seduce you when you wouldn't tell me what I wanted to know."

"Yes, and that's what I was reluctant to tell you. That I had cast a spell over you. As you'll recall, you weren't in a particularly cooperative frame of mind."

"Yeah, well, I finally came around," he muttered, dragging his gaze back to her face. "What does this spell have to do with our situation?"

"Because of the spell, once you leave Sanctuary you'll forget me and everything that's happened here."

"That's impossible!" he declared, his eyes somber. "Not even a spell could make me forget you."

She gave him a sad smile. "Yes, Ryan, it will. The moment you leave coven land, I will no longer exist for you. You'll be free to love again, to mate again."

"*Dammit!* I don't want to be free to love again, and I don't want to be mated with anyone but *you*," he stated angrily, passionately.

He reached out and clutched her arms. Pulling her against him, he stared deeply into her eyes. "You can't do this to us, Shana. We were fated to be together. You said yourself that if that weren't true, I couldn't have accepted the witch's vow from you. So don't do this to us. I love you, and I need you. If that means having to fight Moira in another five hundred years, I don't care. Having you will be worth it."

"But it won't be worth it to me!" she cried in frustration, pulling away from him. She began to pace, and then she stopped to look at him, her eyes filled with such torment that it broke his heart. "I also love you, Ryan. You're the very essence of my soul, and just the thought of losing you is killing me. But can't you see that if you stay, you'll be giving Moira a double victory? She'll not only have another chance at your soul, but because of her, every moment of happiness we share will be overshadowed by her lurking presence. For the rest of my life, her threat to you will be my first thought when I wake up in the morning, and my last thought when I go to bed at night. Losing you will make me miserable, but it won't compare to the anguish I'll suffer if you stay with me. Surely, you can understand that I can't live with that."

He crossed his arms in front of himself, feeling he had to somehow protect himself from the pain. "I do understand what you're saying, Shana, but you have to understand my side in all of this. Until I met you, I was nothing but an empty shell. I had no reason to live, and if I leave, I know that that's what I'll become again. You say you love me, so how can you let that happen to me?"

"That isn't going to happen, Ryan," she said, stepping forward and placing her hand against his arm. "Now that I have my powers back, I know what you've been suffering through since Samhain. Moira was the cause of your torment, and now she's gone. With her no longer lingering over you like a death sentence, you'll go back to being a doctor. With each child's life you save, you'll come closer to fulfilling the karmic debt you owe for the death of Aric's child."

"And you think that will be enough for me?" he demanded, jerking away from her touch.

"When compared to the alternative, yes, it will be enough," she answered.

"So that's it," he stated in defeat as he noted her resolved expression and the determination glittering in her eyes. "It's over between us, and you want me to hit the road."

She gave him a look that was part chastisement and part torment. "As far as I'm concerned, it will never be over between us, Ryan. I am a witch, and I can mate only once. Every moment of my life you'll be in my thoughts and my dreams. But, yes, I want you to hit the road, and our timing is perfect. Sebastian just returned with the car."

He wanted to grab her and jerk her back into his arms. He wanted to kiss her until she was swooning, and then make love to her until she forgot this crazy plan for him to leave. But he knew he couldn't do that. He loved her, and if his staying would make her miserable, then he had no choice. It would kill him, but he had to go.

"Will you at least go with me to the boundary?"

She shook her head. "It's going to be hard enough to say good-bye here. I couldn't bear to watch you forget me."

"Can I at least have a good-bye kiss?"

"Oh, yes!" she said, flying into his arms.

He wrapped his arms around her tightly and buried his face in her hair. Drawing in a deep breath, he savored the scent of her. So womanly. So mysterious. So sexy. *So Shana.* He didn't care what she said, he could never forget her. There would be some part of her—some essence of her—that would remain with him forever.

Cupping her chin, he tilted her face up to his and sealed his lips over hers. When he did, she opened her mind to him, and all her feelings washed over him. Her love enveloped him and made him whole. Her sadness broke his heart in two.

Reluctantly, he pulled away from the kiss and looked down at her. He brushed his thumbs over her satin cheeks and gruffly muttered, "If I have to go, the least you could do is shed a tear over me."

"Witches can't cry," she replied hoarsely. "We're incapable of tears."

"Then maybe I'll cry for both of us," he said as he felt his own eyes grow damp. "I love you, Shana."

She pressed a hand against his lips. "And I love you, Ryan. Good-bye."

With that, she pulled out of his embrace and ran out of the room. He stood looking at the empty doorway, wanting to go after her. Instead, he walked out and headed for the front door and Sebastian.

Shana waited until she knew that Ryan and Sebastian were almost to the boundary before she returned to the repository. She stood beside the table and stared down at the cards. If Sebastian was right, the moment Ryan crossed over the border, the last card would drop and the images would return. At that moment, Moira would be trapped forever, and Ryan would be free.

As her mind absently tracked Ryan's and Sebastian's progress, she let herself relive every precious moment she and Ryan had together. She knew that this was only the first time for that indulgence. That for the rest of her life, she'd relive the short time they'd had together.

Too soon, the memories ended, and so did Ryan's journey. As the car reached Sanctuary's boundary, she buried her face in her hands and let her mind brush against Ryan's. Though she knew she should remain silent, she couldn't help communicating, *I love you, Ryan, and even though I can't cry, I want you to know that my heart is drowning in tears.*

I love you, Shana, and I want you to know that my heart—

Their contact abruptly ended. Shana looked at the pentagram overhead and let out a wailing keen. He was gone, and it hurt her so badly that she was sure she would die from the pain.

But she wouldn't die, because she had every reason to live. Ryan was gone, but she was carrying his child. Through it, she'd find the joy and happiness that she should have had with him, she assured herself, pressing her hand protectively to her abdomen.

Drawing in a deep breath, she looked down at the cards. The images had again become visible, and the last card—The Hanged Man, self-sacrifice—was lying on top of The Fool. There was a part of her that had been hoping that Ryan's departure wouldn't make a difference. That the cards would remain black. Then she could run after him, and they could be together forever. But now she knew that forever was never meant to be for them.

With a heavy sigh, she gathered the cards together and carefully wrapped them into the aged silk they'd been in originally. Then she put them back into the carved box and returned it to its original hiding place.

When she was done, she walked to the center of the room and looked around. All her life she had wanted to escape Sanctuary and the restrictions of coven life. But now, as she looked at all the objects surrounding her, she knew that this was where she belonged. She was not only a member of the coven, but she was the caretaker of the repository, and that was an important responsibility. Though her part in Moira's curse had been her destiny and she couldn't have avoided it, she now understood just how critical it was to protect the remainder of the items in here. It was a responsibility that she intended to take seriously from now on.

"I've finally found my way home," she whispered sadly. "But why did it have to be at such a great cost?"

"Who the hell are you? And what the hell am I doing in your car?" Ryan demanded of the strange-looking and rather intimidating-looking man sitting beside him. With his long, dark hair, hooked nose, and odd, glittering eyes, he looked like some primitive barbarian.

The man pulled the car over to the side of the road.

When they were stopped, he turned to look at Ryan. "I am Sebastian Moran. You don't remember why you're in my car?"

"If I did, I wouldn't be asking you why I'm in it," Ryan muttered.

The man gave him a satisfied smile. "Do you believe in clean slates, Dr. Alden?"

"How did you know my name?"

"How I know your name doesn't matter. What does matter is your answer to my question. Do you believe in clean slates? Do you believe that once a man has learned his lesson, he can begin again?"

"I suppose so," Ryan said cautiously. "Why?"

Sebastian stared at him for a long moment before saying, "What do you think about wishes, Dr. Alden?"

"Look, Moran, I don't know what kind of game you're playing here, but—"

"The game I'm playing could affect the rest of your life, Dr. Alden," Sebastian interrupted quietly. "Tell me what you think about wishes."

"I'm not sure what you're asking," Ryan said, confused by the man's serious demeanor. "I suppose that I believe wishes can come true, but . . ."

"But?" Sebastian prodded, when Ryan's voice trailed off.

Ryan glanced out the window a moment, trying to pull his thoughts together. Finally, he returned his attention to Sebastian and said, "But I guess I also believe that you should be careful of what you wish for, because you just might get it."

"But if it's a wish you really want, then what's the harm of its coming true?" Sebastian asked next.

Ryan frowned at him impatiently. "I think the answer to that is rather obvious, Moran. Too many times we make wishes for things we think we need, when in actuality, having those things will only make us miserable. In other words, if you're going to make a wish, then you had better make damn certain it's something you not only need, but something you need so badly that you're willing to handle the consequences if it comes true."

"So, you believe that wishes carry consequences?"

"Of course," Ryan replied with such vehemence he startled himself. "A wish is a form of desire, and we tend to let our desires get out of hand. We often let what we want override what we really need. There is a big difference between want and need."

"And what do you need, Dr. Alden? If I could grant you any wish, what would you ask for?"

"Love," Ryan answered, again startling himself with the vehemence of his reply.

"And you believe that love is so important that it would be worth the consequences of a wish?"

"I believe that love is so important that it's worth risking your life to have it," Ryan replied.

"Congratulations, Dr. Alden," Sebastian said, suddenly grinning at him. "You've learned the lesson well, and now I'm allowed to grant your wish."

Before Ryan could figure out what the hell the man was talking about, he waved his hand at Ryan, and then flicked his fingers. Suddenly, Ryan's mind was flooded with a hundred images, and all of them were of Shana Morland.

When the images ended, Ryan stared at Sebastian in disbelief. "Are you saying I can go back to Shana?"

"The wishing wand's purpose is not to punish, Dr. Alden. It is to teach you the value of a wish. You've learned that lesson well."

"But what about Moira's curse? If I stay with Shana, then will I have to fight her again?"

"You completed the cycle," Sebastian answered. "You fulfilled The Hanged Man's demand for self-sacrifice by leaving Shana. And by doing so, you chose sacred love over profane love, because staying with Shana would have been profane."

"I'm not sure I understand your reasoning," Ryan said, frowning in confusion.

"It's simple, Dr. Alden. Shana loves you enough to let you go. If you had insisted on staying, you would have been considering your wants and needs over hers, and that is not true love. It's self-serving love. By doing as she asked—by leaving to make her happy—you proved that you truly love her. Moira can't fight that."

"And you're sure you're right?" Ryan questioned warily.

Sebastian shrugged. "The only way to know for sure is to look at the cards. If the images are there, then the battle is over. If the cards are black, it isn't over. So, what's it going to be, Dr. Alden? Do I drive you back to Shana's, or do I drive you to the next town?"

"You know the answer to that. Get me back to Shana's house as fast as you can. And, Moran?"

"Yes?" Sebastian murmured as he put the transmission into gear and began to turn the car around.

"If I ever catch you with your arms around my mate again, I'll break your neck."

Sebastian tossed back his head and laughed. Then he looked at Ryan and said, "I think you're going to make a great addition to Sanctuary, Dr. Alden. Welcome to the coven."

Shana stared at the gigantic bowl of ice cream in front of her. Whenever she'd been depressed before, ice cream had seemed to pull her out of it. But today, just the sight of it made her more morose.

"I have to get over this," she mumbled, propping her elbows on the table and burying her face in her hands.

"I have to be strong. I have a baby to think about, and . . ."

She started at the hollow echoing that drifted through the house. Her head shot up, and she frowned. Who could possibly be knocking on her door at a time like this? She knew that all she had to do was touch the person's mind to find out, but suddenly movement appealed to her.

So instead of using her mental abilities, she scooted back her chair and headed for the door. When she reached it and pulled it open, she was sure she was suffering from hallucinations. It couldn't be Ryan standing on the front stoop!

"Hello, Shana," he said, smiling at her. "Aren't you going to ask me in?"

"Ryan! What are you doing here? You left!" she gasped, realizing that he wasn't a figment of her imagination.

"Yes, I left, and now I'm back," he replied, stepping inside and removing her hand from the door knob. He closed the door and said, "Sebastian says it's safe for me to come back. We can be together after all."

"But Moira's curse! You can't—"

He pressed his fingers to her lips. "Just listen to what I have to say."

Shana stared at him in wide-eyed wonder as he explained what Sebastian had said. "Are you sure he's right?" she asked when he finally finished.

"Shana, he's the most powerful warlock alive. If you can't trust him, who can you trust?"

"But—"

"No buts," he interrupted as he grabbed her arms and pulled her against him. "Kiss me, Shana. I love you, and I want to make love to you. We'll worry about Moira tomorrow."

Shana wanted to object, but he sealed his lips over

hers and she forgot everything but being in his arms. This was where she belonged forever.

"I love you, Shana," he whispered as he pulled away from the kiss and swung her up into his arms.

"I love you, too," she whispered back, wrapping her arms around his neck. "Make love to me, Ryan."

"You just try to stop me," he muttered gruffly, heading for her bedroom.

Ryan lay in bed, listening to Shana's even breathing. Sure that she was finally asleep, he slipped out of bed and pulled on his pants. Then he crept out of the room and headed for the repository.

He knew that Shana wasn't going to be satisfied with Sebastian's reassurances that they were safe. She loved him too much to take the word of anyone, even the most powerful warlock alive. She'd probably insist that he leave again, and he wasn't going anywhere until he knew the truth. Were the images still on the cards, or had they returned to black when he came back?

When he entered the repository, he nervously rubbed his hands against his thighs. He knew where the Tarot deck was hidden. Its location was listed in the journals. But even as he walked toward the fireplace, he found himself wavering. He should just take Sebastian's words on faith. If Sebastian was wrong, then he could worry about it five hundred years from now. At least he'd have this lifetime of happiness with Shana.

But even as he tried to talk himself out of looking, he knew he had to do it. If he didn't, Shana would spend the rest of her life worrying about a ghost that might not even exist.

Drawing in a deep breath, he located the trigger for the secret panel. When he pressed it, a section of the hearth slid open, revealing a small, hand-carved box. As he stared down at it, Ryan again rubbed his hands against his thighs. All he had to do was look, and then he'd know the truth. He reached down and lifted it into his hands.

"You know, what you're doing is exactly what got us into that mess with Moira in the first place," Shana suddenly said behind him.

With a startled gasp, Ryan spun around. Shana was leaning against the door frame, dressed in nothing but his shirt. His gaze automatically slid down her, and he gave a shake of his head.

"God, you're gorgeous."

"You're changing the subject, Ryan," she said in a voice that was half chastisement and half amusement. "You shouldn't be sneaking a peek at the cards."

"You're right," he said, "but I have to know the truth. If Sebastian's right, then our future is secure. If he's not, then . . ."

"You'll have to leave," she finished softly, fretfully. "But what if looking will start the curse again?"

"Shana, the curse is either over or it's not. Looking is not going to change that. So, shall we open the box?"

She wrapped her arms around herself and rubbed at her upper arms, as though suddenly suffering from a chill. "I don't know if I can handle the truth, Ryan."

"We have to face it, Shana. If we don't, you're going to want me to leave, and I don't think I can leave you again. At least I can't leave without looking at the cards and knowing the truth. So what do you say?"

"If I tell you to put it back, will you?"

"I love you," he said without hesitation. "If looking at the cards will make you unhappy, then I won't look."

"And if you don't look and I ask you to leave?"

"Then I'll leave," he said simply.

She again rubbed at her arms. "I guess we don't really have a choice, do we? We have to look."

"Yes," he said with a relieved sigh. "We have to look."

"Then let's get it over with," she said.

He carried the box to the table. Opening it, he lifted out the cards. As he started to unwrap the silk, he said, "Well, here goes."

His fingers were trembling, and it seemed to take him forever to remove the silk. When he did, Shana let out a gasp. He immediately looked at her, his heart beginning to thump fearfully. "What's wrong?"

"Nothing," she said, smiling at him. "The backs are white, not black."

"And that's a good sign?"

"Oh, yes," she said, a quiver of excitement breaking her voice. "Turn them over, Ryan."

He nodded and turned the cards over. Subconsciously, he'd been expecting the worst, and it took a moment for it to register that he was looking down at a strange-looking man, who was hanging upside down.

"It's over!" Shana screamed, throwing her arms around his neck and hugging him so tightly that he could barely breathe. "It's really over!"

"God, I love you," Ryan murmured, tossing the cards to the table and pulling her against him. He rubbed his cheek against her hair. "The future is ours, Shana. An entire lifetime filled with love and magic."

"Yes, and the magic has already begun," she said, looking up at him with a shy smile. "If Moira's cards were telling the truth, I'm pregnant."

Ryan stared down at her, stunned. "Pregnant?"

She nodded. "It's okay, isn't it?"

"Yeah, it's okay," he said, frowning at her. "But did you know this when I left?"

She glanced away guiltily. "Yes."

"And you didn't tell me? For God's sake, Shana. It's my baby, too. I should have known."

"And if you had known, would you have left?" she asked, backing away from him and frowning.

"Of course not," he said, hating the sudden distance between them.

"That's exactly why I didn't tell you."

"Dammit, Shana! You had no right to deny me my child."

"I wouldn't have denied you, Ryan," she said, staring at him with such a wounded expression that he felt like a heel. That irked him, because he knew his anger was justified.

Before he could make that point, she continued, "You would have never known about the child, but it would have known about you. When it reached adulthood, I would have sent it to be with you. It would have befriended you, and the two of you would have gotten to know each other. Hopefully, grown to love each other."

Stunned, Ryan shook his head. "And you think that would have been enough for me?"

"No," she answered. "I was being selfish. I wanted to protect your soul, and if that was wrong, I'm sorry. But in all honesty, I have to say I'd do it again. You're my mate, and I'll do whatever it takes to protect you from harm."

"Dammit, Shana, a man is supposed to protect his wife, not the other way around," he grumbled as he walked to her and pulled her into his arms.

"I'm not a wife, Ryan. I'm a mate, and mates always protect each other. Do you forgive me?"

He stared down into her beautiful eyes and shook his head. "I'd forgive you anything, but in the future, promise me that you'll fill me in on important information like this, okay?"

"Okay," she said, smiling up at him. "We're going to have a wonderful life together, aren't we?"

"You're damn right," he said, resting his forehead against hers. "And to think we owe it all to an evil witch."

"We don't owe it to Moira, Ryan. We owe it to ourselves. Love can conquer anything, and we've just proved that."

"Yeah, we did," he said, smiling. "And speaking of love, how about if we get back to bed?"

She grinned impishly. "Remind me to tell Lucien that I was right. If I'd let him cast the spell over you, we would have driven him nuts."

"I don't know what the hell you're talking about," he said, "but you can explain it later."

"Yes, later," Shana sighed as his lips closed over hers.

This was magic, she decided. Pure, undiluted, wonderful magic, and it would be like this for the rest of their lives.

Author's Note

The Tarot deck referred to in this book is fictional, and I have exercised poetic license and applied very limited meanings to the cards used. Tarot decks are rich in symbolism, giving a depth of meaning to the cards that cannot be shown in the limited format I chose for this book. Each card has several different meanings, and its interpretation is determined by the other cards in a spread. Additionally, each deck has its own symbolism, so the meanings of the cards can vary between the different decks. For those readers who are not familiar with Tarot and are interested in learning more, there are several excellent books on the market.

DARKNESS AND LIGHT

Ariel Dantes was alone in the world and desperate to find her lost brother. Lucien Morgret was the only one who could help her, but he was a man of danger, a man of shadows, a man who could touch the depths of her soul.

But when darkness meets light, Ariel's world is turned upside-down as she experiences things that she never thought could exist outside her imagination. And as Ariel falls deeper and deeper into Lucien's spell, she is drawn toward desires she cannot resist, even if it means losing her heart and soul by surrendering to Lucien's touch . . .

Touch of Night

"*Touch of Night* is a thoroughly engaging book . . . Carin Rafferty is a talent to be reckoned with."

—Linda Lael Miller,
bestselling author of
Forever and the Night and
Taming Charlotte

Don't miss Carin Rafferty's
Touch of Lightning,
coming soon from Topaz

Salem, Massachusetts—1692

Ragna Morpeth slid stealthily to the edge of the bed. When her mate, Seamus, suddenly stirred, she froze. As Ulrich Morgret, the coven's high priest, had instructed, she had slipped Seamus a sleeping potion. But what if the dose wasn't strong enough? What if he woke up?

At the thought, her pulse began to pound, and her entire body began to tremble in fear. If Seamus realized that she was about to betray him . . .

She forced herself to draw in a deep, calming breath. Ulrich had cast a shielding spell over her, so even if Seamus awoke, he would not realize her perfidy. All she had to do was tell him she was going to check on their infant daughter. The worst that would happen was that he'd grumble about her overprotectiveness.

No, the worst that will happen is that he'll make love to you, and if that happens, how will you find the strength to do what you must do?

Ragna closed her eyes tightly against the pain that wrapped around her heart and squeezed. Seamus was her mate, and even though he had changed, she would love him until the day she died. She couldn't go through with this! She had to wake Seamus and tell him Ulrich's plans. They would take their daughter and run away. They would go where no one could find them. They would . . .

Ragna gave a sharp shake of her head to stop her ridiculous fantasizing and climbed out of bed. Even if she did manage to wake Seamus, he'd never run away. He'd insist on fighting Ulrich until one of them was dead, and she knew that that battle would create a new dilemma. If Ulrich died they'd all be lost. If Seamus died, then she would have lost him forever. At least this way, Seamus would have a chance to survive, and she'd much rather lose him to banishment than to death.

After she dressed, she turned and looked down at Seamus. As her gaze moved over his face, she made herself see the reality of what he'd become, rather than the warlock with whom she'd fallen in love. His dark hair was tousled, but that was the only softness to his countenance. There was a sinister sharpness to his features that hadn't been there when she'd fallen in love with him, and even in sleep, his mouth had a cruel twist to it.

When they'd mated, he'd been a kind and loving warlock. Sure, he'd had the same pride and vanity that plagued all warlocks, but how could he have changed so drastically? How could he have become this— monster?

Unfortunately, she knew the answer, and she lowered her gaze to the silver talisman resting on his bare chest. It consisted of two large triangles that had been molded together to form a six-pointed star. The star was centered in the middle of a circle that was delicately engraved with symbols that commanded the dark forces of nature.

As she regarded the magical object, a wave of hatred washed over her. It was the talisman that had destroyed Seamus. When he had inherited it upon his father's death, the talisman had changed him, made him evil.

The talisman only enhanced what was already there, Ragna. For it to create evil, the seed of evil must exist inside its possessor. Now, it is time for you to do what you must do. For yourself. For your child. For the coven. And most of all, for Seamus.

Ragna started as Ulrich's voice echoed in her mind. He was using the old language—the secret language—of their race, and his voice was so clear, she jerked her head toward the bedroom door, expecting to see the high priest standing there.

But he wasn't there. He was waiting outside as they'd planned, and he couldn't enter her home until she invited him in. And if he couldn't enter, he couldn't cast the spell over Seamus that would render him immobile to allow Ulrich to safely remove the talisman from around his neck. Nor could Ulrich cast the spell that would take away all but a modicum of Seamus's powers so that he could be banished into the wilderness.

She returned her attention to Seamus. If she just waited until the sleeping potion wore off and he awakened, she could talk to him. She would persuade him to give the talisman to Ulrich. Once he no longer had the talisman, Seamus would revert to the warlock he had once been, and he wouldn't have to be banished. They could remain together and raise their child. They could . . .

Ragna, you know that is wishful thinking, Ulrich interrupted impatiently. _I've already explained that once the talisman has corrupted its possessor, he remains changed forever. Seamus is lost to us. He must be banished so he can bring no further harm to us or to the mortals._

Touch the minds of the sleeping Pilgrims, Ragna, he urged. _Look into their nightmares—their dreaming cries of witch! We must take care of Seamus now. We must flee before dawn. If we don't, we will all die, Ragna. All of us. Including your child!_

_No!_ Ragna screamed in silent denial, even as her mind raced from mortal house to mortal house—mortal mind to mortal mind. By the time she was done, she had to accept that what Ulrich was saying was true.

The witch hysteria was so strong it hovered over the community like a death pall. Though Ulrich had tried to curb the hysteria, his spells had done no good. The Pilgrims' fear was too strong, and in the past few months, innocent mortals had been accused, condemned, and killed as witches because of what Seamus had done.

Now, every mind was focused on the members of the coven. The talisman had done its work well. It had corrupted Seamus—made him plant the seeds of the witch hysteria into the minds of the Pilgrims—and if he wasn't stopped tonight, the talisman would be well on its way to its final goal.

Ragna shuddered as the full impact of that goal suddenly clarified for her. The talisman wanted to destroy all of humanity, and it would concentrate on the coven first. Once they were gone, there would be no one with the power to stop it. It would use Seamus, giving him increasingly greater ability to destroy, until, through him, the talisman had wiped out the human population on this continent. Then it would find a way to move him to the next continent, and then the next, wreaking death wherever he went. Finally, when only Seamus remained on the face of the earth, it would destroy him, and if legend was true, the talisman would make his death the worst of all.

Ragna pressed her hands over her mouth to hold back a keening wail. If she betrayed Seamus, she would surely die. But if she didn't betray him, they would all die. She knew she had to obey Ulrich, but how would she find the strength to do it? How could she see Seamus banished and not go with him? How would she live with herself if she never knew if he was alive or dead?

Ragna, you have no other choice.

You are wrong, Ulrich, she mentally argued. *You're going to break the talisman into three pieces. Give a piece of it to Seamus, and let me have the coven's piece. It will give me the power to know whether he lives or dies.*

You know that's impossible, Ragna. The talisman gains its powers from the energies of the moon and the sun. Once it is broken up, only one piece can remain in our possession. The other two pieces must be buried far apart, so there will be no chance that the talisman can be resurrected. To allow two pieces to remain above ground could prove to be catastrophic.

You are wrong again, Ulrich. Seamus will be forced to go into the wilderness and live far away from here. When he dies, his piece will surely be buried with him. So, the odds of all three pieces surfacing are next to impossible. You must give him a piece that will allow me to be connected with him.

Ragna, even if I did what you are asking, your only contact would be nothing more than the knowledge of whether or not he lives. You won't be able to communicate with him or know anything about his life. You must just let him go. Keeping two pieces above ground is too dangerous!

And what you are asking is too cruel. If you want me to invite you in, you must agree with my terms. Give Seamus a piece of the talisman, and let me have the coven's piece. He is my mate, Ulrich. I cannot let him go without a way of knowing if he is alive. Give me what I want, or find another way to stop him.

Ulrich was silent for so long that Ragna began to wonder if he'd left. Then, suddenly, his mind connected with hers.

All right, Ragna. The urgency of our predicament is too great for me to refuse. I just pray our descendants will not live to regret my decision.

Ragna refused to contemplate his dire words. Instead, she bent and pressed a quick kiss to Seamus' lips. Then she ran out of the room to the nursery. She gathered their daughter into her arms and hurried to the front door.

When she flung it open, Ulrich was waiting on the other side. She looked at him for a long moment before saying, "You may enter my home, Ulrich. Just remember our bargain. A piece of the talisman for Seamus, and the coven's piece for me."

Before he could answer, she rushed past him and headed for the other members of the coven, who were gathered nearby. When Ulrich finished, they would flee, their sacred belongings protected by spells until they had finally relocated. Then, through magic, they would transport everything to their new home.

She hadn't quite reached the security of the coven when lightning suddenly rent the sky. As she watched the ominous bolts gather into an electrically charged cloud, terror swept through her.

Instinctively, she gathered her baby closer to her chest and refused to look at the lightning, even when she heard it striking the ground closely behind her.

Ragna, how could . . . ! Seamus suddenly screamed in her mind. Before he could finish his accusation, the lightning disappeared.

At that moment, Ragna knew Ulrich had succeeded. He had the talisman and she would never see Seamus again. But at least Seamus would have a piece of the magical object, and that would keep him connected to her. She also knew that the day Seamus died, she would take her own life—her final punishment for betraying him.

Black Hills, South Dakota—1974

Shaman Leonard Night Wolf shivered violently, but it wasn't from the cold. He felt as if someone, or rather *something*, was spying on him, and he glanced around his small encampment fearfully.

Other than the circle of trees illuminated by his fire, all he could see was the impenetrable darkness of a cloudy, starless night. He tried to tell himself that it was an animal he sensed, but he couldn't quite convince himself that it was true.

As he had every winter for the past forty-five years, he'd left the Lakota reservation and trekked deep into the mountains. His journey was a spiritual quest—a time to reaffirm his beliefs. A time to feed his soul. But this year, the trip wasn't soothing him. He felt as if the spirits were out of harmony, and that frightened him.

Huddling into the blanket wrapped around his shoulders, he anxiously fondled the silver triangle hanging from a chain around his neck. He had just celebrated his fiftieth birthday, and he knew it was time to select the new guardian for the triangle. It was one of the dilemmas he hoped to resolve on this trip.

Deciding to quell his apprehension by concentrating on the problem, he stared thoughtfully into the fire and continued to toy with the triangle. There were several promising young braves within his tribe, but he simply hadn't found the one that struck that special "spark" of recognition inside him.

But was it really the spark that was missing? he asked himself. Or, as his wife claimed, was he too filled with self-importance to relinquish his hold on the triangle? Not that he'd be relinquishing it soon. It would take several years of training to make his successor ready to assume that duty, and he knew that he couldn't put off the selection much longer. If he died before the new guardian was prepared to take over the triangle, it could mean annihilation for his tribe.

He shivered again, but this time it wasn't due to unseen eyes. It was from the legend of the triangle, which had been taken from the evil magician, Seamus Morpeth, nearly three hundred years before.

As the gruesome details of Seamus's time with his ancestors tried to surface, Leonard closed his eyes and forced back the memory of the story. Now was not the time to remember the past. Now was the time to think of the future—to choose a new guardian, who would protect his people from the curse Seamus had placed upon them just before his death.

"The triangle gives me my power," he had told them. "And it is the triangle that will exact my revenge. It will join together with its other pieces, and then your tribe will be no more."

And that was the guardian's onerous duty. To make sure that the triangle never joined with its other pieces. But every guardian who touched it found himself drawn into a war with evil. That's why his training was so important. He had to be able to fight magic with magic. He also had to be so pure of heart that his goodness would overcome the evil that the triangle tried to wedge into his soul.

Yes, it had to be someone special, Leonard acknowledged, and he wasn't convinced that any of the young braves vying for the honor were that pure.

That is because none of the braves are meant to be the guardian.

Leonard jerked his head up in alarm as the words echoed through his mind. When his gaze landed on the man standing on the other side of the fire, his heart began to race and his mouth went dry. He was looking at a fierce-looking brave dressed in full war regalia of centuries past.

"W-who are—you?" Leonard managed to stammer through teeth that begun to chatter in fear.

The warrior didn't answer. He simply summoned Leonard to follow with a wave of his hand as he turned away from the fire and walked, or rather *glided*, toward the trees.

It was at that moment that Leonard realized he

wasn't looking at a man but a spirit, and he shuddered in terror. Every self-protective instinct he possessed was screaming at him to run in the opposite direction as fast as he could. So why did he feel his body rise on its own accord and begin following the spirit?

Before he could even contemplate the thought, his mind was suddenly filled with the image of a young and beautiful woman standing in profile. She was tall, and her black braided hair, exotic features and dark complexion told him that she was a member of his race. But then she suddenly turned her head toward him, and as he looked into her gleaming, golden eyes, he realized she was a half-breed. No full-blooded Native American had eyes the color of the sun.

Suddenly, she raised her arm, and he gasped in alarm. A rattlesnake was curled around her arm from wrist to shoulder. He shuddered again as he watched it bury its head into the crook of her neck, as if it were settling down for a nap.

But even more astonishing than the snake was the fact that around her neck hung a triangle identical to the one he wore. Who was she? And where had she gotten the triangle? Was this a portent that Seamus Morpeth's curse was about to come true?

As the questions arose, her image faded from his mind. He was dismayed to realize that not only had the spirit disappeared, but he had continued walking into the forest. When he glanced over his shoulder, all he could see was blackness.

How far away was his camp? Could he find his way back?

"My friends and I have been waiting for you."

Leonard let out a startled yelp and swung toward the sound of the childish voice. At first he couldn't see anything, but then an eerie light began to glow beside a nearby tree.

As the light began to grow brighter, Leonard's mouth

dropped open in shock. Beneath the tree sat a girl about four or five years old, dressed in a thin, white T-shirt and a pair of white panties. Curled in her lap was a small rattlesnake, and she was petting its head as if it were a kitten.

Behind her stood the spirit Indian, his body bowed over her as if he were protecting her from the cold. And perhaps he was, Leonard realized, because he couldn't see any sign of gooseflesh marring her skin.

"Who are *you*?" he questioned in wonder.

"Sarah," she said, raising her gaze to his. "I am the new guardian."

As he found himself staring into a pair of large, golden eyes, Leonard shook his head. But it wasn't an act of denial. It was one of recognition. The spark was there, and he knew that she was speaking the truth. She was the new guardian. He also knew instinctively that this child, whom he'd just envisioned as a beautiful young woman, would be the one tasked to fight the curse that Seamus Morpeth had cast upon his tribe nearly three hundred years ago.